RECAPTURING
LISDOONVARNA

Other Books
By
Frank S. Johnson

Available from iUniverse, Barnes & Noble, and Amazon online e-stores

Good Fortune Sweet Journeys
The Sand Mountain Armadillo War
Sailing the Blue-Green Line

RECAPTURING LISDOONVARNA

By Frank S. Johnson
Part II of the Michael Forester Adventures

The Prequel to
Good Fortunes, Sweet Journeys

Note to the reader

Recapturing Lisdoonvarna, a work of historical fiction, is built upon the author's book, *Good Fortunes Sweet Journeys*. To fully enjoy the richness of his characterization and plot it is recommended that *Good Fortune Sweet Journeys* be read first.

iUniverse, Inc.
New York   Bloomington

Recapturing Lisdoonvarna
Prequel to Good Fortune Sweet Journeys

iUniverse books may be ordered through booksellers or by contacting:

iUniverse
1663 Liberty Drive
Bloomington, IN 47403
www.iuniverse.com
1-800-Authors (1-800-288-4677)

ISBN: 978-1-4401-3562-0 (sc)
ISBN: 978-1-4401-3563-7 (ebook)

Printed in the United States of America

iUniverse rev. date: 4/30/2009

The *Road to Lisdoonvarna* is a traditional tune with no known composer.

ACKNOWLEDGMENTS

Geographical and historical notes from the sources in the bibliography have paved the way for my fictional characters to follow. To make it through life and not read *Trinity* by Leon Uris or Michael Shara's Pulitzer Prize winning, *Killer Angels,* would be a great loss for anyone curious in the passion that defines the Irish soul and also in the ongoing American obsession that is our Civil War.

THANKS

Always to my wife and best friend, Theresa, thank you. Thank you also to my readership. They keep pumping me for my next book. Thanks Paul Friend. What a shot in the arm you are.

Susan Parrish has again, with her determined proof-reading and highly constructive interpretative skills, pushed my tale to a level beyond where I might solely have been able to take it. Thank you, Susan. The story was in the rough and your great efforts have given it a chance to shine. The correct usage of French in the dialogue is also attributed to Susan.

Roger Grider also contributed a great deal by going over this story. His literary honesty is solid gold to this writer.

A thank you also goes out to other proof-readers, Rhonda Preston and Lewis Woody, whose interest and diligence are greatly appreciated.

This book's main character is well versed in horsemanship, and much knowledge that surfaces in my story I owe to others. Steve Walker and Kent Parrish are fine horsemen who deserve a word of thanks. Steve, our local veterinarian, has graciously answered my equestrian questions at a moment's notice. Observing Kent's confidence and ability with horses over the years has made a powerful and lasting impression. Another veteran horseman who needs thanking, again, is my neighbor, Paul Friend. Our talks over coffee about his ranching experiences have played a role in this book and others in the making.

I will forever be indebted to early supporters. I won't forget the time and effort of the many who have helped me along the way: Stephen Shearer, my brother James, Ric Mayer, Linda Crane, Angela Myers, Dorothy Farrington, my mother and my mother-in-law, and David Tankesley among so many others.

To those who find themselves constantly searching for their roots and home

CHAPTER 1
A FRIEND RETURNS

An older man rocked gently in his chair as he awaited another warm evening to fade into night. Dressed rather shabbily in work clothes, his humble stature and solemn blue eyes suggested a simple life likely devoid of sweetness. However, his look and manner were misleading, for he had in fact tasted life in extraordinarily rich doses. To anyone who knew him, Michael Forester was far from simple, actually bafflingly so, and sadly during the last year had been the recipient of a full measure of life's bitter herbs.

Others up and down Flat Creek secretly envied his accomplishments but shrugged off his journeys as too risky. All knew that chancing the unknown could prove perilous. The rich spices of adventure were the table fare of those able to look the devil in the eye. They had no stomach for that. But he was a Kelly. No other explanation was needed.

⊕

Michael Forester coveted the familiar creaks and groans of the old deck. Peeling floor boards or not, his rocker's steady cadence soothed him. Tranquil for once, his pondering thoughts brought on a wry smile that suggested all was as it should be. In these southern Missouri Ozarks, the comforting sounds from fields below and

1

forests on the ridgeline reinforced his thesis. He had lived here all his life.

Also the smells, this hill boy reminded himself. A pungent whiff of garlic blew by, and he breathed it in as he had each June for much of his life. Beautiful green and white braids, newly cleaned and sorted, dangled above him from rough cut rafters. Other fragrances that some might not count as such drifted by. The faint tang of manure from his cattle at the nearby gate found him, only to be layered over with the sweet scent of newly cut hay sweeping up from the fields near the creek. Even the earthy essence of the forest on the far hillside carried to him for the moment, pushed by ever-so-slight evening breezes. Michael noted all, for each blew in strongly opposing memories of good and evil. Here, the seasons of his lifetime spent with his grandfather, mother, and wife of nearly thirty years had helped measure and shape him. Now, all three were gone.

The antique rocking chair wrapped around him. Its fragile compassion appeased his troubles as did the new woman's presence at his left. He treasured the rocker's craftsmanship and also the subtle makings of his red-haired companion. Their mutual silence he judged a blessing. Together, as on so many other evenings throughout spring and now early summer they awaited the day's end. He smiled. She returned it. He felt two minds at ease.

The fact that his ancestors, Sean and Nora Kelly, had together sat in these same chairs before the beginning of the twentieth century, biased his sentiment. Conjured images of Sean Kelly carving out the pair of delicate rockers piece-by-piece, and then enjoying long evenings, or taking in the sunrise with coffee in hand, just as he and Ellen had for decades, lingered in Michael's mind. At the present either early or late in the day, Rebecca O'Sullivan's company alone graced his old porch.

The origin of the local cherry wood had been determined by the uncanny eye of a thirteen-year-old Michael. An early search along Flat Creek had revealed the old stump.   His grandfather, John Kelly, had confirmed his guesswork. Cut, then sprouted, and then cut again at a barrel-thick age, the fine wood of the tree lived on as furniture adorning the Kelly house.

Michael imagined a time before the advent of automobiles, radio, and the Spanish American War when Sean cut and sawed the log into thick slabs, and then stored the lumber for years in a barn loft to dry. A full quarter century before the birth of his grandfather, John Kelly, old Sean had fashioned the delicate wooden parts, or so the story went. A foot-powered lathe had whirled in the large cabin of walnut logs, and it bore the evidence still. Shavings of straight-grained cherry wood remained in the dark corners of the ancient structure.

That these two chairs could withstand the rigors of time both in the heritage they preserved and in their solid construction, pleased him. However, her care, Rebecca's care of him after Ellen's death, he wondered about. He was not wood but flesh. Michael understood that he well could become dust long before the chair in which he sat. His quiet companion, he knew, had by her coming saved him from self destruction.

He reflected how he was more at peace since Rebecca's arrival. The silent thought echoed painfully and also joyously through his mind as his sober eyes gazed over the fields below then back. The red-haired woman beside him momentarily caught his look. Then, here, on this small rise in the valley deeply nestled between the two ridges, Michael remembered the stories of another more recent great grandfather. The man had built this simple farmhouse in 1904, a decade preceding the 'War to End All Wars'. Michael also reminisced how still earlier Sean Kelly had locked great walnut logs together with hammered oak pegs in hand-augured holes not a stone's throw away. A sudden sorrowful cloud engulfed him, its icy grayness left over from the winter. The life and the death of his wife rolled nonstop before his eyes.

⊕

The fiftish woman at Michael's side sensed his sudden melancholy and reached for him. *Everyone needs someone to help them grieve*, and she knew that she was that someone for Michael. Fingers gently locked as the consoling rhythm of the rockers continued. She found his blue eyes. Her thin smile implied, as she intended, her compassion but also her contentment. She savored his company and also her task to cancel a debt long overdue. She squeezed his hand. He responded with a growing smile that meant, for the moment, he had forced his sorrow back.

Though slightly younger, trimmer, and with little gray in her long and still lustrous red hair, Rebecca turned her eyes from the western sky and studied a balding Michael as he reached to the trembling, silken fur at his feet. Memories echoed through her mind. *Recent years have certainly not been kind to you my friend.*

She observed as he studied his old dog's shining eyes. His wry grin told her that he sensed loyalty and that his sad mood had disappeared as quickly as it had come. Strong, leathery fingers again stroked the black-and-white fur. As his hand ran along the animal's back she thought how innate tensions known only to a Border Collie were soothed. *His gentleness, again.* She smiled.

Rebecca noticed the long, handsome muzzle, and fluffed head turned up, but for an instant. The dog acknowledged and then just as quickly returned to its mysterious liaison with all beyond Michael's porch. She marveled at what the canine world could sense and understand, and also wondered about those same traits in the man beside her.

⊕

An early summer evening among many, were Michael's thoughts as he turned to acknowledge Rebecca. *It has all become bearable since she came south from Duluth.* He cast another glance down the hill and found the dark shadows that were his herd of cattle. Momentarily, he watched. Then satisfied, he let his eyes drift further to the stream and the rock foundations of the old mill. All the while he kept an appreciative hand below where tense nature betrayed overpowering passion. He felt the essence of the squirms and wiggles in the animal, every sniff of the grassy fields taken in, analyzed in canine code, and repeated. To Michael in many ways, the dog reminded him of himself.

While a colorful sunset gave pleasure to his eyes, his thoughts remained focused on this loyal friend at his feet. *Old,* he thought. *How many more summers will God allow this old dog to sit sentinel here*? Then more soberly, *How many more will He suffer me the same privilege*?

Michael's return to the silent enjoyment of the evening was not concealed from his partner. He saw Rebecca reach down to caress the dog's thick fur. As she did, he detected hesitation and a fidget from both. Studying the vigilant eyes below, he knew that the trust between the dog and the woman had not yet grown. *Her smell must be so different than Ellen's.* Michael chastised himself for negligence. Rebecca had been here for three months, yet he had not allowed himself to hug her close enough to know her smell. He remembered the fragrance of her skin and hair from a friendly but brief encounter in Duluth two years before, but, *Not yet,* was all he could think. *Not yet.* However, he dearly hoped she would stay.

"Don't worry, Rebecca," Michael reassured. He had raised the trusting animal from a pup. His laugh came out with a lilting tone before he said, "Boots will get used to you, and all too soon she'll be underfoot."

With those words spoken and absorbed, Rebecca responded. "She'll be okay, Michael. She's a good dog." Then with mild amusement, "Even if she doesn't accept me, I see how she treats you."

Michael enjoyed Rebecca's easy going manner. He studied her face and dwelt on her beautiful green eyes. *How long would she stay*? he wondered. *Those eyes,* were all he could think. *Anna's eyes, too. Our daughter.*

Michael's ear caught the late evening call of the birds crossing the valley. In fields surrounding the two-story farmhouse and on greening hardwood-lined ridges mixed with tall pines, he heard the familiar hum of insects drumming to their mates.

Also listening closely, Rebecca asked in the dimming light, "What was that bird, Michael? It's different than a whip-poor-will."

"Chuck-wills-widow."

"You're kidding me?" she responded expecting a joke.

"Nope. Wouldn't do that. Both are very similar including their calls. You wouldn't believe the name of the family they're in."

"Try me."

"Goatsucker."

"You're right! I don't believe you." She laughed not expecting an explanation and then continued monitoring the strange sounds of the Missouri night that were loud and noisy compared to her experiences with Lake Superior's western shores. The next sound sent shivers through her. *An overpowering scream from the ridge. A woman's scream.* She squeezed Michael's hand tighter, but she was no closer to this mystery who continued calmly to rock beside her. Surprised by his lack of reaction, Rebecca blurt out, "Michael!"

"Panther," the single word came out mellow, appreciative in tone, an explanation in itself. "Don't worry. If you were a deer, worry. Not you."

Rebecca, while quite frightened, was sure she would lock her door tonight but still watched Michael. He clearly reveled after the big cat's second blood curdling call had come and gone.

His wrinkled smile to Rebecca said, "It's okay." To him, the late evening's opening notes repeated a lifelong symphony, a seasonal marker of life's passage. *All was right, on time, and moving as it should be.*

He turned and focused on the still engaging woman in the other rocker. He enjoyed her wonderment regarding his home and its evening sounds and knew that the calls of the bugs and the birds contrasted radically to the lonely outcry of the loon or the relentless pounding of Lake Superior's waves on its shores. He had no desire to scare her and so offered a few comforting words. "Don't worry. The cat on the ridge is far more afraid of us than you'd expect." Then he grew more sensitive and attempted to relay a thought to her in hope of calming her fears. "But you have wolves up north. You've heard them? No one is ever attacked."

"Yes, I remember the wolves," Rebecca answered. But in silence she was pondering the man beside her who had killed savagely on Bear Island to save their daughter. "Only if you're not scared," she finally said to him. "Only then will I feel safe, and later, only then will I allow myself to fall asleep."

CHAPTER 2
SNORING INSIGHTS

Although they had shared much in the last months and even a child in the remote past, Rebecca still slept in her own bed. She had taken Rachel's old room, down the hall from Michael. In this farmhouse so full of memories, she deemed it the appropriate place. She stored her clothes and toiletries there, also. They did share the single bathroom.

Nightly, his snoring challenged her patience. The overpowering vibrations leaping from his depths could not be ignored. Often standing by his bed or sitting beside him, her still feminine form clothed in an over-sized tee-shirt, Rebecca would gently coax her friend to roll from his back to his side, hoping to stifle the sleep-stopping outbursts.

Many a warm spring night Anna's mother would linger, just sitting, while he slept long and deep after the snoring stopped. Rebecca would watch him if the starlight or moonlight allowed. If not, she listened as the constant call of owls or whippoorwills filled the night. She heard the life force in his breathing and thought it a soothing tonic for her soul.

"It's not your time to leave this earth," she had muttered in quiet sincerity many times as he slept, more so especially in the early spring when he had needed her most. "If only I had not been so stupid and proud."

Rebecca pulled the blanket higher on his shoulders, wishing she had been wise enough so long ago to have held on to this peacefully sleeping man. He had awakened her soul to trust and passion. She felt privileged. She knew full well that she had another chance and hoped this time not to fritter it away.

Her bare feet lay comfortably on the simple pine flooring which was warped and uneven with age. Her toes caressed a board's rough corner. She sensed her feet planted where they should be.

Looking at his resting form Rebecca surveyed his every curve and motion. His breath came easier now, and at a bearable decibel level. *Balding, gray-headed,* she continued in her analysis, but then jolted awake still more, aware of the furious metamorphosis of which he was capable. *A sleeping wildcat.* She tried to imagine his fury to save their daughter. *Like the panther on the ridge*, she bore in mind from the past evening. *If provoked, a hellion to defend his own.* Having seen it long ago before Ellen ever knew him, or Anna, she knew of this sleeping man's violent loyalty to his friends and was thankful for it.

Rebecca and Rachel had talked of the past, too. How Michael had helped defend his mother near the creek had brought on questions. Rebecca had asked about the scars on his back. She had found them much earlier in their lives but not before his dark-haired, childhood friend. Rachel's confirmation of Henry's story again proved the validity of Michael's intense allegiance to friends and family. "He's a Kelly, Rebecca," she had said as if that were the only explanation needed.

Her vigil over a sleeping Michael continued. A recollection of Anna's description of the terrible night when the bright moonlit waters of Lake Superior shone filled her consciousness. Hands with the lithe, delicate fingers of a musician clutched his sheets. She contemplated his dark nature surfacing like a demon. It had forestalled Anna's death not once but three times in as many days, although his life had hung by a thread. Yet, for all Rebecca had heard, she expected no less.

This night, Michael's admiring companion hovered by his bed

much longer than usual. She lingered even as the wee hours pulled closer to dawn. This still beautiful red-haired woman let her mind drift back in time to the mountains of Montana. It had been in those northern mountains that he had so valiantly defended her virtue. It was there she had allowed him to inch his way into her affections, while he had healed in her care. Vivid images came to her. *Those wilds beside the big river with its waters crashing down beside them. There, this country boy from Flat Creek did indeed bind himself forever in my trust.*

Rebecca reaffirmed her feelings that not tonight or in the future would she need to share his bed. Yet she would, if he desired it. She hoped her grieving man, asleep and so close but now on the mend, would allow her to continue sharing his great passion for life. If he would have her, she was determined to stay with him, despite his intermittent foul moods.

She was weary. However, her thoughts refused to dampen, despite the orange fireball on the eastern horizon. Rebecca remembered releasing Michael so long ago. Then, when twenty-one and pregnant with his child, foolish pride had guided her actions. Now, as she sat on his bed she promised herself in a whisper, "Never again."

"I will stay with you along this backwoods creek," she said to no one but the clicking crickets and the chirping of early birds while a cool morning breeze filled the room. Then, only to the wind in the small patch of corn out the window, "There will be no repeating the same mistake."

CHAPTER 3
RECOGNITION

Late the next morning, a smugly pleased Rebecca watched a determined Michael intent on cutting the yard. He had progressed with the push mower up to the log cabin a distance from the house. He had told her earlier in the day, "It's too tight to maneuver the brush hog around the cabin."

Next to the spring creek she heard his efforts slow. She remembered him mention his dread of cutting the knee high orchard grass and fescue, grown so tall with the rains and sunshine of May. It was now early June.

For a moment Rebecca stopped her inside chores to check on him. She walked through fragrant new mown grass between the house and the cabin while following the sound of the mower. The pulsing, chuggidy chug guided her to where he worked at completing the last few swaths.

Satisfied, she circled in quick strides around the cabin back to finish some chores. Before she knew it, curiosity bested her desire not to be nosy. She found herself inside the mid nineteenth century structure exploring its nooks and crannies.

"After almost four months why haven't I investigated this log house before?" came out as she studied the hand cut joists and rough sawn planks. She wasn't sure.

Later, following their lunch, both decided to lounge under the inviting shade of the porch. With a dripping tumbler of iced tea in her hand, Rebecca asked, "Who built the cabin, Michael? It's certainly a solid structure. It appears much older than I originally thought. I found square nails in the stair boards."

"Every board was pegged, actually," Michael answered. "The nails only came later."

Rebecca sensed his interest in talking and lured him to go on.

"They were so expensive," he explained. "You realize pre and post Civil War nails were each individually hand forged and shaped by a blacksmith's hammer? The truth is, the blacksmith was often too busy with bigger projects so slaves and children produced most of the nails in those times. Can you imagine the work that went into forming one nail?"

More interested in the history of the building than a detailed and elaborate history of building materials, Rebecca impatiently countered, "So, who built the cabin?" She was well aware of Michael's interest in history, especially his family's, and caught herself from stopping him. He was talking in paragraphs and that was progress. It was a first since her coming to his home in March.

So, as Michael began his sequential telling of his lineage, he periodically picked up on Rebecca's lowered eyebrows as a sign that a full epic would never do. Her relaxed, but then just as quickly, intense eyes clued Michael that he need not include every cousin's middle name or all the intriguing stories that went along with each.

"The cabin," he began, "was built by my two or three-times-past great grandfather after the Civil War. He traveled here with his family from eastern Missouri. My Grandpa John said that his father had told him stories about my ancestor, the builder, and as a young man my grandpa actually had known him. His name was Sean, an Irishman. He apparently had been quite a feisty fellow both in the Union cavalry and afterward. His mastery of the fiddle was well known in this area, and it seems everyone in my family has or does play fiddle except for me." He paused, obviously a bit perturbed by his inadequacy, but continued, "It was said that Sean played his fiddle when General Sheridan's cavalry charged into battle."

Michael stopped, turned from Rebecca, laughed heartily, and then said, "Getting carried away a bit, sorry."

He noted, to the contrary, that Rebecca was now immersed in the story more than one might expect. She coaxed him to proceed.

"Can you imagine the battle flags flying, the cavalry galloping towards the rebel lines in formation, and old Sean's fiddle in the background providing the beat and melody to lift men's spirits? Actually, it was told that his skill with a fiddle likely saved him in the latter portion of the war. In the early years of fighting he was in the heat of it and only luck or God's will allowed his survival. General Sheridan considered my red-haired relative too valuable to squander on the front lines during the last years of the conflict and kept him close at hand. In fact quite an illustrious history." And he added, "Would loved to have seen it unfold."

Michael paused, reaching deep to remember stories told by his family. His manner began to turn cold and stark. Looking out across the fields he said, "Fierce, Sean was when confronted. My grandfather told me he was like a badger backed up against a wall." He hesitated in deep thought, and then said, "The oldest neighbors told me that my grandpa was the spitting image of his predecessor in more ways than one."

"Sean seems somewhat like yourself, Michael," Rebecca answered with growing authority. She knew there was more on his mind. She had studied him closely as he had spoken the last words. This afternoon's conversation was indeed the most she had gotten out of him at one time since coming to Flat Creek in late winter.

Michael looked over to Rebecca with a kind but empty stare. He well understood that he and his grandfather had undeniably inherited the same emotional traits. He was also well aware it was not a topic for discussion, nor did he have any desire, today, to travel that path.

Rebecca broke the uncomfortable silence after seeing the faraway look in his eyes. She probed gently, "Is there more?" She watched for a reaction, while hoping not to bring out any dark thoughts. She reached for his hand.

She shuddered, thinking there may well be more, then remembered how Anna only the year before had saved Michael's life by shedding blood on this very porch. *Anna was of him*, Rebecca thought, as she remembered the story of how their daughter had sent three men to their deaths within a few steps of where they now sipped their tea. *Like father like daughter*, she quipped to herself, trying to keep her sense of humor. *Anna was a tigress, too. But then*, she thought smugly, *hasn't she always been?*

Rebecca's thoughts came full circle as she realized that Michael's ancestor, Sean, undeniably sat beside her gently rocking in his chair. No, this reincarnation did not have red hair and could not play the fiddle. However, Rebecca understood. She knew Michael Forester also was more than fierce if confronted. Anna was alive today only because this brave man, whose hand she now held, had risen to cold, determined fury to defend her. She persisted in watching his aging eyes knowing he was there now, immersed in memories of past conflict. A deep slow breath brought him back. She was relieved.

"Sorry. I was in far away places I shouldn't go." Then forcing a smile he continued, "Some of my great-grandfather's effects are in a trunk in the attic. On a rainy day you may want to go through them. There are letters, very old letters from before the Civil War." Michael had not read them all since he was a young man, however, he remembered a diary, actually a very descriptive journal, written by one of his great aunts which was not in the barn but stood on a book shelf above his bed.

She looked into her friend's deep blue eyes. He had aged but his eyes seemed forever young. Their gazes locked for a moment. She remembered he had always enjoyed her eyes. He had called them emerald as were Anna's. She smiled at the country boy who humbly sat before her, a country boy who in blatant contradiction read Michener, Dickinson, and Frost for an evening's entertainment.

She shifted back to the story. "Tell me more, Michael. You know that only half my family are from Ireland. My mother's people came up from the eastern Missouri Ozarks during the Great Depression.

First, they tried to find work in the lead mines near Potosi. Then they traveled to the iron fields of northeastern Minnesota."

"Well," Michael started, thinking of Rebecca's more than casual interest. "I don't know much more, except that Sean Kelly mustered out of the army in St. Louis and was bound to an obligation in Van Buren near Big Spring far to the south. That would have been a long and hazardous trip back then, considering the lack of good roads and Missouri's violent nature during the Civil War and after."

With the last few sentences Rebecca's attention had become charged. She reached over to Michael. "Big Spring! Sean Kelly! You didn't mention that his last name was Kelly, but I was so stupid. Of course, it had to be." Then, "Are you sure his hair was red?"

Michael sensed her excitement. He felt her hands tremble.

Rebecca asked, "Do you know if he limped from a wound from the Civil War?"

Michael looked deeply, again, into those emerald pools, their margins lined by the decades, but still sparkling. Rebecca was still beautiful and more importantly to him, her mind remained razor sharp.

He thought long and hard before answering her questions. "Yes, I remember grandpa describing him like that. Aunt Violet's journal tells more of the details I've forgotten. Sean Kelly lived into the early 1930's. The wound disabling him was inflicted by a horse crushing his leg during a battle. A lot of people knew him around here. And yes, his hair was fiery red until he grew old."

"Like Anna's?" And then quickly, "A journal!"

"Yes, Rebecca," Michael answered with a grin, "like Anna's and yours, if my grandpa's stories held any truth to them." And he thought, *Like my mother's and my grandfather's.*

Michael cradled Rebecca's hand as he tried to decipher the feelings behind her penetrating eyes. Puzzled, he asked, "How would you know of him?"

Rebecca could not restrain herself. She rose from her chair and walked to the rail of the porch. She stood lean and tall against it. She stroked her flowing and fiery gray-streaked curls with nervous fingers. Turning back to Michael she said, "Your great-great grandfather was most likely the same man who saved my ancestors from some terrible injustices." She sat down and waited for Michael's reaction.

When, no words came, she said, "He traveled through the Ozarks just after the Civil War. What I know of you and today of your great grandfather only confirms my suspicions. There are some rough stories of a Kelly fresh from the war with a game leg and bright red hair. He took most of my people west somewhere. No one knew what became of them. They were running from the law after defending themselves at my ancestor's mill at what is now Big Spring State Park." She paused, glancing towards Flat Creek. The remains of an old mill lined the stream. "By all accounts this Kelly, his wife, and another woman, an ex-slave, had taken down an entire clan of local ruffians in the process."

Michael asked without enthusiasm, "Killed them?"

"No less," said Rebecca again drilling Michael with an intense stare. "It appears male Kellys share some similar traits." Pausing pensively, but keenly watching for a response, she considered her next words as Michael revealed a tiny smile, his grin.

"This Kelly," she said, "stopped a mob trying to lynch one of my relatives. The man he saved was a millwright and became his father-in-law." She pointed towards the rock foundations below them on Flat Creek, and then continued. "He saved my great-great-great grandfather." Halting her story, but only for a breath, she then quickly went on, "It all happened near Van Buren at Big Spring in 1866. Anything after that is conjecture."

For a few moments Rebecca remained silent, trying to deduce Michael's thoughts. While holding back as much excitement as she could, she finished her animated narrative, "But you know how mountains can be made from mole hills, and how an ounce of truth produces a ton of lies after generations of telling the same stories."

When Michael answered her with a solemn silence, Rebecca said, "The old matrons of my family, who told me these tales, swore on the Bible that they're true. They told me that my great-great grandmother, Emma, was the main source."

Still unsure of all of this, Michael showed Rebecca only a poker face. However, his great aunt's diary told the story, too, and Emma was a name found early on in its many pages.

Watching him, Rebecca forced a laugh, and then pondered all the possibilities as she put the pieces together. The man in front of her was living proof. Michael and her gallant but fierce relative could easily be one in the same. The genes that made up this man before her, whom she had loved deeply but quietly most of her adult life, could truly be linked to her ancestor.

"He played the fiddle, you say?" Rebecca cajoled.

Michael answered with brimming emotion, "Momma Kay thought that only one person could have ever played as well as Grandpa Sean." He looked deeply into Rebecca's eyes before he spoke again. "Only before she died did she tell me. It was Anna."

Rebecca's face broke into a radiant smile. Then she spoke to his eager ears in a charged but happy fury, "Do you realize that my great-great grand mother may be the sister of Kelly's wife! We could be related, Michael! Actually, the talk was that Kelly may have courted more than just one of the sisters. We may well have the same great-great grandfather! It makes sense that only a bloodline from both sides coming together could make our daughter such a prodigy with the violin."

Rebecca finished out of breath, but then rose up and stepped over to the still sitting Michael. She lured him up with open arms. They embraced with more than a friendly squeeze. He asked her, "Did you know my middle name is Sean? Everyone tells me I am a Kelly despite my lackluster father's contribution."

Michael hugged Rebecca again and continued in roaring approval, "Amazing! Are you sure about your facts? This is pretty far fetched. Did your family write down any of this?" Again his mind traveled to the old letters tied up with faded ribbon in the ancient trunk in the log cabin. They had been written by a soldier to his sweetheart in Memphis a century-and-a-half before. He also went over in his mind what he remembered from Aunt Violet's journal.

"No," Rebecca's elated words proceeded, "but the old stories, as I've already said from different old aunties, were remarkably the same, and the source of so much red hair on the heads of so many leads back to the family members who came north from the Ozarks."

"By the way," Michael added, "the wife of Sean Kelly was quite a fighter, too. Her story alone could fill a book. She actually traveled by train from Memphis across the Confederacy to Georgia and enlisted. She fought as a man for two years." He paused and then, "But let's test your theory."

Anna's mother waited uneasily for his questions.

"Do you know the names of Sean Kelly's wife and of the other woman who traveled with him? They bore his children. Three or four I remember reading."

Rebecca thought a moment then spoke with confidence, "Sean's wife was named Nora Melforth. The other woman I am not sure of, Llewellyn, or Lynn-Ann, or Lee Ann. The old aunties didn't agree on her name."

Michael looked hard at Rebecca. When he finally spoke it was as if gently stamping the final seal of hot wax to authenticate a legal document. "Her name was Luanne," he said. Michael also thought of Violet, one of the Melforth sisters, and was glad that her diary described so much of Sean's exploits from Ireland all the way to Flat Creek.

Michael forced a smile, and Rebecca was pleased that his sober mood from months past had vanished.

Grasping Rebecca by the shoulders, he laughed, then said with a grin that encompassed his entire face, "Do you understand that we were unknowingly committing incest along the banks of the Kootenai River all those years ago!"

Rebecca was transfixed. Her eyes riveted on Michael. She snuggled as close as their two bodies would allow, hugging Michael only as a lover could. Into his ear she whispered, "I'd do it all again, if you want."

She noted with pleasure the reawakening in the man considered lost by his children last winter. His old wry grin was back in force. The transformation on Michael's face helped much of her own pain melt away. Part of her debt was now paid in full.

"The journal or diary that mentions Sean Kelly, you need to read it," Michael added knowing that he was interrupting her deepest thoughts.

Rebecca listened and tucked the information away for future reference but her mind was not on books about ancestors and retracing history. At the moment all she wanted was to be closer to the man in her arms.

She silently predicted that by autumn they would be sharing the same bed. She anticipated waking her friend from his snoring bouts in the future, and then once more snuggling together stacked like spoons on their sides, under warm quilts.

⊕

The following day Rebecca took Michael's words to heart. She found Violet's journal tucked away on his bookshelf. In the living room she settled into an overstuffed chair and proceeded to examine it. While she thoughtfully thumbed through the early pages a yellowed newspaper clipping fell to the floor. Carefully, she picked it up. Across the top was printed in bold type, *The New York Herald* 1859. An article by the architect who built Saint Patrick's Cathedral jumped out at her. Delighted with the find, she sat back with smug contentment and imagined the story of New York City street life printed over one hundred-and-fifty years before.

BOOK II

CHAPTER 1
"IMMIGRANTS' FARE"

from the writings of James Renwich
Architect for Saint Patrick's Cathedral, NYC
Begun 1858, finished 1878

The streets of Manhattan on the lower east side are not a place for a young boy or girl of any faith to grow to adulthood. As I compose this letter in the year of our Lord 1859, I fear for their safety and spiritual well being. Overcrowding, filth, and crime are ubiquitous to the development of any child lucky enough to survive the first ten years. Fear and violence are enemies yet often as not an ally of anyone who lives beyond early childhood into his or her early teens. Disease borne from a communal pump over a shallow well is common. Contaminated water supplies and malnutrition lay low many early on and allow consumption to take its toll of those who survive till later. Fighting and thieving for food and other street violence eliminate still more. Armed with ax handles and knives, great gangs of angry men, mostly of Irish extraction, rule the poverty stricken streets of lower Manhattan Island.

The ragged, barely clothed offspring of the poor immigrant multitudes are cast aside and their condition ignored by those with the power to make changes for the better. Bigger prisons are touted as the answer by the warm, well fed, and well heeled although the conditions in the local lockups are little better than the sordid streets.

These same well-moneyed merchants and speculators, whose nose-in-the-air arrogance is easily recognizable on the great avenues of this major city of our young nation, were but immigrants themselves less than a generation before. However, the memories of his or her family's stepping down upon the coarse planks of American piers off the crowded ships from Rotterdam, London, Dublin, or Bremerhaven has somehow faded, and faded dramatically in proportion to their acquisition of wealth.

Thus, for one of the street urchins to see sixteen years or more can prove an order of overwhelming good luck or resourcefulness. Sadly, the prettiest of girls and boys often are reduced to pedaling their virtue for a pittance as their only option for survival. This is nothing new in any large city of the world, now or in the past, and is viewed and accepted by the self appointed 'elite of New York society'. It is just the way of doing business on the many foul smelling streets that run their course to the East River.

The cold winters of New York and its hot summers prove the most challenging obstacle to survival for the newcomers. The month of January now engulfs the city in its full fury, and a steam ferry, seen through the chilling mists on the water, chugs its way plying the Hudson to outer boroughs on other islands near Manhattan. Put to extended use in the harsh winter months, the spacious-decked side wheeler doubles as a mobile morgue for the poor.

The frequency with which its large bow plows the waters of this busy commercial waterfront is a morbid reminder of the times. The macabre load of death is pushed to the entrance of the Atlantic leaving behind only the dark trail of billowing smoke in its wake. The number of bodies frozen and stacked like cordwood, with a one-way ticket beyond the coast to the depths of the ocean, speaks of the harshness of the winter and of the lives of those who crave opportunity on American soil. To state that times are hard in this grand city of ours is an understatement.

Yesterday, I watched an Irish mother and a German father as they witnessed the advance of the death ship in the harbor on its daily trip to the sea. I could see how they held their children closer and tighter knowing their kin had missed the grim reaper if only for this day. However, these destitute people at Mulberry through Worth Street and Five Points, as the area is termed, with such dreams to have been lured thousands of miles from their origin, know better. They know not to be so foolish as to attempt claiming rights for tomorrow or the day after, no matter how indomitable their spirits. As I saw the mother and father turning from the water, the floating morgue passed. I can only hope they are proceeding forthwith into their new day to make the best of what God has seen fit to bless them.

CHAPTER 2
THE PROMISED LAND

It was in early July of 1860 when the Kelly family finally set their feet on firm ground. On a New York shipping wharf after a rough and lengthy voyage, they stood and admired the busy harbor. Farther up the wooden landing the four watched another ship, far greater than their own, tie up and then almost as quickly, embark again. The guttural German in grunts and hollers carried across the steaming water as hundreds of young men left one ship, recently docked from Europe, only to be funneled aboard another.

Mystified at first, the father, Malroy Kelly, cracked a cynical smile as he studied the markings on the ship and identified the men in charge. The ship, battle ready and meticulously organized, bristled with broad-mouthed, black cannons. Men in blue uniforms aboard the ship shouldered rifles. "The insane comedy of it all," Malroy Kelly stated under his breath. "They, like us, have fled their homeland but to what avail?"

The insightful Irishman, with not much more than thirty years under his belt and a family in tow, saw the clear picture. He knew there was no paradise but had hoped to flee Ireland's feudalistic agricultural economy. He anticipated finding political haven from English tyranny that relentlessly squeezed the very life blood from the peasants who worked the land at home. However, Malroy feared he was grasping at straws. Although already chilled by an unrelenting fever, this first view of America from the docks chilled him further.

The other proud members of his family watched, also. The three had seen the herding of the German boys to the nearby boat, and were puzzled by the exodus. They also fostered great hopes, as their painful journey ended. Ill fortune this determined Irish family accepted. Indeed, it seemed predestined to decide their fate on this fabled American shore.

"Malroy, what is to become of us?" his sickened wife said sadly. Both children looked to their father. They watched him shrug his shoulders. Then the Irish family's free spirited patriarch spouted out despite his weakness, "We'll go on, my dear." He looked skyward, "There's blue sky above so we'll go on." Then with more heart than strength, he steadied himself on the railing. "We'll do our best to go on."

Malroy's thoughts traveled beyond his last words and dwelt on how both he and his wife had been set upon by the typhus early in the three week voyage. He remembered the crowded conditions on board the three-masted sailing ship. Its holds had been packed with low fare immigrants hoping for a better life. The stench of the hundreds below decks had stifled his usually stoic spirit.

Sixteen-year-old Sean and his younger sister by two-years, Mary Katherine, for whatever reason or rhyme, had avoided the harsh effects of the affliction. Sean watched his father's withering face and wondered, *How, if half starved and feverish when arriving in New York harbor, will my family from this very dreary beginning have a chance.*

Sean let his mind drift back to Ireland and the farm halfway between the western shore's raging sea and Lisdoonvarna. There he knew for sure they had no chance. His father had told him on the boat about their landlord's methodical approach to silencing labor organizers and rabble rousers. Sean had heard directly the threat made to his father to cripple his children. Sean imagined himself without his right hand, the hand that held the bow of his fiddle. Triggered by the thought, his hands clenched into tight fists.

⊕

Two terrible days later, a steely-eyed Sean Kelly, the last male survivor of the Kelly clan, surveyed his parents' bodies as they trailed further and further away on the death wagon. He shuddered as summer's putrid air, germinating off the filth strewn streets, swept into his lungs. He pondered God's will in having his parents endure the crossing only to die within days of landing in New York. The image of the wagon's slow turning spokes chiseled into his brain like steel on stone.

The young Irishman stood bewildered and lost. His sister, Mary Katherine, and himself had survived so far. *How could this all have happened? Only last month, I was at the fair in Lisdoonvarna, playing my fiddle in the contest and wooing the tavern keeper's lovely daughter.*

"By what grace of God," he shouted in rising anger at the wagon as it turned the corner, "have I and my sister been spared? And Lord, to what end? To what end?"

⊕

Early the next morning on the Sixteenth Street Wharf, Sean Kelly contemplated the foamy waves that swept the blustery shoreline. In tepid air ripe with the thickness of an impending storm, Sean and Mary Katherine waited. Further out they saw the waters of the vast harbor churned gray by the mist laden wind.

These two young faces, forlorn from their loss, studied the edge of the great river. They clenched each other's unsteady hands. Today, Sean and Mary Katherine watched in utter sadness while the death ship left port. The shrouded bodies of their parents they knew to be somewhere on its canvas covered deck.

"So, dear sister, I wonder which way to travel, now," Sean managed. The lean and wiry speaker, barely a man, mustered a smile for his tired sister whose normally sparkling eyes were so diminished. He crossed himself, more in habit than in faith.

With Spartan effort Mary Katherine answered, "We need to find work Sean." She wondered at what deep well her brother drew his courage. Then, "You will find it easier than I, brother. You are stronger." Pausing, her eyes then drifted from the death ship up to Sean. "We will get through this together."

"So much for the promised land," Sean said as the ship that carried his parents gained speed. He watched its paddle wheel churning the East River's dark waters. A plume of acrid black smoke swept towards him and choked the onlookers on the wharf. He coughed.

Mary Katherine held tight to her brother's sleeve when she saw her father. She stifled a prayer for mercy. "He's there!" she finally forced out, pointing with her uplifted arm. She had indeed seen him. The failing younger sister allowed herself to hang from her revered older brother's steady shoulder.

Malroy Kelly lay amongst so many others stacked like cordwood on the open deck of the steamer. No oilcloth tarp covered him. His red hair was brilliant even in death. Again, a putrid cloud of black smoke surrounded Mary Katherine and she lost contact with her entire body. Thankfully, she felt Sean's strong arms catch her before she fell. When her senses returned, the last female in the Kelly clan heaved, and her stomach emptied into the black, forbidding river of opportunity below.

Chapter 3
Cold Shadows

The roaming pigs unnerved him. Grazing in the gutters and alleyways Sean saw them in troops of three and four. He had counted over a hundred since he and his sister had left the two-penny flop house a few blocks from the wharf in search of Five Points.

"Which way to the Irish at Anthony and Orange Street?" Sean asked a passerby. "Some describe it as Five Points." His cracking voice had reached out to a quick-strided man topped-out with a tall beaver hat. Long tails on a bright colored waistcoat rippled side-to-side as the walker hurriedly attempted to put more distance between himself and the poor red-headed young man hailing him. Sean's eyes lay riveted on the shiny brass buttons running down the front of the man's jacket. No force today could make him look up into the rich man's eyes.

Unfriendly out-stretched hands and pointing fingers gave directions to the pair and sent them onward. Once, after Sean had politely asked for guidance again in the street, he judiciously stood back as a haughty woman carrying a market basket freely spat at his feet. He only held Mary Katherine's hand tighter as the woman cursed his poor Irish heritage.

"Worthless scum, keep moving. Can't you see that decent people live on this street." *Even her shoes,* Sean thought again with his eyes down, *are worth more than anything we have to our names.*

The less than easy passing of his parents the day before had drained any emotions he still might possess. Yet, Sean silently struggled on with his sister in tow. He must. He sensed Mary Katherine shuffling beside him to keep up. She deserved all he could give. She deserved a chance.

After endless blocks of walking, Sean and his sister found the Irish community with their noses. They could smell it a block before they could see it. The streets were piled with a greater abundance of garbage and human waste. More swine ran free.

The new arrivals received help at first, but Sean wondered how those who were only one step ahead of the reaper themselves could help others?

Through the summer and fall both found work, but their long hours of labor in first the sweltering and then drafty upstairs garment factory gained them only pennies a day. During the late afternoons Sean gravitated to the broad alleyway market with his fiddle and bow. There, he lost himself in his music and his efforts earned enough to keep the two just beyond the brink of starvation. They built a tiny lean-to in an alley behind a crumbling livery stable and paid a doubtful landlord's fat-fisted collectors two-bits a week for the privilege. When early winter began the brother and sister somehow survived the cold rains and furious winds.

In Sean's eye other dire traits of the immigrant communities quickly surfaced. Great gangs of men kept the peace in brutal ways. Sean wondered where the police force could be! After a cheerless and sad passing of Christmas day, deep winter set in with a fierce blowing snow.

⊕

The boy from Lisdoonvarna was now seventeen, a man by the hard standards set in the streets. He sat in relative peace on a broken caned chair above the crusting snow and leaned back against a sun-warmed brick wall. Despite his cold sockless feet, he made a point of enjoying his daily survey of the passing people before he played his tunes. A deep voice abruptly caught his attention. Sean listened while a well-to-do man looked up and read the tall letters in painted white script. Each spread boldly above Sean's head on crumbling brick, forming broad, if peeling words. For all eyes that had mastered the English language, which Sean had not, the man read, "Clancy's Dry Goods, Emporium of Household Wares", and as the advertisement continued, so too did the wool-coated man's bellow, "the finest tools and clothing on Market Street!"

A hearty, "Ha!" Sean heard while the reader's judgmental face turned first to him and then many others. "Such rubbish, don't you think, boy? Nothing is fine anywhere in this part of the city. And besides, this is just a broad alleyway and no real street."

Dismissing the remarks as self-important bluster, Sean found it impossible to stifle the sound of slapping new leather on stone and crusty snow or the same man's laughs as he walked away into the crowd chiding the conditions of the poorest of the poor. *Shoes*, Sean thought as his cold toes ran over coarse paper substituted for worn bull hide. *We both need better shoes desperately.*

His own shoddy clothes Sean pretended not to see, while he listlessly pulled his revered stringed instrument from its threadbare cloth bag. He adjusted the tuning pegs one-by-one with the fiddle neck lifted to his ear. A few broken horse hairs were trimmed, and then, lastly, he rosined the bow. With rising dignity thought by many to be uncharacteristic of his station, Sean stood, straightened himself to his tallest, and placed the violin's face piece under his chin just as he had months before at the Lisdoonvarna fair. His poise was evident and attracted the attention of many who walked by. A meager band of raggedy people stopped on this winter's afternoon anticipating the music that had become a welcome reprieve to the doldrums of the day.

Expecting the usual street concert to promptly commence, the gathering crowd grew restless. A stamping of cold feet in the snow and watchful eyes awaited the wiry boy who held his time-worn instrument with elegance. Yet, the young musician remained motionless, staring above the crowd. His gaze crossed the wide, cobble-stoned street through the frosty air that hung above the open paupers' market. He somehow awaited a cue.

Impatient, a few visitors to the lane shook their heads in

disappointment and continued their appointed afternoon rounds. However, as soon as these strangers began walking away, a hearty emission of cherub like notes began. The stoic statue of a young man slowly but deliberately set about to pluck his bow across the four strings held in precisioned discipline by his left hand. The signal he had awaited had come unbeknown to anyone else. An increasingly more rapid beat filled the street.

Rich but merry tunes flew like dancing swallows from Sean's fiddle. Across the tattered, booth-lined street, all under a dusting of last night's snow, the music carried cheerfully in toe tapping rhythms. It gladdened the ears of all who peddled half rotten grain, used clothes, and tin utensils from open carts or beneath snow-dusted canvas.

⊕

The talented lad, green-eyed and red-headed, played his fiddle as only an Irishman could, or would have the heart. He saw the change before him in the crowd's lighter steps and growing smiles. Smugly, he took it all in. He sent jigs and then reels out amongst his brethren, many of whom had also only recently been transported from the east across the storm tossed seas.

The boy acted the part of a man. He looked his people in the eye, one-by-one, giving them a confident smile as the lustrous music flowed from his fiddle. The women applauded and the men nodded, pipes clamped between their lips. The language spoken to compliment the fine Irish lad with his fiddle was much older than English.

The entire audience was immersed, nearly hypnotized. Not just his music captivated them but also his proud and elegant style of playing. Like a winter's magic, it lifted their spirits. While down trodden before on this cold winter's day, the fiddler's audience stood taller as each note reached their ears.

The faces of these listeners, McDowells, McGraws, O'Donnels, O'Duns, and Donnahoes sent off approving sighs as toes tapped in the crunching snow and hands clapped in time. Such jubilance on a cold January day had been unheard of until the red-headed boy had brought his fiddle to the broad alley claimed as a market street by the Irish poor.

Men and women, who had been busy at their booths selling their wares, stopped to listen and briefly deserted their tables to catch a glimpse of the young musician. The mid-afternoon sunshine and the music so familiar soothed their hurts and their hearts.

When the musician put down his bow after over an hour of Celtic tunes, the entire audience vigorously applauded. Their dispositions were now warmer and more congenial despite the brisk weather. These pitiable Irish folk lining this crowded street in New York realized they were proud free people. Sean had given them that. The young fiddler had relieved their troubled minds if only for a brief time, on but another of a string of frigid January days.

⊕

Sean Kelly graciously thanked his loyal audience with a formal bow and smile, and then picked up his upturned hat that had lain in front of him during the concert. He noted its extra weight and forced a wry grin as he finished packing up his instrument in its sack-cloth bag. The handful of pennies he had earned would be put to good use and spent all too soon. While Sean had gazed so stoically and solemnly off into the distance before beginning to play his fiddle, few in the crowd realized what his look sought. He had awaited a sign to begin, and a girl sitting on a slatted wooden fruit box at the entrance of an alleyway was to give it. She had watched the young man intently and with pride as she braced herself, too weak to stand to see him better, too weak to sit up straight.

Sean had watched his worn-down sister in tattered dress and shawl. He waited, his fiddle poised to deliver. The sun-lit spot where he had placed her by the wall was slowly shifting, soon to bring cold shadows. *The concert must not be for too long.* Yet, still he had paused immobile, looking out across the crowd so impatient, waiting for the sign. Then with a forced effort the once pretty but now gaunt-faced girl had turned her head towards her brother. She smiled so slightly, and only for him, thus producing the gesture the fine musician had needed to commence with his joyous rush of Celtic tunes.

⊕

With his newly earned pennies in hand, Sean Kelly walked to a nearby clothing cart. There, he purchased a shoddy wool coat with half of his earnings, then moved down to the alleyway where Mary Katherine sat in the waning sunshine. He saw her using all her energy to cast him an adoring smile.

Sean gently wrapped the thick but tattered coat around his sick sister. Then he carried her slight weight into the brighter sunlit street, moving around the carts to the wall where he had played his fiddle with such stirring confidence. There, he lovingly placed the frail girl on the same broken chair where he had sat before to catch the winter sun.

After wrapping her up tightly and leaning her comfortably against the warm masonry wall, Sean set off with two tin cups to spend the other half of his pennies on bread and hot coffee. In a few minutes he returned to the sunlit cobbles and Mary Katherine's side. He helped her drink and encouraged her to eat. She coughed and blood dripped down her mouth to her chin. With his sleeve Sean wiped her lips clean.

Chapter 4
The Loss of Mary Katherine

Sean felt the fine, cutting crystals of snow on his face. The storm's fury had increased and hurled its frozen bits through the cracks in his shanty's ill-fitting door and walls. He had built it hastily, hoping to soon find better. Day-by-day he had crammed the cracks full of newspaper and added scraps to the roof. He thought often how this four-by-eight foot space might well become the final home for the remaining Kellys from Lisdoonvarna. Others, however, had it still worse. Sean saw them at night in doorways and under the spans of bridges holding desperately to life.

On his bed of rags raised up from the scampering of rats with packing crates, Sean listened to the belabored breathing of sister. His only friend in the new world was finishing her final retreat to the after-time. Here, in this tiny haven, Sean held her, trying to conserve her body heat as she dwindled with each breath.

Providing Mary Katherine with more was beyond his grasp. *Dignity is an illusion held by gossamer threads*, he remembered Father O'Daer telling him as a boy. Now he understood. As a tramp from the crowded and perpetually impoverished streets, life's amenities had abandoned him. *I have spent my days since Ireland...*

in a hell… designed by God for dishonest men. Tears flowed down his cheeks as he finished his thought. *Our good priest in Lisdoonvarna could not have imagined.*

Half awake, then dozing, Sean still heard Mary Katherine's shallow breaths. He dreamed of better times when he was a boy and far away from the filth and cold of this city called New York.

⊕

Walking with a twelve-year-old's typically confident gait, Sean passed down the carriage lane of the squire's manor. He stared in awe at the three-storied, imposing stone house before him. Its tall windows of unimaginably expensive glass panes, not oil cloth, held back the drafts. His innocent eyes took it all in. Doors and shutters freshly painted in bright blue stunned his senses. The well-trimmed yard of green grass and varied shrubbery entranced the poor crofter's son. He could not imagine seeing anything finer should he have lived to be a hundred. Even the pea gravel under his shoes seemed rare and novel to his innocent eyes. Except for the cobbled streets in Lisdoonvarna, rocks and constant mud in a road were all he had ever known.

Now halfway along its grand curving entry way, the squire's mansion stood as high as the stately trees around it. Malroy Kelly's only son walked toward the manor's front door unsure of his place but sure of his intentions. It was then that he heard the dogs.

Roaring! he thought, while caught up in a fear he had never known before. The hounds barked in a ferocious chorus as they rounded the corner of the house with long strides. Three leggy, wolf-like canines raced to his scent on the gravel lane. In seconds he found himself surrounded and frozen by fright. Even his eyes locked in their sockets as total panic engulfed him. Tongues hanging long dripped with drool. Finger-long snarling teeth guarded his escape. Yet at that moment, the clanging of an opening metal gate caught his attention. A man in simple work clothes appeared.

Seeing the boy's peril, the middle aged man hollered to the wolfhounds to heel. The dogs readily complied. He watched the petrified lad who surely felt as if he remained a potential entrée for their supper.

Smiling now, he walked across the yard to the boy and asked, "Are you the one our good Father Vincent O'Daer has recommended? I see you have met our four-legged groundskeepers."

Sean Kelly stood rigid in terror, unable to muster a single word. He was embarrassed, but he could do nothing to remedy his condition. He feared he had soiled his trousers. He attempted to speak but failed as before.

After a few moments of silent appraisal, Calhan O'Quinn, the English squire's stable master, hollered, "Off with you!" His words sent the dogs scurrying back to the house. A hard thrown spray of small stones followed his command.

Only then, with the dogs' departure, did Sean sense the air moving in and out of his chest. Finally he managed to speak, "Yes, Mr. O'Quinn, Father Vincent told my father," and he paused out of breath. Then, "He said you have need of a stable boy."

"Well, then, lad," Calhan said gently, hoping to stem the tide of fear in the boy's eyes, but noted with approval a rapid recovery of confidence. "I have good reports about you. Quick to learn was one of the compliments paid you by the old priest."

He went on, "Hard working and honest, I also hear." Calhan O'Quinn put his hands down on the boy's shoulders, looking him squarely in the eye, "The last quality alone would endear you to me, lad."

With that said a smiling Calhan amiably squeezed Sean by the shoulder and then led him across the large green to the low stone building that housed the stables. As they walked he threw phrases right and left concerning horses, their care and riding, and the wisdom one could gain from watching their behavior.

"They're smarter than most people. You know that, lad? Do you know the difference between the forelock and the withers?" The young Kelly's education had begun.

From a distance a pair of young eyes watched. Seeing the two through the stable's opened doors, Keri O'Quinn studied the new boy with curiosity. She was the same age as Sean and Calhan's oldest daughter. In shadows ripe with smells of stale horse sweat, straw, and manure, she stood shyly on a wooden stall with both feet elevated on the bottom board's edge. For days, she had eagerly awaited Sean's arrival.

She inspected the pair, her father so tall but no mystery and the boy skinny, short and unknown. Keri's bright eyes saw the promising chance of companionship cradled in her father's kind hand. She had been at the church when the priest had proposed that her father hire Malroy Kelly's only son.

On that misty day in early autumn, Sean observed O'Quinn's daughter studying his every step as he began an apprenticeship that would span three years, teach him a vocation, and provide the open-hearted friendship of the entire O'Quinn clan.

That morning his work began simply. He cleaned the stables. But within days after proving himself to the stable master, Sean was soon in the thick of deciphering the countless names and uses of the thick leather harness that hung in the tack room.

Sean grew accustomed to the smells of the horses and gained their loyalty. The continual pleasant presence of O'Quinn's auburn-haired daughter became mostly a blessing. He worked alongside Keri as she diligently forked manure, cleaned the harness, and trained the stock with almost the same skill as her father. He admired her because she worked beside a mere crofter's son as an equal, and also because she dared her new found friend to learn all he could from her father. Keri's competitive spirit only made him fonder of her, and her father insisted they ride together when the day's chores were properly completed. Under O'Quinn care, each passing year brought the lowest born of Irishman ever closer to being one with the horse and a good friend of the stable master's oldest daughter.

⊕

Sean awoke shivering. Not twelve now but seventeen, he felt his stiff legs under his blankets of rags and newspapers.

"Mary Katherine!" he whispered. No answer came. He waited and then placed his ear to her mouth. He neither heard nor felt her breath. His sister was vacant of any signs of life. She was a cold statue beside him. He lit his only candle. Its flame tossed side-to-side in the draft. When he saw her gentle face casting an empty stare his way, he reached to cradle her head. Grief stricken but with the most loving of hands, he pulled her eyelids closed.

⊕

So desperately alone, Sean watched, again, as the death cart wheeled away. And on this sad day he knew he must play his fiddle. Those who listened in the street knew of his loss. They had felt it before in their own lives, and now heard it that afternoon woven ever so deeply in his music, thread by painful thread.

Sean's deep pockets of emotion, filled to the brim with sorrow, enabled his music to glow with passion and allowed him to endure. However, on that darkest of days the boy from Lisdoonvarna played his fiddle until only a few horse hairs remained on the bow and a much anticipated darkness brought reprieve. He had lacked the heart to witness the death ship's scheduled passage to the Atlantic and the final voyage of his beloved sister.

CHAPTER 5
A HAND UP

It was a week later on Market Street when Sean cried out, "Halt or I'll flail you!" Two hoodlums had first knocked down a well-heeled gentleman and were in the process of stealing his wallet. The Irishman ran to the man's aid from his perch against the sunlit wall. An oak stick in hand, he arrived only in time to stop a severe beating. The victim had attempted to fight back and the two attackers were not about to let defiance get by without a lesson.

The thieves turned their heads when they saw Sean with his weapon held high and quickly decided retreat was a better recourse. Over a shoulder, Sean heard one running man holler, "We'll settle with you later, red top." Then as quickly as they had emerged from the crowded street, both disappeared.

Sean helped the injured man up, but wondered fearfully how he would pay in the days to come. The streets were dangerous and he now regretted his heroics. The gangs ruled the alleys, minor avenues, and the night, and no sparse scattering of policemen on Market Street said any differently. The two robbers, Sean knew, were threads intertwined in a much bigger web. He had seen them before. Again, he pondered their retribution as he helped the victim rise to his feet.

"Thank you, lad," the obviously Irish voice said with feeling. "If

I just would have given the louts my wallet, you would have not felt obligated to express your chivalry."

Despite a bruised forehead and a bloody nose, the sharp-chinned, handsome man, ten years Sean's senior, extended his hand. "Daniel Payton, at your service."

Sean took it, amazed at its cleanliness, and ashamed for the first time in months of his lack. He gave Mr. Payton his name. The man's entire appearance spoke of his station, not elegant but tidy and above the streets. With a near beaten spirit Sean looked down. No tattered shoes on this man's feet. The shoes of Mr. Payton gleamed with oil. Sean wondered why the fellow was here in the first place. *What would take a man, many steps up from poverty, to such a derelict and dangerous avenue?*

"Sir, Mr. Payton, moneyed folk avoid our street like the plague." Then, rather more forward than expected but spawned by his curiosity, Sean asked, "Why do you travel this way?"

"Well, lad," a grateful and recovering Mr. Payton said, "I hoped to hear the music this broad alleyway is becoming famous for. In late afternoon, I've heard, is the best chance of catching the tunes of a young man people claim is a master with the bow. A slim red-headed lad," and Payton looked more closely at Sean. Daniel Payton's friendly face spoke volumes to Sean as he politely waited for a response. "Are you, he?"

Sean silently acknowledged Payton's heartfelt praise with a smile, the first since his sister's death seven days before. The red-headed boy from Lisdoonvarna said with a now glowing confident grin, "I hear from folks around that the fiddler of whom you speak is soon to play."

⊕

One dreadful day turned to the next as Sean awaited the inevitable. Every street seller expected the gang's revenge and told Sean to hide or run or arm himself with more than a stick. He stewed in fear of the attack that he knew must come.

The confrontation occurred six days later with no warning. Four of the hoodlums came when he least expected it. He was playing his fiddle with a large crowd assembled on a rare sunny day. The hoodlums' goal appeared to set Sean up as an example, and what better place to do so than on a back avenue teeming with defenseless people.

By the time Sean realized his dilemma and brought his music to a sudden halt, it was too late. He was surrounded. Burly gang members were behind him and quickly pinned his arms. Confused but with sudden anger in his soul, he saw the faces of the crowd radically change from enjoyment to disgust.

"You remember us, carrot top? Greetings from the Dead Rabbits," the chief thug said as he held Sean's chin in his hand. He hoped to intimidate not just the fiddler but all those who were to witness the beating.

"You won't need that fine fiddle anymore, Sean Kelly," another hollered as he grabbed the neck of the treasured instrument. With little effort the heirloom broke into splintery halves.

However, Sean was young and not wise enough to see the inevitable. With a sudden movement he broke free and reached under the feed sack normally used to protect his fiddle. There, his right hand found the hidden oak stave. He discovered in the next few moments that he had truly inherited his father's fighting rage. Two of the thugs went down before the other two had him bloodied and on his knees.

An old woman at a cart who had known Sean for months ran up and entered the fray screaming to the crowd, "Don't just stand there! Help this good boy."

It all ended quickly and luckily in Sean's favor. Three well dressed men with stern faces and swinging shillelaghs, the last of them Daniel Payton, broke through the gathering and halted the beating.

⊕

Later, in a modest apartment many blocks away from Five Points, the Irish farmer's son asked, "So, Mr. Payton, will you be taking the gangs on for my sake tomorrow, too?"

Daniel Payton and his pretty wife tended the fiddle player's wounds with hot soapy water. Mrs. Payton tenderly cleaned the wounds of the boy who had so heroically defended her husband just a week before.

Sean relished her gentle touch. It was the first warm wash cloth on his head since he could remember, and he wondered if heaven could be better.

"No, Sean, I've no plans to fight the gangs. However, my friends and I could not just stand by and watch you being beaten most likely to your death."

Daniel looked to his wife but spoke to Sean, "No, I shall not tempt the fates. I have too much at stake. The Dead Rabbits or the Black Birds, call the rabble what you will, are not to be dismissed lightly. Clarissa and I will be on the train for Boston within the hour. We want you to come with us."

Sean was appreciative but also curious. "Dead Rabbits? I have heard this gang at Five Points called the Black Birds, but Mr. Payton...Dead Rabbits?"

Daniel gave Sean a perplexed look, then spoke, "I thought you'd know that name more than Black Birds."

Sean returned his new friend's barb with a blank face and a shake of the head.

"Well, then, my heroic but ignorant countryman," Daniel began. "*Raibead* is Gaelic for 'a man to be feared'." He searched Sean's face for understanding and continued, "*Dead* in *Gaelic* means 'very much'." He waited and received a nod from Sean and finally an answer.

"A man to be greatly feared," Sean said. "That fits, Mr. Payton, but I would have pronounced it differently in the old tongue."

After packing on such brief notice, the Paytons and Sean plowed through the frosty air and the multitude of half starved humanity lining the streets. The train station seemed an impossible goal. Sean's two new friends, now bound for Boston carrying belongings of mere necessity, were soon lost to him in the tight spaces and the hustle and bustle of the narrow thoroughfare. Cheerless, Sean could only think that the Paytons thought him close behind. Yet, quickly he was far worse than that. He was miserable. Some one had grabbed his arm and pinned him. The Dead Rabbits were to have their settling of scores as Daniel Payton had predicted.

Rapidly tossed on his backside in the icy muck of rotten vegetables and sewage, Sean attempted to ward off cruel blow after cruel blow. Short sticks and shoulder-high shillelaghs pounded him. He saw the long knife blade moving towards his belly.

⊕

Daniel Payton looked over his shoulder. Sean was nowhere in sight. The thought of going back for him instantly faded when he saw his wife. He could not leave her alone on the street in this melee. Besides, he was no hero. Saddened but considering there to be no other options, Daniel turned and with authority led his struggling wife towards the train station despite her pleas to go back. "Daniel, we must help the boy!"

⊕

Remarkably, gunfire halted Sean's execution. A cloud of dark smoke erupted from nowhere and covered him. It was the last thing he could have expected. While quite dazed and bloodied, he still managed to look up. Through the parting smoke, a trim, bearded man in a blue jacket pointed a big pistol at another of the gang members. Powerless, Sean could only watch. He noted that the blood from his attacker's chest was pooling onto the cobblestones, and the knife meant for him had clattered unused onto the street. A second loud discharge from the weapon again filled the broad street with black smoke. Far up the crowded avenue Sean saw only the scurrying retreat of his remaining attackers.

"Thank you," a beaten and bewildered Sean cried out as each new moment produced still newer perplexing drama. Ten other men in dark wool appeared and circled the first with bayonets fixed. Pointing outward in all directions, the flashing blades faced into a swarm of both innocent and guilty onlookers. Sean recognized other members of the gang slipping away, quickly blending into the maze of busy people who seemed indifferent to the two dying hoodlums in the middle of the street.

Sean relished the power of the gun in the hand of the officer and the rifles of his troops. He heard the leader say, "Yes, sometimes we come into the city and silence a few ruffians."

"But the law? Won't the constables or the Rabbits be after you?"

The officer reproached Sean with a laugh that raised a cloud of frosty breath. "Why, son, I am the law! And we shoot rabbits, especially Irish ones, on sight."

Amazed by his deliverance and the bearing of his deliverers, Sean asked, "Is there a way I can join your band?" And then on second thought also inquired, "Are your men fed every day?"

The officer with yellow braid brightly set off on the blue wool of the shoulders of his coat answered Sean again with a rousing laugh, "Son, that's why we're here, to sign up young men like yourself for the Army of the Potomac. And yes, you'll be fed three times a day. Meat once a day."

⊕

While less than interested the enlistment officer took down Sean's name and had him make his sign. Along with fifty other men of many origins, he found himself herded onto a ferry and taken to a unit forming across the Hudson in New Jersey. "And what can you do, lad?" a sergeant had asked and then speedily added. "You can always be a foot soldier." The same question and answer had been raised for the hundredth time by the sergeant to a hundred young men on that cruelly cold morning.

Sean stumbled with his words then fell back on strong memories of the stable master, O'Quinn, his daughter, and then also the English squire who had burned out his family's farm. "I'm good with horses. Worked them at the squire's stables from the time I was twelve." Then with confidence, "I know horses, sir."

The sergeant, a burly man as Irish as Sean, snapped back, "That we'll see, boy. That we'll see."

⊕

Later, another blue wool covered soldier used a shining blade to point. "And this? This? And this?"

Sean answered without hesitation, "Pastern, fetlock, cannon."

A cruel late winter wind cut his face and his rag covered body. Sean hungered for the felted great coat that hung down below his interrogator's knees.

Then, lifting the left fore hoof of the docile horse, the soldier pointed to the underside, "This, this, and this, and this?" finally pointing at the long swelling on the rear of the hoof. Sean answered without error. "Wall, sole, bar, and frog." He waited for more questions. This was fun despite the cold.

"Sergeant," the man with the sword conceded to the higher ranking soldier standing aside, "the boy knows horses."

"Good, then. Now we'll see if he can ride."

Interrupting but respectful, Sean asked, "When do we eat, sir?"

"First, we'll outfit you with a uniform, son." And with those words Sean was thankfully whisked out of the wind into a giant tent, where braziers of coal burned red hot. Men and boys like himself stood in rags or bare skinned, or in a stage in between, while in long line others were roughly being fitted with thick blue shirts and trousers. Loud, coarse talk filled Sean's ears as his clothes were discarded onto a growing pile.

Naked but warming in the heat, Sean waited in line until his hair was shorn close to his scalp. A doctor sat in a chair and examined him with only a look. "He'll do corporal," Sean heard the doctor say. Then the corporal motioned him on. Finally, Sean felt the delicious, scratchy worsted wool against his back. Soon afterwards his bare legs felt the trousers, too big but warm, and finally a set of boots, not new, but not too tight.

Within the hour Sean sat in another noisy tent with a hundred other men. The steaming smells of beans, cornbread, and real ham nearly made him faint. His body shook in eagerness as he sat down. On the table his overflowing tin plate had food, the likes of which, he had not seen since leaving Ireland.

On that same cold February day Sean quickly showed his ability to sit and command a horse. Without question, he was placed in the cavalry. There, he learned to be a soldier, and among boys much like himself he feasted three times a day. His recruiting officer's promise to the hungry, Irish boy on the dismal streets of New York City had been kept to the letter.

CHAPTER 6
HUMBLED

A mounted Sean Kelly, properly armed and confident, rode with his regiment across the mud of north Virginia. The night before, the Union Army had crossed a swollen Potomac on hastily erected pontoon bridges. He had grown strong during the spring and was now a strapping young man. There, in the homeland of Lee and Jackson the fight had been broiling. The year was 1861. Sean Kelly had been in America for less than a year.

"This will put an end to them, you think paddy boy?" Sean's self righteous Sergeant Blakemore bellowed to everyone who might hear him. The cocky sergeant from upstate New York rode among hundreds and trotted beside Sean's horse in line two abreast. "So, what do you think young Irishman? Today, will we see the rebels scatter?"

Sean listened but said nothing. He had seen the strange multitude of spectators. The silhouette of carriages and people on foot appeared to his left far distant on the ridgeline. Sean had also observed the mass of gray, thousands of men and the frightening gleam of their weapons. *Sergeant Blakemore is a fool*, he thought. Many others in his cavalry platoon felt the same. Blakemore had made no attempt to learn even a few words of German, or Polish, or Hungarian, or attempted to treat any of the immigrant soldiers as anything but trash. *Even so*, Sean finished in his assessment. *Food is plentiful. I sleep warm and dry, and some of these men in front and behind me are my friends, German, Polish, or Hungarian. It makes no difference.* How it made such a difference to Blakemore, he had no idea.

His regiment was on the march to meet the Confederate Army of Northern Virginia under General Johnston, and indeed they had. Sean again took note of the Yankee and rebel sight-seers on the far hill expecting a quick victory and an end to the war. He wondered, *Will it be so easy? Is such a victory possible?*

Later, as the day grew warmer Sean felt the need to drink but held back. He knew that his canteen must last the day. Holding the reins of his horse, Sean stood as did so many of his regiment, on firm ground but quaking in fear. They had withstood the cannonade. Now he saw them, ten thousand men moving his way, not a quarter mile to his front. Few were dressed in gray and many were barefoot. Most looked like simple farmers. Then the thought ran through his mind over and over. *They want to kill me. They want to kill me.*

He had first heard the rebel yell earlier that day and had been terrified, then, as now. Quickly he looked to his right and left at many more thousands in blue. He could see that they were less than inspiring. The blood-curdling scream of southern boys pounding the dust toward the Union Army and demanding his death left Sean frozen in horror and powerless. There, that day when the well-dressed on the hillside cheered on the Army of the Potomac under General McClelland, Sean and thousands more galloped or ran in retreat along the little stream called Bull Run.

Sean became but a tiny part of the general chaos that reigned. He knew little of what was happening. Most of the time smoke and dust made it impossible to see the enemy. But always, he heard them and always they were closer. The shrieking sounds were unbearable. To their credit his cavalry unit turned and fought bravely for a few moments, but quickly rode for their lives again. His hopes, the hopes of eighty thousand men in blue, and the hopes of a union of American states looking southward were disappointed.

Grape canister from enemy cannon wreaked havoc. Sean became the undesired witness of Sergeant Blakemore and other soldiers being torn to pieces. During the Union's panicked on-again off-again retreats a stray mini-ball ripped through Sean's left ear. Blue-clad infantrymen had fired through the din on their own retreating cavalry. He felt tears mix with the blood that dripped down his neck. But the tears covering his cheeks were from far more than the pain of his wound. He was not alone in his suffering. The surviving Union soldiers rode away stung deeply by their cowardice.

CHAPTER 7
OVER A YEAR OF WAR: LATE 1862

Sean Kelly fought his way through major battles and minor skirmishes in this war between brothers. His experiences taught him how these rebels who clashed with their northern adversaries, most recently immigrants, were but poor farmers themselves. Arrogant, glory-seeking officers on both sides conveyed ignorance that knew no bounds. During his regiment's many actions Sean searched for glory but found none. The simple alternatives, survival or death met him eye-to-eye. Images of thousands upon thousands shot or hacked down in brutish battle filled his memories. Thousands more he saw die in the hellish heat for lack of a cup of water. Under the hospital tents or on blood soaked tables in the open air, he saw surgeons casually take their toll while practicing the accepted medicine of butchery.

⊕

On one snowy November day, a great battle unfolded as a brigade of Sean's cavalry regiment awaited orders. Held in reserve outside the small Virginia town of Fredericksburg, he and hundreds of shivering horsemen watched the debacle from across the Rappahannock River. Sean had observed one but now witnessed a second sea of blue infantry cross the cold waters on pontoon bridges. Snow was blowing in the frosty air. Again, he knew, they would attempt to move forward up the hill to the already infamous, fog-enshrouded stone wall. "Ten thousand ragtag southern soldiers with muskets," his captain told them, "lie in wait behind that pile of rock dividing a farmer's field beyond a broad ditch and Marye's Hill."

On snowy ground near the river, Sean restlessly gripped the reins of his horse. Above him spread waves of blue on the attack. Throughout the afternoon and early evening, he witnessed the conclusion to the slaughter of thirteen thousand Union infantry. Later the next day in a retreating action, a rebel mini-ball cut deep into the muscle of his lower neck and passed through. Wounded for the second time, he considered his options as one of his comrades closed the gaping hole in his neck with darning thread. Sean refused to be led to a hospital, where, he figured, his recovery would be unlikely.

By good luck Sean had survived this far. He did not wonder if, but when his time on this earth would be finished. With each skirmish and battle he lost old friends and did not allow himself to grow too close. There was no doubt that many of his comrades-in-arms would be killed or maimed before the month was over. He was astonished to still be alive, but being so only spawned guilt. He knew he would answer to God for his good luck, good luck to survive a fight in which better men had died. Then also, there was the stench of unburied horses and men and the sounds of the dying. It could not be forgotten once the day had ended. The smells followed Sean even in his dreams.

Later in the month after a harrowing midnight ride around the enemy flank exhaustion claimed him. When Sean awoke among many hundreds of snoring men in faded blue, the sun was high in the branches of a nearby tree. He was stiff and groggy as he shifted under his single blanket. He touched his aching neck. His belly growled for food. The gentle tug of his horse's reins on his belt reminded him that the animal hadn't strayed.

Sean stood up to stretch his cold legs and again lifted his hand to his neck. His fingers encountered flesh too warm to be healthy. Yesterday, a comrade had told him that his neck looked worse than before. Down the hill a mess sergeant called for men to lineup. However for now, Sean's desire for hot food fell second to his hope for the healing sun. He laid down, again, and changed position until he felt the delicious warmth on his neck.

Above him his eye caught the chewing side-to-side action of his horse's jaw. For a moment the gentle animal's head shaded him, and he moved a bit to maintain contact with the sunshine. In time his neck grew less achy, and he silently thanked his Maker for the curing warmth. He also thanked Him for the rare dreamless sleep that had come at the end of the late night ride.

Shortly, Sean spotted a surgeon from the corner of his sleepy eyes. In a blood spattered apron a gaunt faced officer stepped carefully among the resting troop of cavalry. He held a violin in the air.

Sean heard him ask, "Can someone play?" Then, "If anyone can play this fiddle it will be yours to keep. The owner of this fine instrument has most recently left us. I promised the good man to find another to take possession of his instrument."

No one answered, but many sullen but curious eyes turned the doctor's way.

Not to be moved from his task the doctor scanned the hillside of lounging horse soldiers. His determined voice shouted out, "He was an infantryman with the 10th Maine." Disappointment began to show in his words, "Surely, one of you can play this fine instrument?" A long silence passed. A final appeal was made, "I say, who can play? Surely, one of you?"

From beneath the haven of his horse's long neck, Sean hesitantly spoke out. "Surely, sir, but it has been awhile. I'll not guarantee you a concert until after I'm fed."

A chorus of quiet laughter followed Sean's words. Coffee had been doled out a little earlier but rations had not.

The persistent doctor redirected his efforts and stepped over several sleeping soldiers towards Sean. He placed the fiddle in the

Irishman's hand and leaned back on his heels awaiting proof. The bow remained in his possession.

Sean fondly clutched the fiddle to his chest. Above him, he saw the stern, blood-spattered bone cutter unmoving, with bow in hand. Finally, it came to him. Despite his sleepy stupor Sean now understood that the officer was expecting him to play before the dead soldier's instrument would be relinquished. Now more awake and looking deeply into the serious eyes above, he thought of the honorable doctor's dilemma, *A promise to a dying man.*

Sean Kelly sat up and attempted to clear his head. Still under the muzzle of his horse, he raised the fiddle with loving hands. He thumped the shell of the instrument with his finger and heard what he had hoped. In moments he reacquainted himself with the simple pleasures of holding the curving, contours of the fiddle. It had been two long years since his love affair with the violin had ended abruptly on the streets of New York. He turned the tuning pegs with the fingers of his left hand on the strings. Gentle vibrations captivated this man with no home or family, just an ornate wooden box. He looked up and nodded as he reached for the bow.

"How long have you played?" the medical officer asked with a guarded smile. He handed Sean the bow.

"Since I was a small boy… in…" but his sentence went unfinished. The bow had found the strings. A jubilation within him ran out of control. The music, so long held back, gained precision much faster than Sean expected. The dead Mainer's fiddle was alive and singing. A hillside covered with tired and hungry men dressed in blue-worsted wool suddenly had only eyes and ears for the fast-stepping melodies cascading unexpectedly from one of their own.

"Who's playing?"

"It'd be that damned, red-headed Kelly!"

"Bless his soul! The boy's hands are magic!"

"I've never seen him touch a fiddle. I've ridden with the Mick since last fall."

All over the hillside men were sitting up, tapping out the rhythm, and smiling.

A soldier stood and spoke for the many, "Wonder of wonders! Pray be he won't stop!"

Sean's spirit had revived. Each thrilling run of eighth notes or sixteenth notes whirled in a harmonic parade from what he had found in his hands to be a finely crafted box. His uncallused but driven fingers raced to find the positions on the strings. The bow's stretched horsehair traveled as if in control of itself. Sean sat taller and lifted his chin. He looked first to the doctor and then around to his comrades. How he could possibly remember after such a lapse of time amazed him and also the pleased foot tapping doctor. Around the grassy knoll, he saw an audience of three hundred men relaxed and in high spirits the likes of which he had never seen. Smiles filled faces that only yesterday he had witnessed as distraught with fatigue and pain. No fiddle had been in his hands yesterday. He grinned as a jig and then a reel appeared from the blue. Finally, a slow ballad played itself out. Only then he realized it. He had not been so happy since a fine spring morning in May so long ago.

Throughout that day and the next, despite sore fingers, Sean's new fiddle proved a delightful reprieve for the wounded on the cots down the hill and also for the hospital staff. His joyous re-acquaintance with cat gut, rosin, and long, stretched horsehair soothed his lonely heart. His many troubles of the past years were tucked away in hiding while his fingers and bow ran in a rush over carefully tightened strings.

In those first days with his music again, he grew to feel that no tune was beyond his whirling fingers and dancing bow. His music quickly made him new friends and helped the many in the hospital whose spirits needed lifting. Asked but actually ordered he found himself playing his instrument in the hospital more than with his regiment that was soon to be on the move.

Immediate success brought attention to Sean from unexpected avenues. His minor wounds were treated with vinegar three times a day and began to heal. His confidence again shone in his smile as it had once so long ago at a county fair at Lisdoonvarna and on a wintry street in New York City. Hearing and appreciating his music were not only the patients but also the staff officers under General Sheridan. The doctors and the few nurses, too, found his tunes a pleasant distraction.

⊕

"And you, young red-haired soldier, shall you be playing again soon?"

Sean turned his head and saw her, older but pleasant to look upon, a gentle voice. The slender woman in nurse's apron asked of him again, "A song today to stifle death?" Her stark words and tone jarred his thinking. He had seen her before, yesterday perhaps. She worked in another tent across from the convalescents, where he usually played. He studied her long hair pinned back in a bun, her dark penetrating eyes, and the gentle voice that hid her pain. A tiny smile had grown on her face when she inquired again, "Or as you say, a tune?"

A wry grin blossomed as he answered, "Surely, my lady."

Obviously, an educated woman from the North, Sean learned the following day that Mrs. Whitworth was more open to conversation than he would have expected. He played that morning, as was now habit, and afterwards dipped a cool cup of water. The pretty nurse sat beside him on one of the many overturned barrels.

"I am sure you guess me forward and I admit to being," a dry-eyed Caroline Whitmore began. She sat still straighter after her words, but her gaze that had left Sean and wandered over the multitude of hospital tents and their wounded occupants hurried back to him now wet with tears. "My husband was killed," she began, "at the First Manassas or Bull Run. I volunteered after that. Forgive me, Mr. Kelly, but I must tell you. I see him in your eyes."

The thought unsettled Sean. He witnessed her sad voice replaced with one more cheerful. "Your music fills me with hope." Then suggestively, "I am lonely for a man's conversation."

Sean wondered about her purpose in singling him out. On the surface it seemed clear but there were troubles in her eyes. She could easily earn the attention of any man, especially the doctors and other officers. The woman beside him was beautiful. Somehow, he forced his ears to listen to more than his fast beating heart.

The story told by the pretty nurse from Massachusetts unfolded chapter after chapter. He politely took note, and another lazy afternoon passed. Sean heard Mrs. Whitmore tell her private tale of sadness and of being accepted into the small close knit group of nurses. Her husband, Captain Bertrand Whitmore, also of Massachusetts, had found her at church while on leave. They had courted and been married shortly after. Her family had approved. But now she was lost and hoping to find herself by helping others.

"Bertrand always loved to touch my hair," she reminisced. "He called me his raven-haired beauty." With these words her pale feminine hand traveled the short but terribly trying distance to Sean's. She pulled it up gently to her hair, then down to her lap. Shocked, Sean made no attempt at withdrawal but quickly looked around to see who was watching. He caught the eye of a doctor, and Sean detected the slightest of smiles before the man turned away to his duties.

"It's your eyes, Sean Kelly," he heard her begin seriously but in the sweetest of tones. His heart beat faster, but then he sensed it. Her words were too laced with honey. "When you play you look right through me." Then, finally to Sean's way of thinking, her entire manner relented into timid embarrassment. *An actress*, he decided, as Caroline continued, "A woman could easily learn to enjoy looking into your eyes."

Sean avoided the sentiment and probed her to talk. "Tell me more Mrs. Whitmore. Your story has more to it. Your childhood and your training as a nurse in Boston?"

She smiled appreciatively and then spoke of the growing nurse's corps and how a stubborn woman also from Boston, Clara Barton, had brought many widows and other caring women together.

Sean watched fluid doe eyes in a surprisingly tense face. Her prolonged gaze never left him, and he knew he was being studied for a reaction. What he gave her was quickly deemed not to be enough. A timid, "I am sorry, Mrs. Whitmore," rolled off his tongue in Irish brogue for the third or fourth time that afternoon. Her answer came to him in a puzzling tight-lipped smile.

Sean understood. She was troubled, sick from her sadness. Yet, no sensible words in his mind allowed his hand to separate from hers.

⊕

A week then half of another passed. The now nineteen-year-old Sean Kelly savored the attention of the beautiful dark-haired nurse, whom he found to be four years his senior. She had made sure, despite his healing, that the doctors would not release him to his regiment. He had overheard her telling them, "You are glad of the Irishman's music, too." They had agreed that he could stay a bit longer. However, Sean observed their grinning faces once Caroline had turned away. The blood covered surgeons surely understood what he and Caroline had tried so hard to hide. Sean had shelved his honor a week ago, and he made no attempt, now, to dispute their sly smiles.

Two days later, he watched Caroline Whitmore with a more objective eye. She was far too sensitive to be among the mangled and sick. Just days after he had met her, she had become more detached by the renewed memories of her late husband. Yet, despite her decline, he continued to allow her to give him her body almost every night.

Since they had first talked on the oaken barrels, he had not pressed himself upon her. Rather, she had come to him. She had found him, he had repeated to himself time and again to bolster his fading good conscience. Inevitably, one dark night Caroline Whitmore called him by her dead husband's name, not once in mistake but time and time again. Sean realized what a fool he had been. Damping his own loneliness with the company of the pretty nurse had been a mistake. There was danger in the web in which he was   entangled, but Sean had told himself, "I am lonely, too. I deserve something."

Finally he suggested they cool their liaison. Sean's words shook his unstable lover to the core. "This must end, dear lady. I see in your eyes what I have seen many times. You must go back to Boston and your family. There, you must allow yourself to heal."

Nurse Whitmore's rebuke came hard and furious despite the heads it turned. Sean saw her eyes, once so sad and lovely, now flashing with hate. "No Irish peasant tells me if we are done!"

Uneasy with the looks from the doctors, Sean left the tent city of the sick and dying and quickly found his regiment. His troop of cavalry, after much rest and boredom, had finally received orders to ride north into Maryland to scout for the great but sluggish Union Army guarding Washington.

Content to be back, Sean mounted and was soon riding again two abreast. Dust caught in his throat as hundreds of horses carried their riders onward once more to what would prove inescapable, their death or the death of others.

Winter passed and then a cold spring. A hot summer set in. It was late June as Sean and his troop of cavalry watched Lee cross the Potomac at Harpers Ferry with seventy thousand men.

CHAPTER 8
MORNING MESSAGES FROM GOD

The branches above Sean's head bustled with life. Leaves waved in the gentle wind, and the flittering birds danced from tree to tree. He heard singing in a burst of countless chirps and twitters.

With the edges of his wool blanket clutched in his fingers, the Irishman rolled over onto his side on the black rubber sheet issued to every Union soldier. He looked to the east expecting to see the morning sun but encountered only the vaguest hint of light. *Just before dawn,* he thought, *the most glorious hour of the day.* The mixed chorus of birds in every bush or tree reminded him that life goes on with or without the human conflict of which he was so much apart. He felt lucky. He had lived through another winter and spring to see summer.

The notion that clouds still formed in white towers of cotton and the rains still fell, despite the daily beast-like actions of men, overwhelmed him. Flowers grew on as soldiers fell in battle or forced others to their knees with bloody swords. Most men, he guessed, especially the generals and the politicians on either side, lacked the eye to behold nature's majesty around them, as well as the insight to detect the tiny place of armies in the scheme of things.

So, with hands stretched behind his head Sean continued his silent morning observations while coveting this lazy but special time. The birds kept up their pre-dawn ruckus and provided a cheery good morning to Sean's ear. Dreamy, but, more than half awake, he recognized the strained battle cries that warned other feathered fleet-wings to beware. He was filled with memories of his father who had taught him all these things. *Do not cross this line,* he heard from the cardinal and chickadee's call with all the bravery that can be mustered from such a tiny breast.

Awaking still more, he considered it comic that men before a battle drew soothing, soulful nourishment from the territorial name calling above them in the trees. An epiphany mushroomed in his sleepy mind. He wondered, as the next thought crossed the last, at a level of philosophy supposedly beyond the mental abilities of a crofter's son. *What other blunders has humankind glossed over with its ignorance to suit its needs?*

Sean's meandering thoughts bored too deeply, too early. He attempted to set his mind adrift, to happier times beyond the endless gore that filled his life. *Today,* he wished. *Today, please bring me only dreamy blue skies, hot coffee sweetened with brown sugar, and the sounds of the fiddle, and then, yes, more steaming sweet coffee.* However, his cheerful images quickly disappeared.

"Corporal Kelly!" A gruff sergeant whose Irish brogue was stronger than his own called him. "Wake up! Colonel Krieger wishes you present at his breakfast. Bring your fiddle."

CHAPTER 9
CHOICES

Two more summers passed, and Sean's cavalry regiment had become the eyes and ears of General Philip Sheridan, the chief cavalry commander under General Grant. Grant was now the leader of the Army in the east after bloody success in western campaigns. Gettysburg was a memory that remained on the minds of the Union Army and its men from Minnesota to Maine. Hope for the northern cause had returned with that great victory. Now, General Sheridan was given thousands of foot soldiers along with his cavalry and ordered to sweep the Shenandoah Valley, Lee's breadbasket, clean of rebels.

Several major skirmishes in the valley had taken place between Union forces commanded by Sheridan and Confederates following General Jubal Early. At both Winchester and Fisher's Hill Sheridan had nearly accomplished Grant's goal but with great losses. This valley that was a hot bed of defiance remained spotted with vast fields of wheat needed so desperately at Richmond by Lee's army in siege. The Union general hoped to destroy the last of any resistance in a final sweep near Cedar Creek.

It was a cool, longed-for beginning to September in 1864. Sean was now a veteran of three years of war. His job was to play *The Gary Owen* as his regiment galloped into battle, not in the charge, but behind. He had made himself indispensable by boosting the morale of men in battle and at night around the campfires. He wondered how he had managed to remain alive, but knew it was only by thin threads of luck that he awoke to see each new day. Good luck early on and his ability with the fiddle had saved him. Tomorrow though, he was to be with his regiment in reserve and, if needed, a part of the second wave of attacking cavalry at Cedar Creek.

⊕

Done with his tunes for the evening, Sean's thoughts were not on music, food, or tomorrow's upcoming battle. The night was unseasonably cold, and he was stamping his feet to stay warm. His fiddle and bow were pulled to his chest as if their mere presence might hold back the damp and the chill. Before him he studied a circle of Union horse soldiers who sat staring into meager flames. The small fire made more smoke than heat and blankets covered their backs and heads. Recollections of the afternoon's pitiless summer heat turned cold and the sudden downpour that had continued into the night were still fresh in his mind. Sean looked to the sky, so tired but afraid to let sleep steal the night, and also pleased to see the stars poking through the clouds.

Sean had eaten his biscuit and beans as had the other nine men and did not count it poor fare. His experience had taught him this. It was no small chore to feed twenty thousand or fifty thousand men in any marching army. Sean had seen the wasted bodies of Confederate prisoners and their dead. He wondered how they could sustain their fighting spirit as they starved in the trenches or force-marched to outflank the Army of the Potomac for the tenth time in a month. Sean mentioned the notion to the men who huddled around their tiny fire like quail in a protective covey. He awaited a reply hoping to postpone sleep. He understood well that the morning ride into the enemy's guns would come all too soon.

"You see," lectured a blanket draped soldier. "They are sure they have God on their side and that Bobby Lee is an angel sent from the Above."

A second countered, "There ain't no God."

Still another added, "Well, God is certainly on our side! Don't let anyone tell you different."

The first soldier spoke again. "Both sides feel God is on their side." The man pondered his own words for a moment and then, "That can't be, can it?"

The godless second soldier threw in, "Proves my point."

The third soldier, clearly seething with anger, spoke as if a lion in a cage. "Let no man here tell me God is not on our side! We are fighting the demon slavery. No one can argue that."

A fourth soldier's interest was aroused. He was accustomed to the endless tom-foolery offered up by his comrades during the long idle time between battles. In a quiet but knowing tone he tested the waters, "God is not what you think."

All heads turned his way.

"Carleton, shut your mouth!" hollered the third soldier, a proud zealot of Presbyterianism. "We aren't in need of your philosophy teacher's nonsense around this fire." A few damp and weary heads nodded in agreement.

"What do you mean?" Sean asked, uncharacteristically entering the quarrel. He stood behind the circle with his hands up trying to catch the heat. Thoughtful but typically quiet, Sean seldom said much. He knew that William Carleton, a New Jersey man, could easily be dead in the battle tomorrow. He was aware of far more than many in the circle understood. Curious, the Irishman broke his silence again and asked, "What did you mean, Will?"

"Well, Sean," William Carleton began as the others sighed in disgust, "and to the rest of you. You are fine comrades, and I have no intention of insulting your principles or your notions of the Almighty. These words are for Sean."

William turned his face to Sean and expanded on his earlier statement. "It's my hypothesis that God is in all things, no more in a church building than anywhere else. God is the vibrant energy in all living things, even in two lovers naked before us. We are..."

"Talk naughty to us, Will!" the second soldier cut in. "You do that best."

An uproar of much needed laughter filled the circle.

William Carleton, immune to the rude but playful talk, started again to Sean, "We are put here with choices to make. God put us here but left it at that. He gave us hands and brains to accomplish great things. What he gave us is good. How we use it can be either for evil or for good, or a mixture of both. Most of us hope to do good things in our lives and have that option. Each of us is here because of choices we made. The armies that fight day in and day out throughout this land, now, for nearly four years are made of men who have used their God-given gifts and have chosen to be here."

With that said, Carleton stopped and looked with a penetrating stare around the campfire. He carefully eyed each man with whom he had ridden into battle and with whom in the future he would most likely die. "Should I stop, gentlemen?" the philosophy teacher from Princeton College asked. He was well aware but not too proud that he was a ripe, red apple mixed in with a barrel of potatoes, although fine potatoes at that.

Sean again spoke. "Please, continue, Will. I for one am glad of your words." The fiddler who knew more than he should about tomorrow and that he would likely die in the battle, found an open space and knelt by the fire. "You are making me think, and I feel warmer when I think," Sean said with his amusing Irish lilt. "I think."

All the soldiers laughed again as one. His simple humor was much needed and contagious. Even the harder-edged soldiers chuckled or at least sighed, knowing if they agreed on nothing else, they agreed they liked their red-haired Irishman, even if he was a Catholic.

"So, my friends and comrades in arms," Carleton said continuing in slow precision, "neither army is right, and neither is wrong. They just are, controlled by the individual choices of two hundred thousand men. God is not in these battles we fight. The abilities he gave us consume the lives of so many good boys from northern and southern families. God has given us the ability to choose and there it ends."

"William Carleton, you're a damn atheist!" the first soldier spat out.

"No, my friend," Carleton reveled. "Look up in the sky now, and behold His makings. Tomorrow as the sun creeps up scattering its life-giving rays upon the earth, look out across the golden fields of wheat. His beauty and creation, evident in tall oaks and their tiny acorns is manifest throughout nature of which we are without fail, just a small part. Yet," and the scholar hesitated before he finished, "different from the trees and grasses, He has given us the right to choose."

The joking around the fire continued after Carleton's well chosen words, but Sean adjourned from the group to find a respectable distance away to relieve himself. Beyond the fire and the string of peaceful horses he studied the hundreds of other glowing dots in the night, fires like their own. Looking up, Sean took in the wealth of stars above him. They seemed extraordinarily bright as he pondered the teacher's words. The Irishman felt Will Carleton's ideas were potent, indeed. They seemed the same in some ways to his upbringing in the church at Lisdoonvarna. One needed to look further. All faiths were similar. Will's words were filled with wisdom. Sean reaffirmed himself as a thinker when he murmured to the grand heavens above, "Searching for truth upon your own hearth is important." Then after a pause, "A man will also need to look beyond his doorstep when truth seems impossible to find."

Stumbling in the blackness back to the circle, the Irishman made his way to the remains of a rail fence. There, a few steps from the fire he settled in for the night with his meager effects. "Tomorrow will bring what it will," he whispered, fearful but accepting of what an earlier waking dream had shown him. To the bright stars as his eyes filled with sleep, the now strapping young man from Ireland's western coast whispered, "Tomorrow, my choice will be life."

"Hush, you silly Irishman!" came a friendly call from the circle. Another in a low tone came from the campfire, "Sean brings good luck to us with his gay fiddle and wit. May he sleep in peace."

William Carleton crooned, "Sleep well, our not so simple Irishman."

A unanimous, "Amen," came from all.

And tonight sleep did come easy to the Irish lad of twenty without the treasures of home or family and with no remote chance of regaining either.

CHAPTER 10
RECKONINGS IN A WHEAT FIELD

Sean was trapped. His dream had foretold it. In great pain he surveyed his predicament. His right leg was crushed. A thousand pounds of horse flesh pinned him down. He ran his hands over his body in search of other wounds and found none, yet, he knew that he lay among countless dead who may have drawn cards far luckier than his own.

A bright sun bore down on the battlefield of ripening wheat. Sean's thoughts were as agonizing as his physical pain. His mind drifted to the casualties in the field who might with luck die a quicker death. Cursing his fortune in being in the front during the second wave of the attack, he thought how no fiddling today could remove him from this terrible place.

Sean found, with difficulty, that he was able to sit up. He did so and surveyed the early afternoon landscape of death and destruction. The first shimmering heat waves danced upward over easily a thousand dead or dying. He remembered so many hours before, during the predawn chill, when he was stomping his feet to warm stiff muscles. Now, as he took in deep draughts of warm air, he wished he could spit it out like a bad spot in an apple. The stench of blood and the laxing bowels of dead men and horses sent a trill of panic to his brain. A growing nausea filled his gut. The thought of escape echoed continuously through his mind, but how he wondered? *How?*

The earlier implosion of battle lines had proven monumental. Sean had experienced this madness, quite remarkably, many times before. However, no description of this screaming chaos could do it justice. *No battle cries now*, he thought as he scanned the dotted field of wheat no longer golden in the sun. No passion remained in broken bodies to send them with their billowing, bright colored standards toward the enemy. Around him he heard neither soldiers of northern nor southern persuasion, only pleas for compassion and water, always water. He looked for his own canteen. It was nowhere to be seen.

When Sean's inspection of the bloodbath was complete, he realized again that he was not mortally damaged but confused. *Where's the medical corps? No litter bearers have come from either side!* Although, after seeing such death in the approaches to Richmond and now throughout the winding path of the Shenandoah River, he expected no less. The tens of thousands already buried and those still marching had well endured the incompetence mixed with bravado of the officers' corps. After three years of war the Irishman could be surprised by nothing a major or a colonel, or especially a general might do or fail to do. Union assaults on Confederate defenses usually failed miserably and today was no exception. The afternoon's building heat pushed his wandering thoughts further. He would die here. His dreams had never lied and the latest had shown him in the sun unable to escape from a field of dying men. It was to be.

Sean pondered any line of thinking to keep from losing his mind. Again an attack had gone off course. "A flanking tactic!" the scholarly Will Carleton had skeptically provided but an hour before, as if that said it all. The Princeton professor was now scattered like chopped liver by enfilading rebel canister. Sean's blue wave of horsemen had swept into the ripened wheat field in a daring right flank maneuver. There at its edge, they had met the power of a thousand muskets leveled, ready, and their possessors not remotely considering retreat.

Earlier before his role in the battle, he had witnessed the slaughter in the middle of the field where Sheridan's other horsemen had attempted to sweep through. The rebel center had held. Sean had waited in the trees with his hillside of mounted blue. Then he had witnessed the attacking Union infantry, forced to climb over bodies challenging unwavering defenders. Then, his regiment had been ordered to charge into the wheat field and crush the southern line.

What puzzled Sean was his state of mind. How could he be so immune to the thought of death? Ordered to march into the spewing black maws of the cannon, he had done so without question. Ordered to march to hell and back, he would. *All individuals, all these soldiers on the battleground must feel the same. To protect their comrades and do their duty remained the essence of what truly mattered.*

Sean's dreaming mind left the battlefield. A blur of memories isolated him from reality. Late night campfires drifted into view. There amongst comrades, he thanked God for the soul soothing music sent from his fingers to the horsehair bow and finally to the catgut strings. He had been the lucky one. Others had little release from the tension of the killing. After a long march or bloody day these bedraggled soldiers talked long into the night. Less and less he heard chatter of their sweethearts and home. More and more he sensed a falling to coldness, a relishing of the next battle's coming. Each had accepted death as imminent, and maybe this acceptance gave strength. *Makes us brave,* he guessed. *Yet, soldiers also speak of inner feelings that the war must end, as they are growing too used to the killing. So if not to relish it, then they accept it as part of a day's work.*

His faraway thoughts rolled on. The total escape into his music had saved him from the madness and he hoped would prevent his eternal damnation. His passionate fiddle had not only entertained the troops but provided a daily cleansing of his soul. His music became his opium. His music became all that kept him from growing to like it all too well.

⊕

Day dreaming now aside, Sean starkly surveyed his predicament beneath the yellow sun. No music, now, would help him. The mid-afternoon's heat had refused to level off to a bearable level. The expanse of ripening grain, trampled by thousands of living feet and by the dead or maimed bodies of those who had fought on this killing field, lay almost non-existent, covered. Like rag dolls and not ever living breathing men, he saw both Union and Confederate forces lying contorted upon the golden shafts of grain. Stray movements of up-raised arms or the legs of horses betrayed the fact that the dying had not ended.

Pain. Sean heard its effects in all directions. He felt it. His horse's weight still pinned him down. Screams beside him. Behind him. Agony of his own. Now, in Sean's murky brain another terror surfaced. At the day's closing, a greater helplessness would enshroud the wounded men around him. He prayed for the litter bearers to appear, for if not, then the two-legged scavengers, the robbers of the dead and dying who came out of the night, would find him.

Dirt and wheat chaff lingered in his mouth from the pounding thrust of his horse into the ground. The sweating Irishman spit to his side. Then just as quickly cursed himself for wasting his fluids on so petty an action. Here in this wheat field, he calculated, his maker would meet him eye-to-eye. With that single thought cemented to the moment, Sean pried himself up with great effort. He again assessed the reaper's harvest scattered across the battlefield. His parched words broke in the baking air. "Yes, here. It will... be here."

A sudden alert came in the air. The breeze had again varied and brought a putrid wind with the smells of death. Higher and higher doses tortured him as the slow arcing of the afternoon's September sun made it worse. His stomach wrenched and heaved. He tried desperately to roll on his side and not choke, cursing once more how   his precious water was leaving him. When finally reduced to a writhing coughing animal, his stomach churned no more. Nevertheless, the heat continued, and his head throbbed while his hope surrendered to the baking sun.

Unable to turn away, Sean constantly moved one arm or the other over his face for protection. Far from alone in his agony, he heard the moans and screams of the many wounded soldiers scattered throughout the field, although as the afternoon progressed, the lessening sounds gave evidence of lives being snuffed out. Sean rose up again on an elbow and looked enviously to the east. There, a few soldiers, with some strength remaining, had crawled into the shade of a walnut grove at the field's edge.

Sean stretched up to his limit. A different smell found him as he peered over his dead horse. Across the carnage the source of a greater horror filled his eyes. Smoke and flame lifted and spread across the field. He guessed how wounded men having a last smoke had unintentionally added to the pain so many already faced. The blaze, now a full fledged fire, raged in a long line among dark lumps of bodies in the distance.

Fueled by the dried straw of the wheat, it made its own wind and burned hot. Sean breathed in its acrid smoke, and as he coughed, heard invisible flames provide heightened cruelty to already broken men. The littering of bodies in the field managed to slow the fire's progress, while another smell crept into Sean's nostrils. Drifting across the once beautiful field, the fire's thick fumes brought the foul odor of burnt hair and flesh.

Listening to each breath from his body and seeing his shaking hands, Sean realized any sanity he retained was rapidly leaving. *A plan*, he thought! *Think of anything pleasant. Cool water. Good times.* His desperate mental search grew and then receded. He found himself slipping into restless sleep. Echoes of his home in Ireland filled him. The salty scent from the sea in the west wind picked up among the green hills where he had been raised. He dreamt of learning to play his fiddle and the priest who had nurtured his talent. Ultimately, his thoughts latched on to a special time, a county fair and the young woman whose love he had won that day. The shining green eyes of a pretty girl from Lisdoonvarna looked up at him, demanding his attention. Her memory mercifully pulled him away to better days.

⊕

It was his sixteenth year, and the heat of the battlefield did not yet exist. Sean worked with his father, Malroy, in the big garden which was spread wide with the thick foliage of potatoes, cabbages, and turnips. It was a Saturday morning. From the corner of his eye he saw his mother, Anna, hurrying through her morning chores. He saw too his younger sister, Mary Katherine, as she did her share by feeding the chickens, a few sheep, the family's milk cow, and a new addition, a small but sturdy cart pony.

While the female members of the Kelly family completed their chores near the house, Sean and his father continued to tend the vegetable patch, their bread and butter. Both wished to be done, yet knew they would enjoy the fair far more with the daily chores not put off but put behind them.

⊕

"So, my son," Malroy Kelly piped up cautiously but probing, "will you be looking for a wife at the fair?"

Sean looked up and ceased his hoeing. He saw the sparkle in his father's eyes and knew he was to hear the story he had heard many times before.

"You know, Sean, I found your mother at the fair." Malroy also halted his efforts in the potatoes, and leaned heavily on his hoe. "It was seventeen years ago." To his dismay, Malroy saw only a faint smile on his son's face. The boy had already returned to a steady rhythm of cultivating.

"It would be time for you to think of such things, Sean," his father said as his tool began again to cut the young weeds that threatened the tender leafy plants.

Sean sensed his family's wishes to finish their chores quickly and so pressed on with his efforts in the garden. It was May Day, the first day of the spring fair at Lisdoonvarna, the only village he had ever known. All winter the family had been anticipating this day of friends, eating, drinking, and music. He would be playing his fiddle in the annual music contest included in the fair's festivities. Sean knew how his mother worried for him. Daily, she had railed at him to practice and also boosted his confidence with sweet words of praise. Her assurances bolstered his courage to stand and hold his own in more pursuits than music.

"Stare them down, boy. You are a prince with the fiddle," she had said.

Malroy's mattock churned the ground below him. His thinking was not on gardening but on his wiry, redheaded son hoeing diligently at his side. *A fine boy you are Sean. May you have all the luck a man can hope for as you grow and when you perform with your fiddle in Lisdoonvarna, today.* Malroy said nothing and only thought the good words. He had not the ability with phrases that his wife managed so easily. "Good luck, today, lad," he barely managed.

Sean looked up from his hoeing and smiled. *A good da,* he thought, then brought his tool back to the dark rocky ground cutting the roots of a young weed below ground level. His thoughts were not about himself either. They lingered on the stable master's daughter and how he would soon see her at the fair. Pretty Keri O'Quinn would be waiting with a red ribbon in her hair, although not just for him.

⊕

Sean had practiced diligently for the contest all through the winter and into the spring. Tough calluses on the fingers of his left hand showed it. He had begun with the instrument at seven when his father had placed the Kelly heirloom warily in his young hands.

He had taken to the violin slowly, so all who listened wondered if he would develop the gift for playing. It had been passed down through the Kelly family skipping a generation now and then. Sean's father played an average fiddle but hoped his only son would have the abilities of other Kellys and the Donnahoes on Anna's side of the family. Their fiddles had lightened many hearts and sent listeners into a foot-tapping frenzy.

Painstakingly, Sean did learn. His music at first was a passing interest overshadowed by watching birds in flight, the delight of seeing growing fields gushing their green upward after a rain, and playing with other boys in a small stream nearby. It was not until Sean was nine that the desire to play became entirely his own.

His fire to learn the instrument was kindled by Lisdoonvarna's priest, Vincent O'Daer. The clergyman had inspired Sean to challenge himself. "Compete against yourself," the old pastor had said. "Let your passion for life be expressed in your music. Don't worry about anyone listening. And practice, Sean. You will be quite the fiddler if you practice each day." He also informed Sean after an initial inspection that his fiddle was no ordinary one. "Hold it close and safe," the priest had said. "It has an extraordinarily fine sound, a rare brightness."

⊕

While the Kelly family worked side-by-side, the subtle morning sunshine turned warmer. When the sun sat three fists high above the eastern horizon, Malroy hollered out to cease labors and make ready for the fair. A happy chorus rose up from his family.

Off they went, over green hills and lush valleys the two miles towards the outskirts of town. Their two-wheeled cart, loaded high with food as well as hay for the small sturdy pony that pulled it, lumbered along. Mary Katherine, Sean, and their mother sat with legs dangling off the back of the cart as Malroy encouraged the sure-footed pony down the rutted road with a gentle but practiced hand. Sean reached his arm around the shoulders of his smiling sister, her long flaxen hair lying soft beneath his hand. Mary Katherine then gave him a gentle look. He pondered his good fortune, *How lucky I am to have a family to cherish.*

While the bouncing cart made its way toward Lisdoonvarna, few words were necessary. He traded smiles with his mother, and to his dear father alone up front with the reins, Sean hollered, "*Da,* tis' a lovely day for a fair."

Malroy Kelly leaned back and turned to his son. So very proud he was of this lad, a boy not so long ago, and now in every sense a man, partially of his making. He dwelt on the emerald eyes of his only son, and began to swing his gaze full circle to his right, beholding the morning sun's yellow light cutting through the fog over the fields. To his left they passed a newly cut pasture.

Continuing his heart-felt survey, Malroy joined eyes with Anna, his love and best friend since being a lad himself. Holding her powerful gaze, Sean's father, whose farming efforts both husband

and wife knew would keep them fed, though no better, said with words as fragrant as the new mown hay, "Sean, good lad, tis' a fine day indeed."

With wheels the height of a man, the simple cart rolled and jolted across the deep ruts and lush grass. All eyes were on the white puffs in the sky that foretold fair weather, none finer for a day at the fair.

It was a more than special day for Sean. He held his fiddle, in its coarse tote sack, firmly to his chest. His free hand braced tightly to the cart's side board. The countryside before him spewed colors that appeared more radiant than ever.

Sixteen-year-old eyes studied the familiar green contours around him. All was for the best despite the land's hard lessons. In Sean's mind, the stone walls lining a road no more than a cow path were sound evidence of the poor ground that lay in all directions. Hard to till, hilly, rock upon rock upon rock, this farmland was good only for grazing. A few fertile spots were walled for gardening but the rest provided grass for sheep, cattle, and horses owned in great numbers by the local squire. Sean thought of his work at the squire's stables cleaning and currying the many horses. There, four years before he had first met the stable master's daughter.

The cart rolled on, and Sean listened as his mother gave him a last minute lecture to help bolster his confidence for the competition in the afternoon. She reminded him to stand tall and proud when he drew his bow over the strings. Father O'Daer's words echoed back to him as his mother spoke. The graying old clergyman had lectured, "A show of confidence will entrance the crowd and inspire the musician."

"Mistakes?" Sean remembered the priest answering him with a question. Then continuing with a hearty laugh, "Why, Sean, you'll make no mistakes! You'll but kindly add wee variations on the melody." Then Father O'Daer had added, "Act as if you know what you are doing and before long you will have people begging for more." Sean had wished for the priest's presence at the contest, for he had inspired him to reach for his best. Sadly, Father O'Daer had turned sickly in April and nothing could draw him away from the fire on his hearth.

The bumpy road continued while Sean's family made their way to town. Along the way they met friends also traveling to the fair. The talk between farmers quickly went from health, to crops, to politics. Malroy Kelly was an outspoken man. The squire had publicly reminded him of his place in the scheme of things on several occasions. If not liked by all the other crofters, Malroy was respected for his hard work and generosity. Sean's father was trying to convince the other farmers in the area to demand that taxes and land lease moneys not be raised as they had for each of the last three years.

"We'll be out in the ditches again, as we were in the famine years, eating grass stew. Poor crop years should be taken into account," Malroy had said. He took every opportunity to sway his friends and neighbors in quiet discussions at the public house in the evenings and on Sundays after Mass. "How can a man be expected to feed his family?"

Many listened and agreed with Malroy Kelly's way of thinking. However, his subversive words of grievance filtered up to the squire. Action beyond hard words was soon taken. Malroy was beaten senseless one Saturday night after leaving the pub called the Tan Cockerel. A clear message was heard by the crofters around Lisdoonvarna. The rich man's justice instilled with boots and cudgels sent a clear message to everyone except Malroy Kelly. As Kelly recovered, he vowed to himself and the other crofters, "It would be wise for all to beware of Malroy Kelly. I'll be ready next time."

So, Malroy had continued his tirade against the squire's land policies, but now always kept his tough, head-high shillelagh close at hand. If the squire decided to persuade the crofter with violence again, Malroy would be able to defend himself. He had not long to wait.

He was confronted on the road home. With stone walls on two sides and the squire's men both forward and behind, Malroy stood his ground. A fierceness had overcome him which he had only heard before in stories of his grandfather. Malroy laid low the squire's three thugs in a frenzy of thrusts and head knocking. Amazed by his maddened zeal, he worked to contain his anger from that day forward, fearing that he might kill someone. In defense of his life or not, Malroy well knew he would be strung up at the Ennis gibbet with no cries of mercy from the law. It had been a month since that attack as his cart pulled into the outskirts of Lisdoonvarna and the fair.

⊕

Arriving at the large, freshly mown field at the edge of town with colorful tents and peddlers in abundance, all the Kellys were jubilant. It was not often they could share such joy and frivolity with their friends and neighbors. The crofter's life entailed long hours of work just to keep the family fed and the rent paid. Little time enough there was for the simple pleasures of life. While Sean unloaded the cart with his father, he noticed the proud presence of the local nobility making themselves known. Squire Mennington stood ramrod straight at the edge of the grassy downs with a pistol in hand. Sean and hundreds of others watched as the gun was lifted to the sky and fired in a puff of gray smoke. All heard the squire command, "Let the fair begin!"

Around him, Sean detected an undercurrent of brooding anger in farmers and shop keepers who lingered by the tents and stages. He knew that these residents of Lisdoonvarna and the multitude of stout hearted crofters from throughout this portion of County Clare had no desire for an Englishman to dictate to them, especially when dealing with the rare pleasures of free time.

⊕

Sean and his father strolled away from the women and examined carts that held the goods of shoemakers and other leather workers. Mistaking the large tent to their right as the property of the Tan Cockerel's owner, Len O'Shaughnessy, the father and son strolled to the back wall of canvas and prepared to walk around to the opening of what they guessed to be the drinking tent. They stopped once their ears began to make sense of the discussion inside. They guiltily eavesdropped while silhouettes of many figures moved to-and-fro over the canvas. The tinkling of fine china and silver tableware, even the smells of good food, carried easily through the cloth wall.

Sean heard a deep voice announce. "I say, Squire Mannington, you and I both deplore the over-breeding of the Irish countryside with peasants."

"Indeed, Sir Quincy," Kelly's landlord countered. "We've discussed this many times over dinner," and Sean heard a clinking of wine glasses, "and will again over such fine food. The famine in the 40's was but a natural culling of the rabble, long overdue to my thinking."

An applause broke out within the tent and Sean noted the grimace of disgust that filled his father's face.

The conversation was continued by the first speaker, Sir Quincy. "One million dying in the ditches with grass stains on their faces and over two million more emigrating to America! What a blessing in disguise! It certainly freed up more land for all of us to run more cattle. And bully beef is what feeds the army. To the army!" Sean heard while he saw the shadows of arms lifting glasses. "To those that feed them!" And finally with the greatest of enthusiasm, "To our good Queen. To Victoria! May she prosper and continue to promote our welfare!"

Sean had the good sense to turn to his distraught father who was shaking in anger beside him. He placed his hand on his father's arm just in time. Malroy had pulled his jackknife and his intentions were clear.

"*Da*, no!" Sean pleaded in a whisper. His strong right hand held tight to his father's straining wrist.

A sudden jerk freed Malroy's knife but sadly nicked Sean's hand.

Instantly, it was over. Sean saw his father's remorse. Blood dripped from his bow hand. "My, God!" Sean heard from his father when they were many steps from the landowner's tent. "What have I done?"

Sean's wound was in the flesh of the hand and not the fingers. The bleeding was quickly stopped.

Later, when the two met up with Anna and Mary Katherine,

Sean's mother saw the damage long before he could explain. "Oh my, Sean! What have you done?"

Sean answered too quickly, "A cart, mother. I stumbled on a cart's tongue and fell on some tools."

However, the wife of Malroy Kelly was no fool. She had seen the blood still on her husband's hands and cuffs of his jacket. She feared the time when her husband would fight for his life again. Despite the turmoil somehow now involving her son, she maintained the greatest of control. Anna sent piercing looks her men's way but then quietly dismissed the matter.

"Oh, well then, you ruffians. Both of you will be in need of a washing. I have water and clean rags on the cart."

CHAPTER 11
THE LISDOONVARNA FAIR

The still dreaming Sean strolled with his family among the multitude of red and brown-haired, simply dressed folk. It was apparent to him that every one was enjoying their brief respite from drudgery. He saw the clearing skies above the green, close-cropped downs and beamed broadly to all he passed. A smile usually greeted him in return. He thought to check the clean rag that bound his injury. It was nothing. His father's knife had done no real damage to his right hand.

Colorfully dressed jugglers and mud flinging horses in cart races filled the lazy but rare sun-drenched morning. Home knit sweaters of spun wool and cottage woven cloth graced nearly all attending. Brighter versions were for sale in several market booths. Many other tables displayed shining trinkets and bold-hued bolts of cloth. Further down the way crofters had laid out the fruits of their labors, from early vegetables to cottage crafts, all soon to be judged for blue ribbons. Opposite the sellers, small corrals of livestock awaited critiques from the judges.

In the midst of the festivities, a roped off area had been staked out. Shirts were off young and middle aged men who waited to show off their bare knuckle skills. Boxing provided a release that many a man needed, and the area championship was well attended. It also provided a cash prize.

"The winner will fight in the county seat at Ennis next," an eager spectator told the family. Malroy Kelly watched with pleasure and disdain from the outer circle of the cheering crowd. His own desire to witness the exchange of blows and to comprehend the mob mentality of the crowd at the beginning of a brawl soon waned. When the blood and teeth began to fly, the Kelly family ambled away to gentler pursuits.

They soon found the knee high wooden stage that had been set up for the musicians. Behind it, Sean observed a scene close to his heart. Flying fingers on the strings of dulcimers and fiddles flooded the gathering with melodies from untold generations. Sean listened and wondered. He was aware that few knew the history of this Celtic music they played. Father O'Daer had told him how its roots were entwined in a culture much older than Roman or Greek, but most important, it rang pleasant bells in the souls of those who listened.

Sean stood a few steps from the stage tuning his instrument. His ears heard before his eyes noticed the result of graceful fingers prancing over another set of four strings. A well figured girl near his age with carrot-colored hair glanced his way. Her brief smile caught his fancy as well as the long shining curls that fell beyond her bare shoulders. What he heard from her fiddle impressed him, too.

Sean's chest heaved with a deep sigh. How could he have not noticed her when he first arrived? Everyone knew of Sydney O'Shaughnessy, the pretty, flirting pub owner's daughter. Shy with girls, but not with his fiddle, Sean was determined to show off a bit. He coaxed a spirited tune from his strings without calculating the outcome. Sydney turned to him and for a moment they held each other's gaze.

The power of her sparkling eyes was all it took. He was smitten, although now totally embarrassed. Mary Katherine and rarely Keri O'Quinn being the only girls in his life that he could stare down without wavering, Sean quickly looked away. However, he sensed that Sydney had not.

He looked up to see a joyous smile on her face before she said, "We'll be playing soon. I'm nervous. Are you?"

Sean was dumbstruck. Then, his faltering, uneven words rushed out. "Yes, nervous... too. Love...ly day."

⊕

The hourglass figured girl knew her sudden effect on Sean by seeing him speechless and then stammering an answer. Sydney turned away to other girls she knew and showed the semblance of a scheming smile. She was well aware of the sway she had on men and was having her fun, but also she was testing him.

Sydney decided it time to check with the judges about whom her stiffest competition might be. She had waited until all the other contestants had arrived and could see her step upon the stage. When one of the three, a gray-bearded judge, pointed out Sean Kelly, she rewarded him with a radiant smile. Known in the community for his musical talent but also for his lapse of faithfulness to his wife in the recent past, the old judge patted the small of her back as a parting gesture.

Sydney was unaffected by the judge's forwardness, being used to common lewdness in the pub, and walked coquettishly away, giving him a farewell smile. Yet, despite her teasing manner, most men clearly understood that she was only playing. They liked that in her, she knew, and also understood that she was no man's easy make. However, in Sydney's mind as she walked away and in that of the leering old judge, the first place ribbon had already been awarded.

⊕

Sean's eyes eagerly hunted the crowd for the stable master's daughter despite the pain which she had recently caused him. Still, he hoped to see Keri's brown hair tied back with red ribbon. She had confided in him as a treasured friend, which indeed he was. She had told about falling in love with a boy well beyond the stables of the squire. Sean had hidden his true feelings and congratulated her good fortune. However, he was heartbroken. So, today, since her arm would be wrapped around the arm of another young man, finding her in the crowd, although strangely compelling, would be torture. Scanning the hundreds of people and the many young girls in the crowd, Sean found more than a few with hair back and tied with colorful ribbons, but to his sad eyes there was no bright faced Keri O'Quinn among them.

Disappointed, Sean stopped his search and prepared himself for his performance. All that he had learned from Father O'Daer and his mother came to play. His concentration and confidence, he knew, would hold the crowd and give him an edge.

The red-haired O'Shaughnessy girl, who had unnerved him with her smiling eyes, was to play in the next to last position just before Sean. At least with that outcome he was pleased. He only vaguely knew of her and had only seen her serving in the Tan Cockerel. He had never talked to her. Sean considered her a goddess, *Indeed me and every other lad. It is the way she carries herself. Though she is a tease, she is no tart. Her magic eyes and her confident demeanor overpower the young men of Lisdoonvarna.* He remembered with a grin and a whisper, "Including me!"

Sean and his father had even discussed it. "Beware of her, son. She does not mean harm but has already broken a long trail of hearts. Older men," Malroy Kelly continued, "when seeing the swooning of every lad she's looked at, often smile to each other and remember the few ladies who have possessed the same enchanting ways in their younger years. Recollecting, we all thought of one and mentioned her merits, although she has been dead these fifteen years. The fair wife of Len O'Shaughnessy lives on in his daughter."

To thwart her power, Sean concentrated on his music. *With the resolution of what a saint might do to fight the devil for a soul,* he recited over and over in silence to push her from his mind. Yet, sweet Sydney hung on tooth and nail, and it took a final mighty shove to jostle her image and send it down the road far from his thoughts.

Fiddling filled the air as the contest began. The earliest players held the crowd, entertaining them with reels, jigs, and sad melodies. Out among the audience, to his credit in leaving the beer tent,

Malroy Kelly listened intently, analyzing each contestant and his or her style of cajoling tunes from the curvy, spruce-topped box. One-by-one the contest continued, and Malroy stood amongst his friends and neighbors smugly knowing his son would have a chance to top them all.

The head judge stood and called out to the crowd, "Sydney O'Shaughnessy," and the next to last fiddle player pertly stepped up to the planked platform, surrounded by applause.

This red-haired girl, who had earlier controlled Sean's emotions, quickly showed she was no shy amateur playing before her first large audience. Casting her head back and with it her long fiery tresses, Sydney began. The beauty of the tune leaped from her instrument in graceful cadence. Her fingers pranced on the strings forming vibrations in the hollow wooden core that resonated out to all listening ears. Her performance was not lengthy as were many of the other contestants, but cut to the hearts of the listeners and wooed with its precision and charm. In Sean's mind, Sydney clearly had leaped to first place with the judges and with the audience. "And being pretty," he whispered to a nearby competitor, "doesn't hurt at all."

The popular pub owner's daughter bowed to the cheering crowd and confidently walked off the stand. As she did so, she brushed shoulders with Sean as he stepped up to play. Sean was now far more in control than when Sydney shook him to the bone with her flirting glance earlier. He confidently smiled at the attractive young woman before him, however now in his own beguiling manner.

While looking into Sean's eyes as he passed, Sidney saw not a school boy easily shaken by a pretty girl's smile but a focused young man on a mission. In her heart she wished him luck but wondered, *How good a fiddler can he be*? She momentarily felt unsure of herself. His look had traveled clean through her. Sean Kelly had passed the test.

Making her way through the pleasant crowd after finding her girl friend and taking her arm, Sydney searched for a good vantage point to watch the final contestant. One of the judges hollered out, "Sean Kelly will be the last to perform in the fiddling contest for youth fourteen to eighteen years."

Hurrying to seek the right spot, Sydney noticed nearby people watching her oddly. Not facing the music stand, she thought it peculiar that she had not heard the beginning of the young Kelly's tune. Even more strange, she noticed, was the sudden hush that overcame the large standing audience.

Finally, Sydney looked up. With a fright, she realized that the eyes of the entire crowd were on her and not on the stage. No one seemed to be paying attention to the handsome young fiddler who was studying her with a steady, piercing stare.

The confident red-headed boy had found her eyes. She looked intently into his, now fully aware that the hush and the crowd's attention were all about her and Sean. His fiddle was up and at the ready, she guessed rightly, awaiting a cue.

Sean maintained the hold on the crowd as he looked long and deep into Sydney's green eyes. It was only when a flushed faced Sydney nodded her approval that Sean's bow enthusiastically embarked across his four taut strings.

Sydney's girlfriend, Llewellyn, produced a knowing look. She turned from the fiddler on the stage and saw Sydney's embarrassed smile. Never had Llewellyn seen any young man make Sydney blush, let alone keep her spellbound as if *she* were caught up in a man's appreciative look. Then, Llewellyn watched in awe as hundreds of eyes turned back-and-forth from her lovely friend to the handsome boy whose lilting tune reminded them of their true Irish passion.

Sean had indeed cast a spell. All in attendance, he easily saw, had opened their hearts wide and let him in. An exuberance of glowing faces filled Sean's view. The lyrical and bouncing jig continued, and by the second repetition the crowd was clapping in time and tapping toes with the beat. When finished, his admirers demanded more, a rare compliment for Sean's age group of musicians from those who knew good fiddling.

One of the three judges stood and proclaimed, "We have not heard a fiddler like Mr. Kelly for more than a generation!" He paused to accommodate the applause.

"Yet, it is a contest and not a concert," continued the judge who looked for support to his gray-bearded colleague who had flirted with Sydney and then to the third judge whom Sean had won over easily.

"However," the standing judge added with a hopeful look which provided a fine compliment in its own right, "maybe the young man would be so kind as to perform for the evening's festivities?"

So, the fiddling contest ended, and two of the three judges congratulated Sean warmly with hearty handshakes. A blue ribbon was pinned on his chest, and a gold guinea for first place laid happily in his palm.

"What call you your tune, lad?" asked one of the two admiring judges.

Sean responded, "The Road to Lisdoonvarna."

Sean's naming of his fiddle tune sent the judges nodding to each other in mute, bright-eyed appreciation, even the earlier grumpy one.

Finished with his thanks to the judges, Sean turned to the dispersing crowd. He searched carefully but was disappointed. The red-haired Sydney was nowhere to be seen. Meeting Keri O'Quinn after the contest had become the last thing on his mind.

⊕

Sydney pulled Llewellyn away from the crowd and walked towards a nearby attraction. To her chagrin the two found themselves at the livestock judging area. Far from being their favorite past time, Sydney pretended to admire a healthy Suffolk ewe. Llewellyn turned to Sydney excitedly, her impatience finally spilling out, "How could you walk away from a fine lad such as Sean Kelly? He played his entire marvelous tune, with all eyes watching, just for you!"

Llewellyn paused, bewildered in her envy. She then pointed to the corral of fine sheep soon to be judged, "Do you see the uncooked mutton there in front of us? Well, dear friend, your actions in comparison make the lowest of the furry beasts appear a scholar!"

Sydney, despite her good friend's brow beating, continued at her pretense of observing the sheep judging, but she squeezed her friend's hand all the tighter. Len O'Shaughnessy's daughter was emotionally shaken. Sean had looked right through her on the steps and certainly during his performance. He had rendered her helpless, not a position she had ever allowed herself to be in. Sydney remembered his eyes and then her own. His fiddle and his manner had captured all who listened.

Swept off her feet instead of the usual opposite, Sydney loitered at the sheep judging. She pretended to watch but stared above the corral and off into the crowds. Her mind was obviously elsewhere. The feeling inside baffled her. From past experience she had learned the power that her beauty projected. It had always given her control. She recollected many a man, not just boys, being stunned, their speech slowed or totally stopped when they saw her smile and her stunning green eyes. She was fully aware and enjoyed their enchantment with her. Now, miraculously, she was the one who had blushed from embarrassment. She didn't like it. The reins had uncharacteristically switched hands. So, as one sheep after the other was paraded past the judges, Sydney pondered her dilemma. Maybe Llewellyn was right.

"Let this Sean Kelly find me," she told her friend with a prideful tone. But to herself she asked, *What will I do if he does*? Then, quickly, *What shall I do if he doesn't*?

⊕

Although unable to locate Sydney or even Keri, Sean did find his father, who stood in the beer tent with his second pint in hand. Sean hoped that the first had washed away memories of the gentry's cruel exchange so recently overheard. To Sean's relief, Malroy chimed out only on pleasant topics to his son and several old friends.

"Tis' indeed a fine first day of May in County Clare. Oh, how the noonday sun has graced our gathering of work-hardened souls and also my son's mastery of the fiddle." Glasses lifted and a cheer was raised to the champion fiddler of the morning. "Here's to you, lad." For the second time that day Malroy Kelly's only son blushed with happy embarrassment.

While Sean watched his father and his friends, he contemplated his success. The day had indeed triumphed over a land where overcast skies and tragedy too often reigned. The festivities had continued unaffected by weather, drunkenness, or mean spirited quarrels. A good time appeared to be had by all, especially his father. Malroy seemed content to finish his glass. Sean saw joy and not hate in his father's face. The lazy afternoon had turned glorious, having moved noticeably beyond earlier misbeginnings.

⊕

Among the fair's great crowd the tavern keeper's beautiful daughter was finally located by the blue-ribbon fiddler. Quickly, Sean's gentle nature gained her confidence.

Normally the one to speak, Sydney found herself laughing and enjoying Sean's company with no charade on her part. To her, their exchange was rare and refreshing.

Malroy observed the two walking past hand-in-hand. He whispered to a friend, "A mixture of the perfect sunshine fills this day, the desires of youth. Love's fairy dust has entranced them both." He clapped his thigh happily and then lifted high his half full glass, clinking it together with his neighbor's.

By afternoon's end Sean and Sydney found themselves stealing kisses. Then a little later, they found themselves searching for private spots between the tents to hold tight to each other. By twilight, Sean guided Sydney very willingly into a hayloft, a stone's throw from the fair grounds. There in sweet scented hay with mutual anticipation, their youthful passions stirred faster after having fermented all afternoon. Quickly, they were released. When their lovemaking ended, both dressed with modesty but with a lack of innocence. Casually they walked hand-in-hand back in starlight to the fair ground. There, glowing torches and the fair's still bubbling activity greeted them as if they had never been away.

Everything was brighter, colors more vivid, and people more friendly in Sydney's eyes. "The stars in the plow are very bright tonight? Do you think, Sean?" The red-headed lovers walked together as only lovers can, relaxed in time and in tune with each other. There was little doubt where their new relationship was destined to travel.

Beside the bandstand, people danced and enjoyed the night and the music, but the young couple's eyes, more than not, glowed like the bond of trust between them. Suddenly, to the couple's surprise, a hysterical Mary Katherine found them.

"Sean, I've been looking for you since supper time! Something terrible has happened!"

In an instant the special mood that Sean enjoyed with Sydney evaporated. Could his father have been attacked again? Fearful for his family Sean asked, "Dear sister, what troubles have you seen?"

Not hesitating for a moment, the crying Mary Katherine rushed into the safety of her brother's arms. Then again Sean asked, "Tell me now sweet sister, what is it? Can it be so bad?" Sean looked over her shoulder questioningly to Sydney.

Her blond head reached only to Sean's chin but turned up to him and gazed tearfully into his eyes. She regained her calm, only for a few moments, and firmly stated, "They have burned us out! Neighbor MacEnid brought us the news. It's blackened and nothing is left. Our livestock are stolen or lying with their throats slit. The well is poisoned, father thinks. Someone hoped we would drink from it. We hurried back home once we heard." She took a deep breath and added "Then, I rushed back to find you."

Mary Katherine's litany halted briefly while she caught her breath a second time. "Father tested the well water on a ewe they missed. The poor animal writhed in misery and was dead in half an hour." Then she demanded, "Sean, what will we do?"

"The squire's mischief you can be sure!" Sydney confirmed, not to be left out.

As the master fiddle player held his sister, he nodded in agreement. He understood the politics of the area and was well aware of Squire Mannington's hatred of his father. It could only have been the squire's men who would do such a thing. Mannington, to Sean's thinking, had gone to great lengths to solve the festering problem of Malroy Kelly.

Sean's hand gently stroked his sister's hair as he asked, "Is anyone hurt?"

"No, but father is worried about you. He feared the squire's thugs might have harmed you. When you didn't show up at our usual meeting place at the end of the day we were all upset."

Sean turned away from his sister to the loving, young woman with whom he had spent the most wonderful day in his life. He was unsure of what to say. Finally, with Mary Katherine in tow he escorted Sydney to her father's beer tent. Before telling her goodnight, he told her sadly, "Our wonderful day is over, dear sweet lass. I wish not on such a sad note." Then with bolstering resolution, "I must go with my sister. I will find you tomorrow."

He kissed Sydney once, lightly, and then took a long moment to look deeply into her eyes. He said goodbye and turned to hurry away through the lingering crowds beyond the torches of the fair grounds. With only the starlight above to guide them the two managed to find the lane that led home. Setting a steady pace they quickly covered the two miles to their leased acreage. Upon arrival, it was all as Mary Katherine had described. The farm, the house, and the animals were destroyed. In the light of a single torch among a gathering of neighbors, Sean listened for advice or direction. He found his mother and consoled her. Finally, off a ways he spied his father sitting on a rock stile. A solemn silence that he had never witnessed filled the chilly night air. *Deep gloom*, he conceded in sad irony, *marks the end to this first day of May.*

⊕

The next morning Sean, Sydney, and her father sat in the Tan Cockerel discussing the past night's trouble.

"I hope never to see you walk away, Sean Kelly," Sydney said as she cradled his hand. "Surely things will work out," she added while looking hopefully from one to the other. The troubled look on her father's face told her something different. In a defeated voice, she asked, "And what now?"

Len O'Shaughnessy frowned, and then breathed a deep sigh before he spoke. "Dear daughter, I must ask you to stay clear of this Kelly boy. I want no trouble with the squire or his thugs. Not only could it be dangerous for you and Sean, but it's sadly also bad for business." He looked to Sean. "Be careful, son. Stay away from here, for now. Be patient. It would be best if your feelings for my daughter cooled a bit."

Sean studied his lover's dejected face and then the Tan Cockerel's owner. Sean could not argue with the logic in his words.

⊕

The Kelly family found shelter in a neighbor's barn loft for several nights. There they had time to plan. When word was received from the squire's stable master, tactics changed. Calhan told of overhearing vile talk from the squire's men. "They will first find your son, Malroy, and make sure that he never plays the fiddle again. If that doesn't do the trick, they will come after your women next."

The Kellys were shaken to the core, but what good and loyal friends the family had! The local crofters took up a collection and purchased the family boat fare. It had been no small feat among a group so poor, but Malroy by his speaking out and organizing had made these hard working Irish farmers realize they were not slaves of the English and Irish gentry. In each he had kindled a spark of pride.

Within the week, deep in steerage, the Kelly family pushed westward across the Atlantic on an ocean steamer to America. "No repayment would be necessary," his neighbor Ian Icas had told them. "You have already given us more than enough. Just go and make a new life." Even so, Malroy and his son, being Kellys as they were, told their friends and neighbors repeatedly how they would come back someday and make things right.

⊕

A cool breeze hit his face and Sean awoke from his reverie. Yet again, he wondered what had happened to the green-eyed girl he had loved for only a day at Lisdoonvarna's fair. Only blackness met his eyes and the refreshing night air gave him a renewed desire to live, postponing his fear of tomorrow's suffering. Heat would come again. His thirst was an unending need that would become only greater when the sun came up.

The melancholy recollection of his homeland remained fresh in his mind as Sean scoured the battleground with tired eyes. What lay before him reawakened his senses. To his relief the stench of dead men and horses had somehow lessened with the sun's retreat.

God, where are you? Sean asked in wonder as he studied the carnage around him under the stars and faint moonlight. But he knew that the deity in disgust had long ago deserted both the faded blue and the tattered gray.

CHAPTER 12
THE NIGHT BESTOWS A FRIEND

Still pinned with his right leg beneath the dead horse, Sean's exhaustion pushed him towards accepting his fate. Death tomorrow afternoon, maybe the next, but no longer. The only positive notion he could draw from his dilemma was the continued feeling in his lower leg. Hoping to increase his chances to avoid amputation, if Union stretcher bearers did arrive, he had massaged his upper thigh muscles to improve circulation. Sean couldn't wiggle his toes but did feel the tiny feet of what he guessed were ants and ticks crawling on the skin of his ankle and calf.

The long night dragged on. Sean thought of the past afternoon's battle. A rebel soldier not ten feet away had politely but desperately asked for his help. "Have you anything to stop the bleeding in my leg?"

Sean had turned to see the gaunt face of the Southerner. The flow of blood from the bullet hole in his leg was easily visible. Then he had inspected the slim soldier's face with greater attention, thinking it almost pretty. Odd he had thought. If not on a battlefield littered with several thousand wounded men, Sean would have thought it was a young woman asking for help. He had taken off his belt and thrown it to the fading grayback. Then pulling his bandana from his neck, he had crushed it into a ball, and also tossed it to the weakened soldier.

He remembered saying, "Good luck Reb. Hope it helps you. I won't need it." The Confederate soldier, a private, Sean noted by his shoulder patch, had smiled a tiny smile of thanks.

Long before dawn, Sean heard a rustling behind him. Startled, he looked over to see the same Confederate soldier crawling near. Fear grew in leaps and bounds in Sean's chest. The soldier was loading his rifle.

While Sean watched, only steps away and helpless, slim hands painstakingly rammed home powder and ball down the rifle's black muzzle. Laying the big caliber weapon on his thigh, the soldier reached to the hammer and nipple of the rifle. There, Sean saw him pull the heavy hammer back, the expended percussion cap no bigger than a pea falling to the ground. Then reaching to a bag at his waist he grasped for an unused cap and placed it snugly on the nipple that carried the fire to the barrel and the charge. Sporadically, as the soldier reloaded, Sean saw him glance up with a crazy grin. Greasy, jet-black hair framed his face.

In vain Sean had reached for any weapon in sight. His horse pistol was nowhere to be seen. The short-barreled scatter gun his regiment carried was locked in its scabbard beside his injured leg. The horse's weight was full upon it.

Sean's world, already dismal as he shivered in the night's dampness, was turning devilishly worse. The compounded fear of literally being blown to Kingdom Come at such short range was beginning to ooze out through every pore with his flooding sweat. The calm he had maintained, despite the horror of his surroundings, ebbed still farther away. It had all changed so rapidly. Only frantic thoughts came from within. But no shot rang out. No bullet came for him.

Moonlight peeped from around a cloud and revealed the rebel private. Sean watched him lay his musket on the lodged swale of wheat straw by his side and felt delight as the soldier took the fingers of his right hand from the trigger guard. The Irishman's quick sigh of relief caught the soldier's attention.

"Don't worry Yank," he heard the scrawny soldier say. "It's not for you. Should have told you before. The scavengers are who it's for. They'll come before dawn. You'd do best to have a weapon ready."

The soldier paused then weakly spoke again. This time his high-pitched voice was laced with subdued laugher. "Did you think it was for you? Sorry, to trouble you red-haired Yank." He paused then took a breath before saying, "But our battle is over. We may need to join up together to survive this night. Could you do that? Could you fight beside a butternut?"

With those last words the rebel lapsed into sleep. Sean noted in the moon's brighter glow that the bleeding from the soldier's leg appeared to have stopped.

CHAPTER 13
SCAVENGERS

A crescent moon directly overhead met Sean's eyes when he awoke. Still trapped and with no help in sight, hope for survival was nonexistent. His head throbbed and his mouth and tongue felt as if he had been chewing cotton. It was cool, though, and Sean thanked God for the night. Much of the screaming had subsided, but some low moans still carried across the battlefield's thick moonlit air. *How many men filled this wheat field, like countless broken logs and feed sacks*, he wondered? *It must surely be thousands.*

With great effort Sean rose to his elbows. He scanned the flattened wheat field and caught movement. Maybe one, maybe three or four stone throws away the increasing moonlight illuminated moving shapes. "Litter bearers," he whispered to no one, but then remembered the rebel soldier close by. They were working to transport the wounded off the field. Why had it taken so long? He only guessed. But he had seen it before at Fredericksburg. The medical corps attendance to the wounded was always slow.

Behind him, a stirring caught his ear. The soldier whom he had befriended was dragging himself nearer.

Holding up a flask of water, the Confederate said, "Before I give you some water, tell me your name." Both exchanged first names then the generous man deliberately trickled only a small taste of water into Sean's parched mouth. "Don't have much. Drank most of it myself," said Eli who then drained the remaining half cup into Sean's eagerly waiting mouth.

Long moments of delight later, Sean finally spoke. "Thank you, Eli. Didn't expect that from a Reb."

"Thank you, Sean. Your belt and bandanna have most likely saved my life, for now." Eli then turned to the litter bearers to the west, but looked suddenly in the opposite direction where Sean had to strain his neck to see. "They're coming," he said. "Here, take this." The soldier handed Sean a broken sword with two thirds of the blade still attached firmly to the handle.

The battlefield scavengers were dark spots among the wounded, and Sean was amazed the rebel soldier beside him had seen them. He knew they were stealing valuables from dead or disabled soldiers. They moved slowly and methodically often as not dispatching either a wounded Federal or Confederate to the next world if it made their work easier. Sean watched with dread as two, maybe three dark forms made their way closer.

Eli was now leaning against Sean's dead horse with his rifle pointing towards the scavengers. He turned to face Sean. "They won't reach us for a while. They're combing back and forth." Then in a gravelly voice Eli asked, "Where are you from, Sean? Do you have family?"

Both shared their stories for nearly an hour describing their past and their families in exhausted whispers. Eli described a great gushing spring in southern Missouri and the mill beside it. While their stories were told the rebel and the Yankee kept a close eye on the litter bearers in one direction and the scavengers in the other. It was the scavengers who worked their way first.

Sean knew they were too weak to put up much of a fight. Eli did have his weapon propped up on his good knee. Sean saw the index finger of his right hand cradling the trigger. The loud click of the hammer being brought back attracted the attention of a dark-form standing only a few steps away. Looking up from his victim then over to Eli, Sean watched the scavenger wait, he guessed, deciding whether or not to wave his accomplices over for help.

Eli hollered as loud as a wounded and weak person could, "Hold! Come closer and I'll blow your brains out." His brave but squeaky voice proved not to have the intended effect.

A good bluff thought Sean, but he was soon disappointed to see the dark silhouette of a man taking a step closer to investigate.

⊕

The scavenger smiled as he turned back and spoke in a loud whisper to one of his partners, "Got another one of those high pitched voices this way, Jed." Then still louder, "There might be some play with this one since she still had enough energy to warn me off." He knew this would not be the first or last woman soldier either in blue or gray he would find on a battlefield. The first one he found in men's clothing had bewildered him, but in the past year he had counted well over ten women of differing ages among the dead and wounded. *She will be no different,* he calculated as his heart beat faster. *Me and Jed will have our fun,* raced through his mind as moonlight poked out from behind the clouds.

⊕

Sean watched Eli use a last bit of energy to swing the rifle's stock up to his small shoulder. A blinding flash filled the night. The explosion of the powder charge in the .54 caliber's breech threw Eli away from Sean's dead horse. On the mark, Eli's bullet doubled the evil man over, and the robber of the dead would rob no more. Sean only wondered why the scavenger had so foolishly disregarded Eli's warning.

Soldiers and litter bearers began rushing over. Long bayonets gleamed in the moonlight. The remaining scavengers melted into the night undetected, and Sean and Eli awaited the soldiers, unsure if they would be saved or shot.

A tall man rushed forward, rifle cocked with cold steel menacingly pointed in their direction. Both froze with fear, but it was Eli who broke the silence. "Please, help us. Scavengers were here. That's why I fired." Eli's voice showed no trace of the burliness it carried before.

A beefy Confederate with the thin moon at his back cast a shadow on the two wounded soldiers. When he finally spoke a strong southern accent colored each word, "Your name and regiment?"

Sean saddened when he heard the southern drawl, but Eli quickly answered, "General Gordon's Division, Third Georgia, Major Burris, Company B." Then came, "Private Eli Melforth, but I'm from Missouri not Georgia." His squeaky voice had reached a steady lower pitch.

Eli was looked over carefully then the eye of examination turned more closely on Sean. Weakly the words came in Sean's strong Irish accent, "Army of the Potomac, General Sheridan's Calvary Corps, Corporal Sean Kelly."

"Damn Billy Yank, I should spit you now! Sheridan's boys brought the fight down on our right flank and nearly turned the tide. It would have forced General Early's retreat from the Shenandoah Valley to the south. We are still hanging on by a thread. Give me a reason Private Melforth to let this Yank live!"

The bayonet's silhouetted shape flashed in the moonlight inches from Sean's chest. He waited to die. There was nothing to do. No longer afraid, he only hoped it would be quick. The sound of Eli's voice, now higher pitched and girlish, beseeched the Confederate soldier and his other comrades in arms.

"Would you kill a brave man? He surely gave me the wound I have, yet as the afternoon sun cooked us and blood streamed from my body, he gave me what I needed to girth and cinch down my leg. He saved my life, good soldiers of Bobby Lee. I implore you to spare him."

The talk from the soldiers with readied bayonets was low and full of questions. "What do we do, sergeant? Looks as if we have a spunky southern lad defending a brave Yank. Couldn't very well leave them here for another day in the sun, can we?"

The sergeant answered, "No, Teasley, it seems we have a clear duty in this. You others, get with me and move the horse. Teasley put the wounded soldier from Missouri on your shoulder and carry him clear." Then the southern sergeant continued to command and spoke to a bewildered Sean, "When we have helped all our boys, then I'll make sure you are the first blue belly to be given medical attention. Your medical corps is nowhere to be seen, so consider this a pardon for your sins in fighting on the wrong side. There must be over a thousand of your corps bloodied and eating dust in this field."

The Confederate soldiers and litter bearers traversed the dead men and strewn equipment. Sean, now free from the mass of the horse but unable to walk, hollered as loud as he could, "Thanks, Eli. Thank you, sergeant."

The soldier who walked away in the night with Eli on his shoulder was the enemy half a day ago, but now, he was Sean's only hope. He heard another soldier questioning Eli, "You certainly are a small lad? We'll get some corn bread and beans in you shortly."

Sean wondered where the Union Army's hospital corps had vanished, and worried whether any doctor, from northern army or the southern, would waste precious time on his broken leg. He knew these war weary doctors would likely pursue the simplest avenue towards a cure. Without a second thought they would cut off his leg before blood poisoning took it.

Chapter 14
Answers Arise

Sean awoke with a start. A bearded man's face loomed directly above him. His talk was loud and his breath stank. Sean had no idea where he was or what was happening. He concentrated on the man's dark eyes and not on the putrid wind that followed each word.

"Guess we won't kill you now, Yank. Heard you saved one of our boys." Sean noticed that the man's bandaged arm was slinged. "The one you saved is over there a ways, eight or ten men over. The word is, he's starting to fever bad. He called for the only Billy Yank in the neighborhood, alive that is."

Tapping hard on Sean's chest he continued, "That would be you!" And the wounded rebel managed a laugh as did many others who, despite their sad physical state, savored the tirade.

Barely awake, Sean ignored the Confederate soldier and reached down his right leg hoping it was still intact. His fingers worked slowly touching first his thigh, knee, lower leg, and foot. There was pain in his knee but none lower. It must be crushed, he thought, and temporarily was relieved of the dread of amputation. He felt with his fingers that it was wrapped in rags bloodied by some injury not his own.

On his elbows, now, Sean scanned the hundreds of men lying

on canvas sheets, blankets, and the bare ground. At least they were in the shade. Several large spreading oaks blocked the sun. The wounded had been placed on both sides of a small dusty lane overgrown with grass much like dominoes laid out opposite each other. He waited. There was nothing else he could do.

By midmorning the smell of death and the sounds of the dying had become commonplace. He watched the limp body of a soldier just a step to his left being rolled face down onto a canvas sheet. While the orderlies hauled the expired man away, another stretcher arrived. A smaller soldier took the dead man's place. *Eli,* he wondered, or was he imagining.

Yet, it was Eli, and the fevered boy turned his sweat covered face to Sean. His dark hair and clothes looked as if he had fallen into a creek. Sean could see into those tired eyes. His shivering betrayed the worst. Eli had little left to give.

When the rebel soldier's tenor voice finally spoke, the words formed slowly and flowed unevenly from his mouth. "Sean, I had the orderlies bring me over your way. You'll see why in a spell." Then he rested, breathing shallow and quick. He paused a great while before speaking again. "I need something from you." With great effort and after a deep breath he said, "I'm most surely dying."

A few long moments later, Eli managed, "The orderlies have seen hundreds in my condition. They told me only a few survive the fever and walk away." Again a deep breath, then a concerted effort appeared to come over him. He tried to gain control as the shivering took hold.

"I want you to take," the trembling soldier demanded between gasps, "my effects to my family." He had blurted it out in a pained whisper. "There's not much to carry, just what I have in my pockets." Then so slowly, "Please, Sean Kelly. Promise you'll do this."

"Surely, Eli," Sean answered. He humbly reached for the handful of personal objects. Then Eli said something shocking.

"The silver dollar was my *lucky piece* until your bullet found me, Irishman. The surgeon pulled it from my thigh." But Sean detected no hatred in these high pitched words or eyes that knew death was near, only a spark of good humor brought on by affection.

Sean tenderly looked to the thin, black-haired boy lying before him that in the attack he had most likely shot. *Surely, Eli is only fourteen or fifteen, if that. How could he have been in the war for three years? He must have been tiny when he joined. How could they have let him enlist?* Sean's thoughts, though sympathetic, grew more skeptical with each passing moment.

In the daylight, Sean had a much better view of this soldier who had saved his life. The loose clothing soaked with sweat could not hide the wider hips and thin waist. Sean noted the swellings that could only be small breasts. The evidence was overpowering. Eli was no man.

Sean held it to himself the rest of the morning, too embarrassed to talk to the wounded soldier and unsure what to say if he did.

By mid-day Eli's intense fever had diminished. Sean was pleased, smug actually as he watched the girl disguised as a man. *Quite an actress*, he thought. *Tough as any man I've ever seen.*

While she quietly slept away the early afternoon, Sean thought that maybe, just maybe, this female soldier beside him yet had a chance. When Eli awoke, Sean drank a dipper of water offered by an orderly and watched his rebel friend do the same. He then spoke aloud Eli's home town several times to reassure her. Certainly, he now knew where to find her family. Only then, it seemed to Sean's war seasoned mind, did she release the tension inside her and relax, now content to let the journey of dying carry on.

After another dipper of water Eli looked with intensity toward Sean. He realized that the girl's penetrating gaze was different.

"You know?" Eli asked pensively. Then, "You do, don't you?"

"Not last night," Sean began, "only after you were carried by the orderlies to my side." He studied the gaunt face of the soldier. *Man or woman, it made no difference. She, an enemy, had saved my life.* He sighed as if in pain before he spoke to the brave woman again. "Your secret is safe. I owe you that, at the very least."

Eli smiled weakly and held out her slim burning hand. Sean grasped it gently wondering how this daring girl ever traveled this far with such deception. How many battles had she fought? How many of his comrades had she killed?

She caught him offguard, "And where is your fiddle if indeed you are Sean Kelly?" A pause and then an explanation, "Last night, while trapped under your horse in delirium, you spoke of it constantly, and of the fair at some town in Ireland that I couldn't say." The weak and frightened young woman, who was unmistakably counting the hours till her death, managed still another smile.

Sean's wry grin answered Eli's as his confidence grew inside. He answered, "I'll play a tune for you when I find another." Sean gently squeezed her hand and said, "Sorry, but my fiddle was crushed under my horse along with my leg."

Another beaming smile she sent him, now stronger, and he thought it striking.

Listening with lackluster fading eyes, Sean saw Eli fall into a deep sleep. Later, field guns in the distance awakened her, and Sean judged her rational though terribly frail. He lured her to talk. She rambled on in whispered phrases.

"The orderlies know, but promised... to say nothing. They discovered... my secret... putting the hot metal to the wound... in my thigh." Eli's attempt at speaking became to Sean a series of mumbles. He guessed she was reliving the terrible pain of the burning to seal the wound and stop the bleeding. He reached over with his hand and stroked her brow. His hand remained on her head.

Changing the subject from anything but dying, Sean continued their discussion from the night before where they had awaited salvation in a field of death. "So, why are you and all these southerners fighting so hard and long, if so many of you don't believe in slavery? I can't come close to understanding!" The night before in the killing field, Eli had told him how in the Missouri Ozarks, where her family lived, few people owned slaves.

Refreshed somehow, Eli answered with overwrought words, "Mr. Lincoln gave us no choice, Sean. The Southern States all decided to fight to keep their rights. We are fighting for our freedom! You are here. We must fight to send you marching home."

The farm boy from Lisdoonvarna found himself glued to Eli's stark words. He could not fathom how both sides were fighting for liberty and justice. *How could the same God be cheering on both sides? Why was this mighty war being fought at all?* He remembered the words of the Princeton teacher around the campfire so long ago. William Carleton's words had lived on. *Choices. We all have choices.*

Baffled, Sean said nothing for several minutes. His thoughts returned to a captured southern soldier he had guarded a year ago during an interrogation. The prisoner of war was an average soldier, low in the ranks, one of tens of thousands who withstood the might of the Union Army day after day, year after year inflicting an inconceivable number of casualties upon the overwhelming and always invading enemy from the north.

Lacking shoes, food, and shelter, these hardy men would not quit. No matter how badly the raggedy armies of General Johnston, Hood, Longstreet, and Lee were bloodied, they had persevered.

This lone captive had been asked why he and his comrades fought with such a vengeance. Sean knew most to be poor farm boys as he. Usually only the Confederate officers owned slaves.

"What are you fighting for?" he had heard asked. The soldier, though chained to a tree, stood as tall as he could despite his restraints. His words were spit out in cold defiance, "You Yanks are here!"

Their loyalty to each other amazed Sean. The men in the Confederate Army had come hungrily from Texas, Louisiana, and Florida, states far from any quarrel but seeking conflict. *As simple as that,* he allowed, *they have a blood lust to kill Yankees. These proud people, too proud at times, came from so many farms and forests, villages and towns, mountains or bayous south of the Mason Dixon Line.* Some, he had been told, had even filtered down from the North.

These sons of the Confederacy were not about to allow anyone to overrun their land and prosper from it. These southern boys thought they were so different from the northerners. Yet, Sean knew. They were much the same. He had shot through many a southern Irishman as they had his comrades.

Sean Kelly had fought at Manassas. At the bridge he had seen the thousands of brave Union troops mowed down. He had ridden with Sheridan at Gettysburg. His troop of cavalry had waited in reserve just east of Cemetery Ridge as Picket's division was decimated by enfilade fire of round shot and grape. Over twelve thousand brave rebels attempted to take the well held position. Amazingly, they did, but for moments before Sean's charging cavalry regiment and massed infantry in reserve counterattacked to fill the breach. In but minutes, less than five thousand rebels still stood and were able to retreat. Northern rifle fire from entrenchments and stone walls had sealed their fate. Approaching eight thousand Confederates lay torn by cannon and riddled by small arms fire.

This War of Northern Aggression could end only one way, the soldier under interrogation had muttered still again, "Ya'll be dead or ya'll be gone." Then with his chain stretched to the limit the Reb had demanded, "Which one, Yanks? Which one will it be?"

Sean remembered the words clearly and nearly two years later he still could not claim to understand, but agreed with what his captain had read to his troop of cavalry on President Lincoln's state of mind. Sean believed, as he knew many more knowledgeable than he, that the nation would remain scattered without that determined man in the White House.

Sean brought his drifting thoughts back to the sick girl lying next to him. It was then he noticed his hand. It lay on Eli's head and touched her hair. He hadn't realized that it had remained there. Oddly, his palm was smeared black like coal. He rubbed the hair at her temple and ran it through his fingers. The short strands appeared golden or flaxen in the sun, certainly not black.

Chapter 15
A Tune Turns the Tide

"We overheard your friend, Yank," a sorely wounded rebel three men over to Sean's left said. "My friend is dead but I have his fiddle." Then after a long pause, "Will you be kind enough to play it? Like I said, we heard the lad beside you. All these boys on this hill deserve a cheering up."

Sean felt his spine straighten then relax. These were men no different than himself, although only a day in the past he had tried desperately to kill them. He looked around and saw the wounded that surrounded him in every state of injury, and with a sigh, realized, *They are enemies no more. If this rebel can produce an instrument with four strings and a bow, I will play it.*

A few minutes later a scratched and hard worn instrument was placed in his hands. The Irishman held the fiddle to his chest for a moment first coveting it and then beginning his examination. Its strings were intact. The bow needed a fresh restringing of horse hair, but it would do for now. Then tightening the bow, the boy from not far between Lisdoonvarna and the sea plucked each string while he held the instrument to his ear. With a skill thought reserved for only symphony musicians, the fingers on the right hand of this low born crofter's son turned one tuning peg then another with a precision few could muster.

⊕

The Yankee fiddler's wry smile was witnessed by perplexed Confederate soldiers. It was not easily understood. Some thought it arrogant or defiant or both. So confidently did he hold the borrowed fiddle under his chin that at first they guessed his mood to be sinister. *The look did grace an enemy's face.* The northern soldier's manner failed to change as his music magically began. Lilting and gay, it quickly infected all who listened. The wounded rebel soldiers who could see him best observed a hidden joy behind the solemn mystery of his face.

Approval came in the form of smiles where there had been none or muted applause when each tune ended. The desire for another was quickly demanded and briefly satisfied. Then again and again, while able only to sit, the fiddler wailed away with his bow. The production of the sweetest sounds from cat gut and horsehair, along with a Yank's rekindling spirit, carried over the hill of oaks, green pasture, and wounded men. Its blessing surely purged the dying and revived those torn men still with chances to see the next day.

CHAPTER 16
HURRAH FOR THE FIDDLE

Two burly Confederate medical orderlies in worn and blood stained aprons approached quietly from behind. Not so gently they slid Sean onto a stretcher. When asked where he was to be taken, the huskier of the two litter bearers commanded, "Hush, if you know what's good for you."

Sean hastily returned his borrowed fiddle and as quickly was bustled away. He had only a brief chance to look back. Eli was shivering terribly but fully awake. Her forlorn stare followed him. He felt his shirt pocket for her effects while he studied her reddened and watery eyes. He nodded his head to reaffirm his promise.

In a short time the long strides of the orderlies left Eli and the open air ward of the Confederate hospital far behind. Over the rolling patch of pasture and trees he was carried. More gently than expected, he felt his body settle into knee high grass.

Before the orderlies left, Sean asked them about Eli's chances. He watched them both shake their heads. "You know Eli is a woman, don't you, Yank?" one spoke up.

"And a scrawny one at that," the other had added. "That lowers the chances."

"Take care of her," Sean pleaded as the two turned to leave.

Neither answered and both soon disappeared over the same hill they had so recently traveled.

Sean had been graciously placed in the shadows of a great oak, and a steady cooling wind rustled through its branches. He lay in the grass glad for the shade and the breeze but found himself more puzzled with each passing minute. Why was he here? His aching leg quickly ended his confusion, and he called on all his willpower to hold back a long overdue moan of pain. Just as he was about to give in to his agony he noticed a single rebel soldier not far away. His guard, he calculated, sat with a rifle across his knees and chewed on a long stem of grass. When Sean detected a subtle smile from the man older than his father, he also observed a tell-tale pat on the big musket aimed his way.

Over the crest of the hill the flap of tent canvas caught Sean's attention. He turned to look. There, two white tents billowed in a gust near another large tree. Unfurled battle flags of reds and yellows told him that he was a stone's throw away from the headquarters of a major command.

Throughout the lazy afternoon he awaited his fate while he dozed. A hawk circled far above. Occasionally, he detected activity near the tents. Uniformed officers in gray arrived on sweating horses and just as quickly, before the dust had settled, rode away on some errand. Something seemed very wrong in Sean's mind. He looked around and studied everything within his view. *What is it? What's missing?* Then it came to him. *The silence.* No explosions from cannon or the popping racket of musketry filled his ears. The day was still except for the breeze in the chattering oak leaves high over his head.

Sean noticed a small group of Confederate soldiers who stood near one of the tents. *Awaiting orders most likely,* he guessed. To fill the time he watched the mud-splattered soldier in the shade who guarded him. The man had no shoes. Sean wondered why he fought.

There could be no mistaking the intention of the rebel's firearm. Its big barrel was pointed at his chest, even though it rested on the guard's knee. The end of the weapon stared with its lone dark eye.

The guard's silence, then again that thin smile, told all, but this time it became the forerunner of a statement.

"Do you plan on leaving us soon, Yank?" asked the aging guard, more to kill the time than to seriously pose a threat. An accent of faded Irish had curled around each word. "Lad, do you think it a shame to ruin this tranquil day?"

Sean pointed to his leg. "You'll be expecting me to be going somewhere?" Curiosity and the desire to talk to another human being egged him to ask, "Where was your home?"

"Near Dublin," was the answer. "My sisters and I escaped the famine. We landed in the Carolinas. Charleston it was." He added with sarcasm trailing away in his voice, "My father told me before we sailed not to expect to be treated much different here than in Ireland. He was right."

While Sean pondered the guard's words, movement near one of the tents caught his eye. An older soldier in gray began walking his way. Shiny, knee-high boots swished through the tall grass. *A pleasant rustling*, he thought, as the sound came closer. What the man carried caught Sean off guard. An old fiddle was in one hand and a bow dangled in the other.

Sean frowned as he questioned himself in a whisper, "Do they expect me to entertain their officers on request?" He was taken aback at first when he saw the tidy uniform of the soldier that approached. Two faded yellow stars graced the collar. Yet, Sean was in no mood to be treated like Irish chattel and convinced himself of the officer's intention and folly before the rebel had a chance to explain. Sean noted the care with which the fragile instrument was handed his way, but he refused it.

Sean observed the thwarted look and heard the officer say, "Can you play this? I mean play it well?" Sean was too incensed to speak. He felt his guard's rifle barrel prod his side.

The rebel officer's strong English features repulsed Sean. The man looked much like his father's haughty landlord. The black boots gleamed at the level of Sean's face and blue eyes on each side of a long, thin nose glared down at him. A full beard covered his chin and cheeks.

It was only then that Sean realized he was in hot conversation with a general. He remembered he was a prisoner and at this man's mercy. He managed with great difficulty to curb his building rage and apologized, "I am sorry sir, but what is this all about?"

⊕

The high ranking officer replied edgily, "You have a choice, young man." The rebel general looked over Sean's head to the grass covered hills in the distance and silently cursed the rabble who fought for him and against him. Finally, he said, "Red-headed lad, we have many like you in our ranks." Then he paused and allowed his face to form a smile before he spoke. "The hospital orderlies over the rise say that you played the fiddle like a devil sliding in shoes of butter on a hot skillet. Yes, those were their words." He managed a small laugh, then, "But now I wonder." The officer studied Sean for a moment until he offered a questioning, "Humph?"

The general looked over Sean like a prize calf at the fair, but his eye stopped at his crippled leg. Then again, locking on the boy's determined green eyes, he asked, "Will it be Andersonville in short order or will you play a song for me?"

Curt and clearly impatient with the unexpected insolence of a prisoner of war, the officer waited and allowed the wounded Yankee soldier at his feet a few more moments to decide his fate. *My old friendship with Philip Sheridan be damned*, he thought, hoping that the surly Irishman would refuse again to take the fiddle and make an end to the confrontation.

Sean momentarily brushed back his pride, "Certainly I will play, sir. But I'll not be entertaining enemy officers at their bidding!" These last words from Sean were as blistering as the afternoon sun, and shot up to the stern-faced officer like hot pokers fresh from cherry-red coals.

"An Irish temper, too, I see!" the general said but then quickly a more approving look covered his face. "But no, boy," the officer relented in a gentle tone, now respecting his prisoner more. "You don't understand. I won't be asking that of you."

The relaxed Confederate handed Sean the bow. "Please, just play something if you will, lad. Philip said you played *The Gary Owen* with a passion. If you are the same Kelly we are looking for, you will be traded for a soldier of our own within the hour. An Irish temper indeed. It seems our Irish lads are much like you." He looked then to the guard who was smiling. "Most are truly fierce warriors in battle," then he added crossly, "and when their liquor rules them."

Sean's emotions lightened. He strained with teeth-clenching pain to sit taller up against the tree. He reached out for the instrument in the officer's hand. With a minimal amount of tuning and acquainting himself with the fiddle, Sean began. He flew into the tune played when his regiment of cavalry charged. Around him a hundred, armed, gray-backed men suddenly turned his way.

From where inside he didn't know, a burst of energy filled him. His chin was leveled, and his eyes focused far away. His fingers ran rampant on the taut strings only to finish the song just short of fainting. The last two days had taken their toll. He was far weaker than he realized.

Within a short span of time Sean was back on a litter being carried not by Confederate soldiers but by broad shouldered boys in blue worsted wool. He was no less astounded that within the hour he was placed in an officer's tent on a cot. The Stars and Stripes gently flapped in the light breeze out front. Although hot and thirsty, Sean felt he must surely be the luckiest man alive.

Later, when a sergeant brought him food, water, and a crutch to help him walk on his own to the latrine, Sean asked what had really happened. The sergeant laughed and told Sean about the trades that occurred all the time. "It just so happens that General Sheridan and the Confederate officer you met are old acquaintances. Many of the officers on both sides served together in the Mexican War back in 1848 after leaving the military academy. I'd be guessing that old Jubal Early himself was the officer with the stars on his collar who handed you the fiddle."

"Oh!" Sean said almost speechless as he noticed the stove black stain still on his hand from touching Eli's hair. He continued listening to the sergeant, but silently said a prayer for her recovery. There was little hope he knew all too well. So many wounded soldiers, many his friends, he had watched linger and die from their wounds or the disease that followed.

"Be glad, Kelly," Sean heard the sergeant say. "You must be valuable, indeed."

Finally, the boy from Lisdoonvarna found his voice. "How so?"

Sean saw solemn eyes study him liberally before his question was answered. "You were traded for a Confederate officer. A major, I heard."

Chapter 17
Invited Home

Over a year-and-a-half later, Sean stood in front of an old four-story brick building off Second Street in Saint Louis. He kicked the snow from his boots and entered the hotel now used for convalescing Union soldiers. He limped but made good time through the lobby. He passed by occupied benches and chairs circling a wood stove. Few of the soldiers soaking up the heat were whole. Many were missing arms and legs. The foul smells of chamber pots by each door in a nearby hallway made him gag. He walked on. There was a chance that his friend was close by, and Sean was intent on seeking him out.

Finally, on the third floor at the far end of the hall Sean found him. The broad-shouldered Wilhelm Hausbach lounged in a rickety cane-backed chair, his boots propped up on the window sill. His strong right arm rested on his knee. The other, Sean knew, had been blown away just months ago while chasing down rebels who refused to surrender. Sean remembered the loyal companion that Willie had been for over a year.

"Good view of the city," Sean offered.

Willie had not seen him or recognized his voice. *"Ja, das ist gut,"* he said without turning around. Sean sensed boredom filling the lethargic reply.

"I suppose you'll wish to be off to Hermann soon?"

His curiosity aroused, the one-armed soldier born in America but of German descent turned to Sean. A grand smile grew across Willie's face.

"You found me!"

"Said I would," Sean replied as his grin grew almost as big.

Willie rose from his chair and hugged his Irish friend. Wilhelm Hausbach, also a corporal of the Union Cavalry, soon to be a private citizen asked, "You'll be coming home with me?"

"Yes, Willie," Sean answered, appreciating the full value of his friend's priceless offer to accompany him home. "Thank you. I have nowhere else to go." In addition, he remembered a promise to a dying soldier. When the snows melted he would try to fulfill it by traveling to Van Buren and the mill by the big spring.

"Good, *mein freund*. Tonight we celebrate. Market Street will hear our songs until as these English say, the cows come home." He smiled broadly, and Sean was pleased that with one arm missing his friend still seemed his old self. "And in a few days I will introduce you to all the beautiful girls of Hermann but one."

Sean smiled back. They had shared their stories as they rode together over much of eastern Virginia. Willie had his lower left arm amputated after their last skirmish. Sean remembered how southern sympathizers simply wouldn't give up despite Lee and Johnston's surrender eight months before. Willie had made it unscathed to the last, and then this.

Sean felt he already knew all the girls of which his friend had spoken. Willie had talked many a night around campfires of the established town of tidy brick homes and shops tucked neatly into the hills on the south side of the big river called the Missouri. He prayed the girl in Willie's dreams would still be there and still love him despite his missing arm. Sean envisioned the big river Willie had described. Their plan after the mustering out, and regardless of the cold weather, was to follow it upstream. In three days, if all went well, they would ride into the German city of Hermann.

"Yes, Corporal Wilhelm Hausbach," Sean Kelly answered his friend, "tonight there will be celebration."

In his tent on the grounds around Jefferson Barracks Sean's

thoughts were far from his German speaking friend and tomorrow's final regimental assembly. He remembered another soldier with whom he had shared stories, descriptions of loving sisters and a father. *A mill*, he remembered her telling him, *the best in the state and a great, clear spring gushing from the foot of a tall cliff.* He reached again for the small leather bag on his bunk that held Eli's effects and tenderly sorted through them. His fingers touched a small clasp knife, a locket with an enameled cameo of her mother and father, and an indented silver dollar she had described as her *lucky piece.* For the hundredth time he let them slip through his fingers and into his outstretched hand. Again, he touched the *lucky piece.* The large silver coin that had lain in her pants pocket and most likely taken the wallop of his Colt's bullet spawned regrets. *Eli's lucky piece had only saved her briefly so that I might know her before she died.*

⊕

A day later, the afternoon's chilling wind cut into Sean as did his uncertainty concerning his future. He was a civilian again and a far cry from being beaten on a muck-filled street in New York. He thought the simple ceremony on the parade grounds too short and impersonal but he *was* allowed to keep his horse, the clothes on his back, and promised one hundred and sixty acres of land. Being a volunteer, he was also given one hundred dollars in Union script which he promptly changed into ten dollar gold pieces and larger silver coins minus a few dollars for the banker's commission on the transaction.

A major by the name of Croft asked him, as he had many other men that afternoon, "Where will your claim lie, Kelly? The West is full of land to be taken." Sean had looked at the map before him and had pointed to southern Missouri. The rivers on the map had attracted him.

"It is of my opinion to be a poor choice, corporal, but land grants remain still in that area of the state. At present you need only to decide which state you wish to settle. No matter, though, you can change your mind."

"Sir, what do you know of the Ozarks to the south, a great spring somewhere near Van Buren?"

"Sorry, soldier, don't know that territory." The major turned to another officer and asked, "You know the south of Missouri better than I do, Captain Loughton. What about that area of which our fiddler speaks?"

"Beautiful, sir," Loughton answered brightly. "Small mountains and big rivers." His attitude changed full circle. "Corporal Kelly, the people there have been ravaged by war as have most in rural Missouri. I'm from Cape Girardeau on the Mississippi to the east. The Ozarks to the west and the prairie part of the state have suffered terribly."

A perplexed look came over Major Croft's face when he asked, "Do you know someone there, corporal?"

A solemn-faced Sean Kelly answered, "I did, sir."

CHAPTER 18
HUNGRY FOR A SMILE

Celebrating on the Saint Louis river front with Willie and hundreds of other Union soldiers, locals, French, Spanish, and even trappers from the far west proved a rowdy conclusion to a long afternoon.

Sean made a point of staying sober and away from the inescapable fights that erupted between townsfolk and the soldiers. He managed to slip away before supper and stumbled upon a gun shop along a narrow cobbled street close to the river. Behind the heavy planked counter, a curly-headed, appealing young woman, he guessed the gunsmith's daughter, met his inquiring look. "Sorry, sir, we're ready to close for the day." Sean showed poor manners and lingered for a moment trying to place her accent. Although he knew he was making her uneasy, he admired the rifles and shotguns that adorned the walls and leaned up against a large cask. In pleasant surprise, he spied a few fiddles that hung from a high beam. His fiddle was average and he hoped to find better. "May I come back tomorrow? I'm interested in a shotgun and a fiddle."

The girl looked over her shoulder and nodded to the vague figure of a man hidden in the shadows of the next room at a work

117

bench. Sean quickly realized that a diligent guardian had been watching him all the while.

The girl's honest smile and sparkling eyes followed Sean as he asked, "Might I play a fiddle before I leave?"

She again looked to the gunsmith. Sean saw him agree with a stern nod. A fiddle was carefully lifted down.

Showing off, the Irishman tried to impress the girl with a few tunes, but his mind was far from his music. He judged the girl his age or slightly younger. She spoke with an accent he could not place. Sean promised to return early in the morning, politely left the shop, and began walking down the street. He eagerly looked back and was rewarded. The curly-haired girl watched him from the doorway. Sean saw her toss him a bold smile before she withdrew inside. However, he saw something else. Beyond the gunsmith's painted shingle, a man, most likely a father, escorted a young child as they walked his way. The face of the man, he could never forget.

As the two ambled by, Sean confronted the man with courteous but feigned enthusiasm, "Hello, Daniel."

The man looked up. Startled at first, Daniel Payton, once of New York City, studied the red-headed soldier before him. Then all came back and he timidly greeted Sean, "Hello, yourself." His next words came slowly, apologetically, "Sean, I'm glad you're alive." Then his manner abruptly changed. "We heard the melee," Daniel tried to explain as more theater came out in his voice than sincerity, "and I could not bring my Clarissa back into that fray. I could not come back for you on that dangerous street. I am deeply sorry."

"Maybe not," Sean answered, wondering what he would have done, but quietly decided that if he were Daniel he would have done something. He tried to let it go but couldn't.

"Maybe you can stop by tomorrow and see Clarissa? We are only a few blocks beyond Third Street."

After almost six years, Sean found himself more disappointed in Daniel Payton than angry. Daniel had deserted him to the street ruffians, and to Sean's thinking their friendship had ended long ago. "Thank you, Daniel. But tomorrow I'm leaving the army and traveling with a friend up river."

Sean ended the conversation politely, wanting only to be gone. "It was good to see you." He began to say something else but changed his mind. As he turned away he offered Daniel his best. "Luck be with you and your family."

With deep remorse Daniel Payton watched Sean walk away and turn the corner at Third and Market Street. He wished the episode in New York had never happened.

His daughter looked up and asked, "Daddy, who was that?"

"Oh, no one really, Prissy. Let's go home. Your mother's waiting." However as they walked, Daniel remembered a brave boy fighting off hoodlums to save him in New York City. He also recollected coming to Sean's aid with two other men but only after being brow beaten by an old woman in the crowd. Indeed, he had been too frightened at first to step forward and help. He was a coward and knew it. He had been the last of the three to assist the boy and only then when success was obvious.

During their brief reunion Daniel had seen the scars on Sean's ear and cheek. He pondered the trials his fellow Irishman had known in the war and thought how bravery must still be in the fiddler's blood. Then he spoke to his daughter as if in need of atonement. "He once played a fine fiddle, Prissy." Yet, Daniel could not bring himself to tell her the rest of the story and would not bring it up for discussion upon their arrival at home. *I have paid dearly,* he thought painfully. *We escaped the street gangs of Five Points, but I have lost so much respect from the one person I love the most.*

Her words at the time still echoed out of his guilt laden memory, "Daniel, how can you desert someone who helped you so?" The image of leaving the fiddler in the sordid streets on the way to the train station came back to him. Brave Clarissa had volunteered to go back alone but he had restrained her. Once he had pulled her onto the train, she had refused to talk to him all the way to Boston.

⊕

Sean continued down Third Street to rendezvous with his friends. The night was young. Images of the gunsmith's attractive daughter soon overpowered his recollections of Daniel Payton and stuck with him throughout the evening. Some things in life could not be undone.

In the morning, as early as was respectable, he returned and found only the gunsmith. Disappointed, he still purchased a fine, bright-sounding fiddle, a modern double-barreled shotgun along with re-loadable brass-cased ten gauge shells, a used percussion rifle, and powder and shot. All were obtained for two ten dollar gold pieces. Before leaving the gun shop he paid a nickel extra, despite the disapproval of the gunsmith, to cut down the long barrels of the shotgun to less than the span of his forearm. Before they parted company Sean respectfully pried into the origin of the man's strong accent.

"Polish," the gunsmith said proudly while pointing to his name painted on the sign outside his shop. When Sean shook his head, the gunsmith spoke his last name with pride and waited for a possible slur.

"I can't read, but thank you, Mr. Kov...es...ches...ski," Sean said as he attempted to pronounce the name as he had just heard it. As final afterthought, "You do fine work, sir," he beamed back as he departed towards a now busy Market Street with the two firearms, his new fiddle, and a waxed canvas sack of ammunition all precipitously cradled between arms, shoulders, and clutching fingers.

Chapter 19
On the Road to Hermann

Sean spied the fresh droppings of horses and oxen sending up columns of steam on the snow-covered road. Other riders and a heavy cart were certainly a short distance ahead. Sean turned in his saddle to his friend.

"So, Willie, you promise me there are pretty girls in Hermann?"

"*Ja*, Seanie boy, our *mädchens*..." he paused. "But I've told you a hundred times before."

"Oh, I know," Sean began, while the steady hoof beats of their horses on the frozen mud that constituted a road continued in mindless monotony. "But there are pretty girls in St. Louis, too. I met one last evening."

"Ah, you met someone last night? One of the bar maids, I think?"

"No, Willie, a decent girl. The gunsmith's daughter or maybe his niece. She was very nice to see and also very nice to talk to."

Willie laughed. "Talk to? Sean you know better than that. A young woman is to be loved. Talking to a girl makes things complicated."

Sean expressed his amusement as the miles of travel piled up and the late morning sun worked its way higher in the sky.

The tiny crystals of ice on the tall grasses and great hardwoods lining the established road began a constant dripping, and the roadway melted enough to make the horses work harder with each sloppy step. However, the lack of a cutting wind and the abundant sunshine made their ride enjoyable in contrast to the many times in the cavalry when staying in the saddle had been an ordeal.

"So, what did you buy at the gunsmith's? We have a fine one in Hermann with cheaper prices."

Not wanting to talk about it, but thinking Willie deserved an answer, Sean admitted, "I found a double barreled shotgun like what we used in the war. I was disappointed when we had to turn in our weapons, yesterday."

"But you saved pistols from the battlefield. I saw your saddle bags then and I imagine now that at least two Navy Colts are hidden there."

Sean studied his friend's face, wanting the discussion to end. "Yes, you're right. I'll be traveling south of Hermann into the hill country when spring comes. I've heard I may need them." A powerful laugh followed when he added, "If you and your family don't kick me out sooner than that."

"Van Buren? You're still thinking of riding into the Ozarks to find that dead soldier's family? What was her name again? Ellenore? Ellyn?"

"Eli."

"Odd name for a woman, Sean. You needn't go, though. You will be welcomed in Hermann. Break out your fiddle and the townspeople will adore you." Then Willie added with a leering smile and a chuckle, "And also all the innocent young ladies will no doubt trample a path to your bed." Willie leaned over to Sean and patted him good naturedly on the shoulder. "Maybe I should warn them, do you think?"

Sean cheerfully shook his head and then gently kicked the flanks of his horse to keep her going. His boots felt the prominent ribs of the old dappled-gray mare. He remembered the order when Major Croft told the regiment to trade in their mounts for others in another corral. To the disgust of Sean and all the other horse soldiers, the corral was full of broken down nags. He felt glad to have picked out one quickly. His at least could carry him. Remembering yesterday made him reach into his coat pocket. Some of his mustering-out-pay clinked between his fingers. The rest lay hidden in his saddle bags.

The long morning had come and gone. The excitement, that day, of leaving the army behind in St. Louis still churned in Sean's gut. He asked Willie to tell him one more time about his village by the great river and all the pretty faces he remembered.

"Bet they will be married with babies on their knees by now, Willie," Sean playfully added as they led their horses off the road in the twilight and into a farm yard. Willie countered, "When we nest up in this farmer's hay loft, I'll tell you more stories."

A light snow was falling as Sean paid the farmer a silver dime for the use of his barn and feed for the horses. Both buried themselves in the loose hay and contented themselves with stale bread and a thin slice of cheese. Sean listened to Willie tell again story after story until both were near sleep. He was envious. Willie had a home and family. Sean had only a broken down horse, several weapons, and two nearly threadbare wool blankets. Then, he thought again. *I have Willie, and Willie is indeed my friend.* Sean hoped his companion's sweetheart still awaited his return to Hermann. He also hoped that the girl would accept Willie's lack of a left arm. Then he thought of himself and his crippled leg. He hoped the staunchly German town would welcome two broken soldiers, one finally finding his way home and the other just a stray hoping not to be turned out.

CHAPTER 20
TERROR ON THE RIVER

The animal was tired but Sean spurred the rundown horse, anyway. Nothing was gained by his action except to kindle guilty feelings. He knew the proper treatment of a horse, and this certainly was not it. Immediately, he relented. "Willie, we need to rest the horses."

Willie answered quickly. He also understood. *"Das ist vahr.* You're right, Irish."

A light snow fell for the next hour while the two soldiers, survivors of turmoil and many bitter winters much worse than this, gently led their animals, step by muddy step towards the west and Hermann. They were walking when they heard it. An explosion's booming concussion swept up from the direction of the river. *Perhaps a mile to our north*, Sean guessed. "What was that?" he yelled.

Willie mounted and then stood tall in his stirrups. He listened. Then asked, "Sean, did you hear it? Another boom."

Sean had heard it. "Sure, I heard it, but what, Willie? Cannon?"

"No, Sean, it was a steamship's boiler. One boiler is bad. Two is a disaster."

⊕

A side trail lead them on a detour to the river and a small village Willie knew to be Wattenburg. Beyond them an immense gravel bar a mile long stretched upriver. Straining his eyes and scanning the outer reaches of the bar Sean found it first, "Willie, to the right of the cut bank. Can you see it?"

"*Ja, mein freund,*" came out slow and cold, colder than death itself. Then, "*Ja,* I see it."

In the distance a tall, dark shaft pumping out clouds of black smoke settled deeper into the gray waters of the swirling river.

"The smokestack," Willie said clearly. "One boiler remains, so the riverboat must have had three. Oh, Sean! I hate to see this. In my lifetime, I have witnessed steamships when they hit another or blow a boiler. Either way, the boat goes down or runs aground."

Long moments passed before Willie announced the scope of the catastrophe. "Sean, do you understand how many people die when this happens?" He looked to his friend, then answered himself softly, "Hundreds, Sean. Hundreds. And in this cold water few will have any chance at all."

Sean heard the croak in his friend's throat, the utter helplessness and regret.

"Maybe there are survivors, Willie!" Sean countered, but then looked again across the cold waters. He shivered. *Who could survive this great swirling river?* Already amidst the debris of the boat's wreckage, lifeless bodies had appeared then disappeared in mid river.

In an instant, though, Sean's eyes caught a flash of movement. An arm raised again and again. Tiny white splashes. Someone was swimming towards shore!

⊕

The two friends, who had together survived so much near the end of the war, tied the horses to some nearby driftwood. They could do nothing but watch in agony and wait. Sean could not swim and he knew that Willie would not attempt the impossible. A one-armed swimmer would most likely die. Sean watched his friend then turned to the splashing that was closer though weakening and still far out into the river. *Finally, so close to Willie's home. The hesitation in his friend's face was plain to see. Maybe Willie was just being smart. He has seen things like this before. Being Good Samaritans could easily get us killed.*

Sean stepped into the water. Despite all his love for the man who had shared hunger, near death, and the wrath of superiors, Sean understood that Willie would not be the one to enact a plan. He eased himself further out in the knee deep water. *Only I have nothing to lose if any of the survivors made it close enough to shore.* The Irishman reviewed his thoughts again while a broken but grandly painted sign floated by. "What does it say, Willie?"

"The *Asa Wilgus*. Its captain has hauled my father's wine downriver to St. Charles many times. I know his family." It was what Sean needed to take another step. The slow moving waters were now thigh deep.

⊕

A steady slip and slide into deeper water went with each new step. He claimed a floating stick and firmed up his balance. The cold water finally reached his chest. He gasped in pain. *The blind rescuing the blind,* came to mind. Then a rock tripped his foot and nearly sent him headlong into the water. Sean screamed, "I can't do this," but went on deeper until his arm pits felt the icy wetness. But the slender branch of driftwood in his hand acted now to steady him as it poked down into the mud, and would, if luck permitted, extend his reach to any survivors.

There, two stone throws into the swirling waters he waited. He watched other bodies float by before he saw one arm, and then he thought another, holding onto a plank. One arm churned the water but slower now. Always slower.

He hollered, "Don't give up! Swim harder. Don't stop!" He was sure that the one in front with a burden heard him. He saw a face.

Ten strides. Five. One. Sean reached out towards deeper water to his limit. An unsteady hand grasped the stick. His body wasn't screaming in pain as it had moments before. He could feel very little. Scared, Sean pulled with his best. His arms were numbing. Soon, there were two bodies in tow, alive but barely.

Sean managed to drag the soppy survivors onto the dry gravel, but no more. He collapsed on the beach in a sprawl and felt himself slipping away. His brain still remembered that he was frozen to the bone. A vague something clawed at his brain. *Death is coming.* He knew it all too well during Virginia winters with General Sheridan. *The coldest would begin to tear off their clothes and stagger into the night mumbling nonsense.*

Rise or die! The words shot through his brain. *Rise or die!* And he forced himself with the greatest of efforts to stand as might a drunkard. He saw Willie. *Dear Willie has kindled a growing fire of driftwood.* Sean tried to speak but words refused him. He tried to say, "Willie, thank you. I'll be there in a minute." Only then, finally, did Sean bring back the memory of rescuing the soaking lumps covered in dress fabric.

And so he tried to think, although his brain was a fog. His actions remained slow. His brain worked but hesitated. Sean squeezed his last remaining strength with the mightiest of mental pinches. First one, he carried. *A young woman,* he thought though not sure. Then between them Sean and Willie managed to drag another much heavier. Sean found himself basking in the heat of a fine bonfire. He shivered uncontrollably, but wondered if he had ever traveled to such a heaven of warmth. Only a little later when the fire had truly begun its job did he notice the two people he had helped rescue.

Sean heard Willie take charge with gentle persuasion, "Your wet clothes must come off. It's your only chance." Then Sean turned his head as his friend did the deed. *They will die where they stand if Willie does nothing.*

He twisted his back to the fire and away from the women he had waded in to save. He listened while his friend hurriedly disrobed the two helpless creatures. Their faint cries told all. Whimpers of defeat, not words of defiance, came to his ears while dreamily he watched the steam rise in clouds from his wool trousers and shirt. Oddly, he saw much more as his gaze traveled across the immensity of the river.

⊕

He was a boy again, and he was there, in the other world of which his grandfather and father had warned him. "Be ready, Sean," the memory of Malroy Kelly was again telling him in low tones as all others in the family slept. "It's a burden but also a boon, my son."

The possibilities had been explained in depth that winter's night while thick mists swallowed their simple home. Before a smoldering hearth fire of peat with only those twelve years under his belt, Sean recollected it all in vivid detail. What he saw now in the fog of the great river was another dream, two women at a distance walking steadily before a team of horses. They carried firearms. He saw no faces as they walked ahead. He realized he was watching from a wagon and was unable to rise. Both were young, able women, one oddly so light-skinned and fair-haired and the other so very dark. His body ceased its shivering. His muddled mind, still slower than cold blackstrap, had noticeably begun to thaw.

⊕

Willie had no time for talk or indecision. An empty look on his friend's face told him of suffering, but the savvy young man from Hermann knew the toughness of the Irishman who had remarkably remained standing and unaided by the fire. Quickly, Willie covered the two freezing figures from the river in worn Union blankets from their bedrolls, and only then, when satisfied with his efforts, Willie stripped off his friend's wet shirt. With a gentle hand he laid the Irishman's thick winter coat over bare shoulders. He saw Sean's eyes and the faraway look.

⊕

Sean propped up a semblance of his wry grin as he studied the decent, scurrying German with appreciation. Despite his cold delirium, he hoped, though embarrassed, that his blankets harbored few fleas or lice. *The irritating biters*, he knew from past experience, *awaited their chance*. However, the pain of the cold still controlled him as his hands and arms reached out to the fiery warmth. In his state of confusion he only prayed that he would have the feeling in his limbs to know to retreat when the flames kindled hotter.

Then he realized, *The wind. It's not blowing.* All was quiet except for the lapping of the river's small waves on the shore and the crackling updraft above the fire. *The wind,* he thought again. *If the wind had been blowing, only Willie would be alive beside the fire.* He had seen it many times in the East during long winters. *The wind would have pulled the life from our soaked bodies faster than even good Willie could warm us.*

Time passed agonizingly slow. Clouds of steam billowed from the mounds of drying clothes scattered over driftwood near the fire. Sean's legs finally found pained feeling. The younger woman, the girl who had grasped his driftwood stick and never let go, moved her bare arm to the fire then withdrew, then reached in again to extract the warmth. Sean had seen her eyes. He stared for only a moment then forced his look away to the great river running just steps away.

He was shaking now but not from the cold. His fear had been under control while he rescued the women. Now he felt powerless. He couldn't push away the thoughts. The great river had nearly swallowed him. Willie had called it by a pleasant Native American name, Missouri, but Sean felt with loathing that Big Muddy seemed to suit the dark, beastly stream best.

Chapter 21
Smitten

"You're all right," the Irishman heard Willie's gentle but reassuring words. He wished they were for him but knew they must be for the two women thawing by the fire.

Finally, a weak but encouraging word came from the younger of the two. "Gentlemen, we thank you." She then introduced herself and her aunt.

It was all that Sean Kelly needed. *Retha, she called herself.* The name spun through his mind and over his tongue. He was just beyond hallucinating from the trials of the cold but was in love.

His German friend had seen Sean's look, and a mischievous grin covered his face. "You ladies must be warned that your rescuer is the stuff of legends."

Two sets of female eyes rolled Willie's way then toward Sean and back.

"No, not me," Wilhelm qualified, pointing to his friend. "No, it's this Irish Yankee before you. I would never have had the courage to save you from the waters. And for years I have seen him use that same courage to ravage many hearts." Then, "So, let you be forewarned," Wilhelm offered while attempting not to laugh.

Sean remained silent, but his head was shaking slowly in response to Wilhelm's friendly accusations. *What women have I*

130

seen in the last few years? Where had there been any that Willie knew of? He looked to his friend, only then to see the young woman's stare and gracious smile.

"And how has this happened, Willie?" Retha asked.

Wilhelm Hausbach played his part, cherishing his role as he had cherished the man and the friendship through this last year. Slowly, he allowed his words to swell into a tone laced with good humor. "Beware, I tell you. When you let this man pull his fiddle from its sack, your hearts will be lost." He paused and smiled all around. "I have seen the bravest succumb to the magic of his dancing fingers on the strings." Corporal Wilhelm Hausbach remembered the hundreds of soldiers charmed by his friend's joyous music, *So for certain it must be that women must fall under its spell, too.* Sean had told him of the fair and playing in the streets of New York.

Both women mustered a laugh, the niece more than the aunt. Willie continued in the most serious of voices, "He will make you cry as his bow pulls the music from the strings." He looked to all three but lingered on his old friend's face. "So, beware when we reach Hermann. There, you can not expect my protection."

⊕

By afternoon, they had enlisted a wagon from a farmer whom Willie's family had known for years. Its lumbering gait brought the now dry river rats up to the front steps of a stout brick home on the corner of Guttenberg and Third Street.

"Nickel's enough," the farmer insisted as he was handed a larger coin. "Be careful, now," and winked first at Sean and then at Retha. "Stories like yours will not wash easily from the soul."

He waved as he began to drive away but turned his head back to say, "Wilhelm, tell your father, hello, and also your dear mother."

Willie only waved. His senses were riveted on the man and two women who stood ready to enter the home he had not seen for three years. *Will this be too much for my mother? My sisters? Even my strong father?* He hoped the shock would be small. He also hoped that his letter had arrived from St. Louis the week before.

Looking at his friend, Willie saw infatuation. *It's in his face.* Yet, now, as he studied the pretty young woman on his doorstep, he pondered the chance that she was truly interested, polite maybe and thankful, but most likely a heartbreaker for Sean. *Besides,* he told himself, *my sisters, at least one, will fall deeply for the Irishman and his fiddle.* It had long been in the plan.

CHAPTER 22
HONOR HOLDS HIM

A week later, Sean Kelly stood sadly on the docks of the river town waving goodbye. A mighty sternwheeler churned the waters slowly moving upstream. Retha and her aunt waved back. Their destination was Arrow Rock and then by wagon to Westport to meet Retha's uncle. From there they would set out for Oregon.

Willie, who constantly was at Sean's side, patted him on the shoulder in consolation. "At least you knew her for a few days, Sean Kelly. Be glad of that. Be glad you saved her life. Jesus loves you, Irishman."

However, Sean's thoughts were trying to conjure the Oregon Territory. Maybe he would follow Retha and her aunt and uncle. Then back into the here and now the Irishman turned his head to his friend. "You saved her, too." And then wondered how anyone could love him, even Willie. He had killed far too many men since he had joined the cavalry in New York City so long ago. *No, Willie, sweet Jesus wishes me dead as do the families of the many rebel soldiers I have slain.*

Then, words from Willie came in a tone that reeked with guilt. "You were not afraid to wade into the water, Sean. I could never have done what you did."

Not afraid! Never have I been more afraid, Sean thought, amazed by his friend's remorseful remark. Sean relived that bitterly cold morning. *Terrified was a better description*, but he said nothing.

⊕

All the while, a pretty girl of seventeen silently observed the two young men on the dockside. Gretchen Westfphal studied her cousin, Wilhelm, and then the man he had brought back from the war. *Such passion with the fiddle*, she thought as she watched them leave the dock. *Such friendship. Later*, she thought as she plotted. Later, she would win this strong-hearted friend of her cousin who had made her cry at the dancing hall the night before. *No one*, to her knowledge, had ever upset her in such a good way. She had been amazed when the Irishman played his instrument at the dance. He held her spell-bound and every other young woman her age. His music had flowed beautifully on and on. *The green eyes of the Irishman.* She had been unable to pull away.

⊕

There in Hermann, Sean found himself seduced by the work ethic of the steady *herrs* and *fraus* and also their sons and lovely daughters. He decided to spend the winter, hoping to recuperate from the trauma of four years of war. His mustering out pay he placed in a hiding place in the wall of the Hausbach barn. He found work at one of the local wineries. Along the river hills he became intimate with a prominent German winemaker's oldest daughter. Accepted for industriousness and because he was Catholic, as were these Germans, life turned routine and pleasant. But sometimes he grew restless.

Sean remembered the debt he owed the family of the rebel soldier from the battle at Cedar Creek two years before. His honor required him to travel deep into the Ozarks along the Current River and to its big spring. Almost daily, he attempted to bolster his courage to strike out alone across the lawless mountainous region. He had heard the stories, during the war and after. Missouri was cursed with unending violence.

Chapter 23
Good Medicine

Late afternoons on sunny days Willie and Sean lounged by the busy docks. The two friends discussed the life of the German town and of course the pretty *mädchens*, who walked the streets or lived next door. There was also, of course, discussion about Willie's sisters.

"So, which of my sisters do you like best, Sean?" He had four on his last count, three that were of age to marry.

"Oh, good friend," Sean began, "your sisters are all sweet." But Sean stopped. He could not find another positive word to describe them.

His best friend waited.

"I won't lie to one who has saved me from death so many times," Sean pleaded.

"Not so many times," a sobered Willie replied. "As I remember it was your words to General Sheridan that kept me out of the last great attack. Imagine a general," Sean's friend said with grave respect but also disbelief, "listening to a corporal."

Willie's thoughts returned to his sisters. He was crestfallen. All his sisters seemed to him a perfect match for his friend. Clouding his mind was the sad outcome of failing to make Sean a brother-in-law. That he would remain a comrade-in-arms until they died was a given.

"Where does it come from, Willie?" Sean asked to change the subject.

Disappointed but not shaken Willie answered, well aware of the origin of the Irishman's question. "Out west, Sean. Out west. They say in great snow-covered mountains." *The question of the week had again surfaced and with perfect timing from his friend.*

"Maybe we should go up river and explore, Willie. Life here has become dull."

Willie Hausbach forced a painful smile and said, "Ah, not so dull, I think." Guilt tugged at his thoughts as he realized that he prized Sean's happiness even more than that of his sisters. "I see the smile on Gretchen's face when she watches you and when she takes your arm." He awaited Sean's reaction but was disappointed when none came.

"What lies up that river, friend? Indians, excitement, gold? I remember listening to the hunters and trappers in St. Louis. They talked of huge herds of wooly bison. Fewer now they said but we'd never go hungry."

"*Ja*, Sean, slow down. Stick with Frau Westfphal. She loves you as much as Gretchen. In her eyes, too, I see attachment." A barreling laugh left him. "The good *frau*, whom I know you respect or even love as a *mutter*, may not let you go upriver or anywhere. She may demand you marry Gretchen just to keep you in Hermann."

"Demand?" Sean asked in disbelief.

"Yes, demand, my friend. Aunt Gabriella has great influence here. You treat her with great respect, and justly so. She has helped you, but beware."

Sean let the threat slide and turned from the river to his friend. He studied the face of the stout-hearted young man before him. Willie had come through with his promise. The German town had welcomed a poor Irish boy. Sean only wished that Willie's sweetheart from before the war had done the same. For weeks Willie had lamented. Once while at the dock on a cold winter's night his friend had stumbled into the swift waters, maybe falling in on purpose. Sean wasn't sure. Quickly the Irishman had pushed an empty cask into the river and rescued his friend. The cold river had nearly ended both their lives. Not long after, Willie found another girl, maybe not as pretty, but with a head full of common sense. She adored Willie, left arm missing or not.

⊕

As the winter progressed, and if there were time after work before dark, Sean sat alone on a gravel bar just downstream of the town. He seldom left his perch on the sand and rock until he counted at least one steamboat passing either upstream or down.

When by the rushing Missouri on cold, clear January nights, the sky became a majestic painting of light. He remembered his father pointing out the pictures made with stars in the Irish night. Bright beauty lured Sean out on many evenings usually with a pretty girl in tow on his arm, Gretchen on occasion. His new found friends joined him in his nocturnal sojourns, but most went to bed early. They scolded Sean for staying up too late since they would be up before dawn preparing for the new day. Sean also needed to rise early to be at the large Westfphal winery at the south end of town. Appreciating their good intentions, Sean thanked his friends. But he often stayed out, if the sky remained cooperative and the stars were bright, wrapped in thick quilts and wool blankets until midnight.

Sean found he often rested better if he consumed some of the local beverages and was glad this good tasting medicine was so readily available. No headaches the next day came from the fine wine and thick beer of the hardy Germans. He thought about this stoutly bricked town where the people brewed with prolific pride but seemed to imbibe with hesitant moderation. *The Irish,* he was sure, *can never live here in great numbers. We would drink ourselves to death.*

CHAPTER 24
RELEASE AND REVELATION

Spring finally came. The evening air flushed with the full fragrance of flowers, and Sean continued his chore of splitting wrist-width pieces of hardwood for the cook fire. While taking a rest outside the wood shed, he watched red birds fashioning a nest in a nearby fruit tree set against a southern wall. *Peach*, he remembered Frau Gabriella Westfphal telling him several months before. He had seen them in Virginia. *Ireland was too cold for peach trees.*

Sean glanced up from the building frenzy of the birds to see graceful, brown-haired Gretchen. Beyond the house and the wood shed she carried the kitchen garbage to the chickens. Many German girls had lured him, but this one, so giving, had entangled him.

Sean relished watching her walk. Her stride was smooth and elegant. The heavy leather shoes on her feet failed to steal her femininity. Even in the faded, ankle-length dress she appeared a slim Aphrodite or Venus. He remembered Will Carleton teaching him the words around the campfire before his life was snuffed out in the blood letting along the Shenandoah.

Frau Westfphal's yell grabbed Sean's attention. She was leaning out the kitchen window down the hill. *"Wie hapt nötig* of more wood in the kitchen. *Bitte*, Sean, more wood, *jetzt."*

He answered the good lady promptly, and was soon on his way down the short trail to the house. Sean marveled at the thick, red brick portal and the lack of logs and mud chinking so common away from the river. This was a real house.

Frau Gabriella Westfphal had been more than kind since his arrival. Willie had introduced him to the family Westfphal on the steps of the church after Mass one winter day. A wet snow was falling. Frau Westfphal, not Herr Westfphal, had seen something deep in Sean's character. Her prejudiced and cynical husband had shrugged Sean off as a worthless Irishman. Gretchen's mother had seen much more, lured Sean to her home to work, and treated him like a son ever after. Only several weeks later in their employ did the fact surface that Frau Westfphal's only son had died in Virginia on the battleground at Fredericksburg.

Sean took simple orders from his benefactor without question. He gave this hearty mother of three a measure of patient appreciation that only he could bestow. Sean's devotion to the matron of the family was apparent to the other Westfphals and not always of their liking. This industrious and nurturing mother, near forty, had taken him in, and Sean's loyalty for her grew each day.

Chopping large oak and maple splits into smaller sticks that would fit in the masonry cook stove was a daily chore. Sean soon had a second armful gathered. He was returning to the house when Gretchen, stepping over to him unnoticed from the chicken yard, caught his arm. She reached her hand to her mouth to shield the sound and whispered in his ear as if out of breath, "Deliver the wood and then come back to me."

Sean smiled, pretended not to hear, and continued on to the house. Before entering the kitchen he looked back to see if Gretchen remained in the woodshed. In-between the cracks of the stacked wood her faded blue dress added to the shadows already growing darker. The evening light silhouetted an hourglass figure through her thin dress. Even though she was mostly out of sight, he saw Gretchen stretching her legs as she awaited him on the upturned splitting log in the darkest corner.

Sean thought about their growing intimacy. She, an attractive young woman of eighteen, had reawakened his enjoyment of life.

They had given and taken as young lovers do. To see her shining hair splayed out in the hay of the barn, or in the back pasture on a blanket was indeed a pleasure. Both hoped to enjoy each other on a clean feather bed someday, but that would be when they were brought together in marriage. They seldom talked but treated each other with care and enjoyed each other's company. Gretchen hoped to prove a tonic for Sean's nearly broken spirit as she day-by-day pulled out thorn like bits and pieces of his pain.

Gretchen's glorious smile was a welcome antidote to rainy days. The bodily pleasures he provided soothed her loneliness and filled her physical needs for a man. She professed to be in love with him, and she let him take what he needed. Nevertheless, Sean wished she would talk more, tell him her dreams and where the two would fit in the future.

When Sean returned along the path to the woodshed Gretchen arms were soon entwined around him. Kissing his neck and unbuttoning his shirt began her ritual.

"Is there time, girl? Will your mother miss you?"

She whispered with an accent, distinctly German, "There is time. Be quiet."

Carefully, his fingers loosened the pull string at her throat, and Sean lowered the fabric of her linen dress from her shoulders to her waist. Then, he gently pulled the blue cloth down over her hips. He allowed it to fall in graceful folds on the wood chipped ground. Not to be hurried, he picked up the dress, placing it neatly beside them on a log. Then standing back a moment in appreciation, he beheld her slim arms and shoulders and full but feminine form.

Sean noticed it, then, the movement. From the corner of his eye he saw Gretchen's younger sister, Sophie, taking it all in from behind the chicken house. A portion of her head peeked around the corner.

Sean studied the nosy, twelve-year-old. Watching from a vantage point at the door with gathered eggs in her apron, Gretchen's little sister remained wide-eyed and attentive. Attuned as if in the classroom, Sean noticed that she watched with a glee unencumbered by embarrassment.

Sean said nothing and Gretchen, who was so blinded by her

passion, noticed nothing. Sean looked again to Gretchen's sister in the low light of the evening from his perch in the dark shadows of the woodshed. He watched Sophie's eyes. She seemed to devour the scene as Gretchen, five years older, gave as Sean took, while still unaware of her shameless sister at the chicken house.

Sean was determined to feel neither guilt nor embarrassment. Their actions were not wicked. What he and Gretchen did together now or had done in the past was, if not holy, then at least pure in form. They both gave. They both took. Each with consent. This was nothing akin to his dismal day-to-day existence after stepping onto the stinking wharf in New York harbor, then the streets on the island of Manhattan, and still later, the horror of war in Virginia.

Calm and mindful only of his lover and forcing himself to not be concerned, Sean allowed Gretchen to persist. For a fifth of his short life Sean had ridden with hundreds of men mounted and armed, horsemen with only one mission, to kill, to maim, or to bear witness to death. Hundreds of sons and husbands from as far as Minnesota or Mississippi, he had led or helped lure to travel death's highway. Through it all, he had watched, and more often than not had been helpless to do anything. Sean did nothing now and held Gretchen tenderly. She gave. He took, and Gretchen's presence eased troubling memories.

On this peaceful, March evening brightened by glowing yellow lilies along the path, Sean sought gentle harmony. Despite the leering reconnaissance by his lover's sister, he again decided that he felt no humiliation. On this delightful spring day's ending not far before the one year anniversary of Lee's surrender, he would have his pleasure with no liability attached. And he felt with heartfelt determination, Please, please, let dear Gretchen's magic never end. Then as if he had inherited Will Carleton's Princeton College eloquence, Nakedness and human desire are no evil but a goodness to behold and so chaste compared with the nightmare of mud and bodies in the battlefields.

Sophie's eyes glowed like hot coals. *Look on, sweet Sophie, look on!* Sean thought in muddled sexual confusion, curious of her lack of embarrassment. *Please, girl with no shame*, Sean screamed inside, *let your dear sister continue! Let her continue to release me from my past, if only for a few moments.*

⊕

Later that evening, Sean and Gretchen strolled on the main street of Hermann. Both breathed deeply as they walked hand-in-hand. Close, as only lovers could be, they   reached Wharf Street and turned towards the river. Proceeding down the cobbled hill, the rushing expanse of the sparkling river fired their senses.

A full moon above them revealed contrasts of light and shadow and outlined brick structures next to the steamboat dock. The couple heard giggles and sighs of hidden lovers nearby. They wandered on by piles of cargo covered with taut, canvas tarps, and then up along the long, planked pier. The bright reflections off the river flowed dark and fast. It was on the dock among the barrels and the coils of thick ropes that they talked.

Long moments to Sean short to Gretchen came and went before the German girl nudged his way and firmly comforted him. Sean realized as she held him that he craved much more than her body. He saluted her loyalty to give so willingly and honestly. Though down deep, he wanted to know her thoughts and hopes. To his disappointment, Gretchen spoke only of the night and the pleasure he had given her.

The late evening passed as they sat hip to hip, legs dangling from the rough-sawn oak. Sean worked up the courage to tell Gretchen of Sophie's presence near the woodshed earlier. To Sean's bewilderment Gretchen spoke with a pointed lack of interest.

"It's all right, Sean. I watched many couples on these very docks when I was Sophie's age." She paused and squeezed his hand then added with a smile, "And perhaps even younger."

Gretchen turned to the man with whom she hoped soon to take the sacred vows. She kissed him lightly on the cheek then looked deeply into his eyes. Even in the moonlight her playful expression shone as she defended her former explanation, "How do you think I learned so well to please you?"

Silence grew between them. Its perilous seed germinated bigger than the great flowing waters of the Missouri before them.

Gretchen could not make sense of the vastness she had created between them. *"Vas ist, mein liebchen?"* she asked slipping into her river town's language.

Maybe he had no need to speak. He must be satisfied as any sane man should be. With that firmly decided Gretchen clamped her arms around her dress covered legs and held her knees close to her chin. A cool wind had come up, and she pulled her shawl tight around her shoulders. She let her eyes follow the shimmering river downstream while she pondered the future.

Crystalline moonlight played its game. Gretchen's illusions for tomorrow, the next month, and the following year became a dreamlike procession. She hoped the river would carry them to St. Louis after they married. There, she was sure that her hard working husband would always have food on her table and coins to buy her pretty dresses.

Gretchen's quiet form spelled out contentment and her faraway gaze did not bother him. Her slim figure suggested a dancing sprite, not the daughter of a stout German vintner. Clearly to Sean, her beauty was not to be contested, as one did not dispute the magnificence of the dazzling waters swirling below his feet.

Sean continued his vigil. The river, the night, and the young woman at his side came together as a subtle, unsettling chorus that told him of the tightening strings in his mind. He watched along the shadowy banks as the mighty river made its way towards St. Charles. He imagined its meeting with the clearer Father of Waters above the booming city of St. Louis.

It was on these rough-hewn planks on the river dock in the arms of a beautiful woman and a comfortable spring night that Sean grasped a stark realization. Gretchen was not to be the woman in his life. She was not to share the precious memories of his sister, Mary Katherine, his parents, and Ireland. Gretchen was not the one. Another would listen to his stories of home and the saving grace of his music. She would not bear children of his name.

Again, Sean pulled the ghostly image to the present. It had come to him last week while hoeing weeds between the long rows of grape vines. Somehow forgetting until now, he remembered that he had rested and leaned his sweat dripping body upon the long, hickory handle of his hoe. It was then, as he looked out across the green, rolling hills and down to the great river, the vision had come.

His mind had filled with vivid pictures of a time when he was older. But it was not here. Sadly, he saw, it was not with Gretchen either. On the far edges of a grassy field, he knew not where, there lay two harsh, boulder strewn ridges. A small winding stream coursed between.

"Accept it, Sean," the tattered and gray-bearded patriarch of the Kelly clan had advised. "Do with this gift as you will." His grandfather, with his far seeing eye, had told him later, "But know it's real. All will ring true from your waking dreams."

And so Sean had accepted his gift as best he could and was alive partly because of his glimpses into the future, even though the images were often incomplete and vague.

Still, in the midst of his mind's eye lay the vineyard above the wild Missouri. Sean leaned harder on the handle of his hoe. He lingered in thought as he had so many times before when the sight had come.

The child that he saw in his arms that day was not of Gretchen neither in looks or character. He was sure. The lovely lass, he guessed of six or seven years in a tow sack dress with hair of gold-like sheaves of new cut wheat, held on merrily as he galloped her pony-like on his knee. Below him across the fields Sean caught sight of three boys, fair skinned and red-headed, and two others whose striking charcoal color perplexed him. All five boys swam naked in the creek.

Immediate was the response of the young girl in his arms. She buried her face in Sean's shirt front. Her high pitched, sincere words escaped her pretty mouth, *"Da, don't make me look!"*

To Sean the evidence could not be denied. The flaxen-haired girl, whose tiny, slim arms wrapped around him then, was far from shameless.

CHAPTER 25
SCORNED?

"You will work miles from town, Sean," Herr Westfphal told him as a cold late March wind brought on by a sudden change in the weather cut deep into their wool coats. "I'll visit you on Wednesdays to gauge your progress."

Sean studied the vintner's face. How the task Gretchen's father requested could be worse than the last four years in Virginia or his time in New York City, he could not fathom. The stern man's words had failed to stump his will. Then he raised the question, "How could your land be so far from town?"

"We came a bit later than many of the travelers from the Fatherland," Herr Westfphal answered. "Our acreage is large but most lies further from the river."

Again, Sean studied Gretchen's father as he painstakingly spoke in English. Sean's fluency in German had progressed from *danke* to *bitte* and not much beyond. He wondered where this long winter in Willie's hometown would lead him.

Insistently, Herr Westfphal stated, "You will be expected to work in the vineyards all week, and then come back to town on Friday." He awaited a rebellious reply from this man he likened to all other lazy Irishmen of the world.

"That will be fine, Herr Westfphal," was all the German heard.

"*Sehr gut*," he answered in pleased surprise. Then, the esteemed vintner managed in English, "You and I will prepare for your week away. Food, tools to prune the vines," and he allowed, as his harsh manner lessened, "a bedroll of thick woolen blankets."

Sean watched the single minded German plod away through the ankle deep snow. The weather was a far cry from the unseasonably warm temperatures of the last week and the scent of blooming lilacs. One white footprint and then another followed the bricked walkway from the house and down towards Goethe Street. A sudden tug on his sleeve surprised him. He turned to find Frau Westfphal at his elbow.

His feisty advocate lectured, "Prove you can work, Sean. Prove to my husband that you can be trusted."

The Irishman looked down to the penetrating eyes that challenged him. Frau Westfphal had been the driving force to take him in. Willie Hausbach's introduction had not affected the man of the house, just its matron. Sean remembered the good woman's generosity as he listened, and allowed her words to find fertile ground. This, he would do. He would prove himself to the people who had provided him such haven. These kind people had opened up their hands and warm hearts to allow him in. Later over a beer, his trusted friend, Willie, wholeheartedly agreed, "This new effort on your part, Sean, will place the Westfphal family at ease." Then sternly came, "I would not let them down."

⊕

Four days later on a blustery Wednesday evening before dark, Herr Westfphal arrived as promised. He clapped Sean merrily on the back after his inspection of the vineyard. He followed Sean into the small one-roomed shed used to store tools. There, he fanned the coals in the small stone and mud fireplace. "You do well Irishman," he said as a tiny flame climbed into the slivers of kindling. "I am pleased. Also, I am relieved. I did not think you would do as I asked."

Sean Kelly leaned back against the rock hearth. Its flaming warmth drew him as well as his employer. The day had been misty and cold. On Monday and Tuesday and then again today, he had slaved to finish pruning all but the last acre of grapes. He had maintained his hardworking pace by dreaming of Friday and his reunion with Gretchen in Hermann.

"You have pruned the vines as I have asked, Irishman. You can easily finish tomorrow or Friday." Herr Westfphal took a deep breath and remembered the sloping field of vine-covered trellises that covered the south and east facing hillside. "You watched me well when I showed you. I can tell. Not much more and you will be finished." Then Sean heard the smiling vintner rattle on in German. He understood not a word, just the man's friendly intentions.

The usually stern but now flushed-faced man smiled and reached into his rucksack. He pulled out a tall clay bottle and a cloth sack. "I am pleased we will be able to drink last year's wine together, Herr Kelly." Never before had he bestowed Sean with the respect of the prefix before his last name.

"Frau Westfphal has sent cheese and bread and dried apples. And I," he added smugly, "I brought the wine to open but only if your work pleased me." Again the German, an American for a decade more than the Irish immigrant before him, slapped Sean on the back, meaning well but causing discomfort. Then, with simple ceremony he twisted the wooden plug free and poured the sparkling wine into Sean's cup.

The boy from Lisdoonvarna, long since a man in anyone's eyes, witnessed with pleasure the change in Gretchen's father. *Acceptance*, Sean realized, *acceptance*. The German had given him a passing grade. And with Gretchen clearly so fond of him, Sean knew that he would be able to settle into this rigid but kindly community as he had no other since leaving his home in County Clare. He would forget his dream. *Surely, it must be wrong*. He would honor Gretchen's plan to announce their marriage when he returned.

Herr Westfphal toasted Sean's health, and both sipped wine from cracked stoneware cups. Though nearly as cold as the wind outside, the wine warmed his soul. *Acceptance*, he chewed on the lovely word. It melted in his mouth like the tasty cheese from Frau Westfphal's kitchen pantry.

"And on Friday you will come down from the hills to Hermann?"

Sean heard the questioning statement of his future father-in-law and then an eager disclosure. "The Poeschels have offered one of their empty wine cellars for the party. The storage area will be cleared and all will dance. The Poeschels of Stone Hill Winery, Sean! Do you understand? My family and you are honored by their generous offer of welcome."

Sean watched the typically quiet German and the firelight in his excited eyes. He wondered what else could come next.

"You will bring your instrument? And play?"

Sean's face lit up. He had guessed the reason for the festivity for which Herr Westfphal had invited him to entertain. Deep in a vast cellar of the famed Stone Hill Winery protected from the cold March winds, his promise to Gretchen would be declared to all. "Certainly, I'll bring my fiddle to the celebration," he said. An uncomfortable silence followed, but Sean ended it by saying, "But only for your pleasure, Herr Westfphal."

A jubilant face greeted him. The proud father of Sean's future wife added, "My daughter eagerly awaits you, Irishman." Then with a chuckle and a wink he added, "Frau Westfphal has told me that you two have much to tell our friends and family."

Eager to see Westfphal's lovely daughter, Sean nodded in agreement. Then he hesitated. His sense of right and wrong had begun to rush for high ground with a surge of confusion in hot pursuit. Yet again, his thoughts reminded him that his dreams had always come true! *Gretchen is not to be my wife nor Herr Westfphal my father-in-law. Or are they? Since coming to Hermann life has been so good.*

The last thought sealed the bargain, and Sean forced his puzzling vision far into a hidden corner of his mind. He raised the already half empty bottle and poured another cupful of wine, first for the jovial man who reminded him so much of his father and then for himself. Within an hour both men were snuggly bundled against bitter winds that whistled through the vineyard's shanty. But Sean was not asleep. Eli's dying words filled him as he once again touched the silver coin she had called her *lucky piece.*

⊕

Friday's labors slowly came to an end. The last few among the thousands of grape vines were pruned. The final rail that supported the trailing, thick arms of a grape cane was split and then set firmly into the soil. Although cold and weary, Sean eagerly prepared to depart. His memories of the past week were not harsh ones. Several days had been sunny and not so cold. These large rolling hills near the Missouri River had caught his fancy. He had seen grouse, a few deer, and once an old sow bear lumbering up a draw. He had promised himself to return later in the spring to see the abundant wild flowers that he remembered from Willie's descriptions.

Not wanting to leave anything behind, Sean checked his horse again. His fiddle in its tow sack hung from the saddle horn. While he finished packing his bed roll and side bags, he imagined the five, long winding miles of muddy trails to the north. The stiff southeast wind whipping against his face told him it would be a difficult trip. Snow or freezing rain was coming.

A pastel sunset came and went before darkness found him on the march. No stars filled the skies. Cold rain began to hit his face. Soon it changed to wet snow.

Sean had ridden the first mile but now walked. In the darkness he was glad for the thin mantle of new snow that made it easier to see. He led his horse towards Hermann, but slowly. He knew riding in the darkness could lead to calamity.

For the next half hour he walked slowly, waiting at times. Finally creeping above a ridge, the new quarter moon glowed and brightened the dark night despite the clouds. Shadows in the forest and hillside appeared differently in the new light. In awe Sean contemplated the beauty and halted his march. It was then the odd sound found him.

A quiet moaning. He listened. Again it came to his ear. *A bear or wildcat*, he guessed. *What else could it be?* But then still again, he heard it, the point of origin clear. He walked a few steps then listened once more. Curiosity blanketed his fears, although his big pistol now hung limply in his right hand against his thigh.

Silhouetted on the ridge by the moon glow the outline of a house appeared, simple, a front porch, little more. *Odd*, Sean thought. *It must be abandoned.* On such a cold night, no trace of wood smoke rose up from the chimney.

Calming his horse with the gentle hand and quiet words he had learned long ago, the Irishman found the path. He followed it in the weak light. He halted, and decided to announce himself. "Anyone home? I bear no troubles."

Silence answered him. He stepped closer. When but a few feet from the porch, a faint sign of movement caught his eye and the source of the moaning.

A sad whining voice came from the darkness.

Hastily tying his horse to a supporting post of the porch, Sean searched for a small canvas packet in his saddle bags. Then he turned to the house. He stepped upon the rotting porch that felt ready to give way at any moment. His revolver remained hanging in his right hand, its death dealing bore for the moment directed to the sagging planks beneath his feet.

He sensed only pain, not danger, and he decided to enter through the open door. Inside, he pulled a long yellow-sulfur match from the folded canvas. He struck it on his flint. Around him, a bright awakening occurred. A glow of the match illuminated the contents of the cabin. A stone fireplace. Cold ashes. A simple bed. Motion caught his eye, then another. He heard a mournful cry and its maker spoke. "*Monsieur, permettez mon fils mourir avec paix, s'il vous plaît. Monsieur, permettez mon fils mourir avec paix.*"

In the corner a woman with long gray hair sat in a chair. She appeared of Indian descent but in the match light it was hard to tell. She also seemed ready to accept any fate that he might deliver. Finally, her words made sense to his tired brain. Sean's French lessons with Father O'Daer came back to him. *Permit my son to die in peace*, he remembered.

The Irishman looked around the spartan cabin for a tallow lamp or candle. None could be found. He searched for tinder or fuel but saw none. He lit his second match. Too soon the inside of the cabin disappeared as the meager light burned out. He warned himself against wasting another. Only four remained protected in the canvas packet. Then he pondered what he might of the dark scene around him. The harsh conditions inside were not much better than the bitter weather outside.

On a mission now, while breaking clouds revealed a bright moon beyond the cabin, Sean gathered twigs and branches before the next wave of dark clouds advanced. He also found a cedar tree and tore off enough stringy, dry bark for tinder. A light snow teased his face with sharp crystals. *From where?* he wondered, looking to the pocket of cloudless sky above him. Then, with the dry tinder inside his coat and packing an armload of finger and arm-sized fuel, he re-entered the cabin.

In minutes a tiny fire crackled on the cold stone hearth. Soon, while a steady flame began to take hold, he spied a lone ax leaning by the bed.

Sean was soon out finding more wood for the fire. Under the moon's glow he attempted to chop and chop, wary of his knees and feet. Smaller dead hardwoods came down. Pleased, he again sent the sharp blade deep into the dry wood. Chips flew. In much less than an hour and in a wealth of sweat despite the cold, Sean carried a final load of fuel into the cabin. The stacks on the porch and by the fireplace would sustain a real fire for at least a day.

⊕

He helped the old woman to a seat beside the flames. He found a blanket and placed it snugly on her shoulders. Warmth radiated from the poorly chinked fireplace, and light flickered off the log walls of the cabin. Sean took a moment to consider the structure and decided it sturdy and well built, although certainly ready for repairs. He watched closely and hoped that sparks from the hot fire would not become a nuisance and wondered what type of tree he had chopped up. With time the blaze settled into fiery orange coals.

"What next old woman?" he found himself asking although not expecting an answer. From the beginning he had expected only death. Remarkably, the woman's voice found strength. *"L'eau est mauvaise. L'eau, mon fils, j'ai besoin d'eau, bonhomme. L'eau est mauvaise."* The French word for poisonous and water caught Sean's ear. Then, again he heard her plead, *"De l'eau, s'il vous plaît.*

De l'eau." Somehow finding a word of English, she added, *"Non strength."*

Sean searched the tiny room for a bucket, saw none and then searched the old woman's eyes now sparkling with firelight as he mimed pouring water. Pointing out the door she said, *"Le seau d'eau."*

"The bucket for water," he translated to the puzzled woman. Then as he walked out the door, tardy but well deserved praise left his lips delivered only to the cold wind and the memory of an old priest, "Thank you, Father O'Daer."

⊕

Sean splashed through the shallow edges of the creek below the cabin. He had disregarded the well. Even in the cold he had smelled the putrid flesh rotting despite the chilling air. To his credit, he had found the bucket in the dark.

He trudged upstream. Finally, the source of bad water became unmistakable. In the sparse light the form of a long-dead horse filled his view. Many steps upstream he found clean water and dipped the bucket full.

Soon back within the cabin, Sean had water boiling and loose tea tied in a rag and ready at the kettle. He glanced towards the bed where not an old man, but a younger person lay warming with the old woman at his side. He remembered. She had said *mon fils*, my son.

With care Sean laid another log on the steady blaze. Half warmed himself, water continued to seep from his soaked boots. Sparks flew but the tall stone and mud-chinked fireplace worked well to force the fire's heat into the cabin. After pouring the steaming water in three clay cups, Sean proudly served tea.

In a short time the woman revived and began to nurse her son with more care. Sean watched the pair and then the comforting flames. While his eyes caught the dancing light, his thoughts strayed to Hermann. He was late. Gretchen and her family anticipated his arrival. The entire community expected his music. Again, he pulled Herr Westfphal's words from his memory. *An hour*, he calculated, *or less on the trail to Hermann.* Responsibilities shook him like strong arms. He must leave these people in need or suffer to offend the Westfphals. But could he? Could he leave these two? Instinctively, Sean rose and seized the ax yet again.

He heard behind him, "*Vous êtes très bon, monsieur, un ange.*" He looked back at the now smiling woman as she tenderly forced hot tea into her weak son and then some of Frau Westfphal's dried apples and bread.

However, on the porch while the cold wind found the holes in his heavy winter coat, he whispered, "No, good mother, I be no angel."

French, Sean thought, as he closed the door firmly. *Not farmers? Why are they here?* But he remembered the residents of Hermann describing the land around their sturdy town. "There are few Osage. French trappers remain but they hide themselves from civilized eyes."

Sean guessed this was the case as he sent the chips flying and another large hardwood tree crashed to the faintly visible forest floor. This time, he carried great chunks of dry wood into the cabin's porch. It would burn hot and long. The moon was almost gone when he finished stacking a week's supply. He was exhausted. It was late and far past the time for the dancing to end in the warm cellars of the Stone Hill Winery.

Inside, the woman offered him tea and a place to sleep. Sean did not refuse. Before letting himself nod off under his thick blankets, he allowed himself to appreciate his dilemma. There would be hell to pay upon his arrival in Hermann and from more than one front.

CHAPTER 26
BITTER REUNION

Gretchen stood on the snow-covered street in front of her home when Sean rode up. "So, where were you?" she demanded.

He heard much more contempt than worry in her voice. He was still mounted and wondered if it would be best to rein up and turn the animal in the opposite direction to Willie's house. But even there he knew he would meet stern faces. He was well aware that his unintentional absence had embarrassed many people.

"I'll tell you in the house."

It was Saturday and well into mid morning, and he wondered from which direction, Gretchen's parents or the community, the next hard question would come. He dismounted and tied the reins of the gentle animal to the cold circle of iron in front of the Westfphal's brick home. He had decided he would tell it only once. He walked to the back door and into the kitchen. There, a crestfallen Frau Westfphal greeted him with a cheerless face and a shake of the head.

"Where is Herr Westfphal?" Sean asked politely but firmly. Gretchen was a step behind. Yet, to the good *frau* of the family he directed his words, "Troubles occurred on the road from the vineyard. I'd like to tell you all together." He knew for now that he owed them both a morsel of the truth at the very least. He waited as Gretchen's mother summoned the man of the house.

⊕

Herr Westfphal was exasperated. "You what? You stopped in the night and made no attempt to travel further? I have made the trip many times. Two hours at the most."

However, Sean saw that Gretchen's mother had listened to his story in detail while Gretchen and her father had only heard what they wanted to hear. Sean's green eyes fell across Gabriella Westfphal, again and again always back to her, his only salvation.

Gretchen let fly a cutting remark. "I was deserted on my special day. The dance was to be where we announced our marriage. Your music on the fiddle would have sealed the bargain." The pretty brown-haired girl burst into tears. In mournful sobs she said, "Sean, how could you embarrass me so?"

Gretchen's father stood beside his forlorn daughter supportive but silent. Herr Westfphal didn't know what to think. *Sean had proven so responsible both this winter with the horses and over the last week in the vineyard. How could he slip so far? People freezing in a cabin on his way to Hermann? Obviously a lie! What was he thinking to not arrive on time?* Westfphal wondered when he would be able to look the Poeschels in the eye, again.

Only Frau Westfphal allowed herself to understand. She had listened to his story and knew of the French family who lived far up the creek. Sean had not mentioned the father. He must be dead or gone on the trap line. Still, she studied the Irishman looking for any signs of dishonesty. Then, the dam cracked. Sean mentioned their names. She completely relented.

"We were worried, Sean," Frau Westfphal allowed despite the harsh words of her husband and the long night of humiliation Sean had brought down on her house. However, the tables had now turned full circle and Gretchen's mother released what had been so difficult for her husband.

"We are glad that you are not harmed, Sean. Next, we are proud to know that you helped the mother and son who surely would have died. Now that the story has been fully told, I see that you have done the honorable thing."

Herr Westfphal's good wife grasped Sean's hand and pushed it into her daughter's. "Gretchen, your disappointment will fade. When our friends find that our Irishman was late to be a Good Samaritan, they will all understand. Your future husband will be held in higher respect when our friends and family learn of this."

Gretchen had no words, nor did her father, although his face had changed from a stern countenance to one of smug pride. "So, when you left the Frenchies..."

His wife interrupted, "The Chalumeau family."

"The Chalumeau family, then!" Herr Westfphal paused but then continued, "Should we take supplies to this family, my future son-in-law?"

Sean's head turned to the family's patriarch, whose question had been one of respect, with no underlying tones of malice.

"Yes, Herr Westfphal. It would be the Christian thing to do."

Gretchen's mother squeezed her daughter's shoulder, not realizing the pain she caused. Gretchen pulled away. Frau Westfphal then again reached for Sean's hand, and cupped it in hers. Her powerful silence held her family's attention. Her smile and bright-eyed look of appreciation for the young man before her could not be denied. *Not only*, Frau Westfphal contemplated, *will I have a son-in-law whose tunes on the fiddle could make you cry or bring pleasure on a cold winter's eve, but also,* she thought with satisfaction, *my sometimes less than honorable daughters and husband would have among them a principled man to show them the way.*

She reached for her husband. *May Day*, she calculated while she held his hand, *would be the best date now for Sean and Gretchen to announce their intentions. More than a full month for the real story of Sean's good deed to filter among the hausfraus and their husbands will provide the time for hurt feelings to disappear.*

⊕

A week later as warmer March winds blew from the south, Sean decided it was time to leave Hermann.

"I'll come back as soon I can, Gretchen. You know why I must go. I've told you several times how I promised a dying soldier. I must do this." His mistake, he would realize later, was that he should have told Frau Westfphal and then slipped away. Never should he have confided in Gretchen. She was beyond furious.

A demon, now, with fiery dark eyes glared at Sean. His lovely Gretchen had transformed. Her anger consumed her, and her harsh words cut heartfelt wounds. A woman's scorn, as he had never seen it before, attempted to swallow him whole, and despite his explanations she would not relent.

Again, he reassured her, "I will be back before May Day, Gretchen. We will announce our plans then. I must go. I leave at first light tomorrow."

Sean attempted to hold the woman who, throughout the winter, had given him so much, the woman he had vowed to marry. However, Gretchen's sustained silence, now maintained two steps beyond his reach, proved as painful to him as had her scathing words of abuse.

CHAPTER 27
REPRIEVE

Hermann's often soft-hearted magistrate, Wolfgang Meier one of the rare elected officials of the town, stared down at the man in chains. He liked Sean Kelly. Nearly everyone did. Then, his eyes slowly arose to his fair niece, Gretchen. He had listened when she insisted Sean stay bound in the cellar for three days until his sentence. So, now three days later the stern *burger* spoke soberly while the two elders who attended as witnesses listened.

"So, what is it to be, dear niece? You have cried violation. What is the truth in your accusations?" Herr Meier had watched his sister's daughter from afar throughout the winter. He had also observed her growing from a skinny turnip to a robust beauty. The wise man of forty also knew that Gretchen and Sean were entwined as deeply as a man and woman could be. The Irish boy, to his thinking, had obviously tried to leave without committing himself to his niece. She had given freely. Others besides him had seen her glow afterwards. He knew there had been no violation.

Against the dripping stone of the cellar set aside for the lawless, Gretchen stood sternly in judgment beside her iron-shackled lover. She watched him stare at the wall. Since being accused he had looked at her only once, and now he acted as if she were not alive. Her true feelings were betrayed in the longing, silent look she cast over him. Herr Meier studied one then the other, trying to find his best avenue of judgment. His family had called upon him to prosecute a man whom he knew to be innocent. *Yet, in the end,* he thought, *who will remain once I decide? Who will I see in the streets or at Mass on Sunday tomorrow and next week, and for the rest of my days? The Irishman, no matter how well liked by the town's folk, will be gone, and Gretchen and her family will remain until I die.* The hard matter when described in these simple terms was easily decided. His people and his family came first.

Before even walking down into the dank cellar with its metal rings hammered into its limestone walls, Herr Meier had made his uneasy settlement. Good could not always rule and sadly would not today. "Herr Kelly," the unhappy man announced. "*Bitte,* stand and face your sentence."

While Herr Meier prepared himself to speak the words that would seal Sean's fate, first to a flogging and then to lifelong servitude to Gretchen and her family, the door to the cellar opened with a screech. With relief the troubled magistrate saw his sister, Gabriella. She stepped down into the cellar, one hand on the oak rail and the other holding her skirts above the wet stone. *What can she say,* he thought? But quickly his memories reminded him differently. Since they were children her conscience and common sense had made her the soul of the family. Difficult decisions, she made easier to understand. He only wished she had come to him sooner.

⊕

The Irishman watched dark eyes much like Gretchen's but full of quiet emotion. Their sparkle suggested anger. Frau Westfphal first glanced at her brother, then her daughter, and finally at Sean. An intense silence followed. He could only think the worst. *Will she have me quartered and thrown in the river?*

Sean listened to Frau Westfphal's words, never to forget.

"Sean is a good man, brother, Irish or not. His music and his heart are loyal and true." She walked to Sean and reached down. Like a mother she held his head between her hands and looked into his eyes. "Unchain him brother Wolfgang. He is a warrior. He has suffered enough in defense of our freedom."

Gretchen's mother turned to look at her brother, again, "I have heard him in the night, Wolfgang. Often his sleep is troubled with pain. It reveals his true self. His duty was served. Many late nights Gretchen and I have soothed his horrors from the war."

Kind but wise Gabriella Westfphal turned stern eyes to her daughter. As if a judge in a courtroom she decreed, "Gretchen has felt no violation of her body, only pleasure. I have pretended not to hear many times. She has been lucky enough to have known the love of a troubled man who has served us all. Without Sean and many like him, the immigrant Irish and the Germans, and yes the blacks would all continue to be crushed. We would have toiled under the boots of the Southern chevaliers and rich slave holders if the war had been lost. It would not have bothered either to make slaves of us all." The fine German woman looked to Sean, "He has sent many of these tormentors to the devil to pay their dues."

"But, Momma!" Gretchen cried out. "I am with child!"

The gracious wife of one of Hermann's premier vintners released her hold on Sean and stepped to her daughter's side. This woman, who was respected by those in the cellar as well as in the town, reached out to her lovely daughter. Her words were rich and pure of heart, making her seem taller in the dank dungeon despite her short stature.

"*Mein schönes mädchen,* we will find you a good German boy," she said gently to a teary-eyed Gretchen. "Many young men will seek your hand." Then she shook her head sternly, "You should have come to me first. Sean told me much earlier of his vow to his dead comrade to the south. I am sure he would have come back."

Frau Westfphal took her brother's arm and with a simple nod compelled him to act. In moments the pounding of Herr Meier's hammer echoed in the small stone cellar. On his knees he worked hard to loosen Sean's heavy chains. He freed one arm and began on the hard iron of the other as he heard his sister's voice. "Wolfgang, our Irishman has a debt to pay the family of a fallen soldier. His dreams do not lie."

Gabriella looked to each face in the cellar before settling lastly on the Irishman. "I only hope you can forgive us." Then placing her hand on Gretchen's belly she added, "And hopefully, good man that he is, he will remember this child."

CHAPTER 28
TRAVELING SOUTH

Any evidence of a trail became more and more indistinct as the gloomy day advanced. A resurgence of frigid March winds, so close to being April's own, rushed through the leafless silhouettes of endless hardwoods along the ridgeline. Patches of evergreens occasionally lined the track, and among the thick, green cedars Sean sought protection from the wind. Well worn, his uniform great coat of faded blue wool kept the cold at bay.

On foot the Irishman led his horse through the crackling leaves that off and on covered the trail. His pack animal followed behind. He knew that allowing his horses a rest every hour was a smart thing to do and definitely good for the rider. His game leg, damaged severely in battle, was sore from being in the saddle. With each step he felt the constant bone-deep pain filter away. A plus, he thought trying to be the optimist. He was alive. Eli and scores of others were not.

By afternoon and riding again, Sean found himself trekking along anything but a good trail. To his dismay it transformed into a mere footpath. Vegetation constantly brushed across his horse's flanks. Low branches forced Sean to bend down repeatedly to avoid being raked off backwards.

"This ever changing trail has magic working with it," Sean

murmured to no one. He sensed that he had strayed unknowing from the well traveled track. His confusion that morning he attributed as no relation to anything mystical but a product of his constant day dreaming while in the saddle. *Escape from Hermann. Escape from Herr Meier's cane on his back. Escape from Gretchen. Two days ago, maybe three*, Sean didn't remember. He was torn and failed to see how he could return to Hermann, although each day's travel brought fond memories of Willie's unconditional friendship and Frau Westfphal's kindness.

In his mind Sean tried to retrace his missteps on the trail throughout the morning. His inattentiveness had allowed his horse to follow its nose. He guessed that he had left the Beemont Road several miles back not long after leaving Stony Hill. If not a fine road at first it was an avenue of commerce, though clogged with ruts. This so called lane was a deer trail, if that.

Despite his complete failure at staying on the road, the Irishman decided against turning back, at least not yet. He was heading south and Van Buren was generally in that direction but half a state away. With care he worked his animals off the winding ridge and onto the steep slopes of a big valley below. Amid low rock ledges and loose, flat stones, his mount made slow progress. The pack horse behind fared much worse, almost going down on several ledges with loose rock.

When he finally reached the valley floor, Sean's goal was to find water for himself and a well-deserved drink for his animals. A few mouthfuls of new grass or early elm leaves for the horses, despite his lost time, would keep the day from being a total loss.

Traces of sarcasm filled his voice when he spoke aloud to an empty forest, "Backtracking and finding the main trail should provide a fine afternoon of entertainment!" His strong Irish brogue echoed through the wooded hollow. Further down the slope, his spirits rose when the wind ceased and small but bright beams of light finally broke through the clouds. On what had become a balmy spring day he dismounted and led his horses the short distance to the bottom of the great hill.

Sean found a clear spring at a cliff base that fed into a large nearby stream. There, in a pristine haven of early spring flowers and babbling waters, he reached down to a clear pool and filled his canteen. The familiar green matt of watercress in the spring water reassured him. He cast a smile up to the sky where the warm rays of the sun continued to find their way through thinning clouds.

Sean picketed his animals in a small meadow. There, sprigs of spring growth shot through last fall's brown grass. Ever watchful in the now sun-filled day, he sensed something different. Further downstream as the valley opened up, the faint image of a building's roofline caught his eye.

Among the shadowy grays of tall hardwood and just a stone's throw away towards the bigger valley, a sizeable log cabin took shape. The dwelling lay to his left, well placed above the potential flooding waters of the broader stream glistening at a distance. Startled for a moment, Sean relaxed only when the cardinals and blue jays ceased to comment on his intrusion. Curious, he hoped for the best and a chance to trade or pay for fresh-baked bread.

A faint trail from the meadow to the cabin appeared. He followed it. *Not well traveled for at least a season,* he decided while moving his arms and legs to avoid the sharp thorns of cat's paw vine and last years blackberry canes. That the cabin must be deserted, settled in his mind.

But Sean did not hope for this outcome as he hollered loudly from a distance. "Hello! Hello!" He welcomed the chance to talk to someone, if only about the weather.

He walked closer, edging around the side of the cabin toward the front porch. Again, he let out a greeting so not to startle anyone. He knew that good manners could mean the difference between open hospitality or a puff of black smoke and a one ounce ball flying past your ear.

Sean spied a man on the top step of the porch. He was gaunt and appeared troubled. Seemingly unaffected by the Irishman's greetings, his arms were spread-out, palms down, bracing himself from falling down the stairs.

The sun on gleaming metal jolted Sean suddenly awake! On a porch plank a shotgun lay loosely in the man's trembling hand. Sean froze. A quick rush of fear pulsed through him. He speculated on the weapon's purpose, but after a few moments he knew it was not meant for him.

His friendliness turned to cat-like stealth, and carefully Sean reached his right hand low and with slow deliberation pulled his pistol. Not cocking it, he put his thumb on the hammer. Then, reaching under his jacket, the fingers on his left felt for the handle of the long blade always at his belt.

He called out another friendly greeting, "Hello! Are you all right? Can I help you?" The man appeared dazed and not to hear. Bewildered, Sean studied the unmoving statue. *Odd*, was all he could think while watching the man's unchanging look from the side and now from the front. An empty-eyed stare continued to greet him.

The Irishman watched only eyes, eyes that did not see, but told a story nonetheless. He wondered whether the man could be blind, deaf, or did not recognize him as anything real. With weapons ready but hidden, Sean approached the man now more curious than fearful.

He reaffirmed his good intentions and asked again with gentle words, "Are you all right, good man? Are you blind?" No response came, and the man's blank look remained leveled on the weed-covered fields beyond the cabin. His gaze then moved slowly upward but Sean saw no threat in his eyes. A sigh of relief or hope appeared to fill the man's face. His right hand, once fingering the shotgun, came up empty, a gesture that could only mean peace.

Sean stepped forward after holstering his pistol. He took the haggard man's hand in his own. It was big but weak. His left hand remained under his jacket on his knife. "Hello, good sir. Is it to your liking if I water my horse at your spring?" The skeletal face before Sean forced a small smile but gave no indication that his question was understood.

Continuing to shake the large hand, Sean was surprised by the man's simple but appreciative first words. "Thank you." Then a wide-eyed brightness replaced the wildness of before and he announced, as if everything was finally settled in his mind, "Ah, you must be a messenger of Jacob or Abraham?"

Sean quickly detected a sudden hesitation. He saw the man studying his belt and his still sheathed knife.

"Or," he added with a sudden intensity, "the archangel, Michael?"

With the man's words came understanding. *Something terrible happened here.* Glancing around, Sean spotted freshly dug graves only a few steps from the house but partially hidden by a corral. *The clouded expression on the man's face and in his eyes is not from hunger but from sickness of the heart. He is grieving and truly must think me an angel. But why, the archangel, the avenger of God? Has the man killed his family or friends?* Sean quickly backtracked. *How have his people died?*

First, the Irishman saw the privy and a little further the uncovered rock-ringed well. He concluded the distance too small. Then, when the man stood and opened his front door everything became clear. A wave of putrid air rolled over Sean, and instantly his mind jumped two years in the past to a muddy field belching its week old stench of death.

The man asked, "Will you help me bury her? My wife was the last to die."

⊕

After placing the blanket wrapped corpse deep in the ground beside the others, Sean lured the man to the meadow. There, with fresh air to breathe, a cooking fire was kindled. Tea water was soon hot, and beans and bacon simmered in the kettle. The weary man, named Isaac, told his story.

"The typhoid," he said.

Sean cringed but had already guessed this possibility. He had seen it many times, soldiers drinking from streams littered with the remnants of battle. Whole families had died near Lisdoonvarna with a privy too close to the well.

"My son fell sick soon after me," Isaac continued between sips of tea, "and they would not listen. My wife and daughters refused to walk to the spring for water once the fever took hold. Their reason left them, and they had only the strength to keep pulling buckets from the nearby well." He stopped, clearly very weak and in pain.

"A visitor was here two weeks ago. He was feverish and constantly needing to relieve himself. He must have brought the sickness."

Sean asked, "Do you have family close by?"

The man silently pointed to the graves.

"No!" Sean said sternly, afraid Isaac was beyond the limit of his help. "Someone who will take you in?"

"A sister. I have a sister a morning's ride away. Just a bit down Barren Fork then up Boeuf Creek at Beemont."

"Then, tomorrow," the Irishman offered, "I'll help you go to her. Beemont is on my way to Bourbon." Captain Loughton had told him of the rail line from Saint Louis to Rolla. At Bourbon he could follow the steel tracks to Rolla and then turn south to Van Buren.

CHAPTER 29
RESPITE FROM THE STORM

After leaving Isaac at his sister's, Sean encountered poor roads as he meandered south. Missing one knee deep mud hole only then to slop through another filled his morning. He passed a man his father's age on the road and stopped to talk but quickly wished he had not. A survivor of the war, the bitter man's anger seethed. His plight spilled out, "My horses were stolen first by sweeping Union and then rebel militia forces." His hot words shot to Sean with a suspicious look. "Your pack horse looks familiar to me, son." Deciding that a brawl was soon to come, Sean hurried away as fast as possible.

Later during a cloudburst Sean met a group in a wagon, a family not far from home who were much more amiable. The road had remained a mire of mud, and Sean asked if there were any shorter routes toward Bourbon. The long arm of the family's patriarch pointed to the beginnings of a ridge road. "There's a ford beyond that ridge. It's fine for horses but a ford of the Bourbeuse River is tricky if a heavy rain comes up. Be careful, son."

The early afternoon rain continued with unrelenting fury. Finally, Sean arrived at the river crossing, and there decided that caution was in order. He spied a broad rock ledge jutting out not far from the raging stream. Pleased at the size of the overhang, he found that even his horses could get out of the wet if they desired, but they proved more content to graze in the downpour near the stream on new grass. Under the broad ledge of lime rock it was bone dry, and the Irishman soon had a small fire crackling and hot coals for cooking. While his gear dried and his food warmed, Sean studied the back wall of the overhang. Rock-hard imprints of sea shells roused his curiosity.

Not long before dusk, movement by the stream caught his eye. Two men stood at the water's edge studying the rising river. Sean first eyed the duo with suspicion, as he would any strangers. Despite the waning light he noted the tattered blue uniforms and the dark color of their skin.

When the pair discovered the creek too swollen to cross, the Irishman offered a greeting more than once and smiled. *These are not thieves*, he calculated, and offered his dry cave as respite from the rain.

Sean took measure of the two men as they walked up. He could see they were more wary of him than he of them. "My fire is yours for the evening," he offered. "I would enjoy some conversation if your business is peaceful."

In silence, no words yet spoken, the burliest of the soldiers considered Sean's proposal from five steps away. He and the other turned slowly and looked to an unseen third man. Behind the trunk of a great sycamore, the leader of the three appeared. Sean could tell he was armed. His right hand and forearm hung down behind his thigh. The man could only be hiding a weapon.

Slim and of a height not much more than Sean's, the third man moved ever closer to the fire and the fine shelter of the lime rock ledge. Sean was not troubled but he was tense. His scatter-gun lay under the blanket in his lap while he leaned comfortably against the dry stone wall.

At last the third man spoke, "We had hoped to cross this evening. A friend of ours lives but a few miles from the river."

Sean watched the man come still closer and realized that his right arm must be wrenched or damaged in some way. He saw the man's hand, empty and useless. "Come up, gentlemen. Take a seat, but know that until we get to know each other better I have a shotgun under the blanket on my lap."

The whites of three pairs of eyes broadened in the firelight.

"I have some extra bacon and beans if you are hungry," Sean added. People had befriended Sean in similar situations, so he felt obligated to pay his dues to these unknown men who were soaked to the skin and shivering. *Maybe they will have news. Their company could make the evening pass more quickly.*

"Certainly, corporal," the third man said as he extended his left hand in a peaceful gesture.

"You sure, Nathan?" the biggest of the black men said to his friend as he remained on the edge of the firelight. "We could swim and be at my uncle's before midnight."

Nathan studied the confident, but sensibly anxious, white man sitting against the wall of the cave. He made his decision and hunkered down alone by the fire while probing the coals with a stick. *Obviously, Irish or Scottish*, the leader of the trio thought. He had detected no reason not to accept the rare hospitality provided. *Under the dry rock by a fire the Irishman had offered food with open hands.*

Within a few moments the four quadrants of Sean's hearty blaze were surrounded, three with dripping wet men. Its heat was readily absorbed by two standing figures and one on his haunches. Steam in clouds left the men's wool jackets and trousers, once blue but now faded in places to gray like Sean's. The three newcomers were jovial towards each other and appreciative of Sean.

"Thank you, sir," Nathan said.

"You're welcome," Sean returned. "Others have helped me. So..."

"However, your kindness is above board, and we thank you."

Introductions soon confirmed that these travelers were most likely harmless. Besides, Sean felt a kinship as all soldiers initially do. "Where did you serve?" he asked, a question offered by a million soldiers a million times.

"Tennessee mostly, under General Thomas," Nathan answered. "Then lastly in South Carolina with Colonel Robert Shaw. Did you hear of him?"

"No," Sean answered finding that Nathan's words were not backward nor difficult to understand as many of the colored men with whom he had talked during the war.

"Oh, thought you would have," Nathan said. His tone showed disappointment. "We were the first, you know?"

Sean looked the three faces over, one by one, searching for a clue to understanding Nathan's statement. Curiosity and good manners forced him to say, "Tell me about Colonel Shaw." He studied the intelligent eyes of the leader with the injured arm, but interrupted himself.

"You men aren't armed? Surely, something besides your walking sticks?"

"Hell, no, Mr. Kelly," Joseph, the big man to Nathan's left grunted. "Our Union Army don't arm niggers when they're set free to return to their homes." Those were some of the last words the big man contributed. Dexter Lee, the lanky man to the right of Nathan nodded and squinted his eyes as he said, "Yes, sir. Yes, sir. Nothing but sticks. We do have knives, though."

Nathan took over. "Mr. Kelly, we have no firearms as my friends have said. But a clasp knife was the only weapon we were allowed to leave with. You?"

Sean remembered the pistols stolen in the battlefield and the shotgun purchased in Saint Louis. He then settled his thoughts on the three colored men's lack of arms. They weren't thieves. He was. They had been naive. He had not. They had trusted the army. He had known to trust no one.

The soaked threesome had shown their sparse hands openly as he had told them almost nothing of his. He decided that they must be good men most likely, and continued his appraisal.

"Nathan, tell me of your colonel," Sean asked again, knowing it was the direction that the men wanted to go. The Irishman set his fry skillet on glowing coals and cut far more bacon than he could eat. He then set it to sizzle against the heating cast iron. His actions brought sighs of contentment from across the fire.

A deep breath slipped slowly from plainly the brightest of the group. Nathan's face had become more and more relaxed as he sensed the gentle nature of the man across the fire with the strong Irish accent and the shotgun in his lap.

"Colonel Shaw, Mr. Kelly," Nathan began but was interrupted.

"Nathan, I am not a sir. Call me, Sean."

A sincere and appreciative smile filled Nathan's face as he answered, "I will." Then, back to business he began, "Colonel Robert G. Shaw was the truest of gentlemen who has ever graced God's good earth. We called him Mr. Goldie to his back. His middle name was Gould." Nathan waited for a reaction from Sean, and when he received none he continued. "Our colonel was given the task of forming a regiment of colored infantry, the 54th Massachusetts. He told us all, a thousand men as black as coal, how his superiors said it was impossible to make fighting men from slaves. Black men in the Union Army were to be used to their best abilities and sent in huge detachments to dig trenches to protect the white troops."

Silence, then, "But, Sean, he understood. It was as if he was color blind, and we loved him for it. The colonel formed one of the finest infantry regiments to ever march off to battle." Then sadly Nathan added, "Most died in the assault on Fort Wagner on the South Carolina coast, but with great valor." Then, a lump in Nathan's throat forced his voice to crack. "The rebel garrison murdered any wounded Negro soldiers that we couldn't bring back with us. There were hundreds. We heard their cries but could do nothing." He paused but then added, "I was severely wounded."

Sean refused to let his eyes leave the speaker. Across the fire from him sat a man, not ordinary, and not affected by his skin color, or that of others. By the way he spoke, Sean gathered that Nathan could surely also read, something he wished was one of his qualities. He couldn't hold back.

"Nathan, you can read, can't you?"

"Certainly, and you?"

That word again. Certainly. Only educated men used that word. He had heard officers, both Union and Confederate, use it as if it were common. Embarrassed by Nathan's question, Sean hesitated. Undeniably jealous, his reluctant answer gnawed at the pit of his stomach before finally being stated in painful respect. "No, Nathan, just a few words. I envy you. By the way you speak, I know you are truthful. Your words come out as easily as many of the officers I have known."

The trio around the fire looked at Sean in disbelief. Nathan asked with skepticism in his voice, "How could a corporal in the cavalry know of more than one or two lieutenants or captains let alone officers of higher rank?"

Sean felt inquiring eyes and a growing lack of confidence. He felt obligated to explain, "Through the first part of the war I survived as any soldier would. In the last half my fiddle kept me alive."

"Your fiddle?" Nathan questioned.

"Yes, my fiddle. I was lucky to be selected to play as our regiment charged the rebel lines and played when the officers needed some entertainment in the evenings. My fiddle did, indeed, save my life near the end."

All arms and legs, gangly Dexter Lee let out a plea as he scooped more bacon and beans into his bowl, "Have it with you?" Nathan and Joseph awaited an answer.

Sean smiled at the threesome and understood their hunger. The depletion of his stores of bacon, beans, and bread could be put to right with small change in Rolla, but a desire for music he had found starving men to require as dearly as food.

"Surely," he answered, and Sean reached into the feed sack leaning with his saddle bag against the rock. With care he pulled the instrument from its scant protection. He found the rosin and applied the chalky substance to his bow, realizing that he had not played since before Gretchen's father gave him the task in the hills to work in the vineyard. Would his fire warmed fingers find the right key again? He also hoped not to break a string on this dank night turned so pleasant. There were no replacements. He played into the night, and after none had broken and a multitude of tunes had left him, he put down his fiddle and slept.

Sean awoke with a start and laid his hand on his shotgun. He looked around, then quickly relaxed. By the ashes of the cold fire, the three soldiers he had befriended snored in concert in their blankets. Sean looked to the east and saw the day begin as a joyous but overdue March sun climbed above the hill. He basked in the rare, warming light.

A little later, Nathan awoke. He spoke first as he lay with an arm holding his head up, "I will remember who fed me and revived my soul with his music. If we meet again, my home is yours, Sean Kelly."

Sean responded in kind and told Nathan, Dexter Lee, and Joseph of his debt to a family near Van Buren. He then asked, "Where are you bound Nathan?" and Sean looked to the other two with questioning eyes as he awaited an answer from his new acquaintance.

Nathan proceeded to lay out their plans. "First, today to the south and Joseph's family. Then I will leave my friends and head to Salem which lies further and south of Rolla."

Sean was surprised as Nathan shook his hand. To his comrades and now to Sean the pleasant man said, "My wife and three children await me near the main road south of Salem to Eminence. I can only hope they are well after three years."

Pleased to have met such a man, Sean asked, "And for whom should I ask to find your farm? I am heading south of Rolla, too."

"Why, Sean," Nathan beamed with pride, "ask for the farm of Nathan Weller. Everyone knows me. You'll always be welcome." Then he laughed and Sean was puzzled. An explanation soon came. "The folks around Salem call my wife a witch. Her potions from local plants have healed many a child or a mother after birthing. Superstition reigns of course. But she is not a witch. She is an herbalist."

During the night the stream had lowered, and soon after Nathan's words were spoken the band of three ex-soldiers crossed knee deep in the stream and then walked out of sight into a dense forest beyond.

Sean leaned back against the warm rock behind his campfire. He listened cheerfully to the joking of the friends until the brisk morning wind in the branches silenced their words. He reflected upon his good fortune to find such honest men in the wilderness and hoped to meet Nathan again on the road.

Soon his gear was packed, tied on his horse, and Sean was on his way. The sun's sparkling reflection on the lowering waters of the river put the Irishman in a pleasant mood that lasted the morning.

⊕

A week later after following the railroad to Rolla, Sean headed south. He rode quietly through what appeared to be a deserted town. A girl running in the street told him, "It's Lacoma, mister." Then, after Sean's question of bigger towns nearby, "Salem lies a day to the south."

The small town seemed too quiet as he passed through. Its outer limits of cabins and sparse gardens were littered with deer bones and carcasses he could not identify. The few people he passed watched him but said nothing despite his greetings.

Wishing to be past the dreary village, Sean set his mount and pack animal to a faster pace. When finally well beyond the last log dwelling, he brought his horses to a sudden stop. He cringed as he looked up. Before him, dangling from a huge oak, hung a body, a black body in blue wool. Sean had seen men and women die in a variety of ways but strangulation he thought the worst.

His route forced him to travel practically under the hanging tree. His horses became skittish. Sean lowered his head as he passed, and pushed his animals faster to quickly put death behind.

Yet, he could not squelch his curiosity. Twenty paces past, he halted his horses and turned. It took no longer than a moment of grisly observation to raise his bile. Sean slapped the reins on his mount and shook in disgust and sadness. His mind whirled in anger. The man, no longer a man but a grotesquely elongating corpse, was unquestionably Nathan Weller.

Chapter 30
Prairie Fire and a Friend

Damp, bone chilling mists had burned off earlier in the morning. Now, under the welcome heat from bright spring sunlight Sean made his way on the edge of a vast prairie. Only a few gnarled, old-growth trees grew scattered here and there. Thick, shoulder high grass surrounded them and stretched out as far as the eye could see. While he rode down the rutted trace, he noticed the blackened trunks of many of the matriarchs, he guessed oaks, and wondered how often fires burned through the area. His horses ambled along on a trail that led him higher and back around through the forests. The trio of beasts and man traipsed through thick oaks and tall pines that lined the ridge tops. From the sparse words of a man traveling north, Sean determined that Salem lay unseen but not far to the south.

The man he had met reminded him of others he had passed along the way. After days of rather routine travel he had come across only a few homesteads. The people he did meet stood off with their guns cocked. They were leery, he realized, of the drifting, possibly dangerous Union soldier that he must appear to be. *And I am*, he chuckled with cold assessment. His thoughts rushed back a day and dwelt on Lacoma and Nathan's death. *Was no one to be trusted?*

By late morning Sean reached another large expanse of rolling prairie. No tree was in sight. He turned his head and studied each horizon. The sea of brown grass stretched miles in all directions. Sean relaxed knowing that here there would be no confrontations. Crossing the alternating tall then shorter grassed prairie, he rode from wetter to better drained ground. All along he marveled at the game. Small bands of deer and then a turkey with her nearly grown offspring crossed his path. Once, a group of six elk emerged from nowhere and then vanished like ghosts in the tall grass. The abundance of game perked his hunting spirit. Soon the boy from Lisdoonvarna had his dinner in the iron sights of his rifle.

Later, when the sun shone straight above and after the bent-over labor of dressing a deer, coaxing a small fire near a muddy trickle, and eating his fill, Sean stretched out in the tall, dry grass. He awoke coughing. The acrid smell of smoke filled his lungs. He quickly glanced to his cook fire. No sparks not even any smoke was coming from its cold ashes. Jumping up, he searched for the source as a huge cloud of gray blew over him. Fearful, he promptly mounted up, hoping to sit taller and reach his head above wither high grass to spot the origin of the fire.

Looking upwind, a great dark wall filled the sky. Gray clouds swirled higher and then lifted. His anxious green eyes beheld a wide front of burning prairie along the northern horizon. Flames as high as small trees and less than a mile away were pushing rapidly nearer.

Caught unaware and hypnotized by his fear, Sean continued to watch the advancing fire. Being burned in the scorching fury was not the end of which he had dreamed. He could see the taller grasses in the distance sending cruel flames three times taller than the head high grasses that surrounded him. Sean knew full well that the thick-stemmed grasses would be fuel enough to roast him alive. He watched the line of fire gallop across the prairie, now less than half a mile away.

A survivor of the streets of New York and so many battles in a deadly war, Sean's mind came down from panic-stricken to a buzzing frenzy for survival. What should he do? With no time to ride away from such destruction, Sean began running to his picketed but frightened horses close by. He had a plan. But whether it would work or not depended on time, and there was little of that.

Groping in his saddle bags he found his fire kit of matches, flint, and steel. "Damn!" came out as he knelt in the grass. The matches refused to strike, damp from earlier exposure to the morning dew.

He cursed, and then quickly dropped to the ground on his belly. He deliberately laid the stripped cedar bark from the kit, already twisted into tinder, on a trampled portion of the grass. Striking earnestly with his flint the sparks flew, and smoke soon began to rise.

Picking up the cedar fiber and cradling the dry tinder in his hands, he blew gently. He looked upwind. The fire was closer, a quarter mile. Then again, he blew with steady air, not too much or too little, hoping for a flame. Sounding like muskets on a battle line, the crackling fire storm on the prairie grew closer and closer as the tiny tinder finally flamed before his face.

What a fool, he said to himself, remembering then pulling the black powder flask out of his saddle bags. He poured it cautiously but to hasten the burning of a ten yard line. It caught in a flash. His only hope, a backfire, began to roar away. He waited, and prayed that he was not too late. The Irishman walked downwind a few paces and lit up more of his defensive line with a torch of prairie grass.

Within less than a minute, Sean's backfire howled away leaving blackened ash and mineral soil behind it. Acting swiftly, he moved his horses and gear onto this still smoky but quickly cooling ground. A raging wind, generated by the fire itself, blew from nowhere. To his grief it suffocated sections of his backfire that had attempted to travel upwind. Sean observed the full front of the advancing maelstrom closing in as if an unstoppable rebel attack. Uneasy but knowing it his only option, he awaited his doom or his salvation.

Downwind, he saw his safety valve of blackened prairie swell quickly in width and length, and he inched his way further into the protection of the gray-black ashes. As close as he dared, he placed more and more bared soil between himself and the advancing flames. The fire upwind from him crackled loudly, sounding again much like gunfire from a battle. His careening horses screamed furiously in the blinding smoke. Barely, he held onto the reins. Then one pulled free. His pack horse bolted.

In a sudden swoosh the main fire wrestled his black line. Twenty steps either side of Sean the maelstrom's attack continued. The firestorm, he had so desperately tried to avoid, leapt in bounds but died in a hush just as quickly as it had come forward. Prairie fuel now exhausted, dwindling smoke, not searing heat, advanced onto the relieved Irishman and his remaining mount. He was singed but unhurt. His pack horse was another matter.

Sean rode up onto a blackened rise and caught a glimpse of his frightened pack horse scampering away into the smoke. Coughing but alive, he cursed vehemently in Gaelic to the wind, the smoke, and the retreating wall of fire.

How far would the animal go before succumbing? All his important gear was tied on the horse's back. *How could the animal still live after such a hellish melee?*

With a determined gaze Sean searched the charred landscape that now surrounded him in every direction. His best hope was to find the dead animal and salvage some of his belongings. Again, optimistically, he listened. *No explosions. A good sign.* The two pounds of black powder that remained on his fleeing animal had not found the flames, at least not yet.

While he waited impatiently for the smoke to clear, Sean remembered the antics of rebel skirmishers last fall. They had lit fires in the prairies many times to cover their escape from his company of Union cavalry. Luckily for Sean's troop of horse soldiers, the older veterans had known what to do and do quickly. Today, Sean had done the same. Then, only one man had been lost. A foolish sergeant had chased his panicked mount thinking he could outrun the flames.

The wind around him settled. Yet, downwind Sean watched the backfire continue to sweep across broad grassland. Behind it the earth was bared to a raw dark soil. He sighed in relief. He had escaped a horrible death. Upwind he looked at mile-after-mile of blackened, rolling landscape.

Turning again to observe the fast-moving flames, Sean thought his Maker was indeed still on his side. *A merciful, forgiving God still exists despite the evils of war.*

Coughing all the while, he swung around in soot-covered boots to survey yet again his dilemma. He was surprised to see the line of fire in retreat. The flames downwind were dying, and the massive plumes of black smoke had diminished. He could only think that a creek or gully must be slowing the fire's progress. The smoke cleared in places and revealed to his amazement a plowed field not a quarter mile away. Remnants of corn stalks in chocolate soil littered the earth like straight broken sticks thrown haphazardly across a table to start the game. Beyond the open field of several acres his wondering eyes detected the faint shape of log cabins and the steep pitch of rooflines. Through the thin smoke, the split rails of corrals became visible.

Sean led his lone horse, packed with his little remaining gear, towards what only could be the town of Salem. The curling, gray haze from chimneys mingled with the remaining smoke of the prairie fire. He saw groups of people gathering and understood why they watched him with curiosity. His reconnaissance continued while holding tightly to the reins of his frightened animal.

He saw his pack horse. Near the burned field's edge its lead rope lay securely in the hands of a boy. *A devil,* Sean guessed the boy's thoughts, *has appeared leading his horse from hell.*

Sean stared at the boy. Further away he saw the curious crowd at the edge of the village. The unsmiling youth studied him with wary eyes. Sean's pack horse was calm, and its reins remained firmly grasped in small hands. The last wisps of smoke blew past them. Their gazes locked over ground that had so recently been a great sea of grass cast up in an inferno.

Relieved, Sean worked at leading his prancing horse towards the boy. *How had he tethered my pack animal?* Only moments before the Irishman had thought his valuable animal lost to the fire or spooked beyond finding. Sean spoke into his horse's ear. Its frolic lessened, and he continued towards the boy.

Before the Irishman had a chance to say a word of thanks, the boy who Sean figured to be no more than ten years of age called out in a fearful tone, "If you be the devil, stand back!" Sean, earlier, had guessed right.

The Irishman's mount panicked again, and once more he whispered in its ear, calming it as before. He smiled. He knew his face must be smeared with soot. Anyone seeing him walk out of the fire could well conjure up demons. He laughed heartily, and then said with the least Irish accent he could muster, "Thank you for catching my horse, and no, good lad, I am not the devil." But to himself he said, *Not today*, and paused before speaking again. "Would you take a penny for your efforts? I was in a great worry that my pack animal was lost." It was then he noticed the loose horseshoe on a left fore hoof and added, "Another penny for you to hold my animal while I tighten that shoe."

The boy looked to the horse's foot, and then looked squarely at Sean. "My father can fix the gelding's shoe much better than you."

Taken aback by the boy's confident manner, Sean listened for more. He did owe the boy for catching and holding his pack horse. He took its bridle rope and asked, "Can you truly lead me to a strong-armed smith at his anvil?"

"My father will be glad to speak with another like him."

The boy's speech held little to determine its origin, but Sean questioned him no more, thinking he might meet an Irish blacksmith. It would be nice to talk with someone from home.

CHAPTER 31
INTOLERANCE THEN DECENCY

Reaching a muddy side alley, Sean and the boy followed deep wheel ruts to a main street lined with board walks and wood-framed storefronts. Before ever seeing the livery, Sean heard the repeated pounding of a hammer on metal. At the large entrance to a corral, dark fumes from a coal burning forge circled a burly, bearded blacksmith.

Sean approached the simple workspace that did little more than shed the rain. He glanced up to see a small family on a stout, high-wheeled cart with two broken spokes. Two very young, curious boys, black as the coal from the forge, smiled at him from above. A girl, older than the boys, gave Sean a stern look.

The eyes of the inquisitive Irishman dropped to the front of the cart. A lighter-faced adult of slight build stood in trousers, a work jacket, and a worn, broad-brimmed hat. Sean studied the person calmly holding the reins of the mule, expecting an old grandfather or a brother not quite grown.

A woman, not a man, turned and peered at him with dark, piercing eyes. Her shining skin was a dusky honey-hue, a woman of color. Sean saw her look him hard in the eye, and then slowly circle away withdrawn and defiant. He said nothing and walked on but decided that the face beneath the floppy hat was the most beautiful he had ever seen.

Glad to finally see the blacksmith face to face, Sean expected a kind greeting, but despite the son's introduction, the metal worker's gaze met Sean's with a surly stare. The powerful man rolled his eyes as he spat to the side. He continued without a word to forcefully pummel a rod of red-hot iron.

Sean waited. After the smith had placed the flattened, black metal again in the furnace, he asked, "Will you have time to shoe my pack horse?" Sean did not wish to offend this man who seemed clearly upset already.

The smith set his hammer on the broad anvil with a clank. He spat again, closer to Sean's feet this time, and then looked up to survey the lean Irishman before asking. "Be ye a Papist dog?"

Sean scolded himself for not expecting it. Certainly, the blacksmith's words told him that he was from Ireland, and from the north, Scots-Irish, and by his question an overly zealous Protestant.

Sean had wished to leave religious bigotry behind when his family left the Irish homeland, but its ugly face had appeared and reappeared in New York City, the Union Army, and now here. He knew well that to be Irish, with the second strike being Catholic, placed him at the level of slaves or dogs in the eyes of people with English or Scottish ancestry. He had found many soldiers to be tolerant but inevitably a Protestant radical, usually from Northern Ireland or Scotland, would sour the day with their hate-filled language. *The squeaky wheel gets the grease*, Sean thought, and forced a cynical smile.

"Well?" the blacksmith asked again.

Sean replied, "I am truly Catholic but not so proud as to put my boot onto another man because of his faith."

"If that's the case, so be it. I charge Papists and darkies double."

Sean took a deep breath and let it out slowly trying to maintain control. His anger swelled and slowly deflated. He would not do business with a hypocrite if he had the choice. Turning his horses towards the livery's entrance, he saw again the woman in man's clothing and her children on their cart. *No wonder,* Sean thought, *she was most likely in dire straits without the silver to pay double.* He also guessed by her proud look, which stared down anyone who passed, that the blacksmith may have demanded more than money for payment.

He would as soon nail the shoe himself, not cleanly as the blacksmith most likely, but honestly. Sean's disgust with this little town was growing even though he was not yet sure of its name. He walked his settled horses to a hitching rail on the main street and tied them. Behind him, much too close, he heard the blacksmith's harsh voice but could not understand his words except for, "Papist!"

Sean looked to his weapons and readied his nerves for a confrontation. Taking a deep breath he turned in the direction of the smoky stable where the smith stood out front with hammer in hand.

To his unanticipated relief he heard the smith's words repeated. "Papist, if you are as good with horses as my boy says, I'll shoe your nag for free."

Sean answered the man simply, swallowing his pride. "Surely, I know horses."

⊕

After several dusty hours taming two very jumpy stallions, dealing with a lame animal, and having the smith scour his memory clean of horse doctoring remedies, Sean confronted the blacksmith. He stood by the horse trough washing away the layer of soot from the prairie fire and the most recent caking of dust. "I will be deserving much more than the shoeing of a single hoof. Don't you agree?"

Sean could not doubt the smith's honest dealings when the brawny, square-faced man consented without an argument. "You've done well, lad. There will be no denying that. Setting my stifled mare right is worth much to me. Knowing to push down and back on the animal's kneecap did the trick. I wouldn't have guessed to do that." With clear respect in his voice the smith offered, "Would feeding you a fine home cooked meal satisfy our trade?"

Sean relished the idea. A good meal from a good hearth he had not seen since Hermann, but before he could answer the smith spoke again.

"Now, let it be known my dear wife will not let a Papist in the house. But I will be sure you are fed a hearty meal on the back stoop."

A knowing smile lit Sean's face but he said nothing. Then, looking beyond the smoky blacksmith shop he saw the broken cart. Its owners were nowhere in sight. Sean turned back to the iron worker while trying to avoid showing anger in his words. "Fix the cart outside your shop and we'll be even on our trade."

The sturdy blacksmith kicked back on his heels and hemmed and hawed, then after a moment of indecision said, "I'll not ask you why, but you have a deal."

During the next half hour as the cart's wheel was rebuilt, Sean searched for the owner and her children along the long, broad street of the town without success. He asked at a dry goods store and received an answer from its owner ending in a leering grin. After telling Sean the direction of her farm, he said, "She's a pretty one for sure but be careful, Mick. She'll take a knife to what's below your belt if you have what I think you have in mind. And beware," he added. "She's a witch."

Sean shook his head, acknowledging the man's coarse reply and walked out onto the dry, wooden walkway still intent on finding the woman. At least he had the direction she might travel. When nearly a mile out of town and ready to turn back, he finally saw her plodding through the mud along the road. He easily caught up with the slow-gaited mule she was leading.

The reins were steady in her hand when she looked up. Her daughter straddled the bare back of the animal and two young sons held on behind. Sean saw her quickly take notice of him trotting up. Instantly, he caught the smooth motion of the large-gauge shotgun sliding from a feed sack hanging from the mule's tack.

"Pardon me, lady," he said slowly but was unable to hide the fear in his voice. "May I speak with you?" His polite words did little justice to his noble intentions.

The mule abruptly stopped. The woman's dark eyes cut him to

the core. She cocked her shotgun. Already, it pointed squarely at his chest.

Both boys dropped to the ground and scrambled for the ditch. The young girl slipped away into the roadside brush without a single word from her mother. Sean heard the snap as the second hammer came back. His hands went higher in the air.

Surprising Sean, the woman spoke with slow confidence, "And sir, what business might we pursue on this far from illustrious road at this late hour in the afternoon?"

Odd, he thought, still able to think despite the black maws of death before him. The woman's speech placed her among the few ex-slaves who were literate, only the second he had heard in as many weeks. Few people of color were educated, few Irish folk either for that matter.

Then Sean realized that the intelligent woman had recognized him from the smithy. Doubts filled her unyielding eyes. Sean knew she had overheard the blacksmith's words. Uncomfortably, he watched her await his answer. Her resolute eyes and shotgun demanded a response.

"Pardon me, lady," he repeated again a bit too nervously. Then he managed, "At this moment your cart is being repaired."

Gripping her heavy weapon tighter, the woman spoke with evident suspicion. "But, I don't have the money to pay for the repairs."

Using the pressure of his legs Sean backed his horse a step while his hands remained high in the air. "It's all right. My intentions are not evil." He paused wondering what else to say, then went on, "I was treated much as you were. The blacksmith made a point of his hatred of Irish Catholics as well as colored folk."

By the time Sean had explained the arrangement, the woman smiled with relief. To Sean's pleasure they began the ride back to town together. A brief sharing of stories took place. Only then did Sean see the woman notice the faded yellow stripe on his equally faded blue pant leg. She leaned out from her mule and extended her hand. "My name is Luanne Weller. My husband was in the army. Pleased to make your acquaintance, Mr. Kelly."

Sean tried to hide his shock when he heard the last name,

Weller, but he had already guessed it. Nathan's description of his wife came back to him. Uneasy and feeling guiltier every moment, he could not tell Luanne of Nathan. Sean said little on the return trip to town.

Within the hour Luanne's cart was ready for travel. Sean remained at the livery to be sure the bargain with the blacksmith was finalized. He was pleased. His pack horse was shod too. The smith was a complete bigot but an honest one. His work proved to be of the highest quality.

Afterwards, Sean listened as Mrs. Weller thanked him. Then, with her two young boys and daughter she ponderously wheeled away along the main street, while her big mule steadily pulled through the thick mud. He wished there were more to say to his new found friend, but anything else would have been too forward. The stark image of Nathan hanging from the tree came back to him. All he could suppose to do was that somehow he must help Nathan's wife. *But how?* He had already figured a way to fix her cart. *What else can I do?*

To Sean's pleasant surprise Luanne halted her mule and turned in the high seat towards him. "And should you be in need of work, I can give you that. But I can only feed you for pay, and there is no fancy food on my farm."

Sean could see in Mrs. Weller's determined face that she had made a supreme effort to speak to him. She had pushed down her pride and had gambled on his integrity. He could tell she wanted him to follow her, wherever that was. He also could see that she was frightened.

He answered respectfully, "Mrs. Weller, I will come work for you for a while," then finished in a wayward tone for the crowd that had gathered, "but only on one condition."

The woman of color sat straighter in her seat. She held her children close and prepared for the Irishman's expected response. Luanne Weller's stalwart eyes bored straight through him. In this town she had heard it all before, many times.

Meanwhile, Sean saw more men and even a few women, both white and black, empty the stores and fill the boardwalk. He saw people stop in the street on their horses and heard the mischief developing behind him. He guessed right in thinking that they had expected entertainment. What they seemed to demand of the Irishman proved to be some form of sexual proposition. *The haughty black woman doesn't know her place*, he heard more than once. He detected in the townspeople a festering resentment.

Sean threw his best smile to the swelling crowd of rowdies on both sides of the mud-rutted street. Previously upstanding citizens gawked and made lewd gestures. Thick clouds above him parted and sunshine broke through while every deluded soul, now walking that disgusting avenue of a town whose name he only guessed, chanted for him to speak. He heard the *witch* word, again, many times. Then the Irishman turned to the subdued woman on the cart who sat as tall as ever. Later, he would remember that even then he loved her, respecting her courage to face this mob alone. And he understood how Nathan had loved her, too. However, then a notion caught hold of him. *She is not alone, today.*

Sean repeated, "I'll only work for you, Mrs. Weller, on one condition." He glanced back across the excited faces and then allowed his eyes to return to the dignified mother of three.

Leering men roared with delight. Sean heard two shopkeepers chuckle in anticipation of his next words, surely carnal. "The fun-loving Irishman is making my day!" Wagers passed between them, and another jeering bystander pealed out, "Hallelujah, we're about to have us some fun!"

"What fine amusement," Sean heard from a man with lathered soap still on his face in front of the barber shop. Still another, well dressed with a cravat tied neatly at his neck, waved his arm high. Others shouted mean words to the woman who deserved no one's scorn.

On the sunlit main street Sean observed it all as he had anticipated. All the while the vulnerable mother on the cart drove unrelenting daggers from her eyes into his. The three frightened children hugged her knees awaiting the outcome. He also noticed her hand reach under a blanket. It lay on the butt of her shotgun.

Theatrical since his early fiddle playing days, Sean held up his arm to the loud crowd. The broad street fell silent. Mouths opened in anticipation. Reins on horses dropped to the withers and into the mud. Nothing short of a circus thrill was expected.

Sean's answer bellowed out for all to hear, "You must teach me to read!" Then in a moment, "And only that!"

Luanne Weller's beautiful face instantly relaxed. A smile grew where before there was only grief. The crowd was stunned. Silence and blank expressions filled the board walk. This was drama unexpected. Sean had controlled the crowd as at the fair in Lisdoonvarna and on the back alley in the Irish market street in New York City. However, now, his fiddle and bow lay secured on the bedroll behind his saddle.

He gladly watched a grand smile fill Luanne's perfect face. He bore witness to her hushed radiance dominating the main street as only mud and ugly thoughts had before.

Sean mounted his horse and rode up beside the silently jubilant lady. His pack horse was in tow. He had decided that Mrs. Weller's smile meant *yes*.

Together on that warming April afternoon, the three children, the beautiful lady dressed in men's clothing and a forlorn hat, and the hungry but content Irishman left the fuming town behind. Sean asked Luanne Weller, "Please, if you will, the name of this town?"

"Salem."

"I guessed as much, and am delighted to have found it," only made her smile continue. As a final gesture Sean turned back. He cocked his head and his familiar wry grin appeared. The disgust and disappointment that he had cultivated in the crowd was evident in every face, and Sean Malroy Kelly was pleased of it as any man could ever be.

"Mrs. Weller," Sean said, "you have a field hand for a time, if for no other reason than to spite those ugly souls in that ugly town behind us." He looked to bright, proud eyes. In them he saw acceptance.

CHAPTER 32
EQUALS

The outline of a small dwelling arose in the trees around the bend in the road. Then as the distance narrowed, the stone foundations of a burned out house became evident, and Sean detected the presence of the hardscrabble, make-do or do-without farm that it was. To Sean, the Weller homestead was dreary. However, closer inspection revealed a neat garden enclosed by a woven wattle fence. Newly spaded soil awaited planting while tiny potato leaves were breaking through to the light. In another corner spinach leaves were doing the same. "Well, Mistress Weller, you've planted seed! Good for you." Yet, always lingered the fact that he must tell her the horrible truth about her husband. But he could not, not yet.

Sean tied his horse to a porch post and dismounted. In a survey of the grounds he studied the small barn in need of repair, the tiny two room log house, and the rocked well. *Good,* he thought, *someone, probably Nathan, built soundly but for the last few years the hammer has rarely swung if at all.* The well, he saw, lay below a roof, protected, but needed mending. The outhouse, to his satisfaction, stood back beyond the barn. Jokingly he asked, "A one or two holer?" At the moment Luanne looked to her children who already were drinking from a bucket freshly drawn from the well.

Shotgun loosely in her hand, Luanne took it all in stride and cracked a tiny smile. She saw Sean's smile, too. "Let me show you the barn," she said. There, a skinny, sway-backed milk cow and a mature sow stood contently in their stalls. "There is still a little hay in the loft." She faced him again. "It will be your place to sleep." Her words had been straightforward but mostly her hard look told him clearly her mind.

Sean saw the pain and the hope in the woman's tired face. He had no desire to disappoint her. "I'm your hired hand, Mrs. Weller. I understand it will be nothing more."

Sean followed her. It was evident that Luanne Weller trusted him or wanted to. She showed off the lone milk cow, the sow ready to have piglets, a handful of chickens, and then pointed to a weed-filled field behind the barn. Sean saw that it sloped gently up the hill towards a dense forest of tall oaks. She mentioned growing corn there when her husband had been home. "Your job will be to plow it and ready it for seed. Last year I had a terrible time with it."

From nowhere the question came to him while a large grin filled his face. "You make corn bread?" Then he demanded with mock scorn, "I mean good corn bread."

Sean watched with pleasure as the handsome woman took off her floppy hat and tossed her head back to clear the long, dark hair from her eyes. She stood tall, eye-to-eye before she asked, "And I suppose you can play that fiddle?" She pointed with her slim arm to his horse. "It sits fine behind your saddle on your bedroll, but is it just an ornament for conversation's sake?"

Sean let out a hearty laugh. Luanne had not given an inch. "Corn bread first, then after supper we'll see about some music. Limbering up my bow will take a full stomach." He watched for a reaction while he prepared to throw down his final ace, "I've bacon to add to the skillet if you won't object."

He liked what he saw. Luanne's face had lit up with a smile.

CHAPTER 33
MUSIC IN THE BEDROOM

As evening set on, the wind turned cold and blustery. Luanne had served the Irishman a simple but filling supper on the porch. Now, she politely gave her new hired hand permission to enter the house. "If you will, come out of the wind."

Sean took off his boots and set them beside the door. He walked inside and found it Spartan but clean, and not meager to a crofter's son. The three children watched him bug-eyed from a straw ticked bed in the corner. Their mother sat on the only chair. Sean could only think, after his eyes adjusted to the light, that a beautiful creature was before him. Luanne sat facing him in a clean but simple dress, her hair combed with a ribbon holding it back. The light from the fire defined her high cheek bones and other fine features. Her manner was not of any ex-slave he had ever seen. But then he remembered New York. There in the city he had seen free men of color with their families in the streets. She was of them.

Still taken by Luanne's image that reflected not just her beauty but her faith in him, he well understood the privilege of being allowed into her home. Sean wondered further concerning her lineage. Mulatto was the description he had heard in Virginia. Trust in him or not, he also noticed within arm's reach of the woman a shotgun leaning against the wall.

Sean lifted up his fiddle and bow in one hand, "I think I may remember how to play this pretty wooden box." With a simple wave of her hand he was directed towards the fire to sit on the raised stone hearth. In only a minute his fiddle strings were adjusted, and soon his flowing melodies held all the family's attention. After a few tunes Sean stopped and prepared to leave, thinking it the proper thing to do.

"Oh, no, Sean Kelly! You sit and play more," spilled out from the delighted mother of three. Then more composed and a bit sassy, "You ate far too much corn bread and butter to stop playing now."

Much later as the fire burned low, Luanne intently watched Sean put his fiddle down. The children were asleep. She sat beside them with her knees to her chin. Her eyes were sparkling and appreciative when she bid him good night. "We'll be up at dawn, Sean. There is much to do."

Sean looked back over his shoulder as he opened the door. The lamplight showed the seriousness of his face. "You won't be working me like a mule," he said, "unless you truly teach me my letters." Luanne beamed back. It was the only answer he needed. As she stood up and began to politely close the door behind him, he took note that her hand lay far from her shotgun.

CHAPTER 34
THE OLD LANGUAGE

Sean cursed in Irish as he had learned from his father and grandfather. "The pain will go in its sweet time," he gasped while trying to regain the calmness of a few moments before. He lifted a half rotten board with his right hand as gently as possible, and pulled his crushed left forearm from the fallen stack of rough cut oak. He again moaned in pain and quickly wondered if Luanne or the children had heard his swearing. Then it dawned on him. They would not have understood, although, Luanne would have easily recognized the tone.

Amy, the eldest child, came running first. "Are you all right, Mr. Kelly?" When she saw Sean sitting against the lumber pile in obvious distress she blurted out a compassionate, "I'll get Momma."

Very soon, Luanne was kneeling at Sean's side. From his shoulder to his knuckles she sensitively squeezed the muscle to bone. "Wiggle your fingers, please," she commanded and competently awaited the outcome.

Sean did as he was told. It hurt, but the last digits curled and uncurled. To his mind no doctor could have performed better.

Luanne's words were sober. "Nothing appears broken, however it will bruise." She looked up and caught his gaze. The smile on his face bewildered her. Only a few moments before she was sure she had hurt him while searching for a fracture.

"You stopped your gardening to bother with me?" Sean said playfully. "I'll be fine." He forced a pleasant but pained, "Thank you."

"What were you hollering?" a curious Luanne asked as she looked straight into Sean's green eyes.

"Oh, nothing really. Just a little ditty my grandfather taught me. You don't speak the old language do you?"

"The old language?" rolled out off her tongue as questions filled her eyes.

With that Sean knew his secret was safe, and his blasphemous words had not hurt any feelings.

"What did you say, Sean? I have already guessed that you were cursing in Irish. Don't try to fool me too much. I read books."

Then in Gaelic, he answered her, "Pretty lady, I'll not be telling you that today," and the wiry Irishman stood up and flexed his injured arm, rubbed it, and walked to the barn in search of the saw and auger. There, he began to fashion oak pegs, first splitting thin dry kindling and then trimming each stick to roundness with the spoke shave. He knew if he drove these snugly into drill holes the new boards on the barn would be tight for many years to come.

He heard Luanne holler from the garden, "Tonight after dinner, Sean, we'll work on your reading."

CHAPTER 35
LUANNE

Cold, wet weather had held them back until today's bright sunshine lured them out. This was their first excursion together beyond the boundaries of the Weller farm. Sean carefully observed his new friend on a rocky, open hillside pulling roots from the shallow soil.

Standing with an early flowering plant in her hand Luanne looked Sean's way. She gestured with her other over the wild meadow, "This is what we call a bald knob, Sean. High grassy areas like this harbor a great number of medicinal plants."

So, it would be work after all, Sean shrugged, having hoped for a simple holiday. Sean thought Luanne's ability as a task maker rivaled Herr Westfphal's. He watched while she continued to scour the hillside for slender roots the likes of which he had never seen. His job was to follow and to bag up the surplus harvest.

"How can you know so much about plants?" he asked as one hand uneasily cradled stems of tall grass at his side and the other held her tote sack of freshly dug herbs. It had been two weeks since meeting Luanne at the blacksmith shop. Still, Sean had avoided telling her the terrible truth about her husband. Today's sincere but abrupt question helped him forget for the moment, because he knew Luanne's lengthy explanation would be a sure distraction.

Each day that he waited only made it increasingly more difficult, and he hated himself for being so deceitful. Foolishly, he hoped with time that his guilt and perhaps the terrible story might fade away. Although, neither, to his satisfaction, had shown any signs of disappearing.

She answered him this time only with a smile and kept on with her work.

While disappointed at her lack of conversation but never with her smile, Sean dwelt on the grace of this woman on a mission. Bewildered described Sean's feelings as he watched. *How, indeed, can she know so much about all these flowers and roots?* Her nimble fingers harvested the fresh leaves, roots, or colorful flowers, and sorted them on the sack lying across his arms. Next, she labeled each with a tiny slip of paper tied to the stem or root, accompanied by words so similar to those he had heard in Mass as a young man in Ireland. Lastly, she sent each carefully to its final destination in her side pack. All the while the screaming trio of Amy, Jeremiah, and Quincy chased basking lizards across the sun-warmed, lime rock ledges.

"So, you know how to use these plants for medicine?" Sean asked. "You don't write that on the label as far as I can tell." His education of useful plant lore began soon after and the cool but sunny morning passed even easier.

A smiling and normally shy Luanne spewed out first scientific name, then common name, then season to flower, habitat, and finally, medicinal application.

Sean simply allowed himself to enjoy her presence. He understood little that she said, and there was no question that she was the lecturer and he the student. He could only deduce that this honey-skinned woman was brilliant.

"This herb," she added a bit later in words he understood, "will make my harsh lye soap smell nice and fresh. It's spearmint. Crush it between your fingers and hold it to your nose."

Finally, after several hours of traipsing over rocky glades and along the moist, shaded sides of streams, Sean forced himself to ask the inevitable, "But how and where did you learn so much?"

"You mean to say, Irishman," she quickly answered, "that I was a slave and should know nothing?"

"No," he countered in defense. "It's not that, Luanne. Please, don't think that. I feel you should be teaching not a country bumpkin like me but a hall full of eager students."

Apparently settled by his answer, Sean watched her continue to gather and methodically sort the herbs as if she had not had the chance for years. Her earlier outpouring convinced him that she may well have hidden her talents from others for a long time. But her desire to shed no light on the origin of her knowledge confused him.

They rested for lunch on a jutting, gray ledge high on a bald knob. Luanne confided in him, "We were lucky, Sean." Her expression was the most serious he had encountered from her yet. "My husband and I were sold together a few years before the war started. Our new master even allowed us to keep the children."

Sean saw grief in her face that he had never seen before. He stopped eating his dried apples and prepared to listen to whatever she had on her mind. He watched her slowly wrap her piece of uneaten cornbread in a clean cloth and place it in a broad pocket of her dress before she looked up. *How difficult it must be with so few people to talk to*, was all he could think.

Luanne gazed out across the rolling hills and spoke again but this time with a sad faraway look in her eyes. "For slaves to be allowed to keep their children was rare. For the doctor who purchased Nathan and me, there will always be a kind place in my heart. I was only fifteen then, but I already had Amy. My new master taught me to read and write and could have gone to jail for doing so. I recorded notes in his journal as we searched out medicinal plants on prairies, in forests, and especially by the springs. He decided I was a quick learner and spoke to me as if I were a revered colleague in knowledge. He told me everything. I learned quickly."

Dark sparkling eyes studied Sean. "Am I boring you? I feel I must have bored you all morning."

Sean leisurely shook his head and took her all in. *Such intelligence and decency, more than Sydney O'Shaughnessy and an ocean beyond Gretchen. How special this woman truly is.*

"We traveled," Luanne said with enthusiasm, "through much of the countryside in the adjoining counties. We would be gone for several days at a time. Nathan and the doctor's wife kept the children." She took a deep breath and continued. "The kind doctor's methods were scientific and well intentioned. He never laid a hand on me although we spent countless nights in all seasons camping under the stars."

Luanne continued but now in a cheerless tone, "Neighbors and men from Salem burned down his fine house when it became common knowledge he had taught us to read. Two years into the war Doctor Weller died. He failed to recover from a bad case of croup, but before he caught the sickness he helped my husband escape. Nathan was ferried north by an abolitionist to a German town on the Missouri River, the same town where you said you spent the winter."

She looked intently Sean's way and wondered what secrets he held and then added, "He rafted down to St. Louis and enlisted in the army. Letters came at first. Doctor Weller had taught Nathan to read and write, too. After the summer of 1863 we did not hear from him again. Word came with returning soldiers that a regiment of colored troops had died valiantly trying to capture a rebel fort on the Carolina coast. I can only hope he died quickly."

Memories from another battle filled Sean's mind, horrible images of hundreds of black soldiers dying in a brave but hopeless attack on a rebel fortification. Then it faded away as the pleasant remembrance of good-natured Nathan sitting out of the rain by the fire echoed back to him. Then came the anguish of seeing his hanging body. *How will I ever tell her?*

Changing the subject when she saw Sean's blank look, Luanne pointed with her long and slender arm to another plant only a step away. She pulled it up by the roots before Sean could say a word. She offered it to him for inspection. "Horehound," she said. "It soothes a cough. The medicine's in the root."

Sean reached over but instead of the plant he gently clasped her hand, tall stem and all. With green eyes full of respect, the young man, so far away from his lost Irish home, dwelt on the remarkable woman he had been so fortunate to find. He asked again but this time expected no answer. "How you can know so much?" Then his free arm raised and pointed over the prairie. "I could never remember as you do."

A commotion among the children suddenly began and Sean withdrew his hand.   Jeremiah was terrorizing his little brother, Quincy. Then, in silence he witnessed how good of a mother she was as he listened to her firmly take control of the children. In only a few moments she had them back to eating their lunches and discussing the best ways to stalk a lizard. *Her husband,* Nathan, Sean thought, *had indeed been a lucky man.*

Luanne glanced his way then looked out to the hills. She smiled to no one and then answered Sean by reaching for his hand. She squeezed it gently before speaking. "I would trade all I know of herb lore for your gift of playing the fiddle."

Sean listened and took it all in. He locked on the large doe eyes that now stared back at him. A confirming nod finalized Luanne's admission.

Her compliment appreciated, he could only think to say, "Thank you, dear lady. If you so desire I'll play for you and your family, again. Tonight if you wish. I'll even teach you to play if you'd like."

All afternoon they searched the open hilly ground for new plants. "So, what is this new one in your hand, and how will it cure sickness?" He listened as she picked another and another and lectured, but his thoughts focused only on her, all of her movements, to him, having become a graceful dance.

"An herbalist," she described herself as she packed away the last specimen, "and I seek to learn more each day."

Herbs, Sean thought. He knew the word, of course. Nathan had used it. Not since working with his mother and sister, in the tiny garden just beyond the back door, had it been a familiar term. The smells of thyme and rosemary, basil and chives and his youth swirled foggily through his mind. Sean counted the time. *Six long years. Lisdoonvarna. The fair. Winning the prize. Sydney's smile.* Then he remembered his other fiddles and playing tunes among the Confederate sick and dying. *Eli. There is still that promise to keep.* He watched Luanne again, and his heart grew heavy. He had no desire, today or even soon, to leave the Weller farm.

CHAPTER 36
TRUST

A cherub faced Amy giggled as she sat on the edge of the bed. Her fist smothered much of the amusement that she attempted to hold back. Jeremiah and Quincy rolled on the floor laughing out of control. By the fireplace a silent but pleased Sean sat cross-legged twirling a twig in the flames.

In the other small room under the light of two precious candles, Luanne had listened on-and-off throughout the evening. She was pleased that Sean had offered to entertain the children. Peace for her, a rare commodity, often meant precious time to herself.

Since their simple supper of beans, new spring greens, and cornbread, Luanne had carefully sewn one colorful, rag square to another. While her skillful fingers worked she allowed herself to remember her husband, their good times, and the emptiness caused by his absence. Three years it had been. Tearful eyes guided her needle strokes as she pulled the thread around again and again.

Sean's lengthy but quiet storytelling she heard only off and on. A sudden uproar, though, summoned her to motherly duties. She rose to her feet, settled her dress, and placed herself in the doorway. Arms akimbo she asked in a tone that smacked of suspicion, "Pray tell, what are you all doing in here?"

She bit her lower lip to stifle her own amusement while Sean's gleeful eyes in the firelight said all that was needed. Her attempt to project a disciplined face quickly grew to a semi-smile as she continued to study the red-headed man across the tiny room. When both his hands lifted palms up in a gesture of innocence, she shook her head slowly, acknowledging defeat.

Luanne had suspected it before, but truly realized it now. She trusted him with her children. His heart had told her in Salem. Trusting a man with your children was special and akin to love. Her dearest of dearest continued their delightful writhings on the floor and giggling in the corner.

"Sean Kelly!" she exclaimed not able to be the actress she had hoped. "What have you told them?" Luanne was happy and sad as she asked. Here was a man who asked for nothing but food and friendship but gave her so much more. She felt safe with him although was not sure why. She had heard him scream while he slept. She had run to the barn with the shotgun and then thrown it down in the hay. There, she had comforted him as his nighttime horrors of war tore him apart. It had only been a few weeks, but she knew that he had won her and was pleased. He had not demanded her in his bed, but to keep him, Luanne thought, she would have allowed it, wanted it.

"What, Amy? What?" the exasperated mother asked, while ready to join in, just glad that her children were happy.

Skinny-as-a-rail Amy, playing her big sister part, looked up at her mother with jubilant eyes. "Sean told us a story, Momma. A silly farmer in..."

Quincy, the youngest, joyfully interrupted, "A farmer in Ireland, Momma. He sold his milk cow for a bean. One brown bean!" His laughter erupted again, and his bigger brother joined in.

Relenting, Luanne turned to the glittering, green-eyes of the Irishman sitting on her hearth. His face had formed an unbearable smirk. "Sorry," she said, "I thought, you must have been telling them a naughty story." Then she drank him in, all that she knew, his decency in fixing her cart, his eloquence in Salem's main street taming the mob, his remarkable ability with the violin, and his modesty, and yes also, the fear he inspired in the shopkeepers' and malingers' eyes when they had seen his face and his weapons. She watched him and tried to hold back, but her eyes, she knew well, had told him all.

"Goodnight, Luanne," she heard him say in his strong Irish brogue. His eyes refused to leave hers until he turned for the door.

You can have me when the children fall asleep, she silently mouthed the words to his back. *Please, stay.* Again the words refused to come. She watched the door close behind him but realized that he had understood before he had arisen to leave, and had silently but honorably declined.

Later, as Amy, Jeremiah, and Quincy curled together in sleep like puppies, Luanne sat with contentment beside the dying fire. She poked at the orange embers before she laid on another log. In that quiet time she pondered the presence of the good man who slept in her barn. She prayed devoutly that he would stay.

CHAPTER 37
SIREN BY THE STREAM

Sean gasped in guilt but also in delight. Luanne's exquisite form with silken legs, thin waist, and bare shoulders glistened in the warm April sun. He felt it impossible not to stare. Standing at the edge of the woods, he quickly glanced downstream and saw that the children were safe and harmlessly skipping rocks into a quiet pool. Nevertheless, he allowed his head to turn back towards her. He watched as she laid her threadbare dress on the sunlit rocks and on tender feet entered the cold river without a scream. He was ashamed of himself but would not look away.

First wading, now chin deep in the swirling eddy, her long hair streamed in all directions around her, then disappeared. He watched her splash and then rise from the water. She sat with her knees to the side upon a large flat rock combing out her ebony hair in the sun. Sean had thought this before but confirmed it here and now. *Luanne is the total essence of feminine beauty.* But in shame he backed away. A noisy stumble followed. He looked her away again. She appeared not to have heard.

His unintended hiding place on the forest's brushy edge fell back into the distance. He stepped lightly and made his way along the trail to the cabin, rattled by his wickedness but reliving the memory of the perfectly sculpted form at the stream. *A beautiful statue,* he thought, *like the one of bronze seen in New York City, the rock, the perfect base, holding her up, her perfect body to admire. Even after three pregnancies,* he marveled. Then he walked into the farmyard.

Guilt hung like a cloud over Sean's head while he stopped for a cool drink at the well. Refreshing water passed down but refused to wash away the image at the stream. He conjured memories from the past and how he had taken women before but never like this, never without their consent. There was no denying the disgust he felt in himself for lingering and not turning away sooner. *It was an accident to come upon her,* he told himself to push away the guilt. *Or was it?*

CHAPTER 38
THE DEATH WISH

In 'the long night beneath the wheels of her cart Luanne had given Sean all she had to give. Still bare-skinned to the cold but with a blanket draped from one shoulder, she held him as he slept. She wanted only to give him more.

Their bed between the tall wheels was snug with quilts and blankets on dry, tightly-woven cattail mats. The floor of the cart above them was their poor defense to hold back the cold of the star-filled night. Although she listened as Sean squirmed in his sleep and his fearful words described images of death and war, her deepest hopes echoed back to her lost husband. She prayed that he had never known such horrors so common in the dreams of the Irishman. Yet, she knew better.

So new to her life, yet Luanne comforted this man as a woman might a lifelong spouse. He had defended her and her children with no thought for himself. No shame, no remorse, nor pity did she feel three nights before, or now, for the five evil men who had arrived at twilight.

She had witnessed Sean's raging green eyes change to steel-gray and would never forget. How could she? He had faced them in unchallenged fury, alone. She hoped never again to see it, this evil in him that had erupted from nowhere but had saved her children.

She shrugged her shoulders and shook her body as if to dispel the bad luck she had inherited. Being a woman on her own and also having ancestors from Africa set her in a difficult place. Her fingers stroked the hair on his temple. *We've gained so much from you, Irishman.*

Luanne continued to hold Sean as he flailed in his sleep. "Wake up. It's a dream," she cooed, then dreamed herself, but bright-eyed and awake, retracing the Irishman's pathway into her life.

Only a month before, this strange man with skin so lily white and with hair so red had joined her family with open hands and heart. *Those had been special times.* But try as she might the hurtful memories of three nights past crept back. The real nightmare whirled wildly before her eyes.

⊕

Two explosions echoed through the evening turned upside-down. Then two more and another. The gunfire had come from the barn. There was no mistaking it. Held down by three men, she strained to turn her head toward the cloud of black smoke drifting her way. In torment she watched Amy, clutching her dress, run naked towards the woods. Her boys screamed from somewhere beyond the smoke. She squirmed and struggled to be free but was slapped again into almost senseless submission. Yet, again, she managed to turn her head back towards the barn. *The boys? Jeremiah and Quincy must still be alive?* The good mother grasped on to impossible hope. There was no more she could do.

But, it was not to be. She saw him. His silhouette appeared through the lingering haze of smoke. Each step through the barn's wide doorway brought him closer to her. Two men lay sprawled at his feet. His big pistol hung in his hand almost to his knee. She witnessed a harsh look fly past her to the men who had her down. They had seen him, too, and hollered above her. She screamed for justice, and then mercy. The last hard slap came down. Finally, her arms were free, but she could not move. Blood trickled into her eyes.

Remembering the foul smells of her drunken assailants made the memories stronger. Two strong men held her while another violently took her body. She felt the hard boards of the porch beneath her. Minutes before, they had laughed as they had beaten her down on her back. Her dress was pulled up around her neck. Now though, she saw panicky eyes and frantic hands reaching for weapons and trousers. Oddly, everything flowed ever slower, seeing only the faded blue legs with the yellow stripe take each new step, one then another, closer. "Too slow! Why is he so slow?" she screamed over the chaos, then found control. "Hurry, Irishman. Hurry!"

She heard a dull thud. Something heavy hit the dirt. She remembered yelling, "Irishman, hurry! Don't let them kill you!"

She wiped the blood from her face and looked up. He was there. She saw the coldness in his eyes as an attacker's head met his pistol barrel with a dull crack, and then the first, already down, was left with a smoking hole in his chest.

She saw quiet fury in him daring anyone to interfere, and she saw only panic in the last man's eyes. Fear swept over her, too. *Who is this man standing over me with steel gray eyes?*

Not able to watch, she heard another swoosh that could only be the long, black barrel sweeping down again. Nothing happened. *He must have missed. When will he say something? Surely a weapon is about to find him.*

Helpless to retreat Luanne saw the stark image of the long knife slashing up, then, the blade dripping wet. A long desperate moan from the final man told her it was done. A warm gush of blood spewed over her chest and legs. The man fell lifeless on her. She gasped in pain as her eyes were forced to open wider. Frozen in place, the stench of death was overwhelming. She had no strength and remembered how she could not have moved if God had commanded her to rise.

⊕

The memories continued to flood back. Her eyes had remained locked on the rafters of the porch roof and its oak shingles. She was terrified and could not force herself to look Sean's way. She heard and felt the thumps and groans of the dying man being lifted from her body.

A few moments later, she saw her two sons and daughter run from the side of the cabin. They knelt weeping beside her. She heard his voice above, "It's not her blood. I think she's all right. Amy, find your mother a clean dress. We'll need clean rags. A sack full."

Luanne remembered how her children appeared convinced and watched the Irishman totally unafraid. But she was afraid. Terror consumed her as she saw his hard eyes in the twilight.

Again, she forced herself not to see and allowed a great hope to settle over her, a warm blanket in winter. She looked up again. He was studying her! *Why? What will he do? What is he thinking?* And the briefest of moments stretched so long that she counted the first few stars in the new night sky.

Her humiliation kept her naked, filth-covered body rigid. Only when she again heard his voice did she understand that the horror truly had ended. Sean's gentle words gave her peace.

"Please, dear woman, take my hand." He held tight to her arm as he spoke, "I'm so sorry that I could not stop them sooner." She heard his concerned voice pause and then say, "But know, Luanne, the boys and Amy were not violated."

She remembered his eyes, emerald green now, shining in the weak light of the partly risen moon and the candle lantern brought by Amy from the cabin. Slowly, Sean pulled her up and led her to the well. There, he loosened her soiled dress and let it drop to the ground. She had only been able to watch, barely able to stand, while he drew up a pail of the most silvery water she had ever seen.

Exhausted, she did not want to go on. She wanted to die. Quivering muscles in her arms and legs reminded her of thrashing limbs and the beating that had subdued her. She had fought off the three attackers, if ever so briefly, and defiant tears ran from her eyes while she stood and studied this man now at her feet. He carefully soaked a rag in clean water.

On his knees he began. A strong male hand, absent of lust, washed away the blood and stench from her shaking body. Then she sensed it, when her shivering stopped. The warmth, as now under the cart, surrounded her despite the chilling night and the cold water that cleansed her skin. *Forever more*, she promised herself as her eyes rose to find the purest of light from a now fully risen moon. *Forever more*, she repeated in silence to the quiet of the fresh night and her *Maker*, who she knew had sent him. *Forever more, I will cherish this man as no other.*

Under the big-wheeled cart Luanne watched the stars of another night and continued to remember. She felt his reverent hands as they moved over all of her bare body and mopped away, so gently, the filth and her pain. *No one can hurt me, now*, she told herself. *No one can hurt me.*

The wet rag, soaked clean so many times, traveled her every contour, somehow cleansing more than just her skin. He soaped her down and rinsed her clean. She relished the reprieve rising from the soap's minty, strong perfume. "Kneel down on these clean rags, Luanne," he had gently asked of her. "Let me wash your hair and we'll be done." She did, and soon, the last clinging vestige of death was washed away.

Unmoving, she watched him. *Safe. His hands meant safety.* They again rinsed away her fear, and magically, she recalled, her humiliation. She also remembered with relief, how the vile man on her had not had enough time. There was little chance that he had impregnated her.

Luanne shivered again. She saw her skin glistening in the light of the stars, the moon, and the candle lantern. His sad smile and his tears she also witnessed and felt her own, now as well as then. He had kissed her on the forehead and backed away. By the well Amy had handed him other clean rags, and he had dried her. *The Irishman treats me like a queen.* He had allowed no one but himself to pull the fresh dress over her shoulders. Another surge of warmth surrounded her.

Now, three nights later, Luanne bent down and kissed his sleepy head. She whispered in reverence to the darkness, remembering his playfulness with the children, "A queen to you, my silly Irishman." The moment that the last word left her lips, a shiver unrelated to the cold night air pulsed up her spine.

She remembered how later in those desperate hours he had hitched a rope to his horse and dragged the five bodies one-by-one across the dusty yard deep into the barn. Luanne's memory of watching him on the porch, when his grizzly job ended, returned. With his back to her he sat on the rough boards clenching and opening his fists as if to cast away demons. She heard the ebb and flow of his breath in steady rhythm on that dark spring night. Only a step away she wondered what kind of man sat before her? Again, she pondered how *He* had known to send him.

Luanne allowed her mind to drift further back to the afternoon before the wicked men had come. She thought about Sean returning from the fields in time. He had worked at plowing through the late afternoon sunshine. A few rocky acres were to be sowed in corn. A sweet recollection came. She had brought him cool water from the well to ease his thirst. He had smiled, touched her hand holding the gourd, and drunk his fill. There had been no words between them. None were necessary. He had returned to his task. She had known then but could not tell him. Her mind remained in the field, unsure but really understanding. She pondered the question that probed her very essence. *Who is this man I see on such a beautiful April afternoon?* Sweat had stained his shirt as his arms forced the single blade of steel to hold its own in the furrow. *This soon to be planted corn is not for him*, she knew. *He will be gone.* His giving was only for her and her children, food for the coming fall and winter. *Our paths?* she wondered, while watching him return to his work. *How long and entwined will they be?*

⊕

Beneath bright stars and still leaning against the cart wheel, the stalwart mother-of-three conjured him again on the porch on that horrible night. She remembered her lack of will, and then her courage to speak.

"What kind of man are you?" Luanne asked Sean's silent silhouette as she posed the question in a whisper, "An avenging angel?" When no response came, she walked across the creaking planks of oak and laid a gentle hand on his shoulder.

"Sean Kelly," she said, gently turning him so her tearful eyes met his.

"Know this, Irishman," came softly as she tenderly reached for him and touched his cheek. "I have loved you since Salem when you first asked me to teach you to read."

⊕

And so, now, she held him. Her bare skin was against his on this cold spring night under her cart. Luanne was glad to have said those words. It had come out, finally. It had begun and was not to be stopped. Since the afternoon in the field when he drank her cool offering and touched her hand it had come and before. She knew it must be. To tell him on the porch of her love on that terrible night had proven the hardest of tasks. *But will he stay?*

⊕

Again Luanne was back in time. Not long after sunrise the following morning, she and the children had packed their provisions. Beside her two young sons on the cart were stowed several bushels of corn, one of potatoes, and a crock of corn meal. A precious cured ham, rolled in a feed sack, lay hidden in the hay. Three clay jugs of water hung on a side pole tied with thin cord. The sow, heavy with unborn piglets, and the milk cow followed behind.

By early evening they had put several creeks and valleys behind them. A string of tethered horses brought up the rear as the cart's tall wheels left narrow, telltale tracks. Luanne felt they were lucky to have met no travelers. All day they had crept slowly along on this narrow, muddy road,

She rarely allowed her eyes to leave the Irishman. He rode usually ahead. However now and then, while one of her sons sat on his saddle, he led on foot. She knew that as many miles as possible must be at their backs before nightfall if they were to have any real hope of escaping.

Hour after hour, Luanne felt her cart bouncing up and falling into the ruts, yet unceasingly her eyes followed him. His weapons, she saw, lay close at hand. She prayed quietly many times that day, "Lord, please, let my Irishman stay."

⊕

Sean awoke but Luanne calmed him. She wrapped the blanket

more tightly around them both. The cart's tall wheel remained her support, and she leaned back and studied all her possessions in the world. Under the night sky with the damp-before-dawn glistening on their blankets, her children slept soundly at her feet. The other precious person in her life she held tightly to her breast.

Chapter 39
Wisdom of a Prophet

As one day ran into another, Luanne taught Sean more about the medicinal uses of Ozark plants and during the long evenings spent more time with his reading lessons. Deer were plentiful near the creek crossings on the rough road south. Sean and his adopted family ate venison, wild greens, and a large tuber remarkably like potatoes that Luanne dug along the bottoms by the streams. She hoarded the food brought from the farm.

Sean played his fiddle to make the long evenings pass. It was near the end of one of those quiet evenings that he finally decided it was time. "I must tell you." His words caught in his mouth but he somehow got them out. "I...met...your husband."

"You, what?" she asked while her bright eyes squinted in the firelight.

"Before I rode into Rolla, before Bourbon, I met three men. One called himself Nathan Weller."

Luanne's muscles cramped in place. But she would not be quieted. "Tell me more," she directed while trying to hide the hardness settling into her words. In the darkness her hand reached for her shotgun.

"Three black soldiers were heading home," Sean reluctantly continued. "We camped together in a shelter cave as we waited for the river to fall for safe crossing." Sean watched Luanne's face turn to stone in the firelight.

"Go on!" she firmly commanded.

"We camped together, Luanne. Nathan, told me to visit his farm if I traveled south of Salem." Then with apprehension as he looked into her eyes, "He was a good man. His words were of an educated man. In the morning I bid him and his two friends good luck and farewell."

"What do you mean good luck, Sean Kelly?" Luanne's words were suspicious and sharp. She had returned to the real world where many white people hated others with darker skin for no more reason than their color.

"I don't want to tell you this," Sean said, "but I must, Luanne. He was killed, I guess by a mob. I passed his body hanging in a tree, south of Rolla. I'm sorry."

He tried to reach for her, but her shotgun swung menacingly to his throat. Her right thumb pulled back. The click of a hammer cocking rang like a bell. Her chest was heaving. "Before you met me at the blacksmith shop you knew his name and his story. You found me under false pretenses. You maneuvered me, Sean Kelly, knowing I needed a man so desperately."

Sean saw that she was truly ready to pull the trigger and hedged backwards. He looked into Luanne's eyes, now dim and hateful. "No, Luanne. Please, no." And then his mind began to work. "At first, I did not know your name was Weller. I swear." Unseen, he felt the heavy barrels slam against his head and instantly a veil of blackness fell.

When he awoke, he saw Luanne leaning against a tree with her children at her side. She was weeping. Her shotgun was nowhere to be seen. Instinctively, Sean reached up to the side of his head. A prime knot of swelling and soreness greeted his probing fingers.

He managed, "Nathan and I talked through a rainy evening. I played my fiddle for him and his friends. I swear, Luanne, I had nothing to do with his death. I was sickened by it."

He heard her sobbing words, "I know, Sean. I know."

A puzzled look filled his face.

He watched her chest heave with sorrow. When Luanne finally

spoke, Sean thought he was receiving the wisdom of a prophet. "Only cowards lynch Negroes, Sean Kelly. And you I know are no coward."

⊕

The entire day nothing was said. They made ten miles by early afternoon. That evening as their fire blazed, a rider challenged their camp. Sean cradled a weapon, and smiled at first when he saw the traveler's hand outstretched palm up. The other held something unseen.

"I'm a preacher, a circuit preacher. Reverend Limes is my name."

Sean slowly saw the black book in his other hand materialize in the firelight. Quickly, the traveler was befriended. Over a hefty ladling of steaming-hot corn soup, the Methodist minister spread any news he had of the area. In the morning he gladly gave them directions and was on his way.

Luanne asked Sean as the preacher rode out of sight, "He knows about us, doesn't he?"

Sean answered slowly, "I think he might."

CHAPTER 40
ABANDONED

Soon after breakfast forty miles south of Salem, her cousin's farm came into view on the outskirts of the tiny town of Rector. *Surely, they'll be safe here,* Sean hoped.

He appealed to her as he prepared to leave. "I have an obligation, Luanne. I've told you about it before. You know I care about you and your children, but my whole reason for traveling south from Hermann is in the balance. I have a debt to pay. It's something I must do. I'll come back for you." But he hesitated. "If you still want me to." He watched for a reaction but saw only a face of hard stone.

"I will return to protect your family," he promised hoping to appease her anger. Still, there was nothing in her eyes. He looked to the Weller children and then back to the woman he loved so dearly. The sad eyes of Amy, Jeremiah, and Quincy said one thing. There, he saw true affection. In Luanne's he detected a fiery emptiness that grilled him on the spit. *She must truly hate me,* was all he could think.

Sean mounted and halfheartedly looked back. No longer did she watch him. *She seems like a grand queen of Ireland. She has no time for a crofter's son, and her proud silence is meant to dismiss me from her service.* He was broken and barely managed to ride around the first bend before the emptiness came and wrung out his insides.

⊕

Luanne's mind raced to find answers. She was no man's fool. *A white man and a black woman homesteading one hundred-and-sixty acres on land the army guaranteed him? It will be impossible. What could I have been thinking? Maybe women shouldn't be educated but kept ignorant, better to stand the brunt of hardship. Reading and writing make us dream of better things, better times, better possibilities.* She watched his eyes swing to the children and again to her. Her spine stiffened and she proudly stood her ground. *He'll not be back. Besides, beating him senseless yesterday has obviously distanced him. He will never forgive me.* Painfully, she watched him mount his horse. She turned away unable to witness this awful ending to something so beautiful.

But it didn't last. She had to have one last glimpse. Without a sound she spun about to follow his departure. The hooves of his horses slowly pounded the road. His back and curling hair on his collar she expected to be the last of him she would see. She memorized the faded cloth of his great coat, the red of his hair, and the rolling hindquarters of his big roan pack horse as its tail swatted the ever present flies. Finally around the bend and out of sight, she continued to watch the emptiness of the road. The Irishman was gone. Her family was alone, again. The tears, she could not hold them back.

Luanne tried to break her silence and yell for Sean to turn around and return. For every second lost to indecision, a portion of her crumbled away, making it still more difficult to speak.

The fading sounds of creaking leather and hooves ceased. Now, too late and well beyond his hearing, she finally spoke quietly to all that remained of him, the tracks of his horses in the dust. "I'll wait for you, Sean Kelly. I will wait for you as I would wait for a long sought August rain."

Aching moments passed. Luanne gathered her children and turned dismally to the farm. She saw her cousin. His face glared at her without remorse. Her hopes shattered. *He heard me,* she thought, and sagged sadly in her worn shoes. *His scorn and that of the others will be difficult to bear. Loving a white man is not allowed.*

Then she saw it. Sean's fiddle sack hung full and bulky from the rail of her cart. *Maybe he'll come back for it.*

⊕

The ripples in the small pool raced outward in all directions then were lost in the twigs and leaves at the water's edge. Had he done the right thing this morning? Sean was dejected, nearly destroyed. He cast another pebble into the backwater of the clear stream. He had been on the trail alone for most of the afternoon. His fiddle was gone. Had it fallen off his horse? Then he remembered. *No, it's tied to Luanne's cart more than half a day's ride away. Should I go back?* But he could not face her, not today. The promise he had made to return caught heavily in his throat, and unknowingly he clenched his teeth. He cursed. The salty taste of blood filled his mouth.

Gazing beyond the clear waters of the creek, he watched with an experienced eye as his new horses, a dark Morgan and a heavier roan packing his supplies, reached for lush spring grass. They wound their tongues around the leaves then cut the stems with forward teeth. The distraction helped him. He had left Luanne and her cousin with the army nags and three others. He had kept the best animals from Luanne's attackers as his own. Both were hobbled, now, but he knew better than to let them out of his sight. He had stopped to fill his canteen and allowed them to drink. He lingered by the stream and considered a nap. But falling asleep was not an option, although the afternoon's warm sunshine enticed him.

Lost in thought Sean let his mind wander back through the day. The morning had blossomed with spring color and hope. Leaving Luanne and her children had ended that and had proved as agonizing as anything he had ever done.

⊕

Later along the trail, Luanne still plagued Sean's mind. Leaving her with relatives less than warmed by her appearance had generated mixed feelings. He had befriended the woman and her family on the streets of Salem only a month before. He realized how much they had become a part of his life. Sean told himself again that as soon as he delivered Eli's effects he would return to her. *She may change her mind. Maybe by then she'll need me.* Then optimistically he thought of the future, *If so, we'll trek to the land that awaits me on the other part of the state.* However, yet again, he relived her cold silence when they had parted. *Was it sadness or hatred?* He calculated the latter. *How could it be anything else? I was such a fool not to tell her about Nathan. Too much on my part suggests misuse of her from the beginning. But it's all water under the bridge now. It can't be fixed. What can I do?*

After a lonely sleepless night he was again in the saddle. The morning sun was warm but glared in his eyes. In the northwest a faint line of dark clouds grew larger. Trying to keep a tight rein on his animals, he looked back from time-to-time to his pack horse as it plodded along behind. The prime animal and his mount were working out. He was pleased with his progress to Eminence, although, his state of affairs with Luanne was no less painful. He brooded on his worse fears, her never forgiving him. The sad thoughts pushed him to others, and he drifted back to Hermann and Gretchen. Despite the devil in her, he acknowledged that she had soothed his pain throughout the winter. Guilt rode heavily on his shoulders for leaving his unborn child in Hermann, but his sorrows from the Missouri River town were little when compared with leaving the little village of Rector behind. His feelings came full circle. He pondered the dilemma he and Luanne faced. Her stern silence and turning from him could only mean one thing. It was done. He had begun to let her go. It was that or else wither away.

A rumble in the darkening sky foretold more misery to come. A cold rain began to fall. A dismal Sean halted his animals and dismounted. He unpacked his tattered oilskin cloak and pulled it tight around him. He rode till dark, making the best of a very bad day.

CHAPTER 41
SUSPICION AT THE CROSSING

In cheerfully anticipated sunshine Sean entered the small town of Van Buren. On the north shore of the Current River, many miles and three long rainy days since leaving Luanne, he rode down its quiet main street. He found a dry goods store and purchased beans, flour, coffee, and five pounds of bacon with a few pennies more than a silver dollar. Outside the store, he asked about the mill on the big spring that belonged to Eli's father.

"Don't know an Eli," an ancient lingerer in a cane-backed chair told him, "but have heard of Melforth." The man cleared his throat, spit, and then said, "Everyone has heard of Melforth." He added, "Sure, boy, the mill is just a few miles downstream."

Sean watched the gnarled twig of a figure twirl his pipe in his fingers as he spoke. Sean also could not miss seeing a musket leaning by his chair.

"You're no rebel by the likes of you, but beware. The miller is of that persuasion." And then as if the millwright's life was of no consequence, he finished with, "He needs hanging."

A sullen, "Thanks," passed the Irishman's lips. "I'll remember that." Then he continued on his mission and carefully stowed his provisions in the saddlebags on his big roan. When no further conversation developed, he nodded politely to the old man, and then turned his horses in the direction of the river.

Behind him, he heard an irreverent holler. "You're not the Irishman we've heard about from Salem, are you?"

The old man let out a great, "Ha!" Then a big smile crossed his weathered face as he saw Sean briefly look over his shoulder. "We may be hanging you, too, boy!"

The harsh words drew several residents to the boardwalk. One with a white apron around his waist carried a sidearm. Together the group watched with guarded suspicion as Sean rode his dark Morgan and led his pack horse slowly away to cross the swollen ford. When the Irishman had found the river road and worked his way out of sight the store owner said, "You know boys, it's probably not him. Supposed to be traveling with a slave woman and her pups. Preacher Limes told us two nights ago when he came through. He said he camped with them for a night."

The entire time the old man in the chair had kept his eyes glued on the spot in the trees where the lone rider had disappeared. Then he gave his companions a sober look. "If he were the one, it might be wise to let him be."

⊕

Sean found the Melforth grain mill before noon. He tied up his horses beside a mule in the shade of a great walnut and shouted a loud greeting to any unseen ears. "Hello there! Anyone about?" Hearing nothing but the singing red birds above him and the roar of water at the mill race, he walked up three steps to a broad-planked loading dock. A few strides later, while looking to the dark shadows inside, he called out, "Hello!" His words echoed through the great oaken timbers of the mill but went unanswered.

A sudden sound caught his attention. He listened trying to determine its origin. Muffled, bantering voices and a scuffle of sorts came from a dark corner. His instincts flared and he grabbed a rough but sturdy tool handle from a pile near the door. Sean hesitantly edged his way towards the commotion. The floorboards under his feet creaked with each step. The wooden club in his hands probed into the deep shadows as he hesitantly maneuvered toward the fray.

A maze of grinding wheels, large hand-hewn wooden gears, and multiple flour sluices, that reached up to the second floor, became visible as his eyes adjusted. A wide trap door gaped open as if luring him in. Sean slowly poked his head below the squared entrance and peered into the dark. *Just a poorly lit storage area*, he thought. A floor of sandstone flagging lay at the base of the ladder. A damp, earthy smell hit him, reminding the Irishman of sodden trenches in Virginia and then another more pleasant, apples.

Shuffling feet and a muffled scream met his ears. Sean hollered into the darkened opening, "Is their trouble, there?" While he awaited an answer, he thought over what he had heard. Clearly a woman was in distress.

A deep voice yelled up from the cellar, "Go away!" Then in broken cadence the same voice bellowed, "There...will be...no milling...today!"

The sharp slap of a hand on flesh rushed to Sean's ears. Dark laughter followed.

"Please, help me!" a shrill voice pleaded, only to be silenced by another loud smack.

Chapter 42
Meeting His Second Melforth

Sean climbed down the cellar ladder. The ax handle reached out in front of him. After few moments he saw the form of a girl half clothed and whimpering in pain. She lay on her side at the far end of the stone foundation. A dark shape loomed suddenly from the blackness. A silver gleam came for him. His holstered Colt was useless. Barely in time, the wooden handle flew up. A big-bladed knife landed, but sliced deeply into the thick handle.

Sean managed to speak but only in a whisper, "It would be best if you … ."

Amazed at his slow reactions, he barely pulled and cocked his big Colt. He eyed his attacker and made little effort to avoid this second sweep of the Bowie that arced on a deadly path to his throat.

A hesitant finger yanked the trigger. The gun's recoil pushed him back ever so slightly but enough for the thrust of the big knife to miss its mark. The echoing explosion filled the close quarters of the cellar with sulfury, choking smoke. The collapsed figure at his feet was stark proof to Sean. *Death follows me still.*

⊕

Long moments later, the smoke cleared. Sean saw the victim meekly walk forward. She stepped into the shaft of brilliant yellow light below the trap door.

"Why did you wait so long?" a curious but steady female voice asked.

Sean heard no whimpers now.

"Willis nearly cut you in half. Are you hurt?"

Sean didn't hear her. His thoughts had slipped far away. Her lips had moved but he had heard nothing. Bringing himself back, he studied her, as she him. Her words vibrated in his ears and finally registered.

"Are you all right?"

The Irishman nodded as he watched her. *What a beauty.* The oddest of thoughts filled his brain for such an unusual time. *Pretty girls often receive the worst of it, flirty or not. They need to be more careful.* To him, this one seemed to be one of those.

The young woman hesitated, unsure, but trusted her rescuer nevertheless. "You're all right?" She looked to Willis, bloodied and near motionless on the stone floor, then back to Sean. "Who are you?"

The young woman's fears brewed as she studied the slim, red-headed man in the darkness. When he stepped closer to the column of light coming down from the trap door, she saw him better. *But he says nothing. Is he no better than the animal at my feet? Will he lead me safely away?* She looked more closely at Sean and in his eyes saw only confusion.

"Yes, I'm fine," came out slowly. Then she heard, "Did he hurt you?"

The Irishman beheld long, brown hair unbound and draped in stunning disarray over soft bare shoulders. An ankle length dress and a thin petty-coat were torn in all directions revealing a bare chest covered only with slim arms and shielding hands.

"You'll be all right," he managed. Then, in gentler tones, "I'll do you no harm." Sean could tell instantly she was relieved. Behind him the man she had called Willis stirred.

Sean's breathing became deeper but easier as he relived the last few minutes. He realized how a death wish had nearly come to pass with the swift attack in the darkness. Angered with himself, Sean cursed in quiet but angry Gaelic. It had been very close this time. He had nearly allowed himself to be killed.

The last of the smoke lifted as did the cloud in Sean's thinking. Again he told himself how the man laying sprawled face down on the stone floor deserved much more than a bullet in the chest. Sean thought with maliciousness but also envy, *The villain was lucky to fall so quickly.*

The young woman covered herself as best she could with the tatters of her torn dress but hesitated to make the attempt at crawling up the ladder. Sean studied her as she made a determined effort to stand taller and extend him a hand.

Looking into Sean's eyes she said, "My name is Emma and you?" When her rescuer only nodded, she totally put herself at his mercy and reached up with her foot for the first step. A few rungs up the ladder and her legs tuned to jelly. "I can't go higher. I need your help."

Sean moved to the ladder, and there, he gently braced Emma as she climbed from the cellar. His right hand still firmly grasped his revolver.

Making the last step and out, Emma disappeared into the shadows. He reached up to a rung and prepared to pull himself into the sunlit room above. Abruptly, he felt something hard and cold against his temple. The painful pressure of cold steel pushed his head sideways. His eyes moved to the right. There, he saw what could only be the long black barrels of a shotgun.

"Move and you are dead!" The command came unseen and believable but in a feminine tone. The convincing voice kept on, "Should shoot you where you stand!"

Sean's head was just above the level of the mill floor and the large gun was all he could see. His Irish mind was racing. *Have I come so far through all these years of bloodshed only to fall back into the hole with the animal that I have sent to hell? And by an unknown woman, to boot?* He felt he must be blushing in embarrassment but he was beyond caring for his own safety to feel fear.

A sudden urge prompted the Irishman to demand, "Fire away, madam. I suppose I deserve his hell."

"Stop, Nora! Don't shoot!" Emma screamed. Sean guessed her position near the outside door.

"Nora, stop! He shot Willis."

Sean vaguely made out the shadowed figure of the handsome woman that he had saved from dishonor. He heard again a plea for the pardon of his sentence of death.

"Sister, one of the McLauds is in the cellar shot through, and rightly so!"

The big barrels at his head remained, and Sean focused on a chin high mill stone with uneasiness. He could see little else. Nevertheless, ever so slowly he saw the gun lift. He sensed the bearer's hesitation, but he knew she would have had no qualms in blowing his brains out just as she had said.

"Come up, red-haired man," the hard voice commanded. "Show yourself!"

The Irishman complied. Steadily, he climbed out and his arms perched on the floor boards above the ladder. His revolver still dangled from a little finger but now touched on the dusty, mill floor. He set it carefully down while the protector's lethal weapon remained pointed his way. Studying the dark recess in the room, he finally found the shaded but steady eyes above the shotgun. Sean fruitlessly searched their depth hoping to see compassion and gratitude. What he saw confused him.

⊕

Rising up another rung, a beam of sunlight from a high window glared in his eyes. He could barely see the bearer of the shotgun. Only as she stepped toward the brightness did he observe the woman called Nora with any clarity at all. The long barrels remained trained two fists from his head. A quick breath, he was sure she took in. Her hair, the furthest from brown as was possible, hung long and golden below her shoulders, the only portion of her in the sun.

"Nora, all is well!" came quickly from the shadows, he guessed, from the dark-haired sister. "This man saved me from Willis McLaud."

Nora spoke again but now with wavering confidence, "Up you! Out of the cellar! I must see you better!" A pause, then, "Be quick!"

Sean obeyed. He pulled himself the final steps from the musty darkness.

⊕

Nora gestured to her dark-haired sister to move. "Outside, Emma, away from him."

Emma sensed unknowns concerning the young man whom she guessed to be Irish. In a sudden rush she saw Nora back up against a wall as if seeing a ghost. Emma heard her sister's breathing come heavy, yet forced a smile and saw her confused rescuer catch it. Still cocked, she saw that her sister's shotgun still pointed at the man.

Sean again heard from Emma in the shadows, "Don't shoot him, Nora! Lower your shotgun! My God, sister, the man saved me. Haven't you heard anything I've said?"

By now Sean's hands were high in the air. His pistol remained on the floor to let anyone else, if there were others in this mill, know his peaceful intentions. He pondered in deep, silent examination. *What have I done to stir up this brave, fair-haired woman*?

"Shoot me if you must, dear lady," he finally said, caught in the cold, questioning look of the hellion on the other end of the scatter-gun. "End my pain, or please, put down your weapon."

Each held the other's eye, then gradually Sean watched the smooth bore dip to the floor. Gladly he heard the hammers let down. To his amazement, the mysterious young woman who had completely held him at bay turned in a flurry and ran from the mill. Puzzled, he looked through the open door and saw her glance toward his horses. He heard a jumbling of words as she held her skirts up with one hand and the shotgun in the other. "If you... be .... where is...?"

Baffled not by Nora's defense of her sister but of her flight, Sean recalled her determination only moments before. There had been no question in his mind when he looked in her eye. *Without a doubt the fair-haired Nora had been prepared, if the need arose, to take my life. Yet, when she knew her sister safe, why so suddenly had she lost heart and run away?*

⊕

Nora Melforth raced across the loading dock and then down the steps to the road. She spied the Irishman's mount and pack horse. Her words were muted but came fast and furious, "If you be Sean Kelly, where is your fiddle?" There was no evidence of the fragile instrument on either animal. Barefooted like her sister and laden with the heavy shotgun, a puzzled Nora jogged up the dusty lane and quickly left her father's mill behind.

⊕

Emma spoke first. "Don't know what's happened between you two. You scared her." She studied Sean with more than a casual look. "Nora doesn't scare easily. It's as if she knows you." Emma had allowed her words to come out slowly as her clever eyes ran over her rescuer.

To Sean the pretty girl before him appeared with each moment more beautiful. Surely, the girl was not over sixteen or seventeen. Bewildered but alive, he attempted to regain his mental footing. Her bare breasts were only covered with an arm. With great effort he forced his eyes up to the young woman's face.

"My sister is gone, now," Emma said. "Best to holster your revolver. My father might be here any moment. He has been known to shoot first and ask questions later, especially concerning his daughters."

She laughed and he liked it. "Truly!" she added to speed the process. Then, turning her bare back to Sean but seemingly more worried with her hair than her exposure, two hands reached up to straighten the long tangled strands. Finally, she looked over her shoulder with glittering dark eyes and said, "My name is Emma, Emma Melforth."

After her exhibition, Emma covered herself with one arm holding up a shred of her damaged dress while her other hand reached towards Sean. A confident smile filled her face. She took his arm. "Let's walk to the house. The McLaud boy may lie where he will until my father decides what to do with him."

Emma promenaded with her arm latched tightly around Sean's elbow. Out onto the grist mill's large loading porch and into the bright sunshine they passed. The lovely girl that Sean beheld with adoration adjusted her torn dress, stopped, and then, with the confidence of a queen bestowing favors in her court, rose up on her tip toes and placed a delicate kiss on his cheek. All memory of the incident in the cellar left him.

His mind swirled. He barely heard Emma say, "I thank you, sir. You are a good man. Please, escort me to my family and the safety of my home."

Sean formed a wry smile. *This one has spunk.* They walked and finally his thoughts raced back to the cellar and the man he had shot down. His insides caved into jelly, and he grasped her arm for support.

"Thank you," he said.

Sean guessed that she heard him but his thinking was dreamy and far away.

"I don't know your name, but my family will welcome you when they hear how you came to my aid. Come. It is but a short walk on the wagon track. There, through the trees." Then Emma noticed his limp and questioned, "Are you hurt?"

Sean held firmly to her arm and managed, "I'll be fine. Your fine company has me on the mend."

Lovely Emma strolled with him down the small road. She pointed to a cabin.

With one arm still holding the remains of her torn dress and the other in Sean's, Emma smiled as if nothing of interest had happened. She kept on the track to her father's house nonetheless, more concerned whether the man on her arm was of Irish or Scottish lineage. Her father despised the Papist Irish but loved the Presbyterian Scots.

Then from Sean's point of view, *Splendid is the word that best describes this young woman.* He finally found the sense to answer her question, "No, pretty lassie." His Irish accent and manner came out strong. "Not hurt today, but at other times during the war." Sean paused while any courage within him drained away and added, "It was indeed lucky I had business at the mill today."

Emma's radiating essence held Sean spellbound. Knowing that her power did not include reading his thoughts, she exclaimed, "Lucky indeed! Pray tell what business was that?" She squeezed his arm and gave him a doubtful look. "I saw no grain sacks tied to your pack horse."

When no answer came, Emma accepted his silence. She gave Sean a bright smile, and then continued leading her rescuer up the wide green valley cut in two by a clear rushing stream.

Chapter 43
Nora Hides Her Story

Sean listened as Emma cupped a hand by her mouth and called loud and long for her father. From the covered front porch of the broad cabin the unlikely pair anxiously awaited the millwright. How to politely tell the man about Eli and surrender her effects baffled Sean, but he told himself to deal with the painful issue as soon as possible. Only then would he be free to find his way back to Luanne and her probable wrath.

Who could be no other than Melforth suddenly appeared. In long strides the broad shouldered man paced from the barn armed to the teeth. A double-barreled shotgun lay pointed threateningly towards the newcomer. Sean saw two hammers back on the fearful weapon, and wondered how many menacing Melforths remained and with how many shotguns.

Sean looked again with despair at yet another tool of death leveled at his chest,   and the man holding the weapon was not alone. His fair-haired daughter was at his side and also armed. Off to the side of the cabin a younger dark-haired girl held a pistol while she shooed the rest of the brood deep into the field.

Gradually, he felt his heart return to a slower beat when the black maws of the miller's weapon moved slowly from his chest and found targets in early May's blue sky. That Nora still appeared belligerent struck Sean as odd.

Upon seeing her older sister and father greeting her rescuer in such a threatening manner, Emma burst out angrily, "Papa, has Nora not told you what happened?"

Emma's graying, steady-eyed father nodded acknowledgement. He then motioned Sean to a sawn stump a few steps from the porch. He in turn walked to the edge of the porch with a daughter at each hand. His strong southern accent was apparent as he broke his silence, "Sir, please, sit." Then realizing other unfinished fatherly duties, he commanded, "Emma, get another dress! Modesty has never been your greatest virtue." He turned towards the three young faces that he expected to see in the knee high wheat. The millwright called, "Come, children! The stranger is no robber!"

Last of all, while he examined the outsider and then Nora, a perplexed look came across his face. He had caught the intense look of his fair-headed eldest upon the man whom he guessed might be Irish or Scottish.

Silence held a heavy hand as Robert Melforth and Nora sat together uncomfortably on the porch, studying the newcomer on the log before them.

Sean caught Nora's eye for a brief moment, only for her to turn quickly away. *There was no doubt she could be Eli's sister*, he thought, but he couldn't tell for sure. It had been well over a year, closer to two, since he had promised a dying soldier to bring her effects back to her family. He had no cameo or scissor cut paper silhouette to help him remember.

How exactly Eli did look, he couldn't say, now. Time erased faces. He had known her for so little time, during a single night a year before the war ended. Sean cast a broad smile to the one sister by her father and the other parading out the cabin's door. Sean knew the brave woman he had left dying in Virginia on that hot summer's day certainly had left some high spirited sisters behind. Had Eli Melforth said four or five? He couldn't remember.

That the journey from Hermann to the mill on the big spring was completed gave him satisfaction. He studied the three Melforths before him. Eli had not been a dream after all.

The Irishman glanced at the small green patch of corn and the larger field of heading wheat beyond it, and he beamed a big smile to the youngest girls of the Melforth clan who watched him. Then Sean remembered his fingers blackened by the dye from Eli's hair and his gaze fell on Nora. Her flaxen tresses fell down beyond her shoulders but were not nearly as long as the other girls. Her figure was slight as was Eli's. Questions filled his mind.

"Pardon me, good man," the stout miller began with ponderous politeness. "These are trying times."

Sean was pleased to see the father's shotgun lying across the man's knees.

Then with quiet dignity the miller said in his strong southern accent, "My name is Robert Melforth. These are two of my daughters, Nora the oldest, and Emma, second. Both it appears, you have already met." The royal return of the dark-headed, now fully dressed Emma, moments before, had fully garnered Sean's attention.

Pausing, Melforth then asked with a deep and steady voice, "And yourself?"

As always when he spoke, Sean's Irish brogue betrayed his heritage. A slow and diminutive, "Sean Kelly, sir," left his lips as he raised his hand to Melforth's. "Sorry, we have found each other on such distressing terms. However, I was seeking you," and he countered quickly, "and in good faith, sir." Sean saw the questions grow in Melforth's eyes as their hands firmly came together.

Perplexed, Melforth asked, "What business would you have with me? Millwork I could only suppose. Are your sacks of grain awaiting me?"

Surprising all present, Nora interrupted, "Milling, I am sure." Her family threw her strange looks as she studied hard the man sitting across from her. She found the scars on his face where they should be, and then fleetingly looked to her sister. She demanded of Emma, "Tell us what happened at the mill."

Robert Melforth merely nodded, settling back. His eldest daughter had again taken charge. He formed an understanding but proud smile. *When had she not?*

Sean watched the millwright and his daughter's exchange and

sensed that ruling the roost seemed Nora's way. The Irishman wondered about the strong bond Eli and this other fair-haired sister must have shared. However, why had she run away? It wasn't fear in her eyes he had seen. He asked, "Your other daughter, Mr. Melforth? I've come..."

And again, Nora interrupted with a chorus of demands for her other younger sisters, "Bring the visitor to the well. The very least we can do is give him a cool drink." To her father, "We'll deal with Willis later." She didn't leave Sean's side as he was shown the path by Lilly, the youngest of the sisters.

Sean found himself escorted behind the cabin, near the garden. A fine stone-encased well lay at his feet. A shingled roof covered it. Before he knew it, a bucket was thrown and drawn up. More thirsty than curious of what remained hidden from him and apparently her family, he waited for the appearance of more clues, but soon found himself uncaring. A cooling gourd of clear water from the freshly drawn bucket slid down his parched throat. Still another over his wrists and face silenced his concern. He smiled to the fair-haired daughter, "Thank you, Miss Melforth. It was what I needed most." Her smile shot back hard and calculated, encrusted with suspicion. But Sean could neither grasp its depth nor cared to pursue its intention.

Soon, Emma related the dismal tale from the morning. "Mr. Kelly appeared," and as the words were spoken she affectionately turned Sean's way then back to her father and four sisters, "a red-haired angel from heaven." Then a hardy, "Thank you, good sir," fell from rosy lips to Sean's adoring ears.

To her father Emma said, "You know the McLaud boys. Their urges have fermented over much of the winter and spring. You've seen Willis McLaud, father." He set upon us as we passed the old tannery downstream.

Robert Melforth nodded to confirm Emma's allegations.

Sean watched Emma's chest rise and fall before she continued with her story. "He always was getting my attention in any crude or loud way which he could conceive, including threats. He was convinced that I was his woman. He meant to have me, whether I consented or not."

Nora mentioned that once in her presence the hopefully dead McLaud had brandished his pistol in a threatening manner.

Emma interrupted while her eyes admired her older sister, "Only to have Nora, whom he least expected, pull a knife from the deep pocket of her dress."

The father of five daughters found a crack in the competing words of Emma and Nora. "Nora, you didn't tell me of this."

Then Emma reassured, "Don't worry, papa. Nora protected me."

The words jolted Sean but he let them recede. The younger daughters, pixies he conjured, were dancing and pirouetting at the side of the porch as Emma's story had unfolded.

"Don't mind them, Mr. Kelly," Robert Melforth said betraying both amusement and pride in the antics of his youngest girls. The family's patriarch smiled as he said to his visitor, "Pray, continue, my resolute, Nora."

Nora finished the tale in a calm tone as she grinned at her more feminine sister. "I had the blade to his throat before he could level his pistol."

In shock, Sean continued to listen. He expected these words from Eli, but not from his new acquaintance, Nora Melforth. "The McLaud dropped his pistol and fled," Nora continued, "sending curses and threats behind him to both of us." Somehow, Nora's words sent his thoughts along another avenue just beneath the surface. Lovely Luanne, he wondered? How angry was she? Was she in good hands? Were the children safe?

"But what of Willis?" Nora asked her father.

"Let him bleed," were Emma's words.

Her father nodded. "We'll deal with him soon enough."

All eyes came back to Nora. Sean studied her intently. Where had he known her before? Was a ghostly Eli sitting before him? But no, the soldier Eli Melforth was dead. Her loving description of her sisters and father had mentioned no Nora. However, that had been long ago. He could easily be mistaken.

While the girls quibbled back and forth at the end of the porch a vision flowed from the recesses of his mind. Instead of here with the Melforths, Sean saw himself on the porch of a cabin near a fine clear stream with its larger sister flowing below. His daughter's hair was golden in the sun and her nose was long and straight, so much like several of Robert Melforth's girls. So welcome and accepted for the moment with the Melforth's, Sean's bewildered mind refused to fit the puzzle together. *Eli is dead*, rolled over and over in his mind.

Emma acknowledged her elder sister's story, "Nora's a wildcat indeed! A month ago it happened." With a sly smile she continued, "I've noticed Nora carrying a shotgun on a much more regular basis."

Robert Melforth interrupted again. His face was flushed with anger when he said, "Neither of you told me any of this!"

"And for good reason, father!" Nora exclaimed. "Our time here on the banks of the Current River is marked. To have you killing or harming a McLaud for any reason would only give our vengeful neighbors an excuse." Clearly upset as she spoke, Nora explained how the Melforths' position as southern sympathizers after a war they had lost created a difficult and dangerous position for all in her family.

"You and father's southern pride will get us all killed," Emma spoke up again. "Except, dear sister, I'm pleased to have you come to my aid, even though," she turned and smiled at Sean, "you almost filled the man who saved me with Missouri mined lead."

To Sean's mind too swiftly, Nora again took charge, "Daddy, you and Mr. Kelly need to deal with the body in the mill and his mule. Hopefully, no one passing by has taken notice."

With those words from Melforth's most outspoken daughter, both men preceded back to the mill with Nora a few steps behind.

"I thought you wanted us to take care of this, daughter," the miller said to his trailing first born.

"I should best be along, too, Daddy," Nora countered as her fast moving bare feet kept up. Her ever-present shotgun was slung over her narrow, tanned shoulders and bounced a bit with her every step on the rusty colored lane.

Despite the grizzly work that lay ahead, Sean's mind remained on his promise to Eli and also his promise to Luanne, the woman who still held his broken heart. The image of her by the river in early April filled his senses but was quickly painted over by her cold empty stare when they parted.

Nora looked to the far corner of the mill while all three trudged up the steps to the loading dock. "His mule is gone!" she hollered.

Nora's reconnaissance provoked her father to rush into the mill. Sean was hot on his heels through the shadows. Waiting above while Melforth rapidly negotiated the steep ladder down, it took only moments before a call came up from the darkness. "There's no one here, only a pool of blood."

Sean looked down to the planked floor. His eye quickly caught the tell-tale red splatters that ran in a line away from the gaping hole in the floor. Then from the bright sunshine outside Nora's voice rang clear. "Found his mule!"

Both men ran outside. Nora was holding the reins of a nervous animal. Spots of blood smeared its saddle.

"It was in those woods near the river," she reported before they could ask. She pointed towards the fast flowing Current River. Then, she addressed her father with a sassy grin and without a trace of remorse, "I think Willis McLaud must have gone for a swim."

Nora led Sean and her father to the river's edge. The fast flowing spring flood revealed nothing at first. Then all three saw it at once, a bright red patch of blood on a log by the shore.

CHAPTER 44
SETTLING IN

The body of the McLaud boy was never found. Robert Melforth guessed that the swollen river had carried it far downstream to be lost forever in a deep pool. The dead man's mule proved a more difficult matter. The miller and Sean stripped it of tack and took the animal as far from McLaud ground as possible. There, in an impenetrable plum thicket it was shot and quickly covered with brush and leaves and left to the opossums and beetles. They burned the tack on a brush pile near the Melforth cabin. Emma ran through the ashes with a rake to catch any of the metal buckles. They were almost thrown into the stinking mire of the outhouse.

"They'd look there, Emma," Nora said. "Go now to the fastest rapids and cast these last bits of metal to the Current's waters."

Sean, Emma, and her father all silently agreed while Nora added, "The rushing sand and gravel of the river will quickly cover and hide proof of a McLaud's presence."

Melforth worked to rid his mill of any lingering smells that a dog might pick up. He spread vinegar liberally in the cellar and wherever the McLaud boy had walked or lain. Mercifully, a heavy spring rain fell long and hard that evening and then settled in for two days. Any odors outside the mill that a fine-nosed dog might have detected were washed away. However, the blood inside gave

Melforth the greatest worry. Fear of the McLaud clan ran deep. Their hunting dogs were well known along the Current River as trackers of deer, wild hogs, and men.

⊕

Sean's third day in the valley of the big spring produced a fine sun and blue sky, and Robert Melforth asked if he would make himself useful in the mill. Consenting to the miller's suggestion that payment would be in the form of food, the barn for lodging, and two dollars a week, they shook hands on a verbal contract. Before a day's work was done, Melforth's pleasure was unmistakable. He had observed in Sean a natural affinity for machines. Able to imagine the inside workings of a gear box or bran separator, Sean immediately had won over Melforth, even if he was Irish, a Catholic, and a Yankee. A clear lack of laziness also proved a plus, although his crippled leg slowed him down.

A man from up river took Sean aside the third day at the mill. Gaunt and with ancient piercing eyes, Jonas Berryman roughly introduced himself while they stood alone on the loading dock. Then he got to his real business. "Heard you were here. You'll need be worried, Irish. We burned out a settlement of Papists not long ago in what we call the Wilderness along the Eleven Point River." Berryman's implied threat was understood but had caught Sean totally off guard.

Sean shrugged off the man's words and went back to work. That evening after supper he confronted Melforth about Berryman's story. The millwright confirmed the old man's words.

"Were the Irish settlers trespassing?"

"No, they had proper papers for their land."

"So, your friends and neighbors stole their land?" There was no missing the building anger in Sean's voice.

"Sean, no man, woman, or child was killed." Then the miller proclaimed as if it were gospel, "Our raid kept the Papists from getting a foothold in nearby Oregon County."

Sean was speechless as Melforth continued. "You also will be expected to leave in due time. Right now, I owe you for helping

Emma, and I need a good hand in the mill." Then, as if it made everything right, "And you need the work."

Melforth's last words set the Irishman to walking. He made every attempt to hold back his fury while he searched out the source of the clear stream that powered the mill wheel. Sean spent the remainder of the daylight contemplating the upwelling surge of the big spring's waters. While he sat on a huge rock beside the flow his fingers constantly turned over Eli's *lucky piece* in his pocket. Later, a restless night passed to a sleepless dawn as he wondered in disgust how people along this beautiful river could be so filled with hate.

Chapter 45
Alluring Emma

Three days in the valley of the big spring quickly turned into a week, and Sean now claimed a place at the supper table. He put aside the hard words of the miller and his promise to Luanne allowing only the joy of the younger children's innocence, Emma's beauty, and Nora's mysterious ways to fill his thoughts.

Although the Irishman was enjoying the company of the miller's family, he craved his fiddle. One evening as a single candle burned and after Violet, the middle daughter, had read the Bible verses her father had instructed, Sean asked, "Mr. Melforth, do you know of a family along the river who might have a fiddle?"

His words made Nora suddenly more alert. She listened closely.

"You play?" asked the delighted father and millwright.

"Oh, certainly, sir. But sadly my instrument was left behind near Salem."

Lilly and Melanie, the youngest but far from being shy, chimed in, "Hooray, a fiddler! Now we can dance!"

Nora stepped back from the candle light and watched her family and the man she had known so briefly but so well almost two years before. Her thinking was pained but glad. Pained because his presence meant a greater chance for her father to learn of her actions during the war, and glad because Nora remembered well the power of the Irishman's hand on his bow and also on her heart.

Robert Melforth answered, "I'll ask patrons at the mill, Sean. I'm sure a stray fiddle is to be found and needing a good sawing to keep fit."

⊕

Cool nights near the cold, gushing spring always followed hot days. Almost everything went well between Sean and the Melforth family. The Irish newcomer's work ethic and good manners built trust. That no one mentioned Eli still confused Sean. He allowed the issue to simmer. His life with the Melforth's had become too good to spoil in any way.

The younger Melforth daughters proved delightful. Sean enjoyed the good side to their behavior while their father dealt with the stern discipline that was occasionally needed. It became as it was with his sister in Ireland and with Luanne's children. When in the company of Lilly and Melanie he focused on only these two gallivanting little gypsies. Their playful antics helped him to briefly forget his bad memories.

Melforth salvaged a fiddle of below average quality from a downstream neighbor, and the younger daughters and also shy, dark-haired Violet had not forgotten their promise if Sean obtained an instrument. Dancing young princesses, the Irishman called the three. The girls swirled and pranced as long as Sean conjured up time-honored Celtic tunes. Often the girls would hum the melody of a song and would be delighted when he would quickly pick it up. If he played it once, the music became a part of his great store of tunes locked away in his memory to be played again.

Sean wanted to pull his own fiddle from its sack and play, and wished again that he had not left it hanging from Luanne's cart that hard day. He remained unsettled with his distraction of the promise to Luanne. No answers had come about Eli, yet he chided himself for not asking. Regretfully, he realized that fewer and fewer times each day his thoughts returned to the woman he had cleansed at the well. Evenings among the Melforths pleasantly came and too quickly passed. Each added to the lengthy string of time that pressed May to June and then ever closer to July. At arms-length, images so willingly created by Robert Melforth's lovely daughter, Emma, reigned provocatively.

⊕

Sean unwittingly made a fool of himself concerning Emma. A long graceful neck and finely chiseled features complimented her beautiful, dark eyes. She was a magnet that lured him, and his thoughtful appraisal proved hard to control. The rest of the family saw what he could not and inwardly expressed amusement at his infatuation, but not Nora. She painfully looked on pretending indifference.

"Mr. Kelly, more hot cakes or coffee?" Robert Melforth's lovely second born asked. "Well, Mr. Kelly?" Emma asked again as she and her sisters looked on. Violet threw the others a perceptive smile, and the two youngest giggled outright. Emma's sweet voice brought Sean into the here and now. "Hot cakes or coffee, Mr. Kelly?"

Immediately, he broke his dumbfounded look that had been only upon the young woman. "Sorry!" he finally said. Then, he turned to face the others and their knowing smiles. He knew that the fair skin of his face and neck must be beet red.

"Sean is blushing! Sean is blushing!" squealed the nine-year-old Melanie.

So beautiful, Sean thought, pushing his foolish thoughts away. Yet, despite the sisters' joking, his eyes, while pretending detachment, soon found their way back to Emma before the breakfast meal was finished.

After a long day in the mill and a good supper, Sean politely left the gathering. He was embarrassed again concerning Emma. Out the back door he admired the beauty of a setting sun on Robert Melforth's many projects. He began to stroll through the well pruned orchard that filled the side yard. There, among mature apple and peach trees surrounded by the valley's cool evening air, he watched a western sky basted with light. The brilliance of the sunset colors calmed his spirit and his thoughts of Emma. He found his bare feet carrying him slowly in between the trees. His hand repeatedly touched the low spreading branches draped with small fruit.

His curiosity stirred as he reached out to several branches and examined a variety of apples. Interested in the fullness of an apple at such an early time in the season, Sean reached up and pulled one down. The feel of the hard, unripe fruit in his hand took his mind to other times. Growing and harvesting had once been his life. His embarrassment at the supper table was forgotten as he rolled the apple between his fingers and contemplated its early red color. *So different*, he thought, *than the russets and other northern apples we picked while walking over the farm roads of home in Ireland.* Taking a tiny bite, Sean remembered never seeing an apple so large so early. The unripe sourness of the crisp flesh brought back memories of summers on the move with the Union Army. Green apples had caused many soldiers a belly ache.

"Arkansas Black," a mellow masculine voice informed him from the cabin's back door. "It's a dependable late summer variety. Not ripe now but a good keeper. Can be eaten in August but is best in September when it goes black." Pausing, he then said, "Are you familiar with southern apples?"

Sean said he wasn't and the miller began an orchardist's lecture on the merits of the Arkansas Black, Ben Davis, and Grimes Golden or as we call it, Bell Flower. Sean realized this miller knew much more than the mechanics of grinding grain. He asked, "How can they ripen so early? August and early September apples would be a treat. Only sauce apples ripened so soon or so I thought."

Mr. Melforth explained, "Apple trees from Georgia and North Carolina were brought to the river front areas along the Mississippi by settlers who had moved from the East. Several old timers with knowledge of grafting and breeding managed to push the ripening times back to late summer with the help of the warmer spring weather here."

"They'll be sweeter in another month or so," Melforth told Sean as he watched the Irishman cautiously take a second but smaller bite.

He's right, thought Sean. *The crisp flesh speaks of sweetness to come.* Then Melforth continued, "You realize that most of our apples will go into cider, but the later ones will make the better juice. It's the best way, besides keeping some tucked away in the mill's cellar, that we can avoid spoilage. And besides," he said with a laugh, "hard cider is good for what ails you."

Agreeing with Melforth, Sean again found himself thinking of the incident at the breakfast and supper table. He apologized to his host. "I am sorry Mr. Melforth. Emma is very beautiful. It is hard to keep my eyes from her." Then, after of moment of reflection and looking eye-to-eye with Emma's broad shouldered father the Irishman politely added, "Sir, I will try to do so in the future."

The sire of five daughters studied Sean long moments before saying anything. "I appreciate your apology and your honesty," he began. "It's a show of good manners that I did not expect from a Yankee or a Catholic Irishman."

Hesitating and then again choosing his words carefully, the miller spoke in a subdued tone while looking westward to the building colors of the sunset beyond the ridge, "Emma turns the heads of too many young men as did her mother...." He paused and cast Sean a forlorn smile. "You seem a good lad, Sean. Your behavior in these last few weeks has shown me." A long silence proved more than Sean wished. He was glad when the miller finally spoke. "You and your fiddle are welcome to stay with us until my mill stones slow in early winter."

Sean took the miller's words as a tardy thank you for his rescue of Emma. Melforth was a quiet sort and their brief time together was teaching him the importance of kind words from a man with few to spare. Sean couldn't claim to see friendship in the miller's eyes but he did see respect.

Then, Robert Melforth obviously remembered something and said, "These apples are exceptionally early this year. Spring began in late February with no late killing frost." Then as he turned preparing to leave, he paused and pursued another thought. "And Sean, best be wary. A neighbor's bull is loose in the pasture by the river."

Sean nodded, awaiting more of an explanation. Quickly though, the miller's interest turned to his cabin. Inside, the riotous, happiness of young women filled the twilight. Sean watched the effect on the father as he was drawn to his loving brood. In the dusk the Irishman smiled a wry grin only for the sunset. His conversation with the miller had proved an agreeable diversion.

Sean continued to follow the colors until they went to gray. A gentle hand touched his elbow. Startled, he turned about. To his pleasure a smiling Emma stood at his side.

"Hello, Sean," he heard whispered in a sweet tone from the goddess of the household. Together for a few quiet moments they watched the first stars.

Then pulling his arm to follow her and telling Sean to watch for snakes, she led him across the yard. He followed, unable not to.

"This is our time," he heard her murmur.

Pleased with Emma's closeness, Sean tagged along with her to the barn. Abruptly, she turned a corner into the open doorway and stopped. His kidnap concluded, she grasped both of his hands, coaxing them towards her hips.

Emma looked up into his face. The Irishman's eyes reflected only dim reminders of the day. She spoke to the gentle man, "I heard my father talking to you. You have gained high praise from a man from whom praise comes with great difficulty. And the bull he mentioned, Sean, is not to be trusted. It ran someone down before you came into the valley. Later in the week my father plans to help its owner corral and nose ring it."

Emma's easy manner told Sean that she had other things on her mind besides her father and a mad bull. Pleased, he watched the lovely young woman rise on her tiptoes and place her slim arms around his neck. To her kiss, Sean had no trouble in making an expected response.

Pausing, Sean noted Emma's reaction. He touched her chin with his fingers, and she kissed his hand. That Emma found pleasure with his experience in these matters wiped his slate clean. His embarrassment for earlier boyish stares and stumbling in her presence evaporated. He watched her fingers loosen the raw hide tie on his shirt. Luanne was forgotten.

Whether her advances were well planned, practiced, or both, Sean knew not.   Nevertheless, he enjoyed her hands on his body as she allowed him, encouraged him, to hold her waist. Sean was more than hungry for a woman, especially this young woman whose legs were already wrapped around his waist. He leaned her firmly up onto the rounding curve of an oversized log in the barn's rough wall.

Contentment blotted out other obligations as he allowed the smell of the woman in his arms to fill him. His own experience demanded he go slow, but Emma seemed on a different schedule. She cooed into his ear, "Take off your trousers, you silly Irishman." When he complied, her giggling quickly ceased.

Not long after, their dressing in the darkness was hastily completed. Sean noted that Emma held him only briefly before beginning her return to the house. *Already the magic is fading. Would it last past tomorrow?* He doubted it. Her cool reactions to him physically, afterwards, now explained her feelings about their tryst, an act of animal pleasure of the moment or maybe, a payment. So, with disappointment, Sean prepared himself to bid his impromptu lover good night.

Walking arm-in-arm to the cabin, Emma turned her face up and whispered, "Was that a nice enough thank you for your rescue at the mill?"

Sean said nothing. He reluctantly smiled as he watched Emma enter her home, and then retraced his steps. His private nest in the small loft of the barn awaited him, and later while lying on a blanket over loose hay, Sean considered the vibrant woman in his arms earlier, and then the events of the week as the loft's wide doorway framed the bright night sky. Watching the heavens and waiting to see a shooting star, he pleaded with what he hoped was a merciful God. He prayed that his torturous dreams would cease for the night. Brilliant but tiny pin pricks of light shone through the opening and soothed him. *Surely, tonight,* he hoped, *sleep will come easier.* But he doubted it when a wave of buried guilt concerning Luanne rushed uncontrollably into his drowsy thinking.

CHAPTER 46
A PLEASANT EVENING
GONE AWRY

"**B**ut you will annoy Sean to his limits," Robert Melforth scolded. Then to the jovial Irishman who was being tickled unmercifully by Melanie and Lilly, "Sean, you need not consider escorting the princesses Lilly and Melanie to the river. I will take them tomorrow." Always worried about his eight and nine-year-old girls finding precarious circumstances at the drop of a hat, Melforth hesitated. *I seldom let the two out of my sight in the evenings, nor*, he thought appreciatively, *did Nora during the day*.

However, the reluctant miller gave in to his daughters' wishes when Emma whispered in his ear, "Remember his actions in May. His motives are those of a gentleman. You could have no better nanny than Sean, believe me."

Aloud to all, Emma said with a laugh, "Sean, I wish good luck your way!"

As a parting thought the grateful father again gave Sean an avenue to politely retreat from his youngest daughters while the two pounced on Sean with glee. He offered, "I have little worry about Melanie or Lilly. It's you I worry about. You are not obligated to do their bidding."

The girls were laughing while Robert Melforth's gaze drifted to Emma. *Is she getting rid of three more prying eyes to ease her chances of slipping away beyond the mill to another neighbor boy's arms? Clearly, she is providing this young man a transparent view to her feelings.*

The miller was aware that they had been in the barn together and also how quickly she had left him. The kind but insightful father could tell Emma was either yet again using her charms to manipulate this stout-hearted young man or up to some other mischief. She certainly had no serious intent on luring Sean into a marital web. Knowing Emma's conniving mind, he guessed the former. He understood scheming women. He had married one.

"Let's go, Sean!" Melanie hollered. Then reversing her gears and polite as a princess, "Will you take us, now, please?"

Even as Robert Melforth watched the three disappear into the pasture, he   analyzed his thoughts about Emma. He knew the shallow inner workings of many a pretty girl's mind. He had married a lovely one with little common sense but a far reaching ability to bend a man to her will. He could see his dead wife clearly in Emma more than the others. *Pretty girls all*, he thought, *but Emma is indeed more.* Melforth had long ago conceded that Emma often drew in trouble as sorghum syrup lured wasps. He wondered what had truly happened at the mill when she was confronted by the McLaud boy. He also wondered about Nora. She must be of her true father completely. She was nothing like her mother.

The miller let his mind wander to other times. He remembered Memphis fifteen years before the war. There, Rebecca Tarryton, his wife to be, had conjured up her fair share of difficulties before wisely tying the knot with him, the promising son of a talented master machinist. Robert Melforth knew that he was not handsome but plain. There was no denying Rebecca was with child, and not of his making, several months before she agreed to marry him.

Intelligent, hardworking, and frugal, Melforth felt he had met her criteria for security, if not her cravings for love. His goal to build the most efficient grist mill along one of the fast flowing streams in the Ozarks heralded his ambition. However, it was Melforth's compassion that encompassed their union. Marrying his Becky gladly, despite the talk that the child in her belly was not his, proved his worth, and she willingly gave him six more. Two had failed to live as was so common among children of the time.

⊕

Melanie and Lilly merrily walked hand-in-hand to the river, practically dragging Sean along. The Irishman enjoyed the young girls' attention. He laughed to himself thinking how both had demanded, more than asked, their father's permission to go to the river after supper. While moments later with Emma's backing, they had pertly and properly asked how he could refuse any safer escort than Sean.

Sean remembered Violet, the quiet and thoughtful middle girl, leaving the supper table with a gleeful look on her face that predicted her knowledge of the amusing ruckus certainly to follow. Sean remembered the miller's resolution cracking, while out of the corner of his eye Violet safely scouted the lively skirmish from the doorway of the cabin.

While envious of the glowing warmth of this family, he had seen Violet's and now also Nora and Emma's loving study of their resolute but caring father. Still seated, the older girls witnessed his protective arms gently but firmly surrounding each pleading girl. With admiration Sean gazed once again over each sister and back again. He thought how they must see themselves in Melanie and Lilly, having been treated with the same kind discipline when they were younger. Hoping someday to be a good father, the Irishman wished to do much the same. Melforth dealt well with raising children. Then Sean reconsidered and grinned as he thought, *But only if my children are not of the likes of Violet's precocious little sisters. Their father is the only one who truly rules them.*

⊕

The girls first picked a coarse-graveled beach just beyond the trail under a big leaning sycamore. It proved too rocky and the water too fast for Sean. He moved the spirited duo farther downstream where the gravel was pea sized and mixed with sand. He scanned the weaker current of the stream knowing that in the knee deep water he might save one or both if the worst should happen.

At ease with the girls' wellbeing Sean allowed himself to lie back and relax on the comfortable shore. His eyes traveled across the rushing waters of the river and up the towering stone bluffs. *Majestic*, he thought. *That's the word for it.* Downstream in the deep holes he saw blue water eddies swirling in pools that blended to green. His arms cradled his head in contentment while the rolling river lulled his senses. As the early evening passed he marveled at the clear waters, maybe clearer than any he had ever seen in the mountains of Virginia.

Half-an-hour later, Sean still gazed protectively over Melanie and Lilly. The two frolicked in ankle high water near shore with dresses pulled to their knees. *Such skinny little sprites*, he thought, recollecting his sister at their age. His memories crowded out the pain, and he allowed himself to briefly conjure an image of Mary Katherine from better times. His remembrances complimented the youngest Melforth daughters whom he considered so similar.

The girls wheeled around in playful gyrations with long hair cast out in all directions until exhausted. Then they knelt or actually fell in moist sand on the shoreline laughing as they caught their breath. Refusing to waste a second of play time to rest the two merrily formed up the walls of castles with their small hands. Sean watched it all with satisfaction. He was proud to be trusted for a few hours with the children as might an older brother and considered his good fortune in finding such a family. The excitement of Emma now fading, the puzzle that was Nora, the joy of the other three girls, and even their often sullen father added up to a fine stew of which he was pleased to be but a small part. However separate because of his differences, still he was trusted. *It's a good place to be*, he thought as he wiggled his toes in the sand.

Yet, Sean's questions about Nora's words and actions had never ceased. She was a mystery. Eli's last effects had disappeared from his saddle bags within a week of his arrival, and he was unsure how to deal with the theft. Approaching Melforth about Eli seemed unimportant now. No one in the family had ever mentioned that name. He had asked Lilly and Melanie once. Both had told him that the name was new to them. *Let it alone,* Sean had told himself. *Maybe it's best for now.*

Studying the rolling cadence of the waves downstream helped to clear troubles from his mind. They were all minor when he let himself ponder Emma's enticing smile and the memory of love making in the barn. Once more, he thought of Luanne and her family.

Sean hoped she was accepted by her cousin. He dreaded to pull away from this valley of such comfort. Concentrating on the noble woman from south of Salem, he reassured himself, *In early fall I will temporarily return to see her children and make sure all is well. Yet, how can I break away from this family at the big spring? I've known nothing stronger since Ireland,* and then allowing the full truth to surface, *except with Luanne.*

Had her hate for him melted away or doubled? After tallying both accounts he calculated the latter and forced his remorse to trail away like the swirls and eddies in the river. The bright-eyed, high-pitched screamers in dresses not far away helped him forget. Finally, his regrets escaped for a time, lost to the pleasant revelry of the cool summer evening.

Spring fed, Sean knew this mostly shaded stream to be cold and able to pull the heat from the body as well as the air. Rapidly, the sun was being blocked more and more by the high ridges as it leaned into the day. Huge, stately shadows summoned the evening's end. Sean lounged on the wide beach enjoying the frolics of the girls and the sights and sounds of the river but now more restlessly. The gray light and the chill in the air reminded him that they should be returning home. There was no doubt in his mind that Nora and her father would be anxiously waiting.

The briskness of the evening continued to clear his thinking. The question of how long he should stay with the Melforths tugged at his conscience. It would be foolish to wear out his welcome.

The once bright waters had changed to masses of gray. Only the tallest bluffs still caught the yellow sunshine. It was time to go. The Irishman stiffly pushed himself up from the softness of the bar. He shook out his shirt and hat. A wry grin filled his face as sand poured from the thick leather boots he seldom wore, all compliments of a playful burying by the girls. Preparing them to go home, he knew, would be a difficult matter.

Gently, Sean herded the girls along the gravel bar in the direction of the brushy stream bank and trail that they had traversed earlier. It all became a slow game, too slow, considering the resulting darkness. He marveled how the two could make anything they encountered fun and wondered when in his early years he had ceased being a child.

The girls' bare feet kicked up sand until the bar turned to gravel. Then the game of skipping rocks, one or two for every few steps up stream, led the slow procession finally to the well-beaten pathway beside the bent down sycamore.

Melanie announced as they prepared to leave the river, "I need a minute to visit the bushes." As she raced by, Sean grabbed Lilly playfully and lifted her eight-year-old body high. She snickered as she watched her older sister scampering up the trail into the woods. Melanie was quickly out of sight.

Still a scrawny lightweight, Sean placed the youngest Melforth on his shoulders and spun around in the gravel. A coy, poor imitation of a scream erupted from Lilly, and he continued spinning until both were dizzy and laughing.

They waited for several minutes. Melanie failed to return. Holding Lilly's hand he walked to the end of the bar by the sycamore. He hollered into the woods, "Melanie, are you all right? Come back."

Sean's words fell silent on the thickening shadows. He scanned the near darkness of the forest. His feelings of alarm grew. Again, he hollered into the wall of foliage. Silence again. He decided what must be done.

Looking down at Lilly's frightened eyes, he took her by the shoulders and said,   "Wait right here. Do not move. Do you hear me?"

Lilly's look said more than words ever could. She silently nodded her head.

Sean swiftly glanced around the gravel bar and found a big stick. He put it in her hands, and then proceeded to walk hastily up the footpath. Fearing the worst, he then anticipated Melanie playing a little girl's game, hiding until she was found. Mary Katherine had done the same to her older brother many times.

Traveling the trail's short length to the open field and back, a helpless feeling overtook Sean. *Where is she?* He investigated deeper into the woods and began on his left pushing back branches and saplings. In the sunless forest the color of his pants and heavy boots had turned shades of gray. After searching one side of the trail, he came back to within a few steps of the sycamore. There, he hollered at Lilly to reassure her.

"I'm fine, Sean," she squealed in defiance from the river bank. Her words said to the Irishman, find my sister and don't worry about me.

Sean thought Lilly was doing a fine job of sounding brave, and he promptly began the search again. It soon ended. Melanie was frozen in place. In a squat, her dress was pulled to her thighs. One hand held it tight between her legs. Oddly, no sounds came from her usually never quiet mouth. But her eyes drilled Sean. He saw her fear.

"Are you okay, Melanie?" he asked from several steps away. *Why is she locked solid? What's wrong?* Sean watched, unsure of the problem as only her eyes moved when he spoke. *Why would she not speak?* Then, he saw it. Less than a step from her a copperhead as thick as a rifle barrel lay in the leaves, coiled and blending in. *Thankfully, Melanie had seen the snake and not moved.*

Experiences in Virginia had shown Sean firsthand the effect of a copperhead bite on grown men. None had died, though. One had lost a finger. Another had lost a foot. He remembered being told that a small child could easily be sickened by the bite of a snake so large, possibly to death.

The serpent was only a half a step from Melanie's right leg and bare bottom. He saw the understandably scared little nine-year-old begin to quiver. To her credit Melanie had not lost control.

Sean took action. He stepped to the snake and in rapid motion stomped repeatedly with all his weight. The thick leather over his feet protected him while he roughly grabbed Melanie and propelled her up into his arms. The snake's open mouth repeatedly struck the bull hide of his boots and loose fabric of his trousers. In an awkward but frantic dance, Sean pounded down on the writhing body with all his weight.

Throughout the danger, he held Melanie high while telling her gently, "You're all right, little *lassie*. The serpent won't hurt you, not now."

Screaming finally, Melanie then swiftly burst into tears. She hugged Sean tightly.

Not about to let her go, Sean walked back to Lilly. He found a crying little girl, too, but still with her stick in hand, bravely defending the gravel bar from all potential intruders.

"What is it, Sean?

"A snake, Lilly. A copperhead. It's dead. Climb up."

Lilly gestured to her sobbing sister.

"She's fine. Hop up."

Packing both girls on opposite hips, Sean began the short walk through the trees to the field. "Keep your feet up," he commanded. "Wrap them around my waist." He got more than he asked for. Both girls clung to him like leeches. Two sets of legs squeezed tight to his waist. Two pairs of arms clung painfully around his neck.

Every stick or long shadow along the trail became a snake in his mind. Sean tried not to trip on the occasional rock and shuffled ahead slowly because of his stiff leg.

When only a few steps remained to reach the field, he paused to readjust the heavy loads clutching onto him for dear life. The heavy pressure of something sliding over his right foot sent shivers up his spine. When what must have been a rattler or moccasin cut deep into his thigh. He yelled.

But Sean Kelly would not drop the girls, could not. Frozen in fear but determined, he looked to the field so close but long steps away. The safety of its openness seemed a distance he would never be able to travel.

He was well aware of the coiled instrument of pain below him on the trail. Unlike the copperhead, the effects of this snake's bite could prove terrible. He had seen healthy men die in agony.

The snake, so blurred by the advancing darkness, was easily as thick as his forearm. Desperately, he tried to calm himself, but in moments, he was quivering just as had Melanie. Movement would cause the snake to bite him again. His arms were aching from the weight of the girls. Unintentionally, they were choking him. Surely the serpent would slither away. But the poison would soon begin to act, and he would be forced to drop one or both of his precious cargoes.

Despite the horror, Sean allowed his legs to answer his ever more muddled mind. He stepped forward. Again, he disturbed the serpent. Again, he felt the slicing teeth. He hollered in pain again, and in doing so almost dropped Lilly. But, he managed to walk another step. Desperately, Sean wanted to run away but couldn't. The girls remained locked to his waist. Lilly had seen it, now, and was screaming. There would be no letting go. He would not!

A branch in the face here, a near tumble on a stone, Sean moved forward another step. He continued, but how he didn't know. Finally, in what passed for hours but were really agonizing moments, he gained the open pasture. Yet, despite the advancing cloudiness of his thinking, he trudged further away from the forest. The girls remained locked in his arms.

CHAPTER 47
LONG AWAITED PEACE

Before dropping the girls onto the grassy field, Sean turned back to look at his assailant. There, up the trail he saw the thick reptile outstretched, its length as long as a man's height. He watched it slither into the blackness of the undergrowth. Vague checkered markings confirmed his dread.

Sean took a long breath to slow his racing heart. His arms ached from his efforts with the girls, but the pain was nothing compared to the increasing effects of the venom. Light-headed and weaker every second, he tried not to panic.

"Be calm," he whispered to himself. "Take care of these little ones. Be calm." However as his vision blurred he mumbled, "I can't go on."

Gently, he set the clinging then scrambling girls down. He let himself fall on his backside onto the pasture's dewy grass, and reached for the shoulder of each girl. Slow, raspy words came out, "Melanie, Lilly, I've been bitten by a rattler, a big one. Both of you run home. Bring Nora... your... father." Then, "Find Nora. Quick now! Go!"

His plea echoed in his thinking that was slipping every second. For some reason it came out again. "Find Nora!"

His words turned quieter and began to slur. "Hurrrrry... gggggirls. Youuuuu...mmmmmust... hurrrrry."

Sean heard more than watched while the two scurried like rabbits through the pasture and up over a small rise toward the cabin. He chided himself for not telling them to bring a few pieces of salt pork. The meat would help draw out the poison. However, he was done. He knew it. His tongue was numbing. Breathing was harder. Speech had deserted him.

Alone now, Sean's head reeled. A short distance farther into the open field he noticed a large tree. He forced himself to crawl. On all fours the ever-weakening Irishman found his way and leaned himself up against the wide rough trunk. Breathing in short wisps of air, he looked skyward, but found little comfort as his gaze caught the first stars of the night.

Despite his venom jumbled brain he watched the night sky for nearly a minute. He formed words with his mouth speaking to one bright spot in the heavens, then another. However, no sounds came. He knew that the juices from the snake bite continued their evil work. First, into his muscles, then dribbling through his veins, he was well aware that the poison was destined to flow to his heart. Sean's body relaxed. His eyes closed.

His last conscious thoughts repeated in his mind over and over again. *Hey, red-haired lad, you were lucky it was no moccasin. You may live.* However, the dreadful moments on the trail with the girls came back to him before he fell over into the grass. The big snake had bitten twice.

CHAPTER 48
DESPERATE AND ALONE

Luanne led her big mule through the summer downpour. She trudged along on the rapidly muddied road glad of the cooling rain. A sultry morning had built up into an afternoon of sweltering heat. Behind her, the cart rolled slowly, often grudgingly. It had nearly been taken in the night, two weeks before, while she and her family tried to sleep after a long day in the field. Her pointed shotgun had not allowed anyone to steal all she had left in the world. Her relatives had also wanted to take her children. How they could imagine such a thing astonished her. She had nearly shot her cousin's brother-in-law. He had forcefully attempted to bully her into giving up Amy, Jeremiah, and Quincy.

She pondered her shunning by the small community of ex-slaves. Loving a white man was not to be forgiven. Being able to read had not helped, either. She had worked hard on the farm for weeks and weeks but had not been given meat with the others. Luanne and her children were living off the food she had brought from her farm near Salem. Early on she had given away half of her provisions and livestock as gifts of goodwill, but still had been ordered out to a broken down lean-to far from her cousin's snug cabin and spacious dry barn. Two days before with much effort and threatening words pushing her faster, she had left the farm and crossed into Shannon County. Dent County and the unspeakable behavior of her cousin were behind her, but her escape and the many miles of travel had not dispelled her anger.

While Luanne gently pulled the reins and urged the old mule's progress, she briefly looked over her shoulder. Her three children lay curled in loose straw on the cart. The boys were both asleep hugging their groggy big sister. They had passed through Eminence earlier in the day. Thankfully, no barking cur dogs had threatened her passage. She hoped with luck to reach Van Buren within the week.

CHAPTER 49
ANGEL IN WAITING

Awaking woozily, Sean first realized in fact that he was alive. He lay in a bed. It was nighttime, and a single candle flame lit up the inside of a cabin with a hazy glow. He felt as though he had drunk more than his limit of hard spirits the night before. Soon, his head was spinning. Nausea found him and took control. His stomach hurled its contents into a waiting bucket. Long feminine fingers on the bail were all he saw of his nurse. The agony of the dry heaves raged for a time and then ever so slowly lessened. His weakness consumed him. Who was it who helped at his side? He was too weak to ask or to look up to see her face.

Settling again into the heavenly but lumpy mattress he became aware of coarse blankets against his skin. *Odd it is*, were his first rational thoughts. The awareness came to him that he had not slept in a real bed since Ireland, over six long years before.

Having no idea where he lay or what put him down on his back so incredibly weak, Sean attempted only to stare at the rafters and not throw up. In time his eyes moved ever so slowly, roaming the room. He took in blurred images around him and then pressured himself to focus. Clues gathered. In the clouds of his pained mind inklings of understanding seeped together to form a clearer picture.

His eyes dwelt upon the long fingers on the bail of the bucket. He followed the contours of her hand on a journey along a slim arm, up finally to a face he found vaguely familiar. Once again he felt himself pinned under his horse on the battlefield of ripened wheat. There as now, the blue eyes of a Confederate soldier studied him.

The light-haired woman watched him from a chair. With thin but not unattractive features, he saw compassion brimming in her tired eyes. He saw her smile, but still could not salvage her name. No answer or even a strained question grew in his mind. All he could muster were off-and-on blurry images that strained his eyes and aching head.

He tried desperately to concentrate and looked hard again. She wore no gray uniform, only a simple dress. No harsh sun tormented them from above. Again, he remembered the boot black on golden hair staining his fingers. Eli's hair had not been dark. With great effort he forced the smallest of smiles. *What an appealing woman*, he mused, *so giving.* His eyes closed to rest, but his mind labored to set right the confusion.

Don't I sleep in the barn? Why am I in the house? Then regaining some balance he confirmed that he did indeed spend nights in the barn. *A beginning*, he allowed, but still he doubted his reckoning. *Who is this girl caressing my hand? Her eyes are eyes from the past, those of a dead soldier.*

He cast a little of his delirium away, forcing his muddled gaze to follow her. *She must care to be so close.* Nausea then visited him once more, but the light-haired woman was ready. She pulled his shoulder and with it his body onto his side.

"Stay on your side, Sean," she said. "You won't choke."

His name was Sean, a familiar sound. Suddenly, he knew her name, too! *Eli*, he mouthed the words but no sound came. *But if it is Eli, I, too, have gone from this life.*

The flaxen-haired angel at his side whispered quietly, "You will breathe easier." He heard her pause and felt her squeeze his hand more while he gladly absorbed more of her sweet words. "You are healing, Sean. You will live, my dear, dear man."

Sean's clouded mind filled yet again with the old dream among the grape vines overlooking Hermann. The clinging, flaxen-haired child still straddled his lap, however, this time he saw something else he had missed before. An unknown woman worked in the garden. She also had long light-colored hair. He came back in time and thought how the little girl's resemblance to this gentle woman who nursed him now could not be denied. Today, though, if it was a dream it was a wonderful dream of a real woman whose kindhearted presence rekindled his will.

His body ached terribly, but his shadowy mind became clearer. His eyes would not rest from trying to see her. He again tried to speak but could not. His lips formed the syllables, *E...li*, but still no sound came. He resigned himself to adoring observation.

The light-haired woman cleaned his face with a wet rag, and next vigorously swabbed down his naked body with cold, clean water. He had no energy to refuse, and the cold washing told him this was no dream. She pulled another thin blanket over him and then sat at his shoulder smiling. *A tired smile*, he gauged. Leaning over and now at his cheek, she spoke again in whispered phrases. Her words now, all the words from this sparkling blue-eyed woman, Sean interpreted as melodies more beautiful than any he had ever played. *Eli is alive!*

⊕

Nora bent down and kissed Sean's forehead lightly then spoke with tearful emotion, "Again you have provided protection and life, and yet you live?" Salty tears welled up. She refused to move and the wetness dripped on Sean's cheeks. "As you have been in the past you will always be a man close to my heart." Her fingers reached to her face. She tried uselessly to wipe the stream away.

The words were lyrical to Sean's ears, ears that only hours before, or was it days, had appeared ready to catch the vibrations of his own death rattle. *Who is she*? Sean pondered. *Have I known her as Eli in another life?* Then the battle scene arose once more and then as quickly faded in his clouded senses. His uncertainties returned, though, still again, he looked into the depths of the fretful eyes that stood watch over him. Any doubts vanished. *Before when death called my name, I knew this voice. I knew this look.*

⊕

"He's opened his eyes! Sean has opened his eyes!" The calm of the cabin was broken by Lilly's jubilant yells. The two youngest Melforth girls crept up to Sean's bedside after standing so patiently by the doorway.

Both smiled and Sean saw the dark-haired younger sisters. *Oh, yes*, he remembered, *sweet Lilly and Melanie. Marry them both in an instant.* He forced the tiniest of grins but remained too weak to speak. Two other girls, older and also dark-haired, turned their heads and looked over to him from their cooking pots by the fireplace. *Where has Eli gone?*

Still another movement away at the far end of the cabin caught Sean's eye. *A man in the doorway, older and with a gun in hand embraced my angel. Eli, why are you crying so?*

Sean joked to himself in his delirium. *Hope he's not after me. I'm nearly dead. The man need do little to send me to St. Peter's door.* Then in relief, the Irishman grasped that the man with the gun was the miller, Melforth.

The others in the cabin saw a smile on Sean's face, the last thing that any expected from a man awaking from two days of insensible ravings.

Sean's mind briefly became lucid but his caregiver's identity still remained a mystery. He knew it was Eli but why was Eli here? What had happened? But then it all became clearer, the battlefield filled with death and smoldering wheat straw, the cabin near the big spring, his nurse with flaxen hair, and the thick-bodied serpent. A sudden fearful gasp exploded from his chest, and Sean reached high into nothingness. His flailing arms desperately fended off another attack from dagger-like fangs.

⊕

Within an hour Sean drank sparingly, sipping from a tin cup held in Eli's hand. Now more than vaguely he remembered the angel beside his bed. However, still no name came to him other than Eli. He savored the touch of her hand on his head. The water wetted his lips, but he refused more.

She insisted, "Drink again, Sean!" Then in frustration she

commanded, "You must drink more, stubborn Irishman!" knowing the earlier drops on his lips had not been enough.

Throughout the morning the clouds in Sean's brain parted then closed in again despite his body's progress. "Nora," he heard the name from the younger girls. Nora? Eli was here, too. Where was she? His memories came faster, now. His face turned to panic, as the violent evening on the dark trail filled his mind again. A flash of images screamed from his memory. Settling down and then finding energy to speak, Sean's first coherent words were to Eli and came in high-pitched croaks, "The little princesses, I'm glad they're safe!"

⊕

A little later in the morning Robert Melforth gently asked his two youngest daughters. "Please, tell me again, girls. What truly happened?"

Melanie and Lily sat on the bench by the apple tree and watched their father with pensive eyes. He knelt in the grass at their feet. His strong hands gently lay on their shoulders.

"When you told me before you were so excited." He reached up and tenderly stroked her tangled dark hair. "Can you tell me again, slowly?"

Trying to be as grown up as possible Melanie took a large breath and then trying to speak at a snail's pace but failing, said, "Daddy, Sean saved me from the big copperhead. He pulled me up into his arms. Then he carried me and Lily along the path. We were scared. Lily saw it. We were screaming. The big snake bit him. He was screaming, too."

Melanie looked to her little sister and back unable now to decide what to say. Tears were rolling down her father's cheeks. Melanie had never seen him cry and was confused. "Daddy, it's alright. He saved us."

"I know, Melanie. I know," Robert Melforth answered in a whisper.

She watched her father's face while trying hard to understand his sadness. "The snake bit him again," she began once more. "He almost dropped Lily, Daddy. But he didn't!" she added hoping to make him smile. "Aren't you glad, Daddy? I'm so glad."

Melanie felt his big arms reach further around and hug them closer to his chest. She saw his head nod, but she couldn't figure out why the big tears rolled down his cheek. She felt his wet face on hers, and worried when he didn't say anything. "What's wrong, Daddy? We're safe! Sean saved us."

Finally, Melanie saw him smile just a little, and only then knew everything was all right.

CHAPTER 50
A FATHER'S CARE

A little later Robert Melforth stood in the doorway, heart-shaken and concerned. He was stunned that this stricken man's first words were about the safety of his children. For the second time this morning salty tears filled his eyes. He turned away from the activity of his daughters around Sean in the cabin and looked now to his fields and his work. He sighed and then muttered to no one as his many steps drew him closer to the mill. "There is no better test of a man than this. Catholic or not, to this man I will now and forever be indebted." Then louder to the fields and nearby rushing spring creek, "He refused to drop them! He refused to drop my children and save himself!"

A morning of hard work at the mill passed before Melforth could again look in upon his household. The man with hair plastered down with sweat, Melforth contemplated closely. *What will I say to him? How will I thank him?* His feelings had deep restraints, and the sparse worded miller could think of no way to address the Irishman. His eyes moved around the room, first, to his youngest daughters, then to Emma by a cook pot. He watched her ladle turtle meat and boiled potatoes into a bowl.

Emma, dear Emma, Melforth reflected. *You chase every man in britches and then put him off. So much like your departed mother.*

His thoughts wandered to the sad time when Emma's mother had died after delivering a whole and healthy Lilly.

Continuing to size up the moment, Melforth looked intently at Nora. It was his first born, rarely called Elnora, who had alone saved the poor man lying so weak before him. Certainly, he had helped to carry Sean to the cabin, but it was Nora who had cleaned the paired puncture wounds with single-minded determination. During that long night, he had observed Nora suck the venom from the Irishman's thigh and spit it out! *Her eyes. Her eyes could not lie,* not to him.

What prompted her to this caring passion? Maybe a friend, surely family or a lover, but no Yankee drifter would receive such treatment. Catholic, too! Shaking his head in puzzlement, Melforth remembered how she would only stop her aid when exhausted and when he and Emma had pulled her away. Later, he had watched Elnora cover the snake bite with salt pork to draw the poison out. *Where had she learned that practice?* Melforth shook his head again. He knew not.

Certainly she knows him! From another time or place, Melforth continued speculating. *Yet, the Irishman doesn't know her! So confusing. She must, though. Nora went to Memphis during the war. She must have met him there. He knows her. Repeatedly in his delirium he called for Eli. How else could he know her nickname?*

Melforth went back in time as he continued the survey of his home and his daughters. Long ago when he needed a son so badly, his oldest, such a strong-hearted daughter, had delivered in all ways to satisfy the needs of the mill and the farm. Nora literally made herself a slave to help her family once her mother died. She became a man in woman's clothing, yet remained a gentle soul, even gentler, but more starry-eyed when returning from Memphis after a year's absence. *Her limp,* he remembered, *lasted several months.* She had explained it by describing an accident involving a run away wagon. *Oddly,* he had felt then, *she had refused even Emma to look to her healing leg.*

Robert Melforth remained propped up against the splintery door jam hypnotized by the actions of his daughters, especially Elnora. He spoke in whispers to only the cabin's already sultry air.

"She is the one, the best of the brood. She would be the one for a man to court and covet. Maybe, if Sean recovers, he will look her way rather than to Emma. A pretty face is not substance. We will see if this boy is as wise as he is heroic."

The insightful miller watched as first Emma then Violet spooned the richness of turtle soup into the mouth of this man who had in less than a month's time twice handed the devil his due. There was much he didn't understand about this Yankee drifter, but he was glad that Sean had ridden into the Current River valley.

Finally, the meticulously working mind of Robert Melforth took over and pushed away his emotions. There was much he didn't understand. *From the beginning of Sean Kelly's stay with the family, Elnora has been indifferent to him, cold really. Yet, for the first few days she would not let him out of her sight, and interrupted him if he tried to speak. About what? The man's questions were either cut short or unanswered. Interesting? What could he possibly say that would affect her?*

The miller's reflections continued to spawn memories from the last month. Emma's story at the mill was unsolved. Her explanation of Elnora's behavior towards Sean was equally confusing. *Nora recognized the Irishman from somewhere else, Emma had said. It's all that could explain her actions.*

All puzzling. Melforth rolled the thoughts over and over again analyzing the facts as he watched Violet and the older girls hovering over their red-haired Lazarus. *When the boy is better we'll have some answers*, Melforth thought, and then left the house again for the mill. Work remained to be done. It was Monday afternoon. He knew that many in the Van Buren area would still be in need of ground corn or wheat flour.

He walked the narrow lane to the mill as the great mystery of the summer churned within him unanswered. The imprints of his boots followed him in the dust. The windblown field near the spring danced with the afternoon's glaring sunlight. His uneasy thoughts ebbed and flowed, never quite finding solid footing. As he stepped up the few stairs to the loading dock with new sweat on his brow, his reluctance, based upon his lifelong hatred of anyone different than himself, began a massive retreat. Gentler, more charitable beliefs had grown. Undeniable joy filled his voice as his thoughts erupted to no one but the dark corners of his mill.

"Our Irishman is alive! Thank you, dear Lord."

Then his rare exuberance subsided into stern silence as quickly as it had surfaced. His steady hands pulled down a great lever and tied it off securely at a post. Sounds of rushing water filled his ears while the grinding wheels of the finest mill west of Memphis and south of Saint Louis began to turn.

CHAPTER 51
McLauds' Revenge

O ver a twisting hogback ridge, closer to the Eleven Point River and Oregon County than to the Current, the patriarch of the McLaud clan held court on the front porch of his cabin. Silvery-haired Cyril McLaud rocked in his chair in the sunshine while most of his black-bearded kin relaxed together in the shade to avoid the afternoon's suffocating heat. His many sons and their wives debated the dilemma at hand. A few male grandchildren, almost men, looked on, occasionally backing the comments of one uncle or another. The oldest McLaud watched and listened, taking it all in but saying nothing.

The scorching sun soothed the pain in Cyril's arthritic joints. The warmth amplified what he felt in his bones. Foul play was at hand. Over a month it had been since his youngest son had not returned as expected from Van Buren, and the riders to Van Buren and the vicinity of the big spring had ridden home empty handed more than once. There was no evidence of the boy even with the help of dogs. Cyril predicted to his gathered family, "Something in the whereabouts of the Current and Melforth's mill will turn fresh upon the matter."

His youngest son, Willis, the old McLaud knew well. Much like any male member of his family at that age, the boy had never been on time, was always the last in line when work was passed out and the first to eat. He had been more unmanageable than any of his seven other sons. McLaud blamed that on his wife. She had not taken the switch to him enough or he thought, at all, when the child needed it. He let out a haughty laugh and all eyes turned to him. His thoughts were of the day he had pistol-whipped the two older boys into obedience fifteen years before. The idea of fear being important rambled through his mind. Fear was power.

The sallow faced McLaud spit onto the porch, then shifted in his caned seat while he wiped the tobacco juice from his lips and beard with his sleeve. His thoughts again traveled to the big spring. Somehow he felt the miller was responsible or knew something. He remembered his son's words that betrayed his hunger for Melforth's daughters. McLaud knew that lusting young men would travel far to please their urges. He had been much the same.

He thought again of the miller. Melforth had irritated him for years because of his southern sympathies. *The miller should have been hung long ago.* But he was puzzled. *Why would Melforth coddle a crippled Irish Catholic and a Yankee at that?*

Cyril McLaud's vengeful mind was whirling with angry possibilities, options that he would not hesitate to set in motion. He remembered leading the angry mob of horsemen from Carter into Oregon County to burn out the Irish settlement on the Eleven Point. Robert Melforth had been there, too. Nevertheless, he relished the thought of directing his kin to finally silence the traitor whose safety had been too long preserved by his skill at grinding grain. McLaud contemplated the young Irishman with the miller. A ruthless murmur left him, "We'll hang the Catholic cur dog, too!"

Grandpa McLaud had not gone unheard. His first born asked with a whimsical grin, "Hey, Pap, who is it you wish to bury, today?"

Chapter 52
Eli Revealed

Sean's battle with the rattler's poison lessened. By the next morning the miller's inspection determined that the snake bit falsely the first time. "Certainly its fangs entered the muscle in your thigh," he told Sean as Nora listened, "however the swelling and blackness give evidence that the second bite on the back of the leg has produced all the ill effects. If both bites had been fully venomous," Melforth turned to Lilly and Melanie and predicted, "your white knight with a fiddle would not have lived out the first day."

The observant miller turned to the weak Irishman on the bed. "You're a lucky man, Sean. Glad you are here with us today... I think..." He hesitated and then finished, "And in these days past." In his mind Robert Melforth was trying to say, *Please stay with us, Sean Kelly, maybe then, I will figure a way to repay you.*

Rising up from his chair by Sean's bed, his own bed in reality, for he had slept on the floor for two nights as Sean recovered, the father called his family to order. "We need to work in the garden this morning. Nora, please stay with Sean."

A chorus of grumbles poured out of the four girls from eight to seventeen, but they eventually piled out of the cabin, picked up broad sharpened sticks, the wooden spade, and a single iron hoe.

Each proceeded to attack the weeds among the beans, squash, corn, and sweet potatoes either in earnest or in a mock attempt to fool their father. Melanie and Lilly, more often than not, looked up to see if their task maker was paying attention to their efforts.

Once the girls had retreated with their father, Sean noticed with renewed pleasure how the morning sunlight sent brilliant yellow shafts through the cabin's side door. Nearly blinded by the brightness, he barely recognized Nora's dark, seated silhouette. Only glowing fringes of golden hair suggested a living soul in her dark shadow.

He remembered yesterday's confusion and pain. He had awakened in the afternoon. The younger girls and the father had told him of Nora's efforts to save him. Melanie and Lilly stood by as a solemn Violet had said, "She nursed you at all hours and with skills the rest of us have never seen before." The middle sister had squeezed Sean's hand and continued, "Only when she was beyond human endurance did our eldest allow herself to fall asleep in the chair by your side." Violet continued, "Sean, we are so proud of Nora," and then shyly after great hesitation, "and you."

Emma, who had been tending the fire out of sight, had asked, "When you hollered out from your sleep, how did you know Nora's nickname was Eli? We heard Nora in exhaustion during the early part of the second night of her vigil. She commanded you, 'If indeed you are Sean Kelly play your fiddle again for me as when you thought me dying!' Instantly, Nora covered her mouth with her hands while you moaned in your sleep." Emma searched Sean's eyes for an answer and after a long pause asked, "What did she mean?"

Sean gave a weak reply. "I remember nothing of that."

Today, though, her sharp image was being etched in his mind, the stark profile of her nose, forehead, and the hands that held the bail and cleansed him. *Like sharp scissors*, he felt sure, *the bright rays of morning cut with pure light this angel edged in gold.*

⊕

Feeling his stare Nora turned to Sean. She set down the book she was reading, and reached out both hands to cradle his face. She began to speak but the Irishman's words came first.

"Eli!" came out in a weak burst as his fleeting strength faded. His tired eyes penetrated hers.

With a timidness wrapped in growing confidence, Nora Melforth confessed, "Yes, I have been known by that name, Sean Kelly, once in the War of Northern Aggression and before that by my father when he desired a son."

Unbeknownst to Nora the entire family had since returned from the garden and quietly looked on from the doorway. The younger sisters held their hands to their mouths in shock but not their father. He had known since the evening before.

It appeared to the miller that a monumental compassion shared by both Sean and Nora now kept them silent. The simple touch of their hands was earthshaking to witness. Trust, the special entity springing from fingers, he sensed pulsing through, knitting them together. Invisible bonds appeared to forge them even closer. From beyond his thick-barked exterior Melforth coaxed an appreciative smile.

Sean continued to gaze up into the blue eyes of his flaxen-haired angel. "You were on a blanket lying in the grass, your hands outstretched in desperation. That memory and that of your sadness remains with me. There was no hope in your eyes, Eli. I could only think you were to die as so many others we'd seen." Sean waited before he said, "I'm sorry. I thought you'd gone to God all this time."

Elnora, Nora, or Eli, depending on who was calling her, lifted Sean's hand gently from her knee. She raised it high, spreading all five fingers over her face, and then kissed Sean's palm. Speaking into his hand as she touched and retouched his fingers one-by-one with her lips, she said, "You came to my family with an obligation of death to fulfill." With tears in her eyes Nora continued, "Know now, Sean Kelly, that you have reaped life and love not only from me but from my entire family."

Lilly and Melanie looked up to their father. Questioning eyes were followed by Melanie asking, "What has happened, Daddy?"

Embarrassed by his emotion, Melforth felt the mistiness in his eyes and pushed it back. He allowed only a tiny, knowing smile, which for him was a great deal. The youngest girls, he knew, would not understand, and besides there were no words to explain it. The miller placed his hands gently on the heads of his two little girls. He drew them closer. Painfully envious, his heart heaved in his chest as he continued his vigil over the sick man and his nurse. His eldest daughter had found love. Never had Rebecca, his wife for over ten years, shown him her spirit as Nora now revealed hers to Sean.

CHAPTER 53
A CONFUSED ADMIRER

The serpent again hissed in Sean's sweating face. He lay chest down on the cut bank of the creek. He looked directly into the cat-eyed pupils. He saw a scaled, muscular body prepared to strike. A musky smell filled his nostrils. Helpless, he felt the fear lumped in his throat. There was no air. Then, the dark-colored snake struck like a coiled spring unleashed. A huge gaping mouth, white as cotton, flew towards his face.

Sean bolted upright on the bed. He screamed. Pathetic cries exploded from his core. He choked in fear while his throat constricted and sounds refused to obey his commands. A final silent shriek tried to get out. The dream refused to fade fast enough. Perspiration dripped from his face. He caught his breath, but it came too short and fast. Now, firm hands gripped his shoulders. He heard her words, his angel.

"You are safe, Sean Kelly! There is no snake." Nora's reassuring voice found him. "You are in my arms. You are safe." Her words trailed away, each laced with sympathy. She held him and waited.

My dear brave man, Nora reflected in silence, *you have rescued me, Lilly, Melanie, and Emma. Yet, you have survived only to meet the serpent's wrath in your dreams.* Then aloud, "Let me hold you!

In those labyrinths where you find no escape, I will fight your demons!"

Nora held Sean's convulsing body as it slowly calmed, aware that Sean fought off other fiends in his sleep besides serpents. She had heard his screams in the barn loft earlier in the month and had jumped up from her bed in her night shirt to help. But her father's strong arms at the door had restrained her. Nora had struggled as they both heard words that brought terror to their hearts. The heat of battle, the skirmishes, cavalry charges and mindless death raced from Sean's mouth, and his words painted clear pictures for Robert Melforth and Nora of his sleeping fears and the horrid end to the lives of his companions.

Both father and daughter painfully listened, yet, only the daughter truly understood this soldier in their barn. She also had seen the horrors. The ranting continued, and Nora pleaded pathetically to her father to let her go to him. He only shook his head as his strong arms held her tight. She saw that tears dripped down his cheek, too. Her father's next words crushed her. "The man lying in our barn appears beyond repair."

CHAPTER 54
UNSETTLED

All were asleep when Sean next awoke. It was well past midnight and the cocks had yet to crow. No fever or wild delirium today stole his spirit. His sleep had been deep and dreamless. He quietly raised himself from his sick bed and walked out the doorway of the cabin. The water barrel was on the porch. He was thirsty. His snake-bitten leg flexed slowly and painfully, but followed his command. He charged it all to Nora's nursing and her sisters' gentle ways.

On the far side of the yard beyond the barn he relieved himself of the fluids Nora had forced upon him so regularly. He was more than pleased to be up and not having to use a hollow gourd. Glad he was also that Nora had found and given him one of her father's old nightshirts. Being naked under the thin woolen blanket, at first, had not bothered him, but when he regained his wits at the end of the second day, it became embarrassing while the Melforth girls were constantly at his bedside. When Nora had insisted she bathe him, he was too weak and helpless to refuse. Her little sisters had giggled as she and Violet had swathed him down with the warmed water to clean away his sweat. So, this morning he was reassured to be up on his feet with a full measure of clothing covering his body.

A quarter-moon cast its light all around the valley. He watched the sparkling water from the nearby spring rush away to its unseen rendezvous with the Current River. His time here had been eventful. He was sure that if destiny did indeed run true, he had come to the right place. Still, other thoughts plagued him. What of Luanne, her children, and their safety?

Sean felt that the Melforth girls were all now his family, but worried about Robert Melforth's detached manner. Since the incident with Lilly and Melanie at the river he had said little or nothing. Sean thought of his own father, and felt certain Melforth was of a similar caliber. *Why wouldn't he talk to me? What have I done to anger him?* Painful questions filled Sean's clouded thoughts.

Then another rushed at him. How serious had been neighbor Berryman's warning at the mill? How serious should he take the threat? Again the horrible scene ran through his mind of an entire village of Irish homesteaders on the Eleven Point River burned out and fleeing for their lives.

CHAPTER 55
EXPOSÉ ON SWEAT

Their grinding action an extension of the swift moving water of the big spring's constant flow, the head-high stone wheels rotated against each other as Sean watched and listened. The stream's energy set the water wheel into motion. Turning the drive shaft, the large circular mill stones used gears in-between to mechanically change the direction of force produced by the immense flow of the clear spring waters. Sean never ceased to wonder at the inner-workings of the mill and the miller's mind which had conceived it. To Sean, Robert Melforth was certainly an engineer, a genius, or both.

A sudden, "Best be to your work, Irishman," caught Sean off guard. The miller was irritated about something for whatever reason and holding it close. He only called Sean, "Irishman," when he was aggravated.

Sean soon let his mind meander back to what he had seen in the war as he hefted sack after sack of flour to the dock. The work of military engineers had amazed him. Their efforts miraculously had produced pontoon bridges and roads to move an army of fifty thousand men over the countryside at often very short notice. In the poorly lit mill the turning of the wheels, gears, and drive shafts as large as small trees in syncopated interaction, amplified Sean's appreciation of Nora's father as a master mechanic.

Sean had heard stories told about Melforth by local people as they had waited to have their corn, oats, or wheat ground. Their general idea was that despite Melforth's southern sympathies he was tolerated by the mostly pro-Union populace. He was likable, but it was his vast woodworking and milling skills that let him exist in this environment mostly hostile to the southerner from Memphis. His expertise was too valuable for the community to lose. To find someone else to maintain the complex workings of the flour mill was unthinkable. Lingerers at the mill had told Sean with pride how Melforth's mill on the big spring was reputed by travelers to be the best between St. Louis, Memphis, and Little Rock.

Robert Melforth was able to keep his grinding charges to a minimum because of the mill's efficiency. As the locals sat waiting for their ground grain several had mentioned to Sean that Melforth's continued existence was also due to his very reasonable grinding fees. "To barter for grinding is common. He's smart in these difficult times not to be squeezing blood from a turnip."

⊕

The morning progressed to mid-day in a constant flurry of grinding then loading the endless stream of grain sacks. His leg remained sore from the snake bite, and he worked at a slower pace than usual. It was Saturday, the busiest day for a miller, and Sean was glad to see the last bags of the morning filled and set across the saddle or bucked up on the rear boards of a wagon.

Sean appreciated the coolness of the early day. The nearby stream flowing from the bowels of the limestone hills tempered the summer heat for most of the morning. By quitting time as he emerged from the noisy, dark workings of the mill, the ever present cloud of flour dust clung to his dripping arms and face. He was as white as new cotton in the bole. The heat and humidity of the southern Missouri summer teamed up and won out as usual, producing the sweat allotted to each as a daily blessing.

⊕

For a short time before the noon meal Sean rested at the mill pond. The hard work had taken its toll. He dunked himself to his shoulders in the spring water and then sat back and felt the cold run down his back. While he rested, Sean dwelt on the merits of sweat. It was not until coming to America, that he had found it in such quantities. In Ireland the beads of moisture only came with work. To sweat too much was to exhibit poor manners. So, bakers, farmers, and the masons constantly drew a rag to their brows to wipe it away. At home on the rainy isle where weather was so attuned to the cold sea surrounding it, Sean was accustomed to one's body quickly cooling, prompting the inner furnace to burn at lower levels.

Older farmers in Lisdoonvarna, to whom Sean would listen after Mass or in front of the pub, conversed on the subject of sweating with seriousness. The old timers insisted that the virtues of perspiration were many and described how a sauna's heat could invigorate a man deep down to his bones. To work up a good sweat in the sauna or in the fields and maintain its outflow purified the body and even the soul. Yet, Sean's father quickly discredited these tales as being from the offspring of Finnish and Norwegian sailors who were close to the devil.

"Don't believe their stories," Malroy Kelly had lectured his only son. "To roast oneself then plunge naked into freezing water in a nearby stream, if not crazy, then is to be considered shameless and not becoming to a good Catholic boy." Then he had added, "Nor a good Catholic girl."

The blast furnace Virginia summers during the war had tempered Sean's attitude about sweat. The cooling droplets that rolled relentlessly down his cheeks to his chin before falling to his already soaking chest, became a fact of life, a fact that could not be ignored. To survive the heat of the afternoon was a blessing. To be lucky enough to experience cooling evening breezes renewed a man.

Drinking enough to stay ahead of the loss due to a hot afternoon's baking was difficult. Falling too far behind was to tempt death. To see soldiers fall out of ranks and die from the heat was not uncommon. Many times under a sweltering sun, Sean had wondered if he or his horse, too, were to die from the heat. Consequently, after the many hours of labor in the mill, Robert Melforth's red-haired hired hand took ample time to cool in the rousing spring water. Then he returned to the cabin for the mid day meal and the chance to play some tunes.

⊕

The sparse lunch passed in unsteady peace. Sean continued to wonder about Melforth's silent and possibly foul mood. A little later in the sycamore's shade with fiddle in hand, he sat on his favorite upturned log. Many of the Melforths had gathered on the porch but seemed subdued. *The heat*, Sean guessed. *Emma was missing*, and he wondered where she might be, and then with a smile remembered. In the morning he had seen her walking arm-in-arm with a boy beyond the mill near Alexander's cabin. Even from a distance he had seen the straw on her ruffled dress and in her tangled hair. He had seen her with another young man from up river two days before. *Emma*, he concluded thinking with a smile, *obviously has more than one fish on the line.*

"A tune, Irishman!" the miller abruptly commanded rather than asked. His surly tone shattered Sean's reflection. Violet, Melanie, and Lilly threw Sean quick smiles to counteract their father's gloom. Yet, he wondered about Melforth's coldness and what incident might have angered him.

Sean watched as Nora cast her father a startled look and then a frown. She then rose, took Sean aside, and quietly explained, "With you here he is on uncharted ground. He is stewing mostly, I think, about some bad words spoken in church this past Sunday. But there are other things." She paused a moment and then continued, "I overheard Marvin Upland, one of his old friends, make a nasty comment meant for everyone to hear." She repeated the man's remark, "A Catholic in his mill and at his table. Our good miller has stepped down to the level of the devil himself!"

Nora watched Sean for a reaction, and saw a frown. "Father is embarrassed but is trying to stand firm." Nora forced a tiny smile and reassured Sean, "You have shown him so much, Sean Kelly. You surely suspect he was raised anti-Papist and is trying to fight his intolerance? That he has allowed you at our table is on his part a great step."

They returned to the family on the porch, and Sean attempted to readjust his thinking. He knew the miller to be a good man, and too many times had witnessed his generosity with the community. Melforth's word sealed a bargain among the people along the river, and despite his occasional lax moments Sean summed up the case for Nora's father. He had known far lesser men.

Ill at ease, Sean complied with the order of the miller and proceeded to put his bow to good use on the worn strings of his hand-me-down instrument. Immediately, a bright tune filled the air. He allowed his thoughts to wander beyond the tense moments of the last week and speculated about this old fiddle, and also the one purchased the past winter in Saint Louis. Maybe Luanne had saved it. The instrument Nora had provided from a neighbor made music but not well. There was a crack in the back and the tuning pegs occasionally slipped. Nevertheless, this afternoon he coaxed one melody then another from it. The younger daughters had joined in with song. Melanie and Lilly playfully danced before him in the dust. He heard from a now happy Melanie, "Don't stop, Sean! Play all the day through."

Gracefully the gypsy duo revolved in unison to the beat of the music with their hands extended. The little girls held up the hems of their long dresses forming flag-like movements. Both swirled through the air as queens and princesses might. Sean saw the relief in their faces and smiled. Mary Katherine filled his mind. *Just as bewitching*, he thought of the two, while they pirouetted and pranced. Sean caught both of their bouncing smiles, welcoming his success at skillfully persuading the strings of the old fiddle. He looked to the miller and sadly saw him still stern-faced in his chair. Despite this recent sourness Sean reminded himself how close he was to what he had once possessed in Ireland.

To the noon-time royalty Sean beamed appreciative smiles and then glanced up to the porch and Nora's radiance. His heart nearly stopped. Momentarily, their gazes locked. Later, Sean hoped that he and the miller's eldest daughter could find time alone.

The Irishman, whose seasoned exterior had been lightened

earlier by Nora's explanation and the afternoon's dance, quickly found himself waylaid by a harsh summons.

Chapter 56
Intolerance Gives Way

"Come with me, Papist."

Sean turned to the patriarch of the fine family who had allowed him to be surrounded with the love of his children. *It could be nothing else*, he felt. The older man, the father, the protector of such radiant children, had called upon him with contempt, a dislike, Sean calculated, greater even than Salem's blacksmith. *Papist! Robert Melforth, you could have done so much better. After all, have I not served this family well?*

"We need to talk, Irishman," the miller said as he led Sean away from the porch and to the shade on the north side of the barn.

Fearful feelings, not to his body but to his heart cut down the boy from Lisdoonvarna. He had thought Robert Melforth his friend. Grown and toughened, Sean followed sadly, shaking his head in disgust. *What could the man possibly say now? How could this father of such fine girls be so bitter and intolerant?*

Close to the same spot where Sean had enjoyed the brief intimacy of Emma, Melforth let loose in a rant, "Irishman, how can you be a follower of Rome?"

Sean heard the father's words but was bewildered.

"How can you agree with the countless slaughtering of tens

of thousands whose only crime was to believe but to believe in a somewhat different way?"

Sean saw his eyes. They were angry and without pity.

"What can you mean, sir?"

Melforth continued as Sean appeared to him truly dumbstruck.

Melforth implored, "Son, you are a Papist who has watched the burning of so many good people!"

Sean's blank look sent the miller on to more furious declarations then to questions. "You don't know, do you?" And the gentler side of Robert Melforth again took charge. "You don't understand the pain of the Inquisition?"

The empty stare continued from the attentive Irishman. "Inquisi.....? Mr. Melforth I have no knowledge of such a thing. What is it of which you speak?"

Only then, the intense anger in Melforth receded as if a pounding rain had quickly run dry.

"I'm sorry to distress you, Sean. But I needed to free these words from my heart. My children love you so." His hands flew into the air in frustration. "But I understand why. All five! What am I to do?" He paused and studied this new addition to his family before his next words filtered out in calm deliberation, "You hold all their hearts." A deep sigh followed and then, "And I cannot deny you."

Sean watched as the stance of the fervent Presbyterian slumped to that of a troubled man. The fiddle player countered, "I don't know of all these things you speak, Mr. Melforth. My faith I know is imperfect. But mostly it is good, at least from what I've seen. Yet, sir," Sean continued after a moment, "I'll make no airs to know better than you or anyone else."

Stout hearted Nora's, beautiful Emma's, sweet Violet's, little Melanie's and Lilly's paternal defender answered back but provided no understanding. "You don't hate Protestants? Your priest did not tell you to hate us even as a young boy?" The miller studied Sean waiting for an answer.

"No," the savvy Irishman, whose many battles and fiddling had earned him more time to live, answered. "Until I worked at the squire's stable as a boy of twelve, I had never met a Protestant. And even then, while I do remember being smitten by the Catholic stable master's daughter, I do not recollect any trouble with Protestants until   my father was beaten and my family's farm burned. It was then we were forced to flee to New York and yet, in County Clare, I despised no one of different religion. I did hate the squire for his greed and horrid ways with his tenant farmers, but I never knew of his dislike of Catholics. He was English and despised anyone Irish, Protestant or Catholic."

Melforth was aghast! "You don't hate us?"

Sean swiftly answered, "I never knew you. How could I hate you?"

Melforth's answer became only a thick silence borne of his crumbling bigotry.

Chapter 57
Labor of Love

Sweat stains on Nora's threadbare, sack-cotton dress spread across her back and chest. The hot afternoon's berry picking was a success because in Sean's mind he was spending more time with Nora. His eyes took in her modest feminine contours. They turned more pronounced as the fabric began to cling to her hourglass waistline. Curls of her long hair had escaped a binding ribbon, and golden strands were glued to her moist cheek. Occasionally, he observed Nora stop her labors and carefully extract wisps of her hair caught by the ever present canes.

A whirlwind of activity surrounded Nora as she plucked in abundance the black shining berries. In spite of the occasional pricked finger, Nora lost little time filling her pail. For Sean it was a different story. His meager attempts and his curses when his fingers encountered sharp spines were childish when compared to Nora's precise efforts and stoic acceptance of the thorny inevitable.

"Sean Kelly, how could you survive a war," she teased, "when a mere berry patch defeats you?" Nora's laughter filled the brambles by the spring creek, but all the while she never let her fingers halt their speedy task.

Sean beamed but said nothing.

The Irishman worked harder for a time but soon his mind

strayed and vivid colors in the berry patch garnered his attention. Brilliant reds of unripe berries contrasted beside the blue-black of countless clusters that hung from heavily laden stems. Even the purple-green of June bugs blended in among the summer-green leaves and razor-tipped thorns.

"Picking blackberries is a labor of love," he moaned, as he pricked himself again. *Painful in the picking but delight in the eating*, came to mind as he glanced over his shoulder past the berry patch. There, he sensed the cold stream only yards away. It rushed painlessly on, so fresh and remarkably clear.

He then forced his attention to the work at hand. When he heard few if any whimpers Nora's way, he commented in true amazement on her ability, "Eli, you certainly can put berries in the pail faster than anyone I've ever seen. My sister, Mary Katherine, was fast, too, but not as fast as you."

A quick reply came back, "Keep your eyes on the berries, my good Irishman, and they will be in the bucket faster. I've been watching you," and she paused and shot him a flashing smile. "I've seen idle hands and eyes eager for more than fruit."

Finally stopping her near frenzy of movement, Nora smiled again but this time more provocatively. She saw him take her in. She pointed to her berrying bucket then his. "Mine is nearly full while yours, dear man, holds less than half!"

Without comment Sean smiled back. He continued picking in his haphazard style because his eyes remained upon the angel so close with long golden hair.

At length he blurted out, "Being near you is what I want, and if I have to pick a few berries to do it, so be it!" Her sharply profiled face revealed a wry, hidden smile, but Nora said nothing.

A frightful buzzing startled Sean. From a clump of ripe berries upset beetles as big as small coins flew up with their wasp-like sound. One landed on the neckline of Nora's dress.

"Let me get it, Nora!" Before she could answer Sean was stumbling her way through the maze of blackberry canes. He heard laughter as his boyish antics produced scratches and curses before bringing him close behind her.

"Easy now," Sean said more to himself than to Nora as he admired her glistening shoulders and neck.

A satisfied smile graced her lips. "It's nothing, Sean. Just a June Beetle. You know they won't bite."

Still he continued and placed one hand on her shoulder. Immediately he felt her tense up, then relax. His right hand plucked the harmless insect from her coarse-woven garment. He flicked it away but kept his other hand on her bare shoulder. With a fondness beyond words, he laid his right hand on her hip.

Nora neither spoke nor flinched but backed up a small step closer to Sean.

Touching her, he bent his head and gently kissed her neck. The saltiness of her skin tempted him further. Another essence, Nora's own, pleased him still more.

The millwright's eldest let out a pleasant sigh. Sean took it as an admission of approval. Confirmation of her thoughts came quickly. Nora reached her berry-stained fingers around his right wrist and slowly pulled his outstretched hand from her hip. She guided his open palm across her stomach.

Nora let out a girlish giggle that broke any tension between them. She turned her head to look deeply into Sean's excited eyes. She giggled again, glanced in the direction of the mill and towards her home. Satisfied with their privacy she proceeded to undress the man now facing her, the man she had met two years before in a valley of death beside the Shenandoah River. She studied his wiry, naked form. She had every intention of loving this honorable man for the rest of her days.

Deep in the brambles they found a clear grassy spot. Nora let him coax her down and loosen the string at her neck that held her dress. In her heart she sensed their actions as natural and inevitable. Turning her head back to release her entangled hair from a blackberry cane then towards him again, Nora studied Sean's features. Her smile welcomed him.

Their passions ebbed and flowed on that hot summer's day as did the buzz of the beetles and the wind above the fluttering leaves of the berry patch. All became sounds that soothed and would forever remain a symphony to her ears.

Afterwards, Sean and Nora pulled sparse clothing back over heads and feet. They stood hand-in-hand. Sean reached down to Nora's thigh. There, he respectfully felt the scar most likely made by a bullet from his pistol two years before. "Your *lucky piece* saved you, Eli."

Nora searched his eyes and quietly said, "Many things saved me."

Not fully understanding, Sean let silence hold the moment. Then withdrawing his hand from her leg he laid his guilt onto a single question, "Would you consider marrying the man who surely scarred you for life?"

Nora looked up. His face, his green eyes, she probed with a look as deep as time. She let out a quiet laugh, "We'll see! I'll need to be sure that shooting me again is not in your future!"

She grasped Sean's hand and guided him to the stream's edge. There, she reached around him and feigned an embrace. Catching Sean off balance in one swift motion, she locked her fingers, and pulled. Both tumbled into the cold, swirling waters. They screamed in pain and delight. The surge of the spring stripped them clean of the afternoon's heat, their passions, and the ever present biting bugs in the grass.

In the swift waist-deep water their flailing bodies splashed and sank. Briefly clinging to each other below the stream's surface, they came up thrashing. The rapture of the cold engulfed them. There in the waters of Missouri's biggest spring came momentary redemption. The horrors of a conflict, that both had somehow endured, briefly were lost.

Holding hands and beaming huge smiles, their bare feet met slippery rocks. The lovers edged their way to the stream bank. Nora laughed as Sean lost his footing in the shallow water. She reached out to him, unaware of the forces committed. Together as one, they found firm ground. A little later they stood with their feet planted, two refreshed and dripping bodies conformed to the other.

Sean whispered in Nora's ear. "Nothing can shake me from you." Their hands refused to part.

Wandering back through the meadow to the cabin became a silent but jubilant stroll. Sean sensed the joy in Nora's eyes. He knew it was their moment, and soon they found themselves settling as one with feet dangling off the front porch. Their hands were still locked together.

Melanie and Lilly frolicked close by giggling at the couple while Sean remembered again his daydream on the hill above Hermann, the little girl on his lap, her flaxen hair, golden in the sun, and the light-haired woman toiling in the garden that before he could not name. He pondered the flaxen hair before him. It was still wet and curling on the head of the woman with whom he was sure to spend a lifetime. He told Nora nothing but wondered. The dark-skinned children who also swam and played in the stream? From whom did they come? But he knew that, too, and was troubled. How could that ever be?

Nora's sisters continued to gawk and snicker as they watched the two lovers. Newly arrived at the porch, Robert Melforth simply leaned back in his caned chair, smug in his gladness but still a father, "Melanie, Lilly, that's enough. Stop your silly nonsense or I'll give you a chore," but his thoughts were really on Elnora and Sean Kelly. *This new addition to his family,* his mind went on while looking at the two again. *She could do no better. Even a game leg damaged in the war is a minor blemish. He's hardworking, loyal, and fiercely protective of all around him.*

Pleased he was to gain a son, a son whose courage had rescued Lilly, Melanie, and also Emma. *Somehow,* his thoughts continued, *Sean had saved Nora, too. If only,* he cajoled, *if only his political sympathies were different.* Nonetheless, Robert Melforth had already decided, *I can live with Sean's lack of foresight. The young man cannot be perfect. I can only wish the other girls the luck and good sense to know when such a man walks in the room,* then lastly, *and I wish them the power to keep him.*

Sean's Catholic up-bringing had slipped to a lower concern in Robert Melforth's mind. *That will change,* he deliberated. *Nora will lure the heathen Catholic to the proper view.* He smiled knowingly and pondered how women possessed powers to sway the most stubborn of wills.

CHAPTER 58
AN INTRODUCTION

Fond memories of Nora from Saturday's tryst were certainly not on Sean's mind at the moment. It was a windless day and a fine dust from the milling of wheat was thick and almost unbearable. Sean's mouth, covered with the ringing-wet rag, craved more air. His body not his lungs, he hoped, was painted with the white powder. His urge to untie and throw off the simple cloth from his mouth was overwhelming. Sack after sack of white wheat flour, and then later, corn meal from another stone and separator, fell down into the linen feed sacks held tightly around the square, wooden trough.

Throughout the ordeal of dusty air, the boredom of filling so many sacks with flour, and the stinging sweat that dripped down into his eyes, Sean was aware that it would eventually end. Even if the mill remained in operation all morning and into the early afternoon he considered his labors trivial in comparison to other times in his life. His labors in Melforth's mill were but minor irritations. Nora, good food, his fiddle, and the innocent joy of Lilly, Melanie, and Violet awaited him at the end of the day.

The miller and Sean continued their labors into the mid afternoon. The line of carts and mules laden with sacked whole corn and wheat finally diminished to a trickle. It had been a busy Monday.

"Robert," Sean spoke up as the last of the grinding ended and Melforth pulled the big lever to halt the gears to the mill stone, "did Nora stand her ground while working in the mill?"

Melforth's answer was not long in coming. "Yes, indeed, my eldest pulled hard. I am only glad there were others to help later. Local boys soon filled the gap. If not for the others helping later when they did, Elnora would have worked herself to death and never complained once."

Melforth's straightforward words of praise came as no surprise. Sean thought how the caring but tough, flaxen-haired daughter of the miller exhibited a simple beauty on the surface but much more lay deep. Taking a rest on the shaded loading dock, he paused to wonder long and hard about the woman who had saved him on the battle field and nursed him back to life from the rattler's venom.

⊕

When work was finally complete for the day, Robert Melforth lounged on his cabin's large front porch, glad of the fresh breeze on his face. With pleasure he observed his family as the master fiddler's jigs and reels wooed his daughters yet again. Melanie and Lilly danced in barefooted delight unaffected by the heat. Violet and her big sister Nora tapped toes and clapped hands with the bouncing rhythm of Sean's instrument. Especially, he watched his Elnora. She was happier than he had ever seen her. The middle-aged millwright contemplated grandchildren and also, a son-in-law's continued help at the mill.

Melforth's pipe dreams speedily faded. He had spotted a rider in the distance near the mill. *No*, he reassessed while the blurred motion drew closer and clearer, *it's a figure on foot leading a work horse or a mule and a cart*. He watched the slow procession work its way up his lane. His ever present shotgun was already cradled under his arm. He casually stepped off the porch unnoticed and ambled in the direction of the strangers.

For a moment as he walked toward the mill, the proud father looked back to the porch, unable to contain his pride in Melanie's and Lilly's fun loving antics. His family and the fiddler were so entranced, no one else had noticed the visitors.

Emma and Violet soon looked to the activity in the lane. Then ceasing their giggling and tickling, the young girls also focused on the outsiders as their father walked out to meet them.

Long minutes later, a much more sober Robert Melforth stood by the cabin's porch and addressed the captivated couple.

"Sean, you've a visitor." Melforth's words pulled Sean from his worship of Nora and from a rambunctious tune. With firmer words the miller made it clearer, "There is someone to see you, Sean!"

Truly saddened, fatherly eyes watched while the young man finally acknowledged him with a nod. Sean had still not looked up. But Nora had raised her eyes, and the anxious miller wondered what questions she had about the visitors.

Sean dropped his bow arm from his fiddle and finally sluggishly turned his head. There on the road, his dreamy eyes first came to a mule, a faintly familiar beast, pulling a load. Then his understanding catapulted forward. Dumbfounded, he was totally unbelieving of what he saw.

Two young boys and their older sister, faces and arms black as coal, spied him and smiled brightly. Then he watched the tired face of the most beautiful of women appear from under a broad, sweat-stained hat. A worn out smile met his eyes.

A suddenly shy Amy huddled closer to the rear of the cart but not the boys. In an instant, seven-year-old Quincy and eight-year-old Jeremiah jumped down and kicked up a fuss running to the Irishman's side. Then Sean studied Luanne's dark eyes. They stared hopefully his way. She gave him the same look that he had witnessed as her cart pulled away in Salem. No words came, but his mind was whirling. *How can this be? How... can... this be?*

A faraway look filled Luanne's eyes before her words slipped out in a whisper, "I had to come. There was no one else." Then in hesitation came, "Sean, we had nowhere to go." Her pleading eyes never left him.

Sean could hear the desperation in her words but he could say nothing. He turned to Nora's father, sure he had listened closely to every word. Luanne's exhaustion and her womanly condition were easily detected. Sean was certain that Melforth was already trying to calculate how this lovely mulatto woman and her three dark children would interfere with his eldest daughter's future.

Spell-bound but finally able to speak, Sean asked, "You made it here alone with the children? Amazing!" Then, "I'm sorry." Finally, Sean took Luanne's hand. Over her shoulder he observed their only baggage to be two near empty feed sacks tied to the rail on the cart. Her shotgun's wooden stock poked out of a bag. He grinned in respect.

"Yet, even still," he asked, "how did you find me?" Then he also saw the familiar bulk of his fiddle hanging in the sack off the other side. Luanne's clothing was tattered and covered in red dust. Her children were in no better condition.

Luanne's answer came out stiff and slow. "Crossing the river to the west before the Current, we were nearly lost near Alley Spring. Some good people helped us."

"Sean!" Jeremiah piped out before his mother could suppress him. "Can we stay with you?"

Her pride clearly pressed to its limit, Luanne looked solemnly at Sean. She knew there was nothing else to say.

He touched her shoulder with his left hand and whispered, "I thought you hated me." The Irishman watched for her reaction. It rushed at him unstoppable while only Violet, a few steps away, was able to hear.

"Oh, dear man," Luanne whispered back. "I can never hate you." And as she said the words the good mother of three remembered the moonlit night at her farm, where gentle hands had washed her body of blood and shame.

Indecisive no longer, Sean led a stumbling Luanne to the porch. "You're welcome. You must be hungry."

A radiant smile came back in reply. With Sean, Luanne knew, the children would be safe. Then fully realizing the completion of her journey, she collapsed. Strong arms carried her into the cabin, but she would not remember whose. When she awoke in the light of a single candle on fresh hay her fingers stroked the clean, cotton dress that covered her. A young girl with dark hair, not Amy, motioned her to drink. Cool water never tasted so good.

Suddenly remembering, a frail Luanne rose up on her elbows and barely managed, "Where are my children?"

"Fed and asleep," and Violet's arm pointed to the corner. "Look!"

"My mule? Was it left in the sun?"

"Oh, no, Mrs. Weller," Violet consoled. "Sean led your mule to the spring. He hobbled it in knee deep pasture."

Still puzzled but glad and yet also ashamed of begging for refuge she asked again, "But how long have I been here? Whose clothes am I wearing?" Then in a tiny voice cringing with embarrassment, "Who bathed me, child?"

"It's all right, Mrs. Weller. Please, don't worry. He asked me to help him take care of you." Her eyes appraised the dark woman without her father's harsh pre-judgment. Then Violet told more, "He washed you. I saw only devotion in his eyes. I dried and dressed you."

A symphony of adoration spilled from the sweetest of the Melforth daughters, locked in with a brand of innocence Luanne could not imagine, "If Sean loves you, I will love you, too."

Though she thought herself no longer capable of tears, Luanne fell back into her blankets both warm and safe. Blissfully, she allowed the flood to begin. Then she let herself fall into the most delicious sleep that she could remember.

⊕

In the darkness, Nora's father, a long advocate of slavery, and Sean stood in the solitude of the mill's loading dock discussing the troubling state of affairs that had arisen in the afternoon.

"Who are these people, Sean? Do you expect me to put coloreds up on my land?"

Unaffected, Sean said, "Yes, I do. The barn will be fine, Mr. Melforth."

Sean measured Robert Melforth's anger and watched as it simmered quite ready to rise to a boil. Still, Sean remained calm. With clear conviction he said, "Sir, these people are not colored or white, but people. And they are good people. Her husband was killed after the war. They deserve haven on your land if only for a few days." And as a final note, "I will have nothing less, or I shall be forced to leave, too."

The miller was shocked, but well aware that the Irishman's steadiness had forced his hand. Even though he knew his family owed Sean much, he was still furious. Barely under control, he managed to say, "All right, then, Sean Kelly. You've played your aces. Your black friends may stay a while." Then to cover his lost pride, "But do not expect this game to last long."

In silence they stepped down into the dust of the road. Then, as men who had over many weeks earned each other's respect, a still hopeful father and the man he also expected to be his future son-in-law grudgingly walked back together. No words were spoken between the two for a long night and a day.

CHAPTER 59
AN EXPLANATION

The evening sky was filled with gloriously orange clouds as Nora stood on the porch of the cabin awaiting Sean and her father. She wore her only pair of shoes and her best of faded dresses, unsure of the feelings that had come over her. She had combed out her long hair and tied it back with a ribbon. Behind her ears she had daubed a few drops of vanilla.

Across the small hay field the men she loved the most in the world walked nearer. She looked towards the spring in the distance for a moment trying to clear her thinking, then directly back towards the man she was intent on marrying. When he was face to face with her she asked, "Who is this family, Sean Kelly? I didn't pay much attention when you told me earlier in the summer."

Nora sensed more layers to the relationship of her Irishman with the colored family than her father would ever fathom. She had seen Luanne's distraught eyes blossom with hope. Nora had grasped, as only another woman could, the expectant Negro mother's need to seek refuge satisfied. Later, a pensive Violet had confronted her, "Nora, the Negro woman knows that Sean will help her no matter what! Is that right?" Nora had nodded as she gave a sobering answer, "Yes, Violet, I truly believe it is so."

Sean began his explanation as Nora walked with him to the

spring. "They are my friends, Nora. I hold by my friends. You know that. I told you because you needed to understand my feelings. I met them on the way south from Hermann. They needed help. I helped them. I care greatly for Luanne," then after a delay, "and her children?"

The words struck Nora like a two pound hammer. *They needed help. He helped them*, blistered on her brain. She, more than anyone, fully comprehended the mysteries hidden behind Sean's simple explanation. *This dark mother with her children had run to Sean from two counties west as if he were a savior.* Wise Nora recognized, *So, he must have been. It's as simple as that.*

Torn by this conflict for which she found no reasonable settlement, Nora remembered the look that Luanne had cast Sean in the cabin when she revived. The next day Nora had witnessed another silent but intimate exchange, understanding all too well its meaning.

Just around the corner of the cabin and thinking herself hidden Luanne had stared with brief intensity into Sean's eyes as he raised his head from a chore. She was imploring him to do something. The eldest daughter of Robert Melforth fully recognized the implication of Luanne's gesture. *Of my sisters, only Emma*, Nora was sure, *would know what such unspoken communication truly meant.*

Chapter 60
Dilemma

Nora and Sean sat with knees to their chins perched on the large boulder. The rock, as flat as a great table, looked over the big spring's boiling waters.

Sean's explanation continued in earnest. "Please, Nora, hear me out!"

Nora held her thin leather shoes tightly clenched in her hands. Her attempt to probe the depths of her Irishman's sincerity was trying her soul. Before, he had only briefly described the brave woman near Salem and her troubles, while now tried with carefully chosen words to calm her fears. Melforth's oldest dutifully listened but with a nearly broken heart. *How can he expect me to accept this tale*? However, Sean went on and told her more.

Then she burst out, "Sean Kelly, don't take me for a fool! I saw more in her eyes than gratitude. The woman is one of the handsomest I have ever seen. Can you deny the way she looks at you? You know she is with child."

Sean took a deep breath and let it out slowly. When he spoke, it was with deep conviction. "You, dear Eli, are the woman with whom I hope to spend the rest of my days. Know that. Know that now and forever."

Nora mellowed as Sean's words comforted her just as Sean's

eyes had set Luanne's heart at rest that first day. She listened, still fearfully, while gazing into his green eyes. *He is asking me to marry him,* she presumed. Then Nora thought how she, too, may well be carrying his child.

As the out-pulsing spring water roared below their feet, he went on, "I have loved before, Eli, when I was in Ireland, and on a field of dying men, and this spring before I again became entranced by you. Remember, Eli, when I met Luanne I thought you dead." Briefly Sean's words failed him, and he waited desperately for her understanding. His eyes watched the rolling foam of the blue-tinted pool for many moments before he said, "Please, remember that, before you turn me away." He repeated. "Remember, I thought you dead."

Then catching her eye he said, "You are the woman, Eli, who will bear my children and tend me when I am in need. You are the companion, I pray, who will stand beside me through all that life throws in our path."

He let his eyes follow the current to a faraway place before he spoke again. "But you must know..."

Nora's gentle look instantly transformed to one that was wary and unbelieving. Cat-like and ready to pounce, she watched Sean and waited. *Where in this maze of brambles are his words leading me?*

"I will not turn this woman out on her own, Eli," he began again but softly. "She has no one, and I will not deny that I care for her more than as a friend." He stopped, still looking eye-to-eye with the flaxen-haired woman at his side. He waited for what seemed an eternity for her to answer.

Elnora Rebecca Melforth was not a simple woman. She was the intelligent daughter of one of the most respected men in Carter County. She knew her experiences with life were intimately understood by the man beside her. At first glance two days before, she had determined she was no match in beauty for the dark-haired woman with the honey skin and radiant smile who beamed when Sean was near. Nora felt that Sean knew Luanne through and through, and greatly respected this literate and caring woman. Nora had swallowed her pride but was unsure how tolerant she could be towards someone who had strings tied to her future husband's heart.

"So, what is it that you expect of me, Sean Kelly," Nora finally implored of him. Her eyes, blind to the natural beauty around her, were blurred with tears.

Sean clasped Nora's fingers and gently pulled her hand to his chest. "For now, Eli, please, be patient. Allow me a day, maybe two. By then I hope to find a way to help Luanne and not destroy your feelings for me." He paused, and his kindness turned cool. "But know that I will not abandon her."

Nora's long blond hair waved in the constant breeze off the water. Her steady but tearful eyes again scanned Sean's face. His next words shook her to the core even though she had suspected it.

"The child Luanne carries is mine," he said flatly, his words with no hint of regret. His voice trailed away as the heart-rending sentence reached sharp talons deep into the other woman he would not desert except in death. There was nothing but love and sadness in his eyes.

A long silence allowed pieces of the puzzle to fall into place, unshakable. Neither were simple souls, love struck, or prone to hand-wringing indecision. Both had seen life begin with nurturing family ties, and both had witnessed the reality of death in a war between brothers. Both refused to throw away precious love for the sake of pride, at least not hastily, and not yet.

Nora was hurt deeply. But with the strength of an unknown father she often wondered about, she pondered the wiry red-haired man she had saved on a battlefield. Saved from the poison of snake bite and from his horrors in the night. *Nothing*, she felt, *can break the bonds I share with this man before me. The Sean Kelly I know lets no day pass without helping someone. He is oak. I am ash. But what of Luanne, from what is she made?*

Trusting Sean for more reasons than a host of humanity could ever hope to understand, Nora continued her vigil as the gushing spring water flowed by. The pangs of Nora's icy jealousy begin to melt away, but ever so slowly, one crystalline, needle-like dagger at a time. *I will wait*, she thought, as again her eyes searched his for the deception that she knew was not there. *I will wait and I will see*

from what type of wood this woman is hewn. He will have to choose,
but I will wait.

Nora's anger had calmed. She sensed the cement between them set and dried. A serene understanding of her Irishman settled over her like falling leaves in autumn on a bright cool day. It echoed through her, raising goose bumps on her skin. There would be no desertion on her part, nor on his she recognized, only an attempt to understand and accept. Nora decided, *Yes, accept,* and she whispered aloud this time, "I will wait."

They sat in silence and watched the blue surge of the spring. Nora reached back in time to memories of her first love that she had never shared with anyone. A man as dear to her as Sean had held her heart for many months in Virginia. Several soldiers knew her true identity, and one had gained her trust and all else a woman can give. She had worried desperately at first that they had conceived a child. When they had not, she became concerned, but in a different way. Was she barren or was he?

Finally, Nora turned to the living man beside her. Cold as stone, she told Sean, "This sweet southern boy, once in my arms and who I knew so well, will linger for the rest of my life." She watched as Sean reacted to her difficult admission. Yet, he simply took her hand and warmed her heart when he said, "Yours or mine, our memories are sacred. I loved you when you were my enemy. I love you, now. And I will love you forever more."

Managing her emotions, Nora again studied the Irishman on the misty, gray rock, knowing that he had said it best. *Any that might hold a candle to him have long since perished in conflict. Yet, this man, plain in looks and stature, stands out among so many. I have seen it,* Nora told herself. *I will covet closest to my heart those, as he, who have souls so strong.*

Then while quietly looking into each other's eyes, Sean and Nora embraced.

CHAPTER 61
SISTERS

"**H**as he told you?" Luanne asked breathlessly, bravely breaking the silence of over a week, a week of painful uncertainty. Dew and dirt clung to their bare feet as they weeded the garden alone after breakfast. Nora's shotgun and Luanne's lay close at hand leaning against an old apple tree's gnarled trunk.

On this gray Tuesday, the sharp home-wrought tools came down aggressively time and time again chopping grass and young weeds invading the corn and beans. However, Nora's thoughts were elsewhere. She had heard the rumor in church two days before. The McLauds were coming to kill her father, and soon.

Nora's fearful thoughts swirled in confusion as her hoe continued to cut deeper into the hard soil. Beside her, Luanne spoke again but Nora pretended not to hear, unsure of how to answer. All week she had been proper but had avoided Luanne when she could. It was all too painful.

"Has he told you?" Luanne pleaded but this time slightly louder.

Again, Nora heard this gentle question demanding to be answered and finally resigned herself to be done with the silence between them. She motioned Luanne to a split-log bench. There, when she sat down, her feelings ran through her mind once again.

Indeed, her jealousy of Luanne was overwhelming. How could she compete with one so beautiful and educated? The ex-slave before her not only could read and write English like a scholar, but spoke Latin.

Maintaining control by the thinnest thread, Nora asked, "Tell me what? What should I know?" Then finally pushing aside her pride, Nora said, "Tell me, Luanne." It had been the first time Nora had called the unwanted visitor by her first name.

"What has he told you?" Luanne asked again, appealing for understanding and humanity, factors of which only women seemed born to make sense.

Nora answered in frustration, "He said he helped you. He said he helped your family. He wouldn't say what he did."

Luanne's delicate hand reached for Nora's, and Robert Melforth's eldest daughter let her hold it. Then, the story came out. It's power germinated and grew from when she first met him at the blacksmith's shop, to the assault of her children and herself and their rescue, and finally to his confession of knowing her husband. Luanne saved the story of her by the well for last. She described Sean so humbly propping up her shattered dignity. "Nora, he washed me of the blood and filth of rape and death. I stood naked in humiliation, but he washed that away, too."

The appreciative tears in Nora's eyes had begun earlier during Luanne's tale of woe and love.

"He told me only good things, Nora. He made me feel like a treasured queen rather than a brutally raped woman." Pausing, a few hard moments passed before she continued. "He put cool water on my bruises. He touched me only as would our mothers or grandmothers caring for the sick."

Luanne had more to tell. "He never tried to take my body. Many days later I insisted that he must." Luanne and Nora were now embracing as only distraught sisters might. "Please," Luanne pleaded, "do not hate him for loving me, a colored woman. I know he loves you very much, and more than me." She hesitated, wiping away her tears and then Nora's with the long sleeve of her dress. Golden hair ran through her fingers.

Nora tasted the saltiness of her own tears. With a new found grace that had moments before engulfed her, she felt honored to bestow acceptance.

"In his dreams Sean would speak of the light-haired woman who was to bear his children." Luanne continued while running Nora's long hair between her fingers. "His dreams told of children, dark-skinned and light, swimming and playing in a clear creek near his home." Quietly she added, "Our home, Nora."

The teary face of this fierce Melforth woman came up in shock, but only found gentle eyes. Nora was confused, but pressed forward as was her nature. *Yes, somehow, we will get through this, the affront to my father, the McLauds, and my own embarrassment.* Then unfolding in her thoughts the humble question formed as the last barrier to be broken down. Hand-in-hand with the good woman at her side, Nora murmured the ultimate of apologies, "How could I have been so cruel?"

Each new moment, now so glowing and inviting, grew and passed on to the next. Nora felt the worries on her shoulders lighten while, as if on cue, the fog lifted over the valley. In patches, a bright sun shone through. There, under a fruit laden tree, Robert Melforth's finest daughter, but not of his blood, sensed Sean's dark-haired lover to be extraordinary. Luanne had breached the wall in her heart and had knit their fabric as one. In Nora's mind, their rapport had traveled to a rare place beyond Luanne's striking beauty and her abilities with language and medicines. Luanne Weller now held her trust.

CHAPTER 62
EXODUS

No fires were kindled on the hearthstone of the Melforth cabin on mid summer evenings. The days had grown too hot. Outside within a ring of rounded stones a tiny fire glowed while supper simmered in black kettles hung over the coals. The family sat solemnly in a circle.

Nora adamantly had told her father on Sunday evening, "We must leave! We can follow Sean to his land in the western part of the state. We will start again. Father, listen to me! Please, listen."

Now three days later Nora struggled again to convince her family to leave. The powerful rumors of the McLauds coming to murder her father had failed to be smothered by the days of waiting, rather they had grown hotter as local citizens heard news and quickly spread it. Nora watched the head of her clan turn away from her in frustration and anger. His outrage was directed at her for siding with Sean and Luanne. He told her that he had hoped, instead, to have given them some grain and sent them on their way. So, now on this ever darker Wednesday evening the Melforths and Sean sat pondering their future. Luanne and her children watched from beyond the circle on a thick cottonwood log.

"You must leave with us, father," Nora pleaded while gesturing with a small twig in her hand. "Tomorrow by noon they will most likely come. We must leave by first light." In frustration she tossed her stick onto the hot coals.

"And will you try to steal my children from me, Elnora?" the patron of the Melforth clan painfully questioned even though his respect for her was so evident.

Nora looked to Sean then sadly back to her father. A bright glow, sent by a few crackling flames, lit the fearful faces around her. "Please, if they kill you what will happen to Violet and my two younger sisters? Don't you see? It's all or none."

Sweet Violet, who so often was quiet and no competition for the older girls or for the lively Melanie and Lilly, broke the silent stalemate. "I will stay with you, father." Then she bravely spoke to her oldest sister, "You have taught me to handle a firearm." In response Violet caught the stark looks from her sisters and father and attempted to toss them back in kind.

Sean said nothing, knowing it was not his place, not yet.

Nora had spoken her piece, but nonetheless asked, "Where is Emma? This is important." Then with bitterness, "Is she with one of the McAlester boys, again?"

Robert Melforth shook his head and answered in defense, "Emma is where she will be. I am where I will stay."

Sean watched Nora's father. The Irishman saw only growing resolution in the miller's face.

Melforth looked to his three younger daughters. "And I am where I should be. You, all three, will go with Sean and Elnora. Even though Sean's protection of Emma precipitated this, Cyril has always hated me. It would have come whether or not the Irishman had ever ridden south from Hermann." A deep breath came and went as he studied Sean.

"It's my battle alone," he continued. "All of you must leave." A great sigh left the miller before he spoke next. "I will hole up in the mill and hope for the best. God will grant me peace." He paused a moment, and then added, "And maybe justice."

Sean listened. He compared Robert Melforth's words to those of a valiant major who had commanded thousands and had been cornered, back against the wall. The officer had found safe retreat for all but himself.

CHAPTER 63
ALONE HE STANDS

The next day's late morning bliss turned suddenly sour. From the cabin Sean saw the mob of dark horsemen surrounding the mill. With stealth he led his horse to where   Melforth had been intent on battling until the end. Everything began to play out too quickly. From the safety of the great walnut tree, he observed Nora's father being forced out onto the dock by two heavily bearded men. Oddly, a sigh of relief left him. One of his greatest fears had disappeared. The McLauds' big dogs were nowhere to be seen.

Sean had prepared his weapons earlier. He was ready now but knew there was little time. The McLauds would soon have the miller strung high in a tree.

⊕

"I am the killer of your kin, not Robert Melforth!" Nora and Luanne's red-haired Irishman hollered out. "Your lout of a boy tried to force himself on the miller's daughter. He had a knife to her throat. I shot him. It's me you want."

Sean looked ten startled horsemen in the eye. He had managed to walk his horse closer without being noticed. His angry words continued, "You have no fight with Robert Melforth. Kill me if you

313

can. Kill me! Send me to your son's or brother's hell! I will go gladly but with many of you dead at my feet."

The McLauds sat thunderstruck upon their prancing mounts but braced themselves for a fight. Before them, they knew, stood a man unafraid of death. All looked to their surprised father. More than Sean's words set back the McLauds. The two barrels of the Irishman's scatter-gun lay over his horse's withers and were leveled chest high. Another shotgun they saw strapped on his shoulder. Slowed but not swayed, the McLauds' pride refused them the option to withdraw. To ride away in peace when only one man dared to confront them would have made them the laughing stock of the county.

Sean's undeniable Irish brogue and the faded yellow stripe on the outside of his trousers explained his past. Mumbles and fearful laughter broke out among the black-haired men. "Who is he?" Then from another, "The soldier is a fool to try stopping a McLaud in Carter County." A devilish grin crossed the face of still one more before the words came out. "Ten McLauds will send you to hell."

The youngest horseman piped up in a high pitched voice, "Grandpa, can we hang the Irishman, too?"

Cyril McLaud's voice roared above the din of trampling horses, "Of course! We'll let the crippled Papist join the party!"

Sean Kelly paused, taking in a long slow breath and letting it out at a leisurely rate. His rage had passed and a steady coldness had come over him. Unknown to the McLauds, the lion's cage was open.

Hidden determination blocked his fear as Sean had seen laudanum on the battlefield and in the field hospitals dull the pain of the wounded. His acceptance of death settled deep inside while he climbed that mountain to a point of no return. To all these mounted men who listened, he was certainly a madman. Two handfuls of fierce horsemen, foul hearts so evident, against one. For moments that passed for hours, the Irishman thought of his childhood. He also pondered the two women that he held so dear to his heart. In that precious time Sean Kelly prepared to kill and to die.

⊕

The county's most unwavering southern sympathizer closed his eyes in fearful anticipation of the end. Robert Melforth sat backwards on his horse with his hands tied behind him. He was beyond hope. The laughter of his executioners he supposed to be the last sounds he would ever hear. His neck chafed from the coarse hemp rope, and he cursed himself for being taken so easily. A final prayer for his daughters filled the miller's brain. However, the noose around his neck grew tighter with a sudden yank. First, a frozen tongue and then a graying, fogginess filled his brain.

Only Melforth's vision remained, and from the corner of his eye he observed the rope and the horseman who would end his life. The animal had been backed to allow no mercy of a slack line. Strangling while he awaited the drop, the reverent man cried in silent anguish for God's justice to smite these evil men who would no doubt harm his children. With a last futile gasp Nora's father opened his eyes still wider for what he guessed the last time. Across the road the miller beheld an answer to his prayer. Moments before he had heard but had not believed. A steely-eyed angel with a shotgun watched him.

"Loosen the rope, Tiran," Melforth heard. "We have no use for him to die on his horse."

Laughter arose among the horseman as Cyril McLaud's command granted Melforth a much needed reprieve. A tiny single breath and then another rushed to his starved lungs. The cloud covering his thinking arose momentarily, while in bewilderment he observed his future son-in-law, now never to be. However, in acceptance of his plight the miller readied himself to pass on to the darkness. What could one man do against an army of McLauds?

⊕

Underlying the stranger's resolute eyes lay something the two eldest sons of Cyril McLaud seldom witnessed. The McLauds lived by fear, yet a man stood before them unafraid. The two had been in the war. Both had quickly realized their plight, and their worries grew at a harrowing pace. Only *one* against *ten*, but the brothers knew. There were four barrels of buck shot ready to find them, and the *one* stood protected behind his horse.

⊕

Sean soothed the Morgan with a gentle tone, knowing the animal would be the first to feel the agony of the battle. The gentle gelding would prolong his life for seconds, no longer. He craved it, actually, never understanding how he had survived so long. *Dying is so easy*, he told himself. *Living has always proved so hard.*

His next words were fact in his mind, not show. However, the McLauds, he doubted wise enough to heed them. Sean called haltingly but loud to the two eldest brothers, "Cut...him...down!" He had seen it in their eyes, and knew they needed to be the first to die.

⊕

The Irishman's powerful command affected Melforth in a way he did not understand. Maybe in another life and at some other place he would hear this same voice booming clearly in defiance, and then he would know that men were again about to die. However today, Robert Melforth helplessly waited, knowing his death would not be quick.

⊕

On his fidgeting horse, the gray-haired patriarch of the McLauds coldly stared Sean down. Quiet and brooding, there was fire in Cyril McLaud's eyes. He was thinking what the next move was to be. His nine burly sons and grandsons with their pistols and rifles were prepared to silence this sudden new threat that had appeared, it seemed, from nowhere. Could this really be the Irish cripple he had promised to hang? The boy's shotgun would surely take him down, but for that the oldest of the McLauds showed no concern.

He yelled to Robert Melforth's already pale face, "Hang accursed rebel! Die slow!" And as he said the words his hand slapped the horse with Melforth reversed in the saddle. The sweating beast bolted away.

Sean hesitated no more. First learned on the streets of New York, then refined to an art on the battlefields of Virginia, Melforth's angel let fly the slaying sword.

The large gauge scatter-gun erupted with ear-splitting concussion. Flame and then billowing smoke filled the road. First to the left side, the air around the McLauds buzzed with a cloud of three-sixteenth inch leaden spheres racing through space. The dense pellets instantly spread into a killing path two horse lengths wide.

In agony three McLauds fell to the road. Their horses, also wounded, screamed as they bolted. Sean's second shot quickly exploded from the double barrel. His horse let loose a whinnying scream of pain and ran. Unprotected, Sean watched to Melforth's right, where his buckshot had brought down more than horses and had caused a panic. Three more of the black-bearded men were down.

Dropping his scatter-gun, Melforth's old ten gauge quickly found ready hands. As rapidly as possible Sean cocked the hammers, leveled, and fired on two more of the McLauds before fiery pain ripped his side. One of his barrels had misfired.

Staggering, not falling, he pulled his Navy Colt and once, then twice it exploded in his hand. Another black-bearded man dropped from the saddle. Sean was suddenly knocked sideways and to his knees. More pain gripped him. His left arm dripped red, though, worse pain consumed his chest. His actions seemed dream-like and slow. His heavy revolver remained in his hand. He cocked it for the third time.

Two McLauds remained in the saddle while Sean observed Robert Melforth's kicking, strangling form dangle from the thick-roped noose. Sean looked up and easily detected that the oak limb holding his weight flexed but would stand the strain. The Irishman stumbled toward his failing friend, oblivious of the remaining firearms taking aim at his body. Why he was not shot down, he had no idea. The intense sound of a bee passed his ear.

"Let him hang, Mick!" a deep voice screamed in panic above the melee. Sean's pistol was already aimed towards the man behind the words. The pressure on his trigger let loose the hammer. His pistol exploded again, but it was unknown in the cloud of black powder smoke if his target caught the racing lead ball or not.

"Why would you defend a rebel? You're a Yank like us!" the

oldest voice, now alone, hollered in hysterical distraction through the smoke. Rearing in confusion the horses of the remaining two mounted McLaud's twirled barely under rein. Only the grandfather sat upright. The other bent over and cradled his stomach.

Blinding smoke from the discharge of so many black powder weapons lingered on the road. Sean's eyes burned. The dead and wounded were nearly invisible.

His left arm hung limp at his side and dripped a trail of blood in the dust as Sean walked towards Melforth's dangling body. He holstered his pistol and reached for his long knife. From three steps away he muttered to the miller's struggling body, "There is now little chance, my friend." Then, "God, please help me!" Focused on only one outcome, Sean demanded rescue or death and forced himself forward. In great pain he finally stood below the man who had treated him as a son.

Sean looked up but not to Melforth's beet red face. He waited for the wounded McLaud with his pistol nearly ready to aim, and shoot him dead. Half a second later he screamed in hatred to the oldest McLaud, "No, I am not like you!"

Two swipes of his hunting knife sent the sudden weight of Robert Melforth down. Above him Sean heard repeated metallic clicks. He saw the gray-bearded McLaud throw away his pistol in disgust and pull a long black-barreled weapon from its scabbard, all the while gaining little control over his frightened horse. Sean managed with one hand and his teeth to loosen the noose from Melforth's neck.

The sudden drop had sent the stout miller on him. Sean was defenseless. He watched Melforth's face. Nothing, then a sudden retching breath came from the miller's mouth! Sean saw the armed horseman above him and accepted his fate.

Cyril McLaud looked down. In no hurry now, he let loose a fury of curses, "You lousy, stinking Irish son of a bitch! Die!"

Tears of anger wetted the patriarch's face and beard. His horse wheeled. He scanned the scene of death. *None of this should have happened.* In an agony fueled by seeing all his offspring shot through, no questions of mercy struggled in the old man's conscience. He would lay low the *one* man who had slain *so* many.

"How?" the last McLaud asked his dead and dying sons.

His voice trailed off in madness, "In the blink of an eye? All my boys gone! One man! One man! How?"

The old McLaud unleashed a terrifying scream, "You! You! You!" The single barrel of his shotgun pointed down at the Irishman's head.

Sean had cushioned Melforth's fall. He could do nothing but hold the older man in his lap. His weapon remained useless in its holster under the miller's full weight. To Sean's relief, Robert Melforth was gasping for more air. His now unbound hands rubbed at his throat.

When I am dead, thought Sean, *maybe he will still have a chance*, yet he doubted it. He heard the last McLaud above him on his pounding horse screaming insanely. Sean was well aware that the lone McLaud resolutely aimed, unable to miss.

Cyril McLaud's panicky horse did not cooperate. It jumped. The charge of lead meant for a red-headed target pounded with a shudder into the loose dirt beside Sean's leg.

Then to the Irishman's surprise a barrage of musket fire erupted from the trees at the edge of the road. A great concussion rang in his ears. A new cloud of smoke rolled his way.

"My dear God," Sean asked sincerely of his creator, "how many McLauds can there be?"

CHAPTER 64
A LAST FULL MEASURE

Nora and Luanne looked up suddenly from the packed cart and horses. They had heard the powerful roar of firearms as they were preparing for the journey to leave the valley. Nora called out as she grabbed her shotgun, "Violet, take care of the children!"

A cloud of smoke had risen near the mill. The two women ran down the road as they had never run before. Luanne also carried a shotgun. More explosions echoed across the valley.

"Nora, run faster!" Luanne hollered, pleading to herself as well. Already breathing heavily, she held her heavy shotgun while maintaining her pace several strides ahead of Nora. More gunfire met their ears. Puffs of gray formed then mingled as one, pushed together in the still heat of the afternoon air. Down the lane towards the mill the two women raced. Despite their delay Luanne dared to hope that the Irishman might still live.

"I see them!" Nora hollered while she held her dress up and away from her churning feet. "Maybe you should reload for me." The smoke cleared for a moment, and the outcome of the deadly clash filled her eyes. Men and animals lay strewn and bloodied on the road. She groaned while in full stride. At the moment her father was cut free, Sean went down.

Out of breath beside Nora, Luanne yelled out, "No!" Hatred ran through her as the only McLaud still a-horse missed his mark. In desperation Luanne screamed again, "Faster, Nora! We must run faster."

Melforth's oldest stopped. She braced her heavy weapon on the side of the old walnut tree. With an experience earned dearly during the war she surveyed the landscape of death on the road. One then the other, straining, she pulled back the heavy hammers. *It would be now or never,* her thoughts raced. *There is so little hope. No hope at all.* She glanced to the far side of the table wide tree. Luanne was there and ready.

Fire and clouds of gray smoke erupted. It billowed across the road. Firmly stationed, the two resolute women made ready to let off another volley when the air cleared.

Chapter 65
Luanne Takes Note

Sean heard more than saw the last McLaud fall. The double blast boomed in his ears. "Where? Who?" He had no idea. In a blur he saw the hate-filled patriarch hurled back and then down from his saddle. For a moment the shredded body of the still living man writhed on his back in the dust, but one foot remained caught in the stirrup. His horse bolted.

Sean wasted no emotion as he watched. The torso and head of the barely-living man ploughed the dust and rocks of the road. To Sean's eyes all was quickly lost to the lingering smoke and the trail of dust. Hoof beats faded into the distance.

Long moments later, the thick haze cleared. Sean was near fainting as he forced himself to gaze across the dead and dying. He was sure his luck was done. He cocked his head in disbelief and looked across the road to the great, dark tree.

There, he spied dresses first, two women an instant later. *But dresses were never on battlefields! From where had the gunfire come? The question tried his little remaining sanity? Who saved us?* A pained glance this way and that beyond the carnage gave Sean no answers. The smoke cleared. He saw no one else.

Again, he looked in the direction of the last exchange of firearms. Behind the guns at the thick tree, he saw them more clearly, now. Two women were embracing, jumping up and down. A lovely black woman and a white woman with long flaxen hair. Who were they? Then, the cloud in his mind cleared. *Of course, who else could they be?*

Barely able to sit and speaking with the tone of a man beaten and near his end, Sean said through shallow painful breaths, "He is breathing. Take care of him. Your father is crushing me."

⊕

Luanne hesitated by the tree as she saw a blur of fair hair rush across the dusty road. She stood watching the writhing bodies of wounded men and horses. An empty glaze filled her eyes. She could not move.

She viewed the mangled forms of the McLauds, still not believing the death dispensed by the lone man in the dirt. Her shotgun's second barrel was primed and ready, but Luanne knew that she was done.

Her legs gained courage as she walked to the tiny island of living souls through such a sea of dying. Step-by-step she crossed the corpse littered road. Quickly, though, she leaned her weapon against a lifeless horse and rushed to her bloodied Irishman.

Only one image was branded in Luanne Weller's brain. *Save him*! And with those thoughts she mustered all her strength and helped Nora pull the heavy miller from Sean's wounded body. She recovered her calm demeanor and then methodically began the difficult job of tending his injuries.

Briefly looking up from the Irishman's bloody arm and chest, her eyes swept the incredulous landscape of death surrounding her. Astonishment seized in her throat, but momentarily drained away as she worked to stop his bleeding. She had witnessed it before. On her farm she had seen what this man with steel gray eyes would do to evil men. Here, she had experienced its horror all again, although now with grudging respect. *All the McLauds, but one! But how, Sean? How have you alone taken down so many to their well deserved hell?*

CHAPTER 66
DARK CLOUDS

Sean steadied himself but felt the dizziness coming. He had known it before. Covered in rusty dirt, he placed a sweaty hand to his side, and with a painful breath brought it back for his eyes to see. Red with blood, his fingers were dripping but not as much as he expected. He felt Luanne's gentle then painfully probing hands inside his shirt. *No mortal wound*, he hoped, as he searched her sad eyes.

Nora, just a step away, cringed when she saw Luanne's fingers covered in his blood. She attempted to rise.

Sean saw her intentions and said through pain-etched words, "See to your father, Nora! I will most likely live. See to your father first!" He waved her back to the near strangled miller and watched as she returned to holding her father's head back to ease his breathing.

The smell of the dust and blood took hold and the gray cloud again enshrouded Sean's mind. *Yet, what was this healer's name.* He let loose a pitiful cry as he felt probing fingers again in the bullet hole in his side. For a second time he screamed, and the sudden shock from it lifted the cloud again. He tried to stifle his pain, but failed. Then in heaving agony he studied the honey-skinned woman whose hands both healed and hurt. *Beautiful and capable,* he thought as she pressed firmly with torn rags from her dress. He felt his wound bound tight as yet another moan left him.

Once more, he was aware of Luanne's fingers searching for other sources of blood and broken bones, while around him he saw wounded McLauds stirring. He knew that Luanne sensed his sudden alertness. The Irishman, survivor that he remained, listened intently now. He gripped his pistol firmly in his hand, but then his faculties once more failed him. Another layer of fog swirled before his eyes.

⊕

Near to Sean but so far away, the battle-proven rebel woman sat morosely in the road. Nora's knees supported her father's head as he bent his neck back. He was breathing. She reassured him, "You'll be okay, Papa. You'll be okay."

She watched from the corner of her eye as Sean fingered his pistol. She said to her father, "All of the McLauds are shot through. Just breathe. No one will harm you, now." She saw her father's wild eyes calm with her words, and also saw the questions filling them. His lips moved but no words followed.

Glancing over her shoulder once again at Sean, she wondered beyond wonder how he could still be alive. *He may barely be,* echoed through her brain. Luanne's healing knowledge reassured Nora but sent her mind flying to other places where death had been so commonplace. The expanse of combat, the smoke, the deafening sounds of men and machines, flags flying and falling. This litany of unwanted memories rushed from her past. The heroic, she knew, were the first to be struck down. The millwright's flaxen-haired daughter shook her head as she looked to her Irishman. *How can he still live? Heroic is not good enough to describe him.* Yet at that moment she saw the vacant look in his eyes, and she knew even then.

Nora continued watching over her father. She looked towards Sean's bleary eyes with relief, thankful of Luanne's capable hands on his wounds, but also with fear, aware that his sanity was at its limit and drifting away.

⊕

While the empty-eyed Irishman held Nora's worried stare, he took short calculated breaths. The pain in his side told him with every rise and fall of his chest. *Ribs are broken.* The clouds in his mind came and went. He was angry at having no control. A forced smile filled his face and for a few moments generated not his wry grin, but a foolish one. A sudden rush of nausea gripped him, and he dropped his head between his knees. No matter, his stomach heaved and empted it contents onto the already stinking road.

When his belly had settled and he heard no metallic clicks of weapons being readied to kill him, Sean led himself down from his tall mountain of despair. He would go slower. His thinking clouded again, and then cleared a little. He wondered if he could still stand.

Resting for a moment, the rational side of Sean's brain, that remained, understood what must be done. He caught his breath, and the sharp stitch of pain in his side slowed his movement. He forced himself to rise. *The dark-skinned woman*, he saw, watched him with questions in her eyes. She chided him to be still, and he noticed that the light-skinned woman a pace away only watched. *What was her name*? The cloud was back. *She understood*, he thought. *From somewhere we both have been, she understands.* Sean stumbled away on unsteady legs.

⊕

Nora studied the Irishman's actions as he ever so slowly reached for a loaded pistol cylinder from his belt. She watched him place it into his empty and now open Navy Colt. Locking the barrel down tight, she witnessed his hesitant walk through the scattered array of bodies. She knew that Sean was no good omen for any McLaud who remained alive.

⊕

Sean's muddled brain took in the chaos of sprawling bodies, men and horses, and he methodically searched for signs of the living. An arm shifted. He heard a moan. *Nothing hostile*, was all he could think. *Several still lived but none were willing to fight.* He stumbled to his fallen horse, amazed that it still lived despite its terrible wounds. His first shot sent the loyal animal to the great beyond. His thinking cleared.

Now, with judicious strides Sean moved along the road. He checked horses first, and then emptied his large caliber pistol, again and again, each chamber of powder and lead blasting a shockwave through the thick oven-air heat of the July afternoon.

With the horses now out of their misery, Sean reached to his belt once more. He pulled his last loaded cylinder from its pouch. But then the gray mist returned and tore at his sanity. He saw neither the carnage before him nor the two women who had saved him. He saw only Mary Katherine jolting along with him on the tail of the cart, eager to reach Lisdoonvarna and the fair.

CHAPTER 67
DEATH TO MAD DOGS
AND MCLAUDS

Luanne's dark eyes traveled the difficult route on the road over the dead and wounded. She watched in horror. Her hero was turning butcher. Finding three still alive, she watched as Sean coldly dispatched two to another life.

Luanne shrieked, "No, Sean! Stop!" The point blank shots to the chest from his big pistol caused the ground to shake beneath her. Red dust rose around each new corpse. The dark-skinned healer watched the third and final execution. *What kind of man is this Sean Kelly?* Luanne wrung her hands in helplessness. Her head shook in distress. *Must a lone woman's only protector be a devil of a man, a demon destined to dispense death with no remorse as if squashing bugs between his fingers?*

Morose and awe-struck, Nora's father watched, too. His hands pawed the dirt futilely trying to rise. His experience with death was limited to childbirth, disease, and his own near hanging, and the millwright realized with horror that he could do nothing to stop this final slaughter. Melforth, whose anti-Union preaching had led to Nora joining the Confederate host, now had no taste for the killing he had once promoted.

Nora held her father down as Sean continued. Only she

328

understood. The heartless actions of the Irishman were necessary. She, as Sean, realized that no McLaud on this hot summer's day could be allowed to live. Only one survivor riding away would rain down ruin and would unleash an unwinable feud with the many other McLauds to the south at Doniphan.

They came to kill, Nora thought coldly. *Let them pay the ultimate price. Let them die.* The words branded images in her mind. These ruffians were ready to extract such pleasure from her father's death and that of the Irishman. *Let them die,* remained the words dancing over and over in her brain.

She saw him moving again from body to body searching for any last sign of life. He fired a fourth time and silenced forever the last male McLaud in Carter county. Yet, even for battle hardened Nora, remorse finally settled in, and she felt the trembling that always anticipated her own personal terror.

⊕

Sean disregarded the looks of horror from Robert Melforth, Luanne, and finally from Nora. He mumbled, "I finished the last of the bastards." Then, standing as tall as an injured man could, he scanned the gruesome scene. *A shady spot. The sun is too hot.* He searched and found it, then plopped down painfully. His back leaned against the great oak from which still draped the strong hemp meant for Melforth. Then while he sat, the dark mists painfully and completely engulfed him.

There, under the canopy of one of the grandest of Ozark trees, the composer of beautiful fiddle tunes, the loyal brother, the resolute soldier, and the lover of two fine women clasped his head in his hands. His sanity had departed, evaporated in the heat and the stench of death. A hysterical wailing began. It resounded through the trees and up to the cliffs above the big spring and eerily echoed back. "When will this end? God, please let me die!"

Nora understood. He was broken. The dead who littered this dusty road, if they could hear, surely smiled devil grins knowing the violent Irishmen who had sent them to their Maker was in such agony. Would he soon follow them?

⊕

Sean turned his head and blankly studied the powerful pistol in his hand. He looked up to a crisp blue sky and waited for he knew not what. A phrase from his father came galloping in from the past. He nodded in acceptance. *The truth, Malroy had always said. Search for the truth.*

His next words sent chills through Nora. "Mad dogs are best laid low and not allowed to linger."

It must stop, Sean thought. Then he spouted aloud to Nora, who now kneeled before him unrecognized, "The mad dogs are dead!" Then, too sullen, too quickly, "Yet, I, too, am one." Tears filled his eyes before he asked the ultimate of himself, "Why am I still alive?"

With those crazed words the guilt-ridden Irishman brought his revolver's dark barrel to his head. He hollered while looking directly into Nora's eyes, "I can not live knowing of all the blood I have spilled!" But Sean Kelly saw no living human being before him, only ghosts, certainly not the Eli he loved with all his heart and soul.

⊕

The slim figure of flaxen-haired Nora, so resolute at so many other times and troubles, trembled. Her arms outstretched, she reached in desolation toward Sean with open hands, and feared to touch him with the gun at his temple. In dread she watched the hammer go back.

"No, Sean. Please, no," she pleaded. She saw that her heartfelt words went unheeded, unheard, lost in his total withdrawal. Dripping tears dampened the dust at her bare feet. She cringed fearing the worst.

⊕

The pistol hammer fell. In sudden anguish Sean heard Nora wail with a blood curdling cry, but the Irishman's glazed eyes saw nothing, neither Nora nor the dead littering this small dusty trace. He saw only the thousands in the battlefields rushing to meet each other and the many he alone had silenced.

And so, he was seated in the heat of the mid summer day,

shaded by the spreading oak as he heard the firing pin of the pistol meet the expired percussion cap with a loud metallic clap. His only thoughts were that he surely had already died.

Nora fell down on her knees before him. She yelled in jubilation. "The pistol refused fire! Dear God, his pistol refused fire!" She quickly brought the Irishman close to her chest, while her left hand reached for his revolver.

"You poor man," Nora cried. Melforth's favorite daughter pleaded, "Don't dare try to leave me, again, Sean Kelly! Stay! Stay with me. You have only just found me." Consoling the man before her as best she could, Nora then looked dismally to Luanne and her father for support.

Her eyes moved back and locked on Sean. "You are a good man, a gentle man, Sean Kelly. You are my Irishman and Luanne's, and you have been caught in a maelstrom of death and dying. You are not to blame."

Nora Melforth fell silent as her shoulder muscles began to spasm from holding Sean so tightly. His body relaxed in her arms. The pistol fell into her lap, and she quickly pulled it away.

Chapter 68
Come Back To Me

Time passed. She had no idea how long. Moments? A quarter hour? The afternoon? Nora's words resounded, "Know it, Sean Kelly! I love you! Can you hear me?" She paused then rekindled her passion. "I have loved you since you left me to die on the hill under the spreading oaks." Her words quickly caught the attention of her recovering father.

As forcefully as she could, Nora shook the man who had saved her family. "Look at me, Sean Kelly! Come back to me!" Then she screamed directly into his face, sure his insane eyes were not seeing her, only nothingness. "Come to the here and now! Come back. Come back."

In wretched agony, Nora looked to the sky and lamented, "Oh, God, please, bring our good man home from his pain!"

Observing no change in Sean's eyes, she held him tighter as his hand reached for the pistol cradled in her dress. She threw the weapon onto the road.

Finally, Sean's glazed eyes momentarily cleared. A gentle look drifted up to the eyes of the fair-haired woman. She comforted him until, to her surprise and welcome relief, this survivor of so much terror and sadness began to cry. Sean's tears grew into a constant stream and his head fell forward, sobbing onto her breast.

She understood and her tears mixed with those of rushing grief held in by the man in her arms for so many years.

"Please," Sean quietly spoke, looking up to Nora. His words fought their way through his suffering. His voice cracked but now showed a subtle hint of sanity, "Help me return." Then to Luanne, "Both of you?"

Luanne's dark questioning eyes turned and met Nora's. Robert Melforth's resolute daughter wanted no confrontation. She wanted peace.

Downhearted and unsure, knowing how unstable were the leanings of Sean's mind, Nora asked, "Where Sean? Where? I would help you go anywhere but to death's gate. Why? Where should we go?"

His eyes glazed over again, and Nora thought surely that Sean had become forever lost to her. His empty look stared up, beyond her, into the fluttering, oak leaves in the tall tree above.

"Why, where else... pretty...lassie?" were the words that finally filtered through his strained lips. "Lisdoon...varna!" he exclaimed in broken syllables that trailed away. Nora leaned in to him, keeping his head firmly on her chest. A tearful Luanne had taken one of his hands.

Nora wondered what he could possibly mean. His mind was not right. She held on and instinctively, now, watched her father, expecting guidance. While he massaged the growing black-and-blue lines on his neck she wondered how he was alive. The answer, of course, lay in her lap.

It doesn't matter, Nora thought as she turned towards and then away from the putrefying death on the road. Her eyes scanned the few trees scattered over the small fields of corn and wheat. *He is alive. My father lives. Sean is alive.* All that mattered to her had been preserved.

Small birds in the bush caught her eye. High above, a hawk circled, held up by the afternoon's heat. Nora felt she must do all she could. She would work to heal the befuddled man in her arms. She also would work to bring Luanne into this family, despite her father's uncompromising views. Nora promised herself, and then aloud to the incoherent man in her arms and to the dark-skinned woman so close, "I will make it work. We will make it work."

Studying her cherished Irishman again, she vowed, "I will not give up, Sean Kelly. With my stubbornness and Luanne's knowledge of medicine we will bring you back. I will soothe your mind and purge it of demons. Luanne's love will help you, too. You will heal! You will! There will be no other way!"

Nora's breathing deepened. She turned her head and gazed with morbid fascination at the deadly scene before her, but saw far beyond. She then looked down and studied Sean's face and gently smiled at her broken man. "But you are my mad dog, Sean Kelly, and my father's, and my sisters', and Luanne's. Never let yourself forget that. You belong to us." Nora turned to Luanne and saw the flowing tears and a beaming smile on that undeniably lovely face.

The miller's steady daughter reached out to a honey-colored hand and clasped it tightly. She studied her father's reaction to her outpouring of emotion. His simple nod had satisfied the fire in her soul. The rock of the Melforth clan paused a few more moments to let all her words sink in with the others. She then said with no emotion, "Now let me see where they shot you."

Golden hair that had curled into tearful eyes, earlier, was carefully pulled aside. Nora searched all his body for holes and blood. She found herself pleased with Luanne's bandaging and how she had ripped fabric from her dress and staunched the flow in his side. *Broken ribs*, she thought. *What else*? She was unsure. The bullet had glanced off or passed through. Then she found the exit wound. It had been bandaged, too.

Finding another gash in his lower left forearm also bandaged, Nora reached to the cleanest hem of her tattered dress and ripped a strip of cloth from it. She applied pressure to the bloodied rag already there.

Melforth's oldest daughter sat back on her heels, and tossed her head up. The motion threw long hair from her grimy, sweat-laden face. She reached with the cleaner of her two dirty hands, first to wipe it on her dress and then with her fingers to pull the remainder of the matted strands from her eyes and mouth.

Nora again looked deeply into Sean's now green eyes. She

searched for any sanity that might remain and was pleased to see a hint of it, if ever so little. Directed to her brave and loyal Irishman her simple words came still again, "I love you." Then finding Luanne's expectant face so close, she repeated, "We both love you. Your Mary Katherine would have been proud."

CHAPTER 69
UNDENIABLE RESOLUTION

In the cooling shade beneath the great oak Nora Melforth's interrogation began. "My name, dear man, is Nora, Elnora, or Eli. Can you remember me under the spreading oaks of the hospital? Can you remember me holding you in my father's loft on sweet hay? Can you remember saving this fine woman beside me from the depravity of drunken men near Salem?"

Sean's glassy eyes told her nothing.

Then, "My dear, sweet Irishman, can you remember," and her voice reached a trill note reserved for those also so close on the line to falling into the depths, "the blackberries and the thorns, and the loving? Do you remember, Sean?" she exclaimed. "Do you remember?" She caught her father's intense gaze with every word.

A blank faced Luanne watched in admiration as the other woman in her man's life tried to retrieve madness from the abyss. She wished that she also had words. She simply continued to hold Sean's hand and Nora's.

The pillar of the Melforth clan whispered, "Thank you, my love. Thank you for saving my father," her voice wavered, "and my sisters," and then almost whispering, "and me."

A long silence came and went. Then, in frustration, Nora felt the urge to slap him and forced herself to do so. Once then twice across his face her right hand flew. "Can you hear me, Sean Kelly? I am telling you that I love you! Hear me!" Then more gently but embarrassed before her father and Luanne, "I have never told a man such a thing, not ever."

Nora knew only to continue. She never ceased her siren's call to bring him back. Raising her voice she repeated over and over her bold statements of commitment. She refused to stop, although the wetness on her cheeks had long since been replaced with sweat from the heat of this July day.

Unexpectedly, Nora's senses alerted her. She cracked a stern smile as she saw Sean lift his head and truly look her way.

He took in her compassionate eyes. He was now following her every action. Finally, the Irishman truly recognized the woman holding him. He nodded slightly and in quiet abbreviated words said, "I do remember. A field of wheat. A hot day with men dying. The mountains. The Shenandoah."

⊕

The words had come soft and slow, heard by all but understood only by Nora. She saw the wildness in his eyes miraculously melting away. She heard, "Eli, is it you?"

Nora ran her fingers through his hair. She refused to release him. But any position seemed irrelevant to the fine woman who saw the future in the crazed eyes of the man she loved.

Her eyes were wet and red when she said, "You are truly the finest and bravest of men, Sean Kelly." Now, the stern-faced Nora was sure that she saw the grin. She knew the madness had lessened. Her man, their man, her family's mainstay of hope, truly had heard and understood.

⊕

His eyes remained riveted first on Nora's and then on the sparkling dark ones to her left. Sean's own weary voice at last spilled out. "You have done your share, both you and Luanne." Then continuing, his voice trailed away to sound like lyric poetry from a man who knew nothing of verse. "We will live by a beautiful stream. All of us."

He forced his uninjured arm up towards Nora. His fingers touched her face. "We will all grow old together in a stout cabin in the midst of a fine field of sweet hay. The beautiful stream shall always lie before us." Then to Robert Melforth, "A fine mill of your building lies below."

Resting, Sean started again but ended mid-sentence. "You both will bear my children and..." It was then the exhausted man lost consciousness. Nora had been smiling as he had spoken and continued as she held his sleeping form. She gently laid him down. A large oaken root held his head as a pillow.

CHAPTER 70
A WALK OF PENITENCE

Still unable to speak, Robert Melforth rose to his knees. His strong hands rubbed on his bruising neck. Physically shaken but alive, he carefully observed the entire scene. All the pieces of Nora's mysterious time away during the war had come together. She had fought as a man. His ravings against Lincoln had pushed her to it. While Nora had nursed Sean from the snake bite, he had realized that Sean and Nora had come together on the battlefield. Only then had he recognized his shame. *I am responsible for nearly getting her killed.* And then he had rehashed it. *Each had nearly killed the other but then saved each other. Remarkable!* was all he could think.

Melforth forced himself to stand. Then with care he attempted to walk. Hesitantly, he staggered towards the big oak while struggling with his thoughts. Before him he saw Nora, the strongest, standing alone. *Sean has been right. He has braced himself on her shoulder many times. An irony actually, she has been holding our family up all her life, and now again. If she had not saved the Irish lion's life on the battlefield, my family would have suffered a far different end.*

A sudden movement caught his eye. To his left Amy and the other girls now stood on the edge of the road. He saw Luanne's boys, too, and thought how no one, especially the children, should witness such slaughter on the road. Each carried a weapon, axes wielded by Violet and Amy and sharp gardening sticks by stern faced Lilly, Melanie, Jeremiah, and Quincy. Melforth tried to communicate with his hands to shoo them away, but they had already seen so much and seemed as determined to stay as his rescuers.

With new found strength, the miller pulled his oldest daughter up to him. He turned her face with a father's gentle hands and said humorously amidst a world turned upside down, "Dear Elnora, what a strange place to meet your future husband, on a battlefield." Then one of the last rebels along the Current River plopped down on his knees in the dust. He had more to say, and he hoped the Irishman might hear his words.

Luanne and Nora listened as Melforth whispered to a man who could not hear. "You, Irishman, will make a fine addition to my family, Papist or not."

Nora smiled.

The devout Presbyterian paused, deliberated, and found his new direction. "No!" he seethed. Then with a rare curse he finished his thought, "Damn Irishman, keep your devil ways! Just do not leave my family and pray continue to protect our new friend." He paused in his rhetoric and turned to an appreciative Luanne. "As of today, I hereby promise to do the same."

Reaching his hand down, a woozy but powerful Robert Melforth clasped Sean's good arm. With his great strength he gently pulled the wounded and thankfully unconscious man up to his feet and placed the thin-framed body across his broad shoulder.

With Nora and Luanne's support, the stocky millwright proceeded step-by-step. Together, they carried his future son-in-law the short distance back to the mill. After a brief rest on the loading dock Melforth continued alone with his burden up the lane. Finding penitence in his efforts, Robert Melforth knew that he owed the boy far more than he could ever repay. He was glad for the moment that Sean was numb to his injuries, otherwise, the pain in being flopped over his shoulder like a sack of feed would have been unbearable.

Nora followed with Luanne and the children but then, as if

forgetting something, halted her step. She looked back and realized her mission. Her common sense gave commands to her feet, and she retraced her path to the afternoon's carnage. There, in the dusty road, littered with dead men and blood, she reached down and picked up as many pistols and rifles as her hands could carry.

When she caught up with the trudging miller under his human load, an armory of weapons were cradled in her arms and hung from her slim shoulders. She struggled under the weight to her home. Luanne, meanwhile, had shepherded the children back to the cabin.

On the porch, Nora placed the pistols with care on the thick plank floor. She neatly arranged the rifles and shotguns against the cabin wall. Sean's short scatter-gun she hung from a wooden peg by its lanyard.

Luanne's quizzical stare found the confident Nora. The miller's daughter responded to shed light on her actions. "If he lives or dies, Luanne, I want our Irishman or the rest of us ready to fight off an army of McLauds."

Chapter 71
Neighbors Make it Right

Before the shadows had grown too long as that terrible afternoon waned, Robert Melforth watched his neighbors from up river and down flocking toward his house. Mounted and with weapons at the ready, they slowly rode past the mill on mules and horses, some with saddles, most bareback. A cloud of dust arrived with their passage. All appeared set on a task. They were led by his old friend, Marvin Upland.

Still at a distance the miller inspected these people he knew so well. Each, he understood to be decent folk. These hill people, many of Scots-Irish heritage, had so painstakingly farmed this scarce but fertile bottom land along the Current River. Each had past dealings at his mill. For these long years, since over a decade before the war when his grist stones first ground grain by the big spring creek, he had seen no harsh conduct from any of these people. Surely a few were heavy drinkers at times and found their stumbling way to the mill, but overall they were good neighbors. Most disagreed with his vocal sympathies but all had similar values based on the Good Book. Even Marvin's harsh words in church earlier in the week, the miller considered appropriate. He was sure if their positions were reversed he might feel much the same as his friend.

Still, Melforth remained unsure of their intentions. He

attempted to greet them from his porch, but the riders were too far away for his strained whispers. At the tail end of the mob a single horse caught his eye. A body lay face down tied over the saddle.

Nora promptly stepped to his side. She said to her father, "Don't worry. I'll speak for you. Tell me what to say."

Considering his recent brush with death, he wished a few could have come to his aid. *But none are heroes.* His thoughts echoed. *Under the oak tree near the mill, no one risked their lives. But so it is. They come now, at least.* He reassured himself, better late than never, knowing that the only heroes stood on the porch in dresses or lay bloodied on his bed.

His thoughts ran deeper and he mumbled whispered words unheard except by Nora. "Sean did come! He came and I thank the devil and our dear Lord for the damned, Catholic Irishman!"

He laughed as loud as his crushed throat would allow, then mouthed more in raspy whispers. "My friends and neighbors did not come, only the Irishman. Beyond all hopes, one man and *two women* sent ten McLauds to hell."

Nora was listening but was glad her sisters and the neighbors were not. An appreciative smile graced her face, proud the man at her side had raised her as his own, even though long ago her mother had told her, but to punish him in front of his daughter, that he was not her true father.

The miller watched her smile. *Eli, the strong one.* He saw the fire in his eldest daughter not really his own. *Eli,* he wondered turning the two syllables over his tongue. When had he stopped calling her by that name? No words were necessary, but he told her, "I hope the Catholic lives. I hope you will marry him, and we'll pray he survives his present maladies. As for the black family," he conceded, "you, Sean, and Luanne must work that out for yourselves."

Twenty armed horsemen reached the porch and a voice called out. "Robert, the ruckus on the road was heard all the way to Pemberton's place up river." Then old Marvin Upland, also the father of a fistful of daughters and only one son, reined his mount in closer. Melforth saw that a shotgun lay across the pommel of his saddle. Upland's hand lay on the trigger. The hammers were back.

A man of few words, Marvin studied the miller then glanced

back at his son and the rest of the armed band. In the driest of tones, empty of emotion, he addressed his friend of nearly twenty years, "It's a mess by the mill, Robert."

Robert Melforth, fine miller that he was and confirmed holdout of a lost cause, contemplated the eyes of his neighbors, and now doubted their purpose. The lack of peaceful intentions was written over every face. *Are they out for vengeance? How can they sympathize with the death of one McLaud or even the entire clan*? He could not imagine. *But why had they not holstered or lowered their rifles and shotguns*? Tension built in Melforth's mind. He looked again from one to another and, oddly, each seemed waiting for a cue. But from where or whom, he had no idea. He saw the fear in their eyes and on their tense fingers. His body stiffened. There had been enough death this day. He felt helpless. The miller knew that he could not defend his daughters or the injured Irishman. He could only wait. Robert Melforth's observations were only of his heavily armed neighbors. He had not looked behind to his family.

Nora broke the uncertain silence with a stern voice that demanded a quick answer, "How can we help you, Mr. Upland?"

Marvin Upland asked with unsteady words, "Where is the Irishman?"

A hush filled the dusty air. In the yard before the porch unsettled horses circled as anxious riders reined them and awaited a reply from the miller's daughter.

With the steadiest of hands Nora raised Sean's loaded shotgun from the folds of her dress. Her clear eyes never left Upland's. The obvious sound of many heavy metal hammers cocking, behind her, filled the thick air. All eyes were on Nora as she, with a fearless indifference, slowly answered not just Upland but every armed man before her. "He is shot through and may well not live." She stood resolutely and waited, as did Sean earlier in the day, ready to die if need be to defend all whom she loved.

Marvin Upland and the others at his back lowered their weapons. A myriad of clicking sounds announced the release of hammers on many rifles and shotguns. Astounded, Nora watched unbelieving, but Sean's short double-barrel remained leveled at Upland's chest.

Suddenly, it all became clear to Nora. She alone among these men had known battle. The answer to this fatal impasse shone in their faces. It was undeniable. Her neighbors were no longer afraid. By a hair's breadth she suppressed a flood of laughter. Only the tiniest of smiles was allowed to show her amusement. Her Irish warrior might be near death and only, now, could not hurt them.

"We are sorry, Nora, Robert," Upland let out, obviously relieved. "Besides what happened today at your mill, rumors from Salem have followed your Irishman,"

"Don't believe all you hear," Nora's strong voice broke in.

Long moments again passed in silence. Horses continued to be restless before an unmovable Nora and now an armed Luanne. Her shotgun demanded attention. Luanne spoke up. "South of Salem he stopped five men from violating my children and raping me."

Nora felt reassurance in Luanne's presence. She watched the milling of horses and indecision that seemed to rule her neighbors' actions, until a sudden declaration from Marvin Upland finally put everyone at ease, "We are here to help you, Robert."

The old man continued, "None of this can get out," but just as quickly paused, as if his words were silver dollars and he had spent his yearly limit. Then Upland spoke again, "The McLauds on the road need to be buried so no one finds them. Their horses, too."

Together, the barrels of Nora's weapon and Luanne's dropped to the floor. Nora   sighed in relief. *Enough killing. Enough.*

Another neighbor from down river interrupted Upland, pardoning himself as he did, "We should burn the bodies, Mister Upland."

The collection of farmers and trappers, disgruntled with the burning idea, argued with each other for a time. One spoke up with others in agreement, "Let's just toss the bunch of them in the river."

Upland's son noted that the bodies were sure to be found. "Burying would be worse. Bones and parts would be reappearing for years dug up by hogs, bears, and dogs." In consensus, burning was agreed upon to be the only sound course of action.

Then, a nervous Philip McAlester piped up above the discussion, "If it does get out, we won't be able to help you and your family none,

Mr. Melforth. They'll send in the army from Doniphan down river or east from Poplar Bluff. They'll hang the Irishman first, then you for sure, and probably us too." Looking around to all standing in front of Melforth's porch he said with a surety, "There is a McLaud in Doniphan who sits on the bench in the Union courthouse."

Melforth listened. He was unable to contribute his thoughts unless Nora delivered them. Never, in over twenty years had he heard either Marvin Upland say more than two words let alone a litany or McAlester promise to help anyone but his own.

Upland, McAlester, and the others were offering help. Melforth heard a great sigh of relief in the cabin as the story outside unfolded. Unexpectedly behind him, he heard the gentle click of many rifle and pistol hammers being let down. He had forgotten in crisis, but proudly remembered earlier, that each of his children had charged and capped Nora's loot of firearms. His emotion choked him as he saw his two youngest laying down their heavy pistols. "It's okay, dear daughters. It's over." No one heard him but Nora, Luanne, and Marvin Upland.

Philip McAlester, whose cabin lay but a hundred steps from the mill, spoke up again. "We don't know what army you have that took down all the McLauds, but we are all glad the ruffians are dead." The now not so timid father of two almost grown boys and three daughters, still looked to the open windows of the cabin as if the dreaded army of one might attack.

"My youngest boy," McAlester continued, "saw Willis McLaud haul Emma into the mill cellar in May and saw the Irishman go in and rescue her. We have feared for our own long before. The McLauds were a clan of bullies and brutes." Pausing, he then said, "However, what has happened even their women can never know. They are as mean and evil as their men, especially Granny McLaud. She was most likely the one to stir them up to lynch you."

Marvin Upland held up his arms to call for quiet and then spoke to the Melforths and his neighbors, "The Federal horse cavalry out of Rolla is searching the hills for the Irishman and a black family out of Salem." He looked accusingly at Luanne on the porch and then the faces of her children in the doorway.

Melforth and Nora took in the warning but said nothing. They scanned the entire troop of farmers and hunters. Nora said with conviction as she still gripped the scatter-gun, "Sean Kelly is a good man. You all know that. He has rid the valley of the McLauds. Will you help him?"

⊕

Melforth's neighbors had all dismounted and tied their horses. The miller watched them as they came closer to see the markings of the rope on his neck. He heard many say that they wished they could have come to his relief to stop the McLauds. Several, Melforth remembered, especially McAlester, had run from the mill and cringed in their homes surely hoping the McLauds would stop their marauding with him properly hung. The only one who had the nerve to do anything lay wounded and somewhat insensible within the safety of his cabin.

Melforth's neighbors asked him, "How were so many taken down if you were noosed?"

Nora, with Luanne at her side, took it on herself to relate the terrible tale of the afternoon's battle to the gape-mouthed crowd.

With the telling the farmers stared in disbelief. One in the group cautioned, "It all proves the Irishman a devil, a Catholic devil!"

Another known for his steady temperament, a trapper from just upriver, piped out, "And a devil with a fine fiddle!"

A chorus of laughter defused dark, preconceived notions. All remembered Sean's easy way with people and his entertaining music. The more tolerant neighbor added, "At noonday I could often hear Sean carrying a lively tune from the mill's loading dock or this very porch."

Marvin Upland subsequently spoke, amazing everyone with his robust discharge of words that afternoon, "You'd never have thought! He must have expected to die. I suppose the boy saw a lot of killing in the war."

Looking to all the group except for Melforth and Nora, Philip McAlester chimed in, "Ain't sorry for the Rebs he faced!" Seeing the group's sudden grimaces McAlester realized his insult and turned to the miller unaware of Nora's frown. He apologized.

"Sorry, Robert. The war is over," McAlester stated, acknowledging that Melforth had feelings, too. "Forgive me, but that red-headed lad in your home must have been a terror to behold."

Robert Melforth whispered and Nora repeated his words in simple understatement "Indeed, he was an avenging terror."

Melforth's nearest neighbor confessed, "I am sorry, Robert. I wish my courage would have held up."

The miller's memories echoed back to him. After all ten McLauds expressed their intentions to him outside his mill, no one was in sight, except for the backsides of two men running to the safety of their homes far up the main road, McAlester and another neighbor.

Nora's father stepped down from the porch and graciously took the cowardly man's shoulders in his great hands and whispered as loudly as he could, "You are right to say so, Philip. Today and since I have known him," said Melforth pausing and remembering Emma in the mill cellar, Melanie and Lilly with the snakes, and now this. "Sean Kelly has proven to be a devil any of us could love."

The entire group, except Nora, laughed when Upland loudly repeated Melforth's whispered words.

Nora watched the happy commotion from the porch. She would tell her father at a later date of her desire to convert to Sean's faith. She would insist they be married, if they evaded the prowling federal horse soldiers from Rolla and Doniphan, according to his wishes by a priest if one could be found.

While the banter calmed, the group's business-at-hand came forefront and organization for its completion began. Guilt ridden by his lack of courage, Philip McAlester quickly volunteered his wooden sledge normally used to haul rock from the fields. It would be used to lug the bodies away. Its lowness to the ground would make loading easier, especially the horses. All agreed that the side field, not visible from the mill or the house, was the proper place to build the pyre. A small barn there would be used to deposit the bodies. Logs would be leaned up against the walls to fall into the fire as it progressed. The dead horses would be hauled far over the ridge into the wilderness surrounding the Eleven Point.

The gruesome work began, and nearly two dozen grown men

and two women slaved through the evening. They gathered the wood and prepared for the ordeal of burning to ashes the flesh and bones of the McLauds.

While Melforth's younger girls took care of Sean, Nora and Luanne worked beside the men throughout the night. Emma was nowhere to be seen. By the time the Herculean task was complete, many hands were blistered from wielding axes, clothes were soaked with sweat and soiled with dried blood, and many reeked of rancid lard and tallow used to kindle the fires.

CHAPTER 72
INNER TURMOIL

Robert Melforth reached an arm for the jug as weary words slid from his lips. "Thank you for your help, Marvin." His voice ever so slowly was returning. The potent apple jack had been passed around for several hours as the Melforths and their neighbors watched the great logs burn. As dawn approached they lay in short pasture near the cabin as a half moon settled in the west. A cock crowed in the darkness.

"We will need to sift through the ashes when they cool," old Upland advised.

"And find that other horse," chimed in the hunter who had defended Sean.

Marvin Upland again spoke but only to the miller. "You'll need to leave, Robert. You and your family will never be safe here again. Somehow, McLauds will get word. Before they rode off they surely told their women folk where they were bound. If the remaining family can't put the law on you, they'll start the feud."

Marvin's son added, "A bullet when you're tilling the garden. A fire in the barn or the mill. I don't dare think what those vile people will do. Your daughters, Robert. Think of them. You can build another mill. You need to consider leaving and soon."

Melforth reached up and massaged his throat, again. He had felt the effects of the alcohol in the hard cider as it relaxed his muscles and his mind. His whisper had reached a low but audible level, "The devil, as you all call him, must heal or die of his wounds before I leave this place. I owe him that much. I owe the man peace."

Upland rested his hand on Melforth's shoulder. Gently he asked, "I'm intruding but I must ask how you'll handle the dilemma of your daughter and the woman they call Luanne?"

"I don't know, old friend," a dispirited Robert replied. "So many things have happened. The Irishman's coming to the valley in early summer has changed everything."

Marvin added more. "I've seen him at the mill during the past week with both women. It's evident that he has feelings for each. Does the colored carry his child?"

An embarrassing grimace filled Melforth's face. An answer almost never came. When it finally did it was spoken in a broken and frustrated manner. "I know. Lord help me, Marvin, I know. But what am I to do? How can I refuse a man who has fended death from my house so many times?"

Upland and the other neighbors listened in silence and painfully witnessed Melforth's growing despair. The firelight in the distance revealed shiny wetness flowing down his cheeks and dripping from his chin. Uncomfortable for the miller to a man, they politely turned away.

While so doing Marvin Upland spied a standing resolute figure in calico on the porch. Watching him and his neighbors with a hard stare he saw the miller's flaxen-haired daughter. Not unexpected, he noted that her fiery eyes were dry. Upland studied the undeniable commitment of her gaze with envy. He knew Melforth's oldest had more spine than the lot of the men at his side. He had seen her grow from a child. Early in the spring he had seen those same eyes when she had taken the knife to Willis McLaud's throat in defense of Emma. Yesterday, he was sure that he had been very near being riddled with buckshot. *She would have defended her father, family, and lover to the death.*

"Think she heard us?" whispered his son.

Marvin Upland continued his observation of Nora's hard,

penetrating look before he answered, "Certainly," and he paused in respectful awe before he added, "every word."

⊕

The usual morning fog lifted from the valley of the big spring, and Robert Melforth was pleased with his observations. No trace of the violent hill clan remained. He rubbed his painfully sore neck, and echoes of yesterday's anguish and his nightmare returned.

Earlier, he had dozed off with the others near dawn and had then awoken in terror. He remembered sitting up while he gagged on his own spittle. His hands groped in desperation to loosen the noose, still real in his dreams. However, his awakening showed him fear besides his own. The miller's sleep groggy brain managed to register pained faces and unconstrained curses that filled the air when Marvin Upland announced, "The horse that is unaccounted for, we need to find it. Hopefully, the frightened beast has not run the five miles toward McLaud land." Melforth heard Upland continue in sobering tones, "I fear the worst. Our labors to hide the past afternoon's reckoning may have been in vain."

Still later in the morning after a lean breakfast prepared by all the daughters and Luanne, the neighbors, one-by-one despite their exhaustion, made a point of visiting the Melforth cabin before going their own way. Contrived conversation with the miller and his children provided an excuse. Their eyes betrayed their real reason for coming inside. Each stared longer than was polite at the wounded man on the miller's bed.

While the neighbors feigned discussion only to gawk, the miller sipped his coffee and paid little attention except to Nora's words. "Please, stay, all of you and drink your coffee in the shade. My father and I have much to discuss."

Soon after, the lingering neighbors filtered away to tend their horses and sip from   steaming tin cups. The miller gathered his family and Luanne's inside the cabin and listened to Nora's plan. This time her scheme, to maximize their efforts to leave their valley of the big spring as soon as possible, was met with far less of a quarrel.

"Father," Nora proposed, "Sean is feverish but he can ride in the wagon. It will be painful, but his life will not be threatened."

"But Nora, he's sorely hurt!"

Not about to give an inch, Nora soberly lectured, "Luanne and I both agree, father, and she knows better than I. Sean can travel and must, or he will die not from his wounds but from dangling high before the courthouse in Doniphan."

Standing tall, Nora sighed as she surveyed her family's response. She well understood the difficulty of what was proposed. She had left the front door open for a purpose. "And to do so we must load your mill stones in Luanne's cart while help is handy." She pointed to the waiting men outside who she knew were listening to every word. "We must leave before nightfall. The half moon will provide ample light to pass by Van Buren before dawn and be on our way west."

CHAPTER 73
READING LESSONS

Thirteen-year-old Violet scanned the words slowly and clearly pronounced each syllable. The thick black, leather-covered book lay in her lap across her faded dress as she propped her bare feet against the side boards of the wagon. She leaned over slightly. Her index finger followed the words. Violet, whose quiet nature and gentle dark-brown eyes bespoke her shy manner around Sean, was determined. She told herself still again that she would not look at Sean between phrases as she read the Psalms. Seeing him would only distract her.

Sean touched his forehead and felt the small beads of sweat that came and went during the day. His high nighttime fevers were less severe now, and he slept better. Luanne's medicines were working. While he listened to the miller's third daughter read from the Bible, he realized that he was healing, but slowly. Although his broken rib pained him greatly and he was feverish, he looked up from his bed of quilts and straw on the wagon bed. Sean hoped when harm came there would be enough guns ready to halt it. He knew he would be useless in the family's defense.

Turning his thoughts from himself he studied Nora's middle sister, not so little at thirteen. She certainly could read up a storm, but Sean was puzzled why she read from the Bible for the longest time before each reading lesson. Many of the verses taught good values, but he didn't want preaching. He wanted to learn to read. Disappointed in Violet's methods, he wished that Luanne would continue to teach him later when there was time.

⊕

Violet's prayer from Psalms Sixty-Two came out clear and pious. She had begun earlier on Psalms Fifty-Five.

"Oh God, hear my cry for help,
listen to my prayer!
From the end of the earth I shall call to thee,
with sinking heart.
To the rock too high for thee,
lead me!
For thou art my refuge,
a strong tower against my enemies."

Her words flowed smoothly almost delicately, Sean thought, *as a gentle river finding its way to the sea. She can be a scholar if her father allows it.*

Catching himself, he reflected with amusement upon the knowledge of an illiterate Irish crofter's son on such things. *Besides, where in this hill country wilderness of Missouri will she find teachers to help her? But of course, Luanne.*

Violet persisted in her oration from the Psalms. She failed to sense Sean's respect for her abilities or his boredom with her source. He was the strong tower in her mind. She continued as her father had instructed. Bible verses were first to sway his mind, spelling and grammar last.

At first she had been frightened when Nora and her father asked her to teach Sean. How could she, so young, teach such a man, a man who defended her family as if their blood ran through his veins? Unsure of herself but glad of his company, she had diligently though hesitantly pursued their request. Each hot afternoon, when the Melforth caravan rested in the shade, the reading lessons had continued while the Irishman recovered from the jarring morning's ride in the wagon.

Violet cleverly caught Sean's playful wit that came out despite his poor health. She found the confidence to throw it back at him full force. She adored Sean's fun loving ways but allowed him little time for such trivial pastimes and drilled him relentlessly from the worn primer. *Hopefully soon*, she thought while he stumbled over the simplest of written words, *Sean will be strong enough to play his fiddle again*. Violet was sure that his music would go a long way to revive the spirits of her uprooted family. Her father had told everyone but Sean his worries. A slow recovery might change everything. If Sean died on the journey they would have nowhere to go, no land to claim.

As Violet continued to listen to his childlike attempt at reading, she evaluated the man sitting before her for the hundredth time. She was well aware that she loved him as she might her own brother, perhaps more, and his ability with the fiddle was simply a side attraction. It was his selflessness and decency. She cherished him, and if Nora or Luanne cast him aside, she promised herself to take him in a heartbeat. Violet wished she could muster the courage to thank the pained man who so easily joked or flirted with anyone near. For everything he had done for her family, thanks would be a good beginning.

A few long days of hard travel later Violet heard Sean ask pointedly, "What do you see, dear Violet, when you study me with those dark eyes?"

Blushing with embarrassment, Violet looked down at her toes, so wanting to answer but unable to speak.

"No, that was unfair," Sean burst out before Violet might summon her inner thoughts that he knew he had no right to claim.

"Pardon me, Violet Melforth," he said to confirm his mistake. "Know that your efforts to teach me and amuse me as I heal are taken kindly." He paused and lifted her hand in his. "You're a gentle soul, sweet *lassie*, and to think I am ten years older. It's an admirable and difficult thing you do. Thank you for such concern."

Serious eyes rose up to Sean's and never left. No words came to her or were necessary while she allowed neither smile nor childish emotion to surface. Indeed wiser than her few years, she said nothing while Sean's appreciative statements sealed his position forever in her life.

"I'm but an ignorant Irish peasant, Violet, but I have had the luck to be accepted by two wonderful families, yours and Luanne's. Also, I'm lucky to have such a scholarly young woman to teach me my letters."

Violet's reaction would never be totally understood by Sean that day or even later in their lives. Her thoughts could only go to the one fact that the Irishman seemed always to toss aside as trivial, or avoid as if it never happened. He had saved nearly her entire family from certain death, *and yet, he entertains us all with the same good nature as if he has done nothing of importance.*

⊕

Another afternoon when Melforth's middle daughter taught a lesson, he watched Violet speak with confidence. He hoped to learn even faster. He listened as she reminded him, "Be patient." A shy but pretty smile appeared with her words as she assured him, "You're learning, but it takes time. Luanne taught you well, but you must work harder."

Sean put this ever confusing language aside in his mind and looked contentedly at the other members of the Melforth and Weller family. He glanced around the vista of forests, streams, and close by at the lone wagon packed with belongings, the cart with its mill stones, and the horses. Had he lost the language of his homeland? Had English taking its place? He began to name in Gaelic each item he saw, quizzing himself aloud to reaffirm his confidence, but stopped after only a few. Sean saw the Melforths staring at him as if he were chanting incantations. Only Luanne smiled. *The entire clan probably thinks I have mislaid my sanity, again.*

"It's Gaelic, the old language of Ireland," he said to sooth their worries.

With Sean's explanation, the family settled back into their normal activities at the resting spot. He appreciated recovering in the midst of such family. Seeing Melforth take to Luanne's children, especially Jeremiah and Quincy, helped to set his mind at ease. Sean marveled as the mechanical mind of Robert Melforth taught two young boys to fashion tiny wooden gears with mere whittling knives.

Around the evening cook fire, Sean continued to enjoy the antics of the five youngest children. Nora and Luanne were across from him mending the family's travel-worn clothing. He thought it all encouraging until he confronted himself again with the double edged sword that plagued him, the dilemma of loving two women. *And yet, there they sat smiling happily like peas in a pod.* Sean shook his head in bewilderment. He certainly knew he would never be able to share a woman with another man. Occasionally, each looked up and sent him a warm smile that cheered his tired soul.

Sean reached down and stirred the fire. Memories of yesterday's travels came to mind. The two women were far ahead of the wagons, scouting ahead on foot. Both confidently cradled shotguns, while their broad hats shaded them from the harsh July sun. He smiled while visualizing a past dream spawned while going home with Willie along the Missouri River to Hermann. It depicted the same scene, two well armed women, one dark-skinned and one light, walking ahead. But yesterday he saw their faces. He smiled again and thought that any bandit foolish enough to confront the pair deserved their buckshot.

Nora had told him the day before what he already suspected. "I carry your child, Sean Kelly." Even so, the way she had said it had calmed him. Her tone of reassurance had continued, "You need only worry about recovery from your wounds. I have Luanne and she has me when our time comes. And besides, we all have a plucky Irishman that we know will regain his strength."

His image of Nora reaching out and carefully embracing his still weak body was not easily to be forgotten. Luanne had smiled her approval from across the fire.

"I'll not be able to fend off many villains for a while, Nora," Sean said. Nora had quickly laughed. He saw her confidently pat the stock of the double-barrel that was strapped over her shoulder.

"We'll handle it for now, Sean." Then, in a poorly mimicked

Irish brogue, delivered in a puffed up tone intended to tease, "Oh, Sean Kelly, it seems our desire for your speedy recovery hinges rather upon another talent."

"And what could that be?" he laughed.

"Why, my good Irishman, the return to the fireside of your joyous fiddle."

⊕

Around another fire ring two weeks later and only a few days east of Springfield, Nora expressed her worries to Sean. "There is a southern way to bypass Springfield. We've heard from travelers that the federal garrison remains there. They'll be looking for us. The directions given were to take a less traveled road through Galena and west."

Sean acknowledged Nora's counsel but could tell she had more to say.

"Luanne and I have worked things out, Sean," she began, "but I need to know your mind." A long silence came between them before she asked, "Will you marry me, Sean Kelly?" The face of the toughest Melforth hinted at tears. "I dread to think of our children bastards."

Sean looked to Nora with love and then also to Luanne's compassionate face nearby. "I certainly will marry you, Eli, in any church you choose, but know I will forever offer Luanne, if she wishes, my care and affection. If she desires the Kelly name she and her children shall carry it, too."

BOOK III

CHAPTER 1
LETTING GO

It was a cool and cloudy morning in late June when Rebecca O'Sullivan ran her fingers over the twin black barrels. Just the night before, she had finished reading Aunt Violet's lengthy journal. She noticed that the shotgun was amazingly free of rust for its age. She grasped the wooden stock of the scattergun and wondered how it had been used in her ancestors' defense. She cringed imagining how Sean Kelly had used it at what was now Big Spring State Park just after the Civil War, and how Anna herself had wielded it only last fall. Terribly short barrels told even her, the music teacher from Duluth, that this was a force to be reckoned with. She was proud of her daughter, but didn't think she could have performed so well as Anna to protect Michael. *Yet, it all made sense. Anna was indeed a Kelly like her father.*

Rebecca's curiosity overtook her better judgment, and she pulled one hammer back and then the other until each stopped with a hard click. She promptly realized it had been a mistake. She had only guessed it was unloaded. Now, with great care she placed it, still cocked, back into the long narrow box in the old wooden trunk. Her hands shook as she closed the cracked wooden lid. She scolded herself for being the fool but quickly found herself back on her nostalgic journey.

The leather hinges holding the lid of the old trunk appeared newer, oiled, and supple. Michael, or maybe many of the Kellys, had indeed taken care of this old heirloom. She wondered for a moment but then resigned herself never to know all the deathly stories in which Sean's devastating weapon had taken part. Rebecca was aware that Michael's side of the family was alive almost certainly because of it.

The thick-planked stairs creaked on their rusted square nails as Rebecca stepped down to the first floor of the cabin. *Sean Kelly's log cabin*, she thought as she studied the log walls and tools hanging from pegs. *What would he have been like? 1866 was so long ago.* But then she remembered. He slept down the hall from her every night.

She walked across the dirt floor to the doorway. Glad to leave the ghosts of her kin behind, she strolled into the morning sunlight pleased of the clouds' retreat. Still cool, the early summer day would heat up soon enough. She went to find Michael, all the while feeling pangs of guilt. Pleased that she had finally looked through her great-great uncle's effects, Rebecca nevertheless promised herself in the future to keep her hands to herself concerning unknown guns.

A little later she was back at the old cabin with Michael in tow. She confessed, "You'll need to look in the trunk and fix the shotgun."

"You broke it?" was Michael's quick and unbelieving response. He saw remorse in her face. Then, a worried, "There's no way you could you break it." They both climbed the splintery stairway to the loft. The air of the upstairs room had turned sultry. The corrugated metal roof above popped and creaked from the sunshine. Sweat dripped off their chins as they knelt down in front of the trunk. Michael opened it.

Quickly inventorying its contents, he saw that all was in order. Reaching down to the smaller wooden box he pulled out the shotgun. Carefully, he showed Rebecca how to release the hammers to a safe position.

"You did okay. Glad you told me, though. Even an unloaded

gun should never be put away cocked. You did check to see if it was unloaded?"

She looked down while shaking her head.

"The tension on the hammer springs should be relieved. It's just wasn't safe." He showed her the lever that broke open the gun to reveal two hollow chambers. "Promise me next time to check if it's empty. Okay?" He gently squeezed her hand and put the incident behind them.

Michael had grown up with guns, and Grandpa Kelly had taught him well. Last year before Ellen had died, he had shot the old firearm as he had periodically all his life. Grandpa Kelly had told him as a young man, "You never know boy, you might need it someday." At the time Michael had been unsure of the origin of his grandfather's thoughts.

Gently, Michael lifted out the few other effects belonging to his ancestors and laid them on a dusty cane-backed chair beside the trunk. A single leather bag clinked when he set it down. The yellowed pages of bundled letters bulged in an open leather satchel. Both Rebecca and Michael sat on the floor as he pulled several golden coins, twenty-dollar double eagles, out of the bag and placed it on the satchel. Beside the old coin, he set two silver earrings and a brooch.

"Rebecca, this jewelry belonged to Nora Melforth Kelly."

She dipped her head in respect, then said, "Tell me everything you know about each item. Slowly, Michael, one by one."

He sensed Rebecca's interest despite the attic's uncomfortable heat. He suggested they bring a few articles down and continue their discussion in the shade at the house. Included were the thick bundles of letters.

CHAPTER 2
LETTERS FROM THE PAST

A few minutes later on the porch's east side, Michael and Rebecca settled into the rockers as a cool breeze strengthened from the east. Michael gently pulled out the stack of letters and carefully untied the string that bound them. After the discovery of their mutual ancestor earlier in the week, he had refreshed his memory of their contents. Once Rebecca finished reading one he handed her another. He knew she should know the story they told.

"Michael," Rebecca said studying his face for answers, "these are dated before the Mexican War! Some are from 1846. The final one was penned in late 1847."

"Just read on. I'll not spoil your fun."

So, this woman, so dear in the past to Michael Forester and now again, poured her energies into digesting the rambling words of a lonely soldier to his distant lover.

Abruptly her head came up from her reading, "Michael, the girl was from Memphis," but quickly her avid concentration returned to the pile of opened letters that now filled her lap and the small table between the rockers.

While Rebecca lost herself in history, Michael decided to leave her to her reading. "You've quite a stack to go through. Thought I'd head up to the ridge and scout around a bit. When you're finished, holler. I'll hustle back down to the house."

⊕

Over an hour later Rebecca laid down the last letter. She leaned back in the rocker. Her spine tingled thinking of all she had read. She pushed her mind away from the romantic aspect of the story and focused on the cold reality of the times and the situation.

Michael had returned and took a seat beside her. "You know, Michael, that old story in the letters has been repeated innumerable times throughout history."

Michael studied her face. He wondered if the woman he cared for so much had figured out the mystery.

"Two young people, a beautiful woman and a dashing military officer fall in love. The officer is called to duty in a foreign war. He sadly leaves his lover on the dock, but she carries his child. To make it a tear jerker, he is killed and never sees his sweetheart or his baby."

Michael nodded. He realized that she hadn't seen it yet. The question he had been waiting for finally came.

"So, who in your family is connected to these letters?" Rebecca asked with curiosity but a lack of emotion. She watched Michael as he said nothing and studied her with an intensity she rarely saw.

Rebecca breathed deeply. She hoped that his silence was a joke. "Michael, what is it? Are you okay?" She felt her chest again inhale deeply. There was no humor in his eyes. He was as serious as she had ever seen him. She remained quiet and waited. Their eyes never dropped.

Finally, she heard the earth-shattering words leave his mouth, "It's about you, Rebecca."

Rebecca O'Sullivan's thoughts spiraled around in confusion. What could he possibly mean? Was his mind failing again?

Then with slow deliberation Rebecca asked, "About me? What do you mean, Michael?" Scenarios including all of her known ancestors echoed through Rebecca's mind. Each she tried to nail down as being relevant to Michael's statement. None held water. None had lived in Memphis.

"Rebecca is a common name in my family," Michael began.

"Michael, it's a common name everywhere," the red-haired woman at his side fired back.

Michael let loose his own barrage. "The young woman with child from Memphis to whom all the letters are addressed is named Becky. Obviously, Rebecca was her given name." He paused a moment, then he pointed down to Flat Creek, "Those foundations are of a mill built here in the late 1860's by Robert Melforth. Nora Melforth Kelly was his daughter. Nora's mother was the Becky in the letters. Nora's father was Lieutenant Jacob Atchison. The Becky in the letters...."

And the clutter in Rebecca's brain cleared. She was on overload. In her hand she held the written words of her ancestor, the mother of her great-great grandmother, Emma.

Michael asked, "Have you read the last letter?"

"I glanced at it."

"Read it closer now," Michael asked. "Actually, if you would please, read it aloud."

A bit flustered and secretly upset at Michael for being so in control and theatrical, she began, "It's dated January 1847....." and she continued.

Dear Miss Rebecca Tarryman,

It is with grave pain I write this letter. Your fiancé, Lieutenant Jacob T. Atchison, was killed yesterday. His bravery and leadership under fire from a Mexican counter attack helped save two hundred soldiers under my command. Jacob was my comrade and my friend since the Point. My gravest sympathies go out to you.

Signed with much sadness and sympathy,
Your servant, U. S. Grant, Lieutenant US Army
Mexico City

CHAPTER 3
KNOWING FULL WELL

Rebecca stared moodily at Michael but her mind was away in another time, another century. She guided her sight with the help of the descriptions from Violet's stories and saw Elnora slaving at the mill to satisfy a father's desire for a son. She imagined Eli in battle and after, where she lost a war but gained a husband. Rebecca observed a fierce woman ready to die if need be to save the man she loved as well as the man she knew as her father. She had also helped save Sean Kelly knowing full well he loved someone else as much as he loved her.

Rebecca knew that Elnora or Nora, her great-great aunt, must have read all of these letters written to her mother. This young woman in those dangerous times during and after the Civil War knew well the origin of her fire.

CHAPTER 4
LISDOONVARNA

A week later Michael, again, hiked slowly up the ridge. Boots, his Border Collie, was far ahead on the trail of a squirrel. With a slow but measured gait Michael covered the length of the rocky summit and found one of his favorite stony outlooks. A strong breeze held the summer's heat at bay. Here, nearly two years before, he had foreseen Ellen's death. Here also, he had found the evidence of a shooter and his son's hard justice.

His trek through the brush had produced a few crawling ticks on his pant legs. *Nothing to worry about*, he thought, and dealt with the bugs with a flick of his finger. He pushed the past aside and looked out across the green hills and down at the meandering and mostly tree-covered waters far away. Always in awe, he soaked in the wild scene, and its opposite, the pastoral fields below observed a thousand times before. A dark line of thick clouds to his southwest caught his attention. A thunderstorm was brewing, building its towers of clouds. *There's still time*, he calculated, so allowed his vigil to continue.

⊕

Michael remained high on the hill above his home for nearly an hour watching the clouds grow darker. Lightning on the horizon struck the hills. While he waited for the cooling rain he saw and thought of many things but confirmed one old adage his mother had crocheted in colorful letters. Its summarized version still hung above the kitchen sink. "Change what you can but have the wisdom to know what you can't." That he had tried was all he could think.

A steady Michael Forester arose from his eagle's perch. In a sober mood he began making his way back down the rocky, leaf-matted trail, glad of his walking stick. Rebecca would be worried. The wind had picked up considerably. The clouds, dark and threatening, loomed above. Lightning was closer than he would have liked. Then the skies opened up. He looked around for Boots. The old dog was nowhere to be seen.

A foot race in the rain to the house forty years before filled his mind. While he ambled down the now muddied trail, he wondered how Henry was doing. Unable to put up with retirement his old childhood companion had returned to the University of Missouri campus. There, the scholar of history had continued his research into the effects of medicinal botany on rising cultures. Henry had told him his new book should be out within the year. Michael remembered his most treasured friend and distant cousin saying. "Doubt if it will do as well as Pollan's *Botany of Desire* or Diamond's *Guns, Germs, and Steel*, but I'll give them a run for their money!"

Michael's daydreaming unexpectedly ended. He tumbled off the trail while his sudden curses and groans of pain were swallowed by the noisy downpour. He moaned as he made the difficult attempt to pull himself up, only to slide back down. He cursed his old knees and the false step that had upended him and sent him down the hill on his head. *I was lucky*, he reflected as he felt the cushion of thick leaves under him. Young saplings stopped him from rolling further.

A dazed Michael finally pulled himself to the sitting position and attempted to reorder his scattered thoughts. His head had missed hitting a shelf of limestone by inches. All the while his newly returned Border Collie stood protectively with two feet on his shoulder licking his ear.

Michael brushed himself off. Then he reached a hand gently back to his dog and stood up. Again, but this time more carefully, he began hiking down the steep, sloppy trail. To no one but the trees and the storm, he scolded himself in Irish brogue. *"Not what you used to be are you, lad."* Remarkably, despite the din of the storm, faint sounds from Rebecca's violin echoed up from the valley below.

The farmhouse was a welcome destination when his muddy shoes finally clomped on the dry porch. Rebecca's fiddle called from the living room. Her music, while easing the sting of his bruises and hurt pride, abruptly stopped.

Heavy footfalls brought Rebecca outside with fiddle and bow in hand. "You're dripping wet!" she said with amusement. Then while he took off his boots she inspected his ruffled clothing more closely. She saw drops of blood on his forehead.

"Looks like you took a spill. I'll get the first aid kit." Rebecca returned shortly and set him straight with a wet cloth and a daubing of peroxide.

"Were you taking out trees or boulders with your head, this time?"

Michael managed a grin as he looked up, first to Rebecca and then to the storm. He reached to his drenched dog and gave it a pet.

Rain pelted the roof. The blackest thunder cloud Rebecca could recall lingered high above them. "Don't worry," she heard. "Only if you were on the ridge, worry." She had heard that before. At that moment a bold stroke of lightning lit up the hillside. Delayed thunder rattled the house.

A little later when he tread on the kitchen floor with bare feet and in dry clothes, Rebecca had two glasses full of ice and a gallon jar of tea ready. "Glad you made it back before the really bad part of the storm hit, Michael." She meant for her sarcasm to both scold him and set him at ease. It did. "Sweet tea?"

With dripping tumblers in hand, they stood together watching and listening from the protection of the living room. Below the house, thick grass in the hayfield swayed in the wind like a sea of waving wheat.

"I'll need to be cutting the hay soon," he said motioning to the rain swept fields between cool sips. "This rain won't last. The fescue's not much but it's full of clover. Good now. Almost as full of protein as alfalfa."

Seeing the rocking chairs just outside in the shelter of the porch he felt the urge to be a part of the storm. Michael asked like a begging puppy, "Let's sit outside? Okay?" Luring her he added, "It'll be a better place to watch the storm."

He smiled at Rebecca when she nuzzled up to his shoulder. She must have other things on her mind. "Maybe I'll teach you to cane chairs," he said, doubting her interest at the moment. "Would you try? You're pretty good with your hands."

His mind was on much more than the maintenance of the chairs out on the porch. Michael savored it all, the good woman beside him, the suddenly dark afternoon, and the icy liquid in his hand. Its delicious effect was working wonders. Cold downdrafts from the thunderstorm blew his remaining hair as they stepped out and settled into Sean Kelly's delicate rockers.

A heavy torrent of rain suddenly pounded the tin roof of Grandpa Kelly's old house, providing competition to Michael's next soft spoken words. "You don't suppose our ancestor, Sean Kelly, ever truly felt that he had found peace and family here? He had lost so much in Ireland, New York, and the Civil War."

Michael's question gave Rebecca a clear wake up call. "You've been thinking, haven't you, Michael?" Then she added half in jest and half expecting to hear him say yes, "Did you see him on the ridge?"

Michael's forced smile said little. "No," he said but he lied. Then a few long moments later, "You'd be taking me back to the clinic in Kansas City and Doctor Layton, if I did." He smiled broadly, "But, you've always thought I was crazy anyway, right?"

Rebecca smiled, too, and said, "I'll take you as you are." And she reached for his hand.

The storm's fury began to send streams of rain across the porch, and they retreated back to the living room. There, Michael looked out again, his view out of focus because of the waviness of the aged panes of glass in the window. He knew it must appear surreal to Rebecca's eyes. To Michael it cast much the same mood that he had experienced on the ridge earlier and at fourteen seeing the ghostly shapes of his mother by the creek.

Seeing 'beyond' in small doses he had somehow gotten used to, however, the images whirling into reverse, today, had scared him. He was crazy. He must be. It wouldn't be the first time he thought so. But this time there was no gun to his head. Rebecca was near, and he was sure their children would approve.

His conversation on the deserted ridgeline in the heat of the afternoon with Sean Kelly had shaken him to the core. *The building thunderstorm had summoned him*, he supposed. Now, with Rebecca locked tight against his chest, it didn't matter.

⊕

While gazing thoughtfully out the window into the rainy summer squall, Rebecca asked, "You don't suppose your Grandfather John and the other Kellys who came after Sean were the real winners?" She readjusted herself, placing an arm around Michael's waist, then continued, "I mean, Sean's family through the generations has done very well, don't you think? Look at your good years with your grandfather, your mother, and Ellen. Your children. Look at us."

He did. They both smiled.

Rebecca took another drink of tea and said, "Sean would be pleased to see that. Maybe his family has. Lisdoonvarna was a state of mind to Sean Kelly. Maybe it's closer to us than we all know. You should honor his dreams and struggles by holding on and appreciating what he gave with so much effort."

She studied Michael's intent face. "To me," she said, "this land, you and your family, and certainly his music seem quite a gift."

Reassured, Michael gave her a hug. "You're right," he answered slowly as voices from the past and the future filled his mind.

Rebecca listened but knew he was far away and not really with her.

Michael pushed himself to return to the present, and, again, stared down into those emerald eyes whose mantle of fiery red framed such a loving face. The green pools seemed to force him to say, "Rebecca, I am indeed a lucky man."

Turning away from the lure of her eyes, Michael scanned the

rain glazed fields towards the swirling creek he had known all his life, the same view that his great-great grandfather had known. He returned his attention to Rebecca. So very glad he was to have found a small measure of her in his youth and more now. This lady beside him, so sensitive and yet so determined, he realized no longer filled his heart like a wondrous river. He had witnessed the transformation occur since her coming. To him her essence was now of a vast, sparkling sea.

He gave Rebecca a knowing smile, and then he nodded. His words when they finally came drew an appreciative look. "Yes, we are the ones who have recaptured Lisdoonvarna."

CHAPTER 5
RAIN IN LISDOONVARNA

Storms came and went all afternoon, and the leather satchel of letters and other heirlooms remained suggestively on the kitchen table inciting Rebecca's curiosity. The next day, the off-and-on rainy weather continued as did their discussion over lunch.

"So, whatever our parts in this tale," Michael said, "we know there is more to the story than a stubborn Irishman fighting off starvation on the streets of New York City and villains in Missouri. A woman just as strong, he was lucky to find, and lucky also that she stood by him. He also..."

"But bigamy, Michael? Rebecca interrupted. "How at that time did Sean get away with it in Missouri?" Then after a thoughtful pause, "Even if he was far in the back woods of the Ozarks?"

"I've wondered about that too," Michael answered. "Most of the stories I've heard growing up were probably nine tenths lies. However, my Grandpa John had the best answer I heard through the family grape vine, which of course was validated by Aunt Violet's journal. He said that Sean did indeed marry Nora in a church but just as surely married Luanne in the privacy of his home. Probably in that very cabin," and Michael gestured with his hand in the direction of the log house near the spring creek.

A heady silence simmered before Rebecca prodded Michael to continue. "Go on."

"Violet described the exodus to Flat Creek with Elnora's family without Emma but with Luanne and her children. Your great-great grandmother Emma was never spoken of again in Violet's journal. The mill stones and carpentry tools are all Robert Melforth brought of importance. A few of his tools still survive and are hanging in my shed. With these he hoped to build another mill wherever his Irish son-in-law settled the family."

Michael continued, "Violet also wrote how Luanne and Nora got their heads together and formed a *pax romance*, well understanding the stubbornness of the man for whom they both cared so deeply. Nora and Luanne shared the love of Sean Kelly in a difficult but mutual trust. Once at Flat Creek Luanne insisted that he need not have her in his house. She raised Nathan's three children and her child by Sean over the ridge in a small cabin under the Irishman's protection. Many of her grandchildren inherited the musical traits so common in Kellys. By late Victorian times many a wealthy family in Springfield or Carthage would often have a black Kelly in their parlor entertaining guests on piano, violin, or tutoring their children upstairs."

Michael paused to catch his breath and then went on, "Nora gave Sean four children who lived. Much later, she was injured from a falling timber in the mill and never fully recovered. After her death in the late 1890's, Violet was the only remaining Melforth on Flat Creek. The younger sisters had long since married and moved to the city. Aunt Violet never married and remained devoted to Sean. To her frustration, Sean brought Luanne into their home, this very house, but Violet loved her, too, and stayed on. The unlikely trio lived into the early portion of the twentieth century. Sean had many adventures that I've not shared with you. Despite his wounds in battle, he outlived all the Melforths except Violet. She was at his bedside when he died here on the farm on Flat Creek at the ripe age of eighty-seven. I sleep in his room." Michael added with apparent pride, "My mother actually heard him play his fiddle on this very porch when she was a young girl in the 1920's."

"But what about Nora's jewelry? It's expensive. It must have a story."

"Glad you reminded me, Rebecca. As all things concerning Melforths and Kellys it does. Sean was given the broach and ear rings by the appreciative wife of a railroad owner from Tulsa. Sean was in Aurora on business and happened to be in front of a hotel when the woman was robbed. The thieves were getting away with her box of precious jewels. Nora's broach and ear rings were Sean's reward for stopping the robbery."

"Did he shoot them all!"

"No, not this time!" Michael said and laughed as he thought about the episode. "No, Sean was carrying dry goods to his wagon as the robbers tried to run by. He smacked them with a five pound bag of coffee."

Rebecca's eyes sparkled a little more. "Oh, really!" She remembered Anna's story of another Kelly on an island up north doing much the same thing.

⊕

During a lull in the rain they returned to the cabin. While Rebecca watched Michael repack the family relics in the old trunk, she looked out and noticed that the breeze had stiffened in the trees. Still another bank of dark clouds had moved in. Before she knew it, she heard Michael holler, "Race you! Hurry or you'll get wet!" He ran ahead to the house to beat the rain. "Follow me!" But she hesitated and then for a few moments lingered at the cabin, hoping for the rain to let up.

A bright, knowing smile filled her face. Despite the shower, she was sure that the man she had loved for so long had seen it. She pleasantly wondered about all of his explanations of their family ties and how he had sparked her curiosity and imagination.

The downpour only became heavier. Rebecca heard Michael gloating with childish glee while quite dry under the covered porch of the farm house. The rain was blowing in. She was getting wet. She hollered above the hammering deluge, speaking only of the moment but arousing questions from long ago, "You should have made me follow you when I had the chance, Michael!"

She caught his smile and his answer as he yelled back, "Maybe, but I doubted you would come to me when we were younger. Now, I think you will."

She ran to him. The warm rain soaked her to the skin before she finally stepped up on the porch. She reached out and Michael cradled her dripping head on his chest. He led her to the protection of the house.

In a quiet voice Rebecca said, "I am glad we've shared this time." She looked up into his eyes. A gentle look graced her face. "You know we were meant to be together, Michael." Then with uneasiness, "I think Ellen would have approved. Do you?"

The man from Flat Creek found her emerald eyes, and emotion filled his words as he answered, "Yes, I think so, too." He sensed the power that only came with caring deeply for another. Regaining his composure, he escorted Rebecca into the house and down the hallway to his bedroom. There, he laid her down on the white linen of his bed, her wet clothing now in a pile on the pine floor. The country boy who had been through so much could only think, as he studied the long, red hair splayed out on the pale-skinned woman before him, how beautiful she remained.

AFTERWARD

Missouri was a hellish place to live during and after the American Civil War. A local historian filled me in, "People with money left, and did so without looking back." Older ranchers in the southwest portion of the state enlightened me to the fact that farmers for a decade after the war carried firearms over their shoulders when working in their fields. Even now there remain strong loyalties that quickly surface.

When recently researching Missouri bushwhackers for another book, a friend with deep family ties to the area stared me down when I asked questions on the subject. Icy words laced with metal declared, "My relatives were only defending their land and their families from Union atrocities." This reminded me that history is usually written by the victors, and that I needed to dig deeper.

The Ozarks were mostly pro Union, but my research, throughout, always pointed towards strong southern sympathies within a hundred miles of both sides of the Missouri River. Those leaning towards the Southern cause nearly succeeded to pull Missouri from the Union. During those turbulent years, failure to do so was only by a hairsbreadth. Tens of thousands of Union soldiers, garrisoned over the state, were required to quell the rebellion. Untold injustices were inflicted by Federal troops, Red Legs, Jay Hawkers and conversely by vengeful bushwhackers. If I had lived then and possessed the means, there is no doubt that

I, too, would have attempted to flee far from the chaos that was Missouri or hopefully had the courage to stand and defend my land and family.

⊕

Also, it must be noted that numerous historical accounts exist concerning women soldiers disguised as men serving in the ranks of both blue and gray. This thought alone provided the first spark that ignited my curiosity to write this story. Obviously, the kindling of my interests regarding Missouri's part in the conflict and other sparks generated along the way were incorporated, I hope, to the tale's advantage.

BIBLIOGRAPHY

The Beleaguered City of Vicksburg, Shelby Foote, Random House, 1991,1995.

The Border Wars, William Connelley, Smithmark, N.Y., 1909 and 1960.

The Civil War in Missouri, Dino A Brugioni, Sumners Publishing, 1987.

The Civil War, Strange and Fascinating Facts, Burke Davis Fairfax Press, N.Y., 1913, 1982.

The Civil War in a Bottle, Battle at Fayetteville, Arkansas, Kim Scott, Kinnally Press, Bozeman, Montana, 1996.

Civil War in the Ozarks, Philip W. Steele and Steve Cottrell, Pelican Publishing Co., Gretna 1993.

The Civil War, Picture History, Bruce Catton, American Heritage/Bonanza Books, N.Y., 1960.

Cold Mountain, Charles Frasier, Random House, 1997.

Enemy Woman, Paulette Julies, Harper Collins, 2003.

Gangs of New York, Herbert Asbury, Thunder Month Press, 2001 (reprinted from the 1928 ed).

Into the Wilds, Civil War Series, Irish Immigrants during the Civil War, Ann Vernon, *Missouri Life Magazine*, 2008.

Killer Angels, Michael Shara, Random House, 1974.

Kingdom Of Callaway Historical Society, U.S. Army Corps of Engineers Missouri River Maps, circa 1864, Wreck of the *Asa Wilgus*, 1857-60, 212 ft. three boilers, downriver from Hermann, up from Berger Bottoms.

Mostateparks.com/history

The Last Full Measure, Jeff Shara, Balantine Books, 1998.

TheNationalArchives.gov/women-in-the-civil-war, by Deanne Blanton, 1993

Trinity, Leon Uris, Doubleday, 1976.

Printed in the United States
218097BV00002B/8/P

9 781440 135620